Jeffrey Archer

ALSO BY JEFFREY ARCHER

A QUIVER FULL OF ARROWS
THE PRODIGAL DAUGHTER
KANE AND ABEL
SHALL WE TELL THE PRESIDENT?
NOT A PENNY MORE, NOT A PENNY LESS

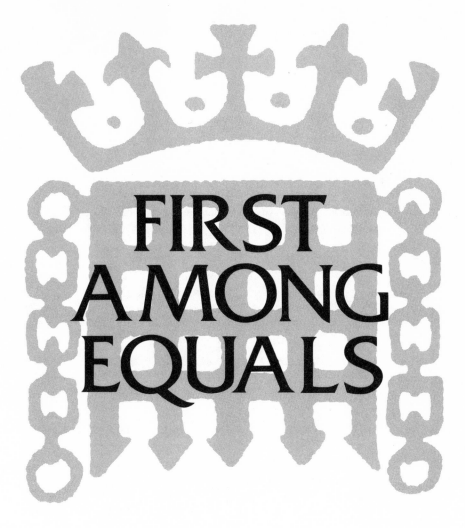

FIRST AMONG EQUALS

Linden Press/Simon & Schuster
NEW YORK
1984

This novel is a work of fiction. Names, characters, places and
incidents are either the product of the author's imagination or
are used fictitiously. Any resemblance to actual events or lo-
cales or persons, living or dead is entirely coincidental.

Published by Linden Press/Simon & Schuster
A Division of Simon & Schuster, Inc.
Simon & Schuster Building
Rockefeller Center
1230 Avenue of the Americas
New York, New York 10020
LINDEN PRESS/SIMON & SCHUSTER and colophon are trademarks
of Simon & Schuster, Inc.
Designed by Eve Metz
Manufactured in the United States of America

1   3   5   7   9   10   8   6   4   2

Library of Congress Cataloging in Publication Data

Archer, Jeffrey, date.
First among equals.
I. Title.
PR6051.R285F5   1984   823'.914   84-11267
ISBN 0-671-50406-1

TO JONI

PROLOGUE

Saturday, April 27, 1991

KING CHARLES III made the final decision.

The election had duly taken place as decreed by royal proclamation. The polling booths had been closed, the votes counted, the computers turned off; and the experts and amateurs alike had collapsed into their beds in disbelief when they had heard the final result.

The new King had been unable to sleep that Friday night while he considered yet again all the advice that had been offered to him by his courtiers during the past twenty-four hours. The choice he had been left with was by no means simple, considering how recently he had ascended the throne.

A few minutes after Big Ben had struck 6 A.M., the morning papers were placed in the corridor outside his bedroom. The King slipped quietly out of bed, put on his dressing gown and smiled at the startled footman when he opened the door. The King gathered up the papers in his arms and took them through to the morning room in order that the Queen would not be disturbed. Once he had settled comfortably into his favorite chair, he turned to the editorial pages. Only one subject was worthy of their attention that day. The Fleet Street editors had all come to the same conclusion. The result of the election could not have been closer, and the new King had been placed in a most delicate position as to whom he should call to be his first Prime Minister.

Most of the papers went on to give the King their personal advice on whom he should consider according to their own political affiliations. The London *Times* alone offered no such opinion, but suggested merely that His Majesty would have to show a great deal of courage and fortitude in facing his first constitutional crisis if the monarchy was to remain credible in a modern world.

The forty-three-year-old King dropped the papers on the floor by the side of his chair and considered once again the problems of which man to select. What a strange game politics was, he considered. Only a short time ago there had been clearly three men to consider, and then suddenly one of them was no longer a contender. The two men remaining—who he suspected had also not slept that night—could not have been more different—and yet in some ways they were so alike. They had both entered the House of Commons in 1964 and had then conducted glittering careers in their twenty-five years as members of Parliament. Between them they had held the portfolios of Trade, Defense, the Foreign Office and the Exchequer before being elected to lead their respective parties.

As Prince of Wales, the King had watched them both from the sidelines and grown to admire their different contributions to public life. On a personal level, he had to admit, he had always liked one while respecting the other.

The King checked his watch and then pressed a bell on the table by his side. A valet dressed in a royal blue uniform entered the room as if he had been waiting outside the door all night. He began to lay out the King's morning suit as the monarch went into the adjoining room where his bath had already been drawn. When the King returned he dressed in silence before taking a seat at a small table by the window to be served breakfast. He ate alone. He had left firm instructions that none of the children were to disturb him.

At eight o'clock he retired to his study to listen to the morning news. There was nothing fresh to report. The commentators were now only waiting to discover which man would be invited to the palace to kiss hands.

At nine-fifteen he picked up the phone. "Would you come up now, please," was all he said. A moment later the King's private secretary entered the room. He bowed, but said nothing, as he could see the monarch was preoccupied. It was several moments before the King spoke.

"I have made my decision," he said quietly.

PART ONE

The Backbenchers

1964-1966

1

IF CHARLES GURNEY HAMPTON had been born nine minutes earlier he would have become an earl and inherited a castle in Scotland, twenty-two thousand acres in Somerset and a thriving merchant bank in the city of London.

It was to be several years before young Charles worked out the full significance of coming second in life's first race.

His twin brother, Rupert, barely came through the ordeal, and in the years that followed contracted not only the usual childhood illnesses but managed to add scarlet fever, diphtheria and meningitis, causing his mother, Lady Hampton, to fear for his survival.

Charles, on the other hand, *was* a survivor, and had inherited enough Hampton ambition for both his brother and himself. Only a few years passed before those who came into contact with the brothers for the first time mistakenly assumed Charles was the heir to the earldom.

As the years went by, Charles's father tried desperately to discover something at which Rupert might triumph over his brother—and failed. When they were eight, the two boys were sent away to prep school at Summerfields, where generations of Hamptons had been prepared for the rigors of Eton. During his first month at the school Charles was voted class president, and no one hindered his advance en route to becoming head of the student body at the age of twelve, by which time Rupert was looked upon as "Hampton Minor." Both boys proceeded to Eton, where in their first term Charles beat Rupert at every subject in the classroom, outrowed him on the river and nearly killed him in the boxing ring.

When in 1947 their grandfather, the thirteenth Earl of Bridgewater, finally expired, the sixteen-year-old Rupert became Viscount Hampton while Charles inherited a meaningless prefix.

The Honorable Charles Hampton felt angry every time he heard his brother deferentially addressed by strangers as "My Lord."

At Eton, Charles continued to excel, and ended his school days as President of Pop—the exclusive Eton club—before being offered a place at Christ Church, Oxford, to read history. Rupert covered the same years without making one honor roll. At the age of eighteen the young viscount returned to the family estate in Somerset to pass the rest of his days as a landowner. No one destined to inherit twenty-two thousand acres could be described as a farmer.

At Oxford, Charles, free of Rupert's shadow, progressed with the air of a man who found the university something of an anticlimax. He would spend his weekdays reading the history of his relations and the weekends at house parties or riding to hounds. As no one had suggested for one moment that Rupert should enter the world of high finance, it was assumed that once Charles had graduated Oxford, he would succeed his father at Hampton's Bank, first as a director and then in time as its chairman—although it would be Rupert who would eventually inherit the family shareholding.

This assumption changed, however, when one evening the Honorable Charles Hampton was dragged to the Oxford Union by a nubile undergraduate from Somerville, who demanded that he listen to Sir Winston Churchill, who was making a rare appearance to debate the motion "I'd rather be a commoner than a lord."

14

Charles sat at the back of a hall packed with eager students mesmerized by the elder statesman's performance. Never once did he take his eyes off the great war leader during his witty and powerful speech, although what kept flashing across his mind was the realization that, but for an accident of birth, Churchill would have been the ninth Duke of Marlborough. Here was a man who had dominated the world stage for three decades and then turned down every hereditary honor a grateful nation could offer, including the title of Duke of London.

Charles never allowed himself to be referred to by his title again. From that moment, his ultimate ambition was above mere titles.

Another undergraduate who listened to Churchill that night was also considering his own future. But he did not view the proceedings crammed between his fellow students at the back of the crowded hall. The tall young man dressed in white tie and tails sat alone in a large chair on a raised platform, for such was his right as President of the Oxford Union. His natural good looks had played no part in his election because women still were unable to become members.

Although Simon Kerslake *was* the firstborn, he had otherwise few of Charles Hampton's advantages. The only son of a family solicitor, he had come to appreciate how much his father had denied himself to ensure that his son should remain at the local public school. Simon's father had died during his son's last year at school, leaving his widow a small annuity and a magnificent Mackinley grandfather clock. Simon's mother sold the clock a week after the funeral in order that her son could complete his final year with all the "extras" the other boys took for granted. She also hoped that it would give Simon a better chance of going on to university.

From the first day he could walk, Simon had always wanted to outdistance his peers. The Americans would have described him as an "achiever," while many of his contemporaries thought of him as pushy, or even arrogant, according to their

15

aptitude for jealousy. During his last term at Lancing, Simon was passed over for Head of School, and forever found himself unable to forgive the headmaster his lack of foresight. Later that year, he narrowly missed a place at Oxford's Magdalen College. It was a decision Simon was unwilling to accept.

In the same mail, Durham University offered him a scholarship, which he rejected by return post. "Future Prime Ministers aren't educated at Durham," he informed his mother.

"How about Cambridge?" inquired his mother lightly.

"No political tradition," replied Simon.

"But if there is no chance of being offered a place at Oxford, surely . . . ?"

"That's not what I said, Mother," replied the young man. "I shall be an undergraduate at Oxford by the first day of term."

After eighteen years of improbable victories, Mrs. Kerslake had learned to stop asking her son, "How will you manage that?"

Some fourteen days before the start of the Christmas term at Oxford, Simon booked himself into a small guest house just off the Iffley Road. On a trestle table in the corner of lodgings he intended to make permanent, he wrote out a list of all the Oxford colleges, then divided them into five columns, planning to visit three each morning and three each afternoon until his question had been answered positively by a resident tutor for admissions: "Have you accepted any freshmen for this year who are now unable to take up their places?"

It was on the fourth afternoon, just as doubt was beginning to set in and Simon was wondering if after all he would have to travel to Cambridge the following week, that he received the first affirmative reply.

The tutor for admissions at Worcester College removed the glasses from the end of his nose and stared up at the tall young man with the mop of dark hair falling over his forehead. The young man's intense brown eyes remained fixed on the tutor for admissions. Alan Brown was the twenty-second don Simon Kerslake had visited in four days.

16

"Yes," he replied. "It so happens that, sadly, a young man from Nottingham High School, who had been offered a place here, was killed in a motorcycle accident last month."

"What course—what subject was he going to read?" Simon's words were unusually faltering. He prayed it wasn't chemistry, architecture or classics. Alan Brown flicked through a rotary index on his desk, obviously enjoying the little cross-examination. He peered at the card in front of him. "History," he announced.

Simon's heartbeat reached one hundred and twenty. "I just missed a place at Magdalen to read politics, philosophy and economics," he said. "Would you consider me for the vacancy?"

The older man was unable to hide a smile. He had never, in twenty-four years, came across such a request.

"Full name?" he said, replacing his glasses as if the serious business of the meeting had now begun.

"Simon John Kerslake."

Dr. Brown picked up the telephone by his side and dialed a number. "Nigel?" he said. "It's Alan Brown here. Did you ever consider offering a man called Kerslake a place at Magdalen?"

Mrs. Kerslake was not surprised when her son went on to be President of the Oxford Union. After all, she teased, wasn't it just another stepping-stone on the path to Prime Minister—Gladstone, Asquith . . . Kerslake?

Ray Gould was born in a tiny, windowless room above his father's butcher shop in Leeds. For the first nine years of his life he shared that room with his ailing grandmother, until she died at the age of sixty-one.

Ray's close proximity to the old woman who had lost her husband in the Great War at first appeared romantic to him. He would listen enraptured as she told him stories of her hero husband in his smart khaki uniform—a uniform now folded neatly in her bottom drawer, but still displayed in the fading sepia photograph at the side of her bed. Soon, however, his grandmother's stories filled Ray with sadness, as he became aware that she had been a widow for nearly thirty years. Finally she seemed a tragic figure as he realized how little she had experienced of the world beyond that cramped room in which she was surrounded by all her possessions and a yellowed envelope containing five hundred irredeemable war bonds.

There had been no purpose in Ray's grandmother's making a will, for all he inherited was the room. Overnight it ceased to be a double bedroom and became a study, full of ever-changing library books and schoolbooks, the former often returned late, using up Ray's meager pocket money in fines. But as each school report was brought home, it became increasingly apparent to Ray's father that he would not be extending the sign above the butcher shop to proclaim "Gould and Son."

At eleven, Ray won the top scholarship to Roundhay Grammar School. Wearing his first pair of long trousers—shortened several inches by his mother—and horn-rimmed glasses that didn't quite fit, he set off for the opening day at his new school. Ray's mother hoped there were other boys as thin and spotty as her son, and that his wavy red hair would not cause him to be continually teased.

By the end of his first term, Ray was surprised to find he was far ahead of his contemporaries, so far, in fact, that the headmaster considered it prudent to put him up a form "to stretch the lad a little," as he explained to Ray's parents. By the end of that year, one spent mainly in the classroom, Ray managed to come in third in the class, and first in Latin and English. Only when it came to selecting teams for any sport did Ray find he was last in anything. However brilliant his mind might have been, it never seemed to coordinate with his body.

In any case, the only competition he cared for that year was the middle school essay prize. The winner of the prize would be required to read his entry to the assembled pupils and parents on Speech Day. Even before he handed in his entry, Ray rehearsed his efforts out loud several times in the privacy of his study-bedroom, fearing he would not be properly prepared if he waited until the winner was announced.

Ray's form master had told all his pupils that the subject of the essay could be of their own choosing, but that they should try to recall some experience that had been unique to them. After reading Ray's account of his grandmother's life in the little room above the butcher shop, the form master had no inclination to pick up another script. After he had dutifully struggled through the remainder of the entries, he did not hesitate in recommending Gould's essay for the prize. The only reservation, he admitted to Ray, was the choice of title. Ray thanked him for the advice but the title remained intact.

On the morning of Speech Day, the school assembly hall was packed with nine hundred pupils and their parents. After the headmaster had delivered his speech and the applause had died down, he announced, "I shall now call upon the winner of the prize essay competition to deliver his entry: Ray Gould."

Ray left his place in the hall and marched confidently up onto the stage. He stared down at the two thousand expectant faces but showed no sign of apprehension, partly because he found it difficult to see beyond the third row. When he announced the title of his essay, some of the younger children began to snigger, causing Ray to stumble through his first few lines. But by the time he had reached the last page the packed hall was still, and after he had completed the final paragraph he received the first standing ovation of his career.

Twelve-year-old Ray Gould left the stage to rejoin his parents at their seats. His mother's head was bowed but he could still see tears trickling down her cheeks. His father was trying not to look too proud. Even when Ray was seated, the applause continued, so he, too, lowered his head to stare at the title of his prize-winning essay: "The First Changes I Will Make When I Become Prime Minister."

2

MR. SPEAKER ROSE and surveyed the Commons. He tugged at his long black silk gown, then nervously tweaked the full-bottomed wig that covered his balding head. The House had almost gotten out of control during a particularly rowdy session of Prime Minister's Questions, and he was delighted to see the clock reach three-thirty. Time to pass on to the next business of the day.

He stood shifting from foot to foot, waiting for the five hundred–odd members of Parliament present to settle down before he intoned solemnly, "Members desiring to take the oath." The packed assembly switched its gaze from Mr. Speaker toward the far end of the chamber, like a crowd watching a tennis match.

The newly elected member of Parliament stood at the entrance of the House of Commons. At six feet four, he looked like a man born with the Tory party in mind. His patrician head was set on an aristocratic frame, a mane of fair hair combed meticulously into place. Dressed in a dark-gray, double-breasted suit, with a Regimental Guards tie of maroon and blue, flanked by his proposer and seconder, Charles Hampton took four paces forward. Like well-drilled guardsmen, they stopped and bowed, then advanced toward the long table that stood in front of the Speaker's chair between the two front

20

benches. Charles was surprised at how small the chamber was in reality: the Government and Opposition benches faced each other a mere sword's length apart. Charles recalled that historically a sword's length had once insured the safety of those bitter rivals who sat opposite each other.

Leaving his sponsors in his wake, he passed down the long table, stepping over the legs of the Prime Minister and the Foreign Secretary before being handed the oath by the Clerk of the House.

He held the little card in his right hand and pronounced the words as firmly as if they had been his marriage vows.

"I, Charles Hampton, do swear that I will be faithful, and bear true allegiance to Her Majesty Queen Elizabeth, her heirs and successors according to law, so help me God."

"Hear, hear," rose from his colleagues as the new member of Parliament leaned over to inscribe the Test Roll, a parchment folded into book shape. Charles proceeded toward the Speaker's chair, when he stopped and bowed.

"Welcome to the House, Mr. Hampton," said the Speaker, shaking his hand. "I hope you will serve this place for many years to come."

"Thank you, Mr. Speaker," said Charles, and bowed for a final time before continuing on to the small area behind the Speaker's chair. He had carried out the little ceremony exactly as the Tory Chief Whip had rehearsed it with him in the long corridor outside his office.

"Congratulations on your splendid victory, Charles," said the former Prime Minister and now Leader of the Opposition, Sir Alec Douglas-Home, who also shook him warmly by the hand. "I know you have a great deal to offer to the Conservative Party and your country."

"Thank you," replied the new MP, who, after waiting for Sir Alec to return to take his place on the Opposition front bench, made his way up the aisle steps to find a place in the back row of the long green benches.

For the next two hours Charles Hampton followed the proceedings of the House with a mixture of awe and excitement.

He marveled at the simplicity and justice of the parliamentary system in lively debate before him. Labour versus Tory, Government versus Opposition, the Minister on the bench and his Shadow Minister on the opposite bench. And as with two soccer teams, Charles knew every position was covered—Government Minister continually scrutinized by his Shadow Minister in the Opposition. He also knew that if the Conservatives won the next election, the Shadow team was well prepared to take over from the outgoing Labour Government.

Glancing up at the Strangers' Gallery, he saw his wife, Fiona, his father, the fourteenth Earl of Bridgewater, and his brother, the Viscount Hampton, peering down at him with pride. Surely no one could now be in any doubt as to which Hampton should have inherited the family title. For the first time in his life, he had found something that wasn't his by birthright or by effortless conquest.

Charles settled back on the first rung of the ladder.

Raymond Gould stared down at the invitation. He had never seen the inside of Number 10 Downing Street. During the last thirteen years of Conservative rule few Labourites had. He passed the embossed card across the breakfast table to his wife.

"Should I accept or refuse, Ray?" she asked in her broad Yorkshire accent.

She was the only person who still called him Ray, and even her attempts at humor now annoyed him. The Greek tragedians had based their drama on "the fatal flaw," and he had no doubt what his had been.

He had met Joyce at a dance given by the nurses of Leeds General Hospital. He hadn't wanted to go but a second-year undergraduate friend from Roundhay convinced him it would make an amusing break. At school he had shown little interest in girls, and, as his mother kept reminding him, there would be occasion enough for that sort of thing once he had taken his degree. When he became an undergraduate he felt certain that he was the only virgin left at the university.

He had ended up sitting alone in the corner of a room decorated with wilting balloons, sipping disconsolately at a Coke through a bent straw. Whenever his school friend turned around from the dance floor—each time with a different partner—Raymond would smile broadly back. With his National Health spectacles tucked away in an inside pocket, he couldn't always be certain he was smiling at the right person. He began contemplating at what hour he could possibly leave without having to admit the evening had been a total disaster. He would have been frightened by her overture if it hadn't been for that broad familiar accent.

"You at the University as well?"

"As well as what?" he asked, without looking directly at her.

"As well as your friend," she said.

"Yes," he replied, looking up at a girl he guessed was about his age.

"I'm from Bradford."

"I'm from Leeds," he admitted, aware as the seconds passed that his face was growing as red as his hair.

"You don't have much of an accent, considering."

That pleased him.

"My name is Joyce," she volunteered.

"Mine's Ray," he said.

"Like to dance?"

He wanted to tell her that he had rarely been on a dance floor in his life, but he didn't have the courage. Like a puppet, he found himself standing up and being guided by her toward the dancers. So much for his assumption that he was one of nature's leaders.

Once they were on the dance floor he looked at her properly for the first time. She wasn't half bad, any normal Yorkshire boy might have admitted. She was about five feet seven, and her

23

auburn hair tied up in a ponytail matched the dark-brown eyes that had a little too much makeup around them. She wore pink lipstick the same color as her short skirt, from which emerged two very attractive legs. They looked even more attractive when she twirled to the music of the four-piece student band. Raymond discovered that if he twirled Joyce very fast he could see the tops of her stockings, and he remained on the dance floor far longer than he would even have thought possible. After the quartet had put their instruments away, Joyce kissed him goodnight before Ray went back to his small room above the butcher shop.

The following Sunday, in an attempt to gain the upper hand, he took Joyce rowing on the Aire, but his performance there was no better than his dancing, and everything on the river overtook him, including a hardy swimmer. He watched out of the side of his eyes for a mocking laugh, but Joyce only smiled and chatted about missing Bradford and wanting to return home to be a nurse. Ray wanted to explain to her that he longed to escape Leeds. He couldn't wait to travel to London. But he also knew he didn't want to leave this pretty girl behind. When he eventually returned the boat, Joyce invited him back to her boardinghouse for tea. He went scarlet as they passed her landlady, and Joyce hustled him up the worn stone staircase to her little room.

Ray sat on the end of the narrow bed while Joyce made two milkless mugs of tea. After they had both pretended to drink, she sat beside him, her hands in her lap. He found himself listening intently to an ambulance siren as it faded away in the distance. She leaned over and kissed him, taking one of his hands and placing it on her knee.

She parted his lips and their tongues touched; he found it a peculiar sensation, an arousing one; his eyes remained closed as she gently led him through each new experience, until he was unable to stop himself committing what he felt sure his mother had once described as a mortal sin.

"It will be easier next time," she said shyly, maneuvering herself from the narrow bed to sort out the crumpled clothes spread across the floor. She was right: he wanted her again in less than an hour, and this time his eyes remained wide open.

It was another six months before Joyce hinted at the future, and by then Ray was bored with her and had his sights set on a bright little mathematician in her final year. The mathematician hailed from Surrey.

Just at the time when Ray was summing up enough courage to let her know the affair was over, Joyce told him she was pregnant. His father would have taken a meat ax to him had he suggested an illegal abortion. His mother was only relieved that she was a Yorkshire girl.

Ray and Joyce were married at St. Mary's in Bradford during the long vacation. When the wedding photos were developed, Ray looked so distressed, and Joyce so happy, that they resembled father and daughter rather than husband and wife. After a reception in the church hall the newly married couple traveled down to Dover to catch the night ferry. Their first night as Mr. and Mrs. Gould was a disaster. Ray turned out to be a particularly bad sailor. Joyce only hoped that Paris would prove to be memorable—and it was. She had a miscarriage on the second night of their honeymoon.

"Probably caused by all the excitement," his mother said on their return. "Still, you can always have another, can't you? And this time folk won't be able to call it a little . . ." she checked herself.

Ray showed no interest in having another. He completed his first-class honors degree in law at Leeds and then moved to London, as planned, to complete his studies at the bar. After only a few months in the metropolis, Leeds faded from his memory, and by the end of his two-year course Ray had been accepted at a fashionable London chambers to become a much-sought-after junior counsel. From that moment he rarely mentioned his North of England roots to his carefully cultivated

25

new circle of society friends, and those comrades who addressed him as Ray received a sharp "Raymond" for their familiarity.

The only exception Raymond made to this rule was when it served his budding political career. Leeds North had chosen Raymond to be their Labour candidate for Parliament from a field of thirty-seven. Yorkshire folk like people who stay at home, and Raymond had been quick to point out to the selection committee, in an exaggerated Yorkshire accent, that he had been educated at Roundhay Grammar School on the fringes of the constituency and that he had refused a scholarship to Cambridge, preferring to continue his education at Leeds University.

Ten years had passed since the Goulds' memorable honeymoon, and Raymond had long since accepted that he was tethered to Joyce for life. Although she was only thirty-two, she already needed to cover those once-slim legs that had first so attracted him.

How could he be so punished for such a pathetic mistake? Raymond wanted to ask the gods. How mature he had thought he was; how immature he had turned out to be. Divorce made sense, but it would have meant the end of his political ambitions: no Yorkshire folk would have considered selecting a divorced man. Not to mention the problem that would create with his parents; after ten years of housing the young Goulds on their trips to Leeds, they had come to adore their daughter-in-law. To be fair, it hadn't all been a disaster; he had to admit that the locals adored her as well. During the election six weeks before she had mixed with the trade unionists and their frightful wives far better than he had ever managed to do, and he had to acknowledge that she had been a major factor in his winning the Leeds seat by over nineteen thousand votes. He wondered how she could sound so sincere the whole time; it never occurred to him that it was natural.

"Why don't you buy yourself a new dress for Downing Street?" Raymond said as they rose from the breakfast table.

26

She smiled; he had not volunteered such a suggestion for as long as she could remember. Joyce had no illusions about her husband and his feelings for her, but hoped that eventually he would realize she could help him achieve his unspoken ambition.

On the night of the reception at Downing Street Joyce made every effort to look her best. She had spent the morning at Marks and Spencer searching for an outfit appropriate for the occasion, finally returning to a suit she had liked the moment she had walked into the store. It was not the perfect fit but the sales assistant assured Joyce "that madam looked quite sensational in it." She only hoped that Ray's remarks would be half as flattering. By the time she reached home, she realized she had no accessories to match its unusual color.

Raymond was late returning from the Commons and was pleased to find Joyce ready when he leaped out of the bath. He bit back a derogatory remark about the incongruity of her new suit with her old shoes. As they drove toward Westminster, he rehearsed the names of every member of the Cabinet with her, making Joyce repeat them as if she were a child.

The air was cool and crisp that night so Raymond parked his Volkswagen in New Palace Yard and they strolled across Whitehall together to Number 10. A solitary policeman stood guard at the door of the Prime Minister's residence. Seeing Raymond approach, the officer banged the brass knocker once and the door was opened for the young member and his wife.

Raymond and Joyce stood awkwardly in the hall as if they were waiting outside a headmaster's study until eventually they were directed to the first floor. They walked slowly up the staircase, which turned out to be less grand than Raymond had anticipated, passing photographs of former Prime Ministers. "Too many Tories," muttered Raymond as he passed Chamberlain, Churchill, Eden, Macmillan and Home, with Attlee the only framed compensation.

At the top of the stairs stood the short figure of Harold Wilson, pipe in mouth, waiting to welcome his guests. Raymond was about to introduce his wife when the Prime Minister said, "How are you, Joyce? I'm so glad you could make it."

"Make it? I've been looking forward to the occasion all week." Her frankness made Raymond wince. He failed to notice that it made Wilson chuckle.

Raymond chatted with the Prime Minister's wife about her recent book of poetry until she turned away to greet the next guest. He then moved off into the drawing room and was soon talking to Cabinet Ministers, trade-union leaders and their wives, always keeping a wary eye on Joyce, who seemed engrossed in conversation with the general secretary of the Trades Union Council.

Raymond moved on to the American ambassador, who was telling Jamie Sinclair, one of the new intake from Scotland, how much he had enjoyed the Edinburgh Festival that summer. Raymond envied Sinclair the relaxed clubable manner that was the stamp of his aristocratic family. He interrupted their flow of conversation awkwardly. "I was interested to read Johnson's latest communiqué on Vietnam, and I must confess that the escalation . . ."

"What's he interrogating you about?" asked a voice from behind him. Raymond turned to find the Prime Minister by his side. "I think I should warn you, Ambassador," continued Mr. Wilson, "that Raymond Gould is one of the brighter efforts we've produced this time, and quite capable of quoting you verbatim years after you've forgotten what you thought you said."

"It's not that long ago they used to say the same sort of thing about you," the ambassador replied.

The Prime Minister chuckled, slapped Raymond on the shoulder and moved on to another group of guests.

Raymond rankled at the condescension he imagined he'd heard in the Prime Minister's tone, only too aware that his nervousness had led him to commit a social gaffe. As in the past, his humiliation turned quickly into anger against himself. He knew that the Prime Minister's words had contained some genuine admiration, for if Raymond had gained any reputation in his first six weeks in Parliament, it was as one of the Labour Party's intellectuals. But he felt the familiar fear that he would ultimately fail to turn his mental acuity into the currency of politics. Whereas some of his peers among the new intake of MPs, men like Simon Kerslake, had delivered maiden speeches that made the veterans in Parliament sit up and take notice, Raymond's first effort had not been well received; reading nervously from a prepared manuscript, he had been unable to make the House hang on his every word.

Rooted to the spot, feeling the familiar blush rise to his face, Raymond was determined to remain calm. His career, he assured himself for the umpteenth time, would simply have to follow an unusual path. He had already begun to work to that end, and if he could pull it off, few members would be able to ignore or challenge him.

Reassured, Raymond moved on to be introduced to several people about whom he had only read in the past; he was surprised to find that they treated him as an equal. At the end of the evening, after they had stayed what he later told Joyce had been a little too long, he drove his wife back to their home on Lansdowne Road.

On the way he talked nonstop about all the people he had met, what he thought of them, describing their jobs, giving her his impressions, almost as if she hadn't been there.

They had seen little of each other during Simon Kerslake's first six weeks in Parliament, which made tonight even more special. The Labour Party might have returned to power after thirteen years, but with a majority of only four, it was proving almost impossible for Simon to get to bed much before midnight. He couldn't see any easing of the pressure until one party had gained a sensible working majority, and that would not happen until there was another General Election. But what Simon feared most, having won his own constituency with the slimmest of majorities, was that such an election would unseat him, and that he might end up with one of the shortest political careers on record.

That was why Lavinia was so good for him. He enjoyed the company of the tall, willowy girl who couldn't pronounce her Ws, and he was angered by the gossip that he knew surrounded their relationship.

True, his political career had been off to a slow start before he'd met Lavinia Maxwell-Harrington. After Oxford, throughout his two years of National Service with the Sussex Light Infantry, he'd never lost sight of his goal. When he sought a position at the BBC as a general trainee, his natural ability to shine at interviews secured him the job, but he used every spare moment to advance his political ambitions: he quickly joined several Tory organizations, writing pamphlets and speaking at weekend conferences. However, he'd never been taken seriously as a prospective candidate until 1959, when, during the General Election, his hard work earned him the post of personal assistant to the party chairman.

During the campaign he had met Lavinia Maxwell-Harrington at a dinner party held at Harrington Hall in honor of his chairman. Lavinia's father, Sir Rufus Maxwell-Harrington, had also been, "sometime in the dim distant past," as Lavinia described it, chairman of the Tory Party.

When the Conservatives had been returned to power Simon found himself a frequent weekend guest at Harrington Hall. By the time the 1964 election had been called, Sir Rufus had passed Simon for membership of the Carlton—the exclusive Conservative club in St. James—and rumors of an imminent engagement between Simon and Lavinia were regularly hinted at in the gossip columns of the London press.

In the summer of 1964, Sir Rufus's influence had once again proved decisive, and Simon was offered the chance to defend the marginal constituency of Coventry Central. Simon retained the seat for the Tories at the General Election by a slender nine hundred and seventy-one votes.

Simon parked his MGB outside Number 4 Chelsea Square and checked his watch. He cursed at being once again a few minutes late, although he realized Lavinia was well versed in the voting habits of politicians. He pushed back the mop of brown hair that perpetually fell over his forehead, buttoned up his new blazer and straightened his tie. He cursed again as he pulled the little brass bell knob. He had forgotten to pick up the roses he had ordered for Lavinia, although he had passed the shop on the way.

The butler answered the door and Simon was shown to the sitting room to find Lavinia and Lady Maxwell-Harrington discussing the forthcoming Chelsea Ball.

"Oh, Simon darling," began Lavinia, turning her slim body toward him. "How super to see you."

Simon smiled. He still hadn't quite got used to the language used by girls who lived between Sloane Square and Kensington.

"I do hope you've managed to escape from that dreadful place for the rest of the evening," she said.

"Absolutely," Simon found himself saying, "and I've even captured a table at the Caprice."

"Oh, goody," said Lavinia. "And are they expecting you to return and vote for some silly bill on the hour of ten?"

"No, I'm yours all night," said Simon, regretting the words as soon as he had said them. He caught the cool expression on the face of Lady Maxwell-Harrington and cursed for a third time.

31

3

CHARLES HAMPTON drove his Daimler from the Commons to his father's bank in the city. He still thought of Hampton's of Threadneedle Street as his father's bank although for two generations the family had been only minority shareholders, with Charles himself in possession of a mere 2 percent of the stock. Nevertheless, as his brother Rupert showed no desire to represent the family interests, the 2 percent guaranteed Charles a place on the board and an income sufficient to insure that his paltry parliamentary salary of £1,750 a year was adequately supplemented.

From the day Charles had first taken his place on the board of Hampton's, he had had no doubt that the new chairman, Derek Spencer, considered him a dangerous rival. Spencer had lobbied to have Rupert replace his father upon the latter's retirement, and only because of Charles's insistence had Spencer failed to move the old earl to his way of thinking.

When Charles went on to win his seat in Parliament, Spencer at once raised the problem that his burdensome responsibilities at the House would prevent him from carrying out his day to day duties to the board. However, Charles was able to convince a majority of his fellow directors of the advantages of having someone from the board at Westminster, although the rules dictated that his private employment would have to cease if he was ever invited to be a Minister of the Crown.

Charles left the Daimler in Hampton's courtyard. It amused him to consider that his parking space was worth twenty times the value of the car. The area at the front of Hampton's was a relic of his great-grandfather's day. The twelfth Earl of Bridgewater had insisted on an entrance large enough to allow a complete sweep for his coach and four. That conveyance had long disappeared, to be replaced by twelve parking spaces for Hampton directors. Derek Spencer, despite all his grammar-school virtues, had never suggested that the land be used for any other purpose.

The young girl seated at the reception desk abruptly stopped polishing her nails in time to say "Good morning, Mr. Charles," as he came through the revolving doors and disappeared into a waiting elevator. A few moments later Charles was seated behind a desk in his small oak-paneled office, a clean white memo pad in front of him. He pressed a button on the intercom and told his secretary that he did not want to be disturbed during the next hour.

Every Conservative member of Parliament assumed that after his defeat in the election Sir Alec Douglas-Home would soon step down as Leader of the Opposition. Now, in the spring of 1965, Charles knew he had to decide whose coattail to hang onto. While he remained in Opposition, his only hope was of being offered a junior Shadow post, but that could turn out to be the stepping-stone to becoming a Government Minister if the Conservatives won the next election. He faced the first major test of his career.

Sixty minutes later the white pad had twelve names penciled on it, but ten already had lines drawn through them. Only the names of Reginald Maudling and Edward Heath remained.

Charles tore off the piece of paper and the indented sheet underneath and put them both through the shredder by the side of his desk. He tried to summon up some interest in the agenda for the bank's weekly board meeting; only one item, item seven, seemed to be of any importance. Just before eleven, he gathered up his papers and headed toward the boardroom. Most of his colleagues were already seated when Derek Spencer called item number 1 as the boardroom clock chimed the hour.

During the ensuing predictable discussion on bank rates, the movement in metal prices, Eurobonds and client-investment policy, Charles's mind kept wandering back to the forthcoming Leadership election and the importance of backing the winner if he was to be quickly promoted from the back benches.

By the time they reached item 7 on the agenda Charles had made up his mind. Derek Spencer opened a discussion on the proposed loans to Mexico and Poland, and most of the board members agreed with him that the bank should participate in one, but not risk both.

Charles's thoughts, however, were not in Mexico City or Warsaw. They were far nearer home, and when the chairman called for a vote, Charles didn't register.

"Mexico or Poland, Charles? Which do you favor?"

"Heath," he replied.

"I beg your pardon," said Derek Spencer.

Charles snapped back from Westminster to Threadneedle Street to find everyone at the boardroom table staring at him. With the air of a man who had been giving the matter considerable thought, Charles said firmly, "Mexico," and added, "The great difference between the two countries can best be gauged by their attitudes to repayment. Mexico might not want to repay, but Poland won't be able to, so why not limit our risks and back Mexico? If it comes to litigation I'd prefer to be against someone who won't pay rather than someone who can't." The older members around the table nodded in agreement; the right son of Bridgewater was sitting on the board.

When the meeting was over Charles joined his colleagues for lunch in the directors' dining room. A room containing two Hogarths, a Brueghel, a Goya and a Rembrandt—just another reminder of his great-grandfather's ability to select winners— could distract even the most self-indulgent gourmet. Charles did not wait to make a decision between the Cheddar and the Stilton as he wanted to be back in the Commons for Question Time.

On arriving at the House he immediately made his way to the smoking room, long regarded by the Tories as their preserve. There in the deep leather armchairs and cigar-laden atmosphere the talk was entirely of who would be Sir Alec Home's successor.

Later that afternoon Charles returned to the Commons chamber. He wanted to observe Heath and his Shadow team deal with Government amendments one by one. Heath was on his feet facing the Prime Minister, his notes on the dispatch box in front of him.

Charles was about to leave the chamber when Raymond Gould rose to move an amendment from the back benches. Charles remained glued to his seat. He had to listen with grudging admiration as Raymond's intellectual grasp and force of argument easily compensated for his lack of oratorical skill. Although Gould was a cut above the rest of the new intake on the Labour benches, he didn't frighten Charles. Twelve generations of cunning and business acumen had kept large parts of Leeds in the hands of the Bridgewater family without the likes of Raymond Gould even being aware of it.

Charles took supper in the members' dining room that night and sat in the center of the room at the large table occupied by Tory backbenchers. There was only one topic of conversation, and as the same two names kept emerging it was obvious that it was going to be a very close-run race.

When Charles arrived back at his Eaton Square home after the ten o'clock vote, his wife, Fiona, was already tucked up in bed reading Graham Greene's *The Comedians.*

"They let you out early tonight."

"Not too bad," said Charles, and began regaling her with how he had spent his day, before disappearing into the bathroom.

Charles imagined he was cunning, but his wife, Lady Fiona

35

Hampton, née Campbell, only daughter of the Duke of Falkirk, was in a different league. She and Charles had been selected for each other by their grandparents and neither had questioned or doubted the wisdom of the choice. Although Charles had squired numerous girlfriends before their marriage, he had always assumed he would return to Fiona. Charles's father, the fourteenth earl, had always maintained that the aristocracy was becoming far too lax and sentimental about love. "Women," he declared, "are for bearing children and insuring a continuation of the male line." The old earl became even more firm in his convictions when he was informed that Rupert showed little interest in the opposite sex and was rarely to be found in women's company.

Fiona would never have dreamed of disagreeing with the old earl to his face and was herself delighted by the thought of giving birth to a son who would inherit the earldom. But despite enthusiastic and then contrived efforts Charles seemed unable to sire an heir. Fiona was assured by a Harley Street physician that there was no reason *she* could not bear children. The specialist had suggested that perhaps her husband pay the clinic a visit. She shook her head, knowing Charles would dismiss such an idea out of hand, no matter how much he wanted a son.

Fiona spent much of her spare time in their Sussex East constituency furthering Charles's political career. She had learned to live with the fact that theirs was not destined to be a romantic marriage and had almost resigned herself to its other advantages. Although many men confessed covertly and overtly that they found Fiona's elegant bearing attractive, she had either rejected their advances or pretended not to notice them.

By the time Charles returned from the bathroom in his blue silk pajamas Fiona had formed a plan, but first she needed some questions answered.

"Whom do you favor?"

"It will be a close-run thing, but I spent the entire afternoon observing the serious candidates."

"Did you come to any conclusions?" Fiona asked.

"Heath and Maudling are the most likely ones, though to be honest I've never had a conversation with either of them that lasted for more than five minutes."

"In that case we must turn disadvantage into advantage."

"What do you mean, old girl?" Charles asked as he climbed into bed beside his wife.

"Think back. When you were President of Pop at Eton, could you have put a name to any of the first-year boys?"

"Certainly not," said Charles.

"Exactly. And I'd be willing to bet that neither Heath nor Maudling could put a name to twenty of the new intake on the Tory benches."

"Where are you leading me, Lady Macbeth?"

"No bloody hands will be needed for this killing. Simply, having chosen your Duncan, you volunteer to organize the new intake for him. If he becomes Leader, he's bound to feel it would be appropriate to select one or two new faces for his team."

"You really are a Campbell."

"Well, let's sleep on it," said Fiona, turning out the light on her side of the bed.

Charles didn't sleep on it but lay restless most of the night turning over in his mind what she had said. When Fiona awoke the next morning she carried on the conversation as if there had been no break in between.

"Better still," she continued, "before the man you choose announces he is a candidate, demand that he run on behalf of the new members."

"Clever," said Charles.

"Whom have you decided on?"

"Heath," Charles replied without hesitation.

"I'll back your political judgment," said Fiona. "Just trust me when it comes to tactics. First, we compose a letter."

In dressing gowns, on the floor at the end of the bed, the two elegant figures drafted and redrafted a note to Edward Heath.

At nine-thirty it was finally composed and sent around by hand to his rooms in Albany.

The next morning Charles was invited to the small bachelor flat for coffee. They talked for over an hour and the deal was struck.

Charles thought Sir Alec would announce his resignation in the late summer, which would give him eight to ten weeks to carry out a campaign. Fiona typed out a list of all the new members, and during the next eight weeks every one of them was invited to their Eaton Square house for drinks. Fiona was subtle enough to see that members of the lower house were outnumbered by other guests, often from the House of Lords. Heath managed to escape from his front-bench duties on the Finance Bill to spend at least an hour with the Hamptons once a week. As the day of Sir Alec Home's resignation drew nearer, Charles remained confident that he had carried out his plan in a subtle and discreet way. He would have been willing to place a wager that no one other than Edward Heath had any idea how deeply he was involved.

One man who attended the second of Fiona's soirees saw exactly what was going on. While many of the guests spent their time admiring the Hampton art collection, Simon Kerslake kept a wary eye on his host and hostess. Kerslake was not convinced that Edward Heath would win the forthcoming election for Leader of the Opposition and felt confident that Reginald Maudling would turn out to be the party's natural choice. Maudling was, after all, Shadow Foreign Secretary, a former chancellor and far senior to Heath. More important, he was a married man. Simon doubted the Tories would ever pick a bachelor to lead them.

As soon as Kerslake had left the Hamptons he jumped into a taxi and returned immediately to the Commons. He found Reginald Maudling in the members' dining room. He waited until Maudling had finished his meal before asking if they could have a few moments alone. The tall, shambling Maudling was not altogether certain of the name of the new member. Had he seen him just roaming around the building, he would have assumed that, with such looks, he was a television newscaster covering the Leadership contest. He leaned over and invited Simon to join him for a drink in his office.

Maudling listened intently to all that the enthusiastic young man had to say and accepted the judgment of the well-informed member without question. It was agreed that Simon should try to counter the Hampton campaign and report back his results twice a week.

While Hampton could call on all the powers and influence of his Etonian background, Kerslake weighed up the advantages and disadvantages of his competition in a manner that would have impressed a Harvard Business School graduate. He did not own a palatial home in Eaton Square in which Turners and Holbeins were to be found on the walls, not in books. He also lacked a glamorous society wife—though he hoped that would not be the case for much longer. He had no money to speak of, but he had scraped together enough from his employment at BBC to move from his tiny flat in Earl's Court to a small house on the corner of Beaufort Street in Chelsea. Lavinia now stayed the night more often, but he hadn't been able to convince her to reside there on a more permanent basis.

"You don't have enough closet space for my shoes," she once told him.

It didn't stop Simon from enjoying her company and remaining aware of her feel for politics. Over dinner the night he had seen Maudling she demanded to know, "But why do you support Reggie Maudling?"

"Reggie has a great deal more experience of government than Heath, and in any case he's more caring about those around him."

"But Daddy says Heath is so much more professional," said Lavinia.

39

"That may be the case, but the British have always preferred good amateurs to run their government," said Simon. And no better example of that than your father, Simon thought to himself.

"If you believe all that stuff about amateurs, why bother to become so involved yourself?"

Simon considered the question for some time before taking a sip of wine. "Because, frankly, I don't come from the sort of background that automatically commands the center of the Tory stage."

"True," said Lavinia, grinning. "But I do."

Simon spent the following days trying to work out the certain Maudling and certain Heath supporters, although many members claimed to favor both candidates, according to who asked them. These he listed as doubtfuls. When Enoch Powell threw his cap into the ring, Simon could not find a single new member other than Alec Pimkin who openly supported him.

Simon made no attempt to influence Pimkin's vote. The small rotund figure could be observed waddling between the members' bar and the dining room rather than the chamber and the library. He would have undoubtedly considered Simon "below his station." Even if he had not been voting for Powell, it was no secret that he was slightly in awe of his old school chum Charles Hampton, and Simon would find himself third in line. That left forty members from the new intake who still had to be followed up. Simon estimated twelve certain Heath, eleven certain Maudling and one Powell, leaving sixteen undecided. As the day of the election drew nearer it became obvious that few of the remaining sixteen actually knew either candidate well, and that most were still not sure for whom they should vote.

Because Simon could not invite them all to his small house on the corner of Beaufort Street, he would have to go to them. During the last six weeks of the race he accompanied his chosen Leader to twenty-three new members' constituencies, from

Bodmin to Glasgow, from Penrith to Great Yarmouth, briefing Maudling studiously before every meeting.

Gradually it became obvious that Charles Hampton and Simon Kerslake were the chosen lieutenants among the new Tory intake. Some members resented the whispered confidences at the Eaton Square cocktail parties, or the discovery that Simon Kerslake had visited their constituencies, while others were simply envious of the reward that would inevitably be heaped on the victor.

On July 22, 1965, Sir Alec Douglas-Home made his formal announcement of resignation to the 1922 Committee, comprised of all the Tory backbenchers.

The date chosen for the Party Leadership election was just five days away. Charles and Simon began avoiding each other, and Fiona started referring to Kerslake, first in private, then in public, as "that pushy self-made man." She stopped using the expression when Alec Pimkin asked in all innocence whether she was referring to Edward Heath.

On the morning of the secret ballot both Simon and Charles voted early and spent the rest of the day pacing the corridors of the Commons trying to assess the result. By lunchtime they were both outwardly exuberant, while inwardly despondent.

At two-fifteen they were seated in the large committee room to hear the chairman of the 1922 Committee make the historic announcement:

"The result of the election for Leader of the Conservative Parliamentary Party is as follows:

EDWARD HEATH	150 votes
REGINALD MAUDLING	133 votes
ENOCH POWELL	15 votes

Charles and Fiona opened a bottle of Krug while Simon took Lavinia to the Old Vic to see *The Royal Hunt of the Sun.*

41

He slept the entire way through Robert Stephens' brilliant performance before being driven home in silence by Lavinia.

"Well, I must say you were exciting company tonight," she said.

"I am sorry, but I'll promise to make up for it in the near future," said Simon. "Let's have dinner at Annabel's on—" Simon hesitated—"Monday. Let's make it a special occasion."

Lavinia smiled for the first time that night.

When Edward Heath announced his Shadow Government team, Reggie Maudling was named Deputy Leader. Charles Hampton received an invitation to join the Shadow Environment team as its junior spokesman.

He was the first of the new intake to be given front-bench responsibilities.

Simon Kerslake received a handwritten letter from Reggie Maudling thanking him for his valiant efforts.

4

IT TOOK SIMON ALMOST A WEEK to stop sulking over Heath's election, and by then he had decided on a definite course of action for the future. Having checked the Whip's office carefully for the Monday voting schedule, and seen there were no votes expected after six o'clock, he booked a table at Annabel's for ten. Louis promised him an alcove table hidden discreetly from the dance floor.

On Monday morning Simon perused the shop windows in Bond Street before emerging from Cartier's with a small blue leather box which he placed in the pocket of his jacket. Simon returned to the Commons unable to concentrate fully on the orders of the day.

He left the Commons a little after seven to return to Beaufort Street. On arrival home he watched the early-evening news before washing his hair and taking a shower. He shaved for a second time that day, removed the pins from an evening dress shirt that had never been taken from its wrapper and laid out his dinner jacket.

At nine o'clock he transferred the little box from his coat pocket to his dinner jacket, checked his bow tie, and as he left, he double-locked the front door of his little house.

When he reached Chelsea Square a few minutes later he parked his MGB outside Number 4 and once again the omniscient butler ushered him through. Simon could hear Lavinia's high tones coming from the drawing room, but it was not until he walked in that he realized it was her father she was addressing.

"Hello, Simon."

"Good evening," Simon said, before kissing Lavinia gently on the cheek. She was dressed in a long green chiffon gown that left her creamy white shoulders bare.

"Daddy thinks he can help with Ted Heath," were Lavinia's opening words.

"What do you mean?" asked Simon, puzzled.

"Well," began Sir Rufus, "you might not have backed our new Leader in his struggle, but I did, and although I say it myself, I still have a fair bit of influence with him."

Simon accepted the sweet sherry Lavinia thrust into his hand.

"I'm having lunch with Mr. Heath tomorrow and thought I'd put in a word on your behalf."

"That's very kind of you," said Simon, still hating the fact that contacts seemed more important than ability.

"Not at all, old boy. To be honest, I almost look upon you as one of the family nowadays," added Sir Rufus, grinning.

Simon nervously touched the little box in his inside pocket.

"Isn't that super of Daddy?" said Lavinia.

"It certainly is," said Simon.

"That's settled then," said Lavinia. "So let's be off to Annabel's."

"Fine by me," said Simon. "I have a table booked for ten o'clock," he added, checking his watch.

"Is the place any good?" inquired Sir Rufus.

"It's super, Daddy," declared Lavinia, "you should try it sometime."

"Those damn clubs never last. If it's still around this time next year I'll consider joining."

"Perhaps you won't be around this time next year, Daddy," said Lavinia, giggling.

Simon tried not to laugh.

"If she had spoken to me like that a few years ago, I'd have put her over my knee," he informed Simon.

This time Simon forced a laugh.

"Come on, Simon," said Lavinia, "or we'll be late. Night-night, Daddy." Lavinia gave her father a peck on the cheek. Simon shook hands with Sir Rufus rather formally before escorting Lavinia to his car.

"Isn't that wonderful news?" she said as Simon turned the ignition key.

"Oh, yes," said Simon, guiding the car into the Fulham Road. "Very kind of your father." A few spots of rain made him turn on the windshield wipers.

"Mummy thinks you ought to be made a Shadow Spokesman."

"Not a hope," said Simon.

"Don't be such a pessimist," said Lavinia. "With my family behind you anything could happen."

Simon felt a little sick.

"And Mummy knows all the influential women in the party."

Simon had a feeling that was no longer going to be quite so important with a bachelor in command.

Simon swung the car into Belgrave Square and on up toward Hyde Park Corner.

"And did I tell you about the Hunt Ball next month? Absolutely everyone is expected to be there, I mean everyone."

"No, you didn't mention it," said Simon, who had never admitted to Lavinia that he couldn't stand Hunt Balls.

Simon saw the cat run out in front of the double-decker bus and threw on his brakes just in time. "Phew, that was close," he said. But a moment later Lavinia screamed. Simon turned to see a trickle of blood running down her forehead.

"Oh, God, I'm bleeding. Get me to a hospital," she said, and began to sob.

Simon drove quickly on to St. George's Hospital on the cor-

ner of Hyde Park and leaped out, leaving his car on a double
yellow line. He ran around to the passenger side and helped
Lavinia out, guiding her slowly to the emergency entrance. Although blood was still trickling down Lavinia's face, the cut
above her eyebrow didn't look all that deep to Simon. He took
off his dinner jacket and put it over her bare shoulders, doing
everything he could to comfort her, but she continued to shake.

It must have been the fact that Simon was in evening clothes
that made the duty nurse move a little more quickly than usual.
They were ushered through to a doctor only a few minutes after
arrival.

"It's all over my beautiful dress," said Lavinia between sobs.

"The stain will wash out," said the doctor matter-of-factly.

"But will I be left with a scar for the rest of my life?" asked
Lavinia.

Simon watched with silent admiration. She was completely in
control of everything around her.

"Good heavens, no," replied the doctor, "it's only a flesh
wound. It won't even require stitches. The most you might experience is a small headache." The doctor damped the blood
away before cleaning the wound. "There will be no sign of the
cut after a couple of weeks."

"Are you certain?" demanded Lavinia.

Simon couldn't take his eyes off her.

"Absolutely certain," said the doctor, finally placing a small
piece of adhesive across the wound. "Perhaps it would be wise
for you to go home and change your dress if you are still planning to go out to dinner."

"Of course, Dr. Drummond," said Simon, checking the name
on the little lapel badge. "I'll see she's taken care of."

Simon thanked the doctor and then helped Lavinia to the car
before driving her back to Chelsea Square. Lavinia didn't stop
whimpering all the way home, and she didn't notice that Simon
hardly spoke. Lady Maxwell-Harrington put her daughter to
bed as soon as Simon had told her what had happened.

When mother and daughter disappeared upstairs, Simon returned to Beaufort Street. He removed the little box from his blood-stained dinner jacket and placed it by the side of his bed. He opened it and studied the sapphire set in a circle of small diamonds. He was now certain of the hand he wanted to see wear the ring.

The next morning Simon telephoned to find that Lavinia was fully recovered, but Daddy had thought it might be wise for her to spend the rest of the day in bed. Simon concurred and promised to drop in to see her sometime during the evening.

Once Simon had reached his office in the Commons he phoned St. George's Hospital, and they told him that Dr. Drummond would be off duty until later that afternoon. It didn't take the skill of Sherlock Holmes to find Dr. E. Drummond's telephone number in the London directory.

"It's Simon Kerslake," he said when Dr. Drummond answered the phone. "I wanted to thank you for the trouble you took over Lavinia last night."

"It was no trouble, no trouble at all—in fact it was the least of last night's problems."

Simon laughed nervously and asked, "Are you free for lunch by any chance?"

Dr. Drummond sounded somewhat surprised, but agreed after Simon had suggested the Coq d'Or, which was conveniently near St. George's Hospital. They agreed to meet at one.

Simon arrived a few minutes early, ordered a lager and waited at the bar. At five past one the maitre d' brought the doctor to his side.

"It was good of you to come at such short notice," said Simon, after shaking hands.

"It was irresistible. It's not often I get invited to lunch when all I have done is clean up a flesh wound."

Simon laughed and found himself staring at the beautiful woman. He recalled the calm poise of yesterday, but today she revealed an infectious enthusiasm that Simon found irresistible.

47

The maitre d' guided them to a table in the corner of the room. Simon stared once again at the slim, fair woman, whose large brown eyes had kept him awake most of the night. He couldn't help noticing men stop in mid-sentence to take a closer look as she passed each table.

"I know it sounds silly," he said after they had sat down, "but I don't know your first name."

"Elizabeth," she said, smiling.

"Mine's Simon."

"I remember," said Elizabeth. "In fact I saw you on Panorama last month giving your views on the state of the National Health Service."

"Oh," said Simon, sounding rather pleased. "Did it come over all right?"

"You were brilliant," replied Elizabeth.

Simon smiled.

"Only an expert would have realized you hadn't the faintest idea what you were talking about." Simon was momentarily stunned and then burst out laughing.

Over a meal Simon couldn't remember ordering, he learned that Elizabeth had been to school in London before training at St. Thomas's Hospital. "I am only working relief at St. George's this week," she explained, "before I take up a full-time post in the gynecology department of St. Mary's, Paddington. If Miss Maxwell-Harrington had come to the hospital a week later, we would never have met. How is she, by the way?"

"Spending the day in bed."

"You're not serious?" said Elizabeth. "I only sent her home to change her dress, not convalesce."

Simon burst out laughing again.

"I'm sorry, I probably insulted a dear friend of yours."

"No," said Simon, "that was yesterday."

Simon returned to Chelsea Square that night and learned, while sitting on the end of Lavinia's bed, that Daddy had "fixed" Ted

Heath, and Simon could expect to hear from him in the near future. It didn't stop Simon from telling Lavinia the truth about his meeting with Elizabeth Drummond, even though he had no way of knowing Elizabeth's feelings. Simon was surprised at how well Lavinia appeared to take the news. He left a few minutes later to return to the House of Commons in time for the ten o'clock vote.

In the corridor the Chief Whip took him aside and asked if he could see him in his office at twelve the next morning. Simon readily agreed. After the vote he wandered into the Whip's office in the hope that some clue would be given as to why the Chief Whip wanted to see him.

"Congratulations," said a junior whip, looking up from his desk.

"On what?" said Simon apprehensively.

"Oh hell, have I let the cat out of the bag?"

"I don't think so," said Simon. "The Chief Whip has asked to see me at twelve tomorrow."

"I never said a word," said the junior whip, and buried his head in some papers. Simon smiled and returned home.

He was unable to sleep much that night or stand still most of the following morning and was back in the Whip's office by ten to twelve. He tried not to show too much anticipation.

Miss Norse, the Chief Whip's aging secretary, looked up from her typewriter. The tapping stopped for a moment.

"Good morning, Mr. Kerslake. I'm afraid the Chief Whip has been held up in a meeting with Mr. Heath."

"I fully understand," said Simon. "Am I to wait, or has he arranged another appointment?"

"No," said Miss Norse, sounding somewhat surprised. "No," she repeated. "He simply said that whatever he wanted to see you about was no longer important, and he was sorry to have wasted your time."

Simon turned to leave, immediately realizing what had happened. He went straight to the nearest telephone booth and dialed five digits of Lavinia's home number, and then hung up

49

suddenly. He waited for a few moments before he dialed seven digits.

It was a few minutes before they found her.

"Dr. Drummond," she said crisply.

"Elizabeth, it's Simon Kerslake. Are you free for dinner?"

"Why, does Lavinia need her Band-Aid changed?"

"No," said Simon, "Lavinia died—somewhat prematurely."

Elizabeth chuckled. "I do hope it's not catching," she said, before adding, "I'm afraid I don't get off until ten-thirty."

"Neither do I," said Simon, "so I could pick you up at the hospital."

"You sound a bit low," said Elizabeth.

"Not low—older," said Simon. "I've grown up about twenty years in the last two days."

Although he wasn't much more than a glorified messenger boy, Charles Hampton was enjoying the challenge of his new appointment as a junior Opposition spokesman in Environment. At least he felt he was near the center of affairs. Even if he was not actually making decisions on future policy, he was at least listening to them. Whenever a debate on housing took place in the Commons, he was allowed to sit on the front bench along with the rest of the Conservative team. He had already caused the defeat of two minor amendments on the Town and Country Planning Bill, and had added one of his own, relating to the protection of trees. "It isn't preventing a world war," he admitted to Fiona, "but in its own way it's quite important, because if we win the next General Election, I'm now confident of being offered a junior office. Then I'll have a real chance to shape policy."

Fiona continued to play her part, hosting monthly dinner parties at their Eaton Square house. By the end of the year every member of the Shadow Cabinet had been to dinner at least once at the Hamptons', where Fiona never allowed a menu to be repeated or wore the same dress twice.

When the parliamentary year began again in October,

Charles was one of the names continually dropped by the political analysts as someone to watch. "He makes things happen," was the sentiment that was expressed again and again. He could barely cross the members' lobby without a reporter's trying to solicit his views on everything from butter subsidies to rape. Fiona clipped out of the papers every mention of her husband and couldn't help noticing that only one new member was receiving more press coverage than Charles—a young man from Leeds named Raymond Gould.

Raymond Gould could be found tapping away late into the night on his ancient typewriter with his phone off the hook. He was writing page after page, checking, then rechecking the proofs, and often referring to the piles of books that cluttered his desk.

When Raymond's *Full Employment at Any Cost?* was published and subtitled "Reflections of a Worker Educated After the Thirties," it caused an immediate sensation. The suggestion that the unions would become impotent and the Labour Party would need to be more innovative to capture the young vote was never likely to endear him to the Party's rank and file. Raymond had anticipated that it would provoke a storm of abuse from union leaders, and even among some of his more left-wing colleagues. But when A.J.P. Taylor suggested in the London *Times* that it was the most profound and realistic look at the Labour Party since Anthony Crosland's *The Future of Socialism,* and had produced a politician of rare honesty and courage, Raymond knew his strategy and hard work were paying dividends. He found himself a regular topic of conversation at every political dinner party in London.

Joyce thought the book a magnificent piece of scholarship, and she spent a considerable time trying to convince trade unionists that, in fact, it showed a passionate concern for their movement, while at the same time realistically considering the Labour Party's chances of governing in the next decade.

The Labour Chief Whip took Raymond aside and told him,

"You've caused a right stir, lad. Now keep your head down for a few months and you'll probably find every Cabinet member quoting you as if it was party policy."

Raymond took the Chief Whip's advice, but he did not have to wait months. Just three weeks after the book's publication Raymond received a missive from Number 10 requesting him to check over the Prime Minister's speech to the Trade Union Conference and add any suggestions he might have. Raymond read the note again, delighted by the recognition it acknowledged.

He began to hope he might be the first of the new intake to be invited to join the Government front bench.

Simon Kerslake looked upon the defeat of Maudling and his own failure to be offered a post in the Whip's office as only temporary setbacks. He soon began to work on a new strategy for gaining his colleagues' respect. Realizing that there was a fifteen-minute period twice a week when someone with his oratorical skills could command notice, he turned all his cunning against the Government benches. At the beginning of a new session each week he would carefully study the agenda and in particular the first five questions listed for the Prime Minister on Tuesdays and Thursdays.

Supplementary questions were required to have only the loosest association with the subject of the main question. This meant that although Ministers were prepared for the first question, they could never be sure what supplementaries would be thrown at them. Thus, every Monday morning Simon would prepare a supplementary for at least three questions. These he worded, then reworded, so that they were biting or witty and always likely to embarrass the Labour Government. Although preparation could take several hours, Simon would make them sound as though they had been jotted down on the back of his agenda paper during Question Time—and in fact would even do so. He remembered Churchill's comment after being praised for a brilliant rejoinder, "All my best off-the-cuff remarks have been prepared days before."

Even so, Simon was surprised at how quickly the House took it for granted that he would be there on the attack, probing, demanding, harrying the Prime Minister's every move. Whenever he rose from his seat, the Party perked up in anticipation, and many of his interruptions reached the political columns of the newspapers the next day. The Labour Party had become painfully aware of Kerslake's contribution at Question Time.

Unemployment was the subject of that day's question. Simon was quickly on his feet, leaning forward, jabbing a finger in the direction of the Government front bench.

"With the appointment of four extra Secretaries of State this week the Prime Minister can at least claim he has full employment—in the Cabinet."

The Prime Minister sank lower into his seat, looking forward to the recess.

No one was more delighted than Simon when he read in the *Sunday Express* Crossbencher column that "Prime Minister Wilson may dislike Edward Heath, but he detests Simon Kerslake." Simon smiled, pleased to find that real results had come from his own efforts, not from outside contacts.

PART TWO

Junior Office

1966-1972

5

THE BRITISH CONSTITUTION remains one of the great mysteries
to almost all who were not born on that little island in the North
Sea, and to a considerable number of those who have never left
its shores. This may be partly because, unlike the Americans,
the British have had no written constitution since Magna Carta
in 1215 and since then have acted only on precedent.

A Prime Minister is elected for a term of five years, but he
can "go to the country" whenever he thinks fit, which inevitably
means when he considers he has the best chance of winning a
General Election. If the government of the day has a large majority in the Commons, the electorate expects it to remain in
power for at least four of the five years. In such circumstances
"to go early" is considered opportunistic by the voters and for
that reason often backfires. But when a party's majority in the
House is small, as was the case with Harold Wilson's Labour
Government, the press never stops speculating on the date of
the next election.

The only method the Opposition has for removing the Government in under five years is to call for a vote of "no confidence" in the House of Commons. If the Government is
defeated, the Prime Minister has to call an election within a few
weeks—which may well not be to his advantage. In law, the

monarch has the final say, but for the past two hundred years the Kings and Queens of England have only rubber-stamped the Prime Minister's decision, although they have been known to frown.

By 1966 Harold Wilson was left with little choice. Given his majority of only four, everyone knew it would not be long before he had to call a General Election. In March of 1966 he sought an audience with the Queen and she agreed to dissolve Parliament immediately. The election campaign started the next day.

"You'll enjoy this," said Simon as he walked up to the first door. Elizabeth remained uncertain, but could think of no better way to find out what grass roots politics was really like. She had taken the few days' vacation due her in order to spend them in Coventry with Simon. It had never crossed her mind that she might fall for a politician, but she had to admit that his vote-catching charm was proving irresistible compared to her colleagues' bedside manner.

Simon Kerslake, with such a tiny majority to defend, began spending his spare time in his Coventry constituency. The local people seemed pleased with the apprenticeship of their new member, but the disinterested statisticians pointed out that a swing of less than 1 percent would remove him from the House for another five years. By then his rivals would be on the second rung of the ladder.

The Tory Chief Whip advised Simon to stay put in Coventry and not to participate in any further parliamentary business. "There'll be no more important issues between now and the election," he assured him. "The most worthwhile thing you can do is pick up votes in the constituency, not give them in Westminster."

Simon's opponent was the former member, Alf Abbott, who became progressively confident of victory as the national swing to Labour accelerated during the campaign. The smaller Liberal Party fielded a candidate, Nigel Bainbridge, but he admitted openly that he could only come in third.

For their first round of canvassing, Elizabeth wore her only suit, which she had bought when she had been interviewed for her first hospital job. Simon admired her sense of propriety, and while Elizabeth's outfit would satisfy the matrons in the constituency, her fair hair and slim figure still had the local press wanting to photograph her.

The street list of names was on a card in Simon's pocket.

"Good morning, Mrs. Foster. My name is Simon Kerslake. I'm your Conservative candidate."

"Oh, how nice to meet you. I have so much I need to discuss with you—won't you come in and have a cup of tea?"

"It's kind of you, Mrs. Foster, but I have rather a lot of ground to cover during the next few days." When the door closed, Simon put a red line through her name on his card.

"How can you be sure she's a Labour supporter?" demanded Elizabeth. "She seemed so friendly."

"The Labourites are trained to ask all the other candidates in for tea and waste their time. Our side will always say, 'You have my vote, don't spend your time with me' and let you get on to those who are genuinely uncommitted."

Elizabeth couldn't hide her disbelief. "That only confirms my worst fears about politicians," she said. "How can I have fallen for one?"

"Perhaps you mistook me for one of your patients."

"My patients don't tell me they have broken arms when they're going blind," she said.

Mrs. Foster's next-door neighbor said, "I always vote Conservative."

Simon put a blue line through the name and knocked on the next door.

"My name is Simon Kerslake and I . . ."

"I know who you are, young man, and I'll have none of your politics."

59

"May I ask who you will be voting for?" asked Simon.

"Liberal."

"Why?" asked Elizabeth.

"Because I believe in supporting the underdog."

"But surely that will turn out to be a waste of a vote."

"Certainly not. Lloyd George was the greatest Prime Minister of this century."

"But . . ." began Elizabeth enthusiastically. Simon put a hand on her arm. "Thank you, sir, for your time," he said, and prodded Elizabeth gently down the path.

"Sorry, Elizabeth," said Simon, when they were back on the pavement. "Once they mention Lloyd George we have no chance: they're either Welsh or have remarkably long memories."

He knocked on the next door.

"My name is Simon Kerslake, I . . ."

"Get lost, creep," came back the reply.

"Who are you calling creep?" Elizabeth retaliated as the door was slammed in their faces. "Charming man," she added.

"Don't be offended, Dr. Drummond. He was referring to me, not you."

"What shall I put by his name?"

"A question mark. No way of telling who he votes for. Probably abstains."

He tried the next door.

"Hello, Simon," said a jolly red-faced lady before he could open his mouth. "Don't waste your time on me, I'll always vote for you."

"Thank you, Mrs. Irvine," said Simon, checking his house list. "What about your next-door neighbor?" he asked, pointing back.

"Ah, he's an irritable old basket, but I'll see he gets to the polls on the day and puts his cross in the right box. He'd better, or I'll stop keeping an eye on his greyhound when he's out."

"Thank you very much, Mrs. Irvine."

"One more blue," said Simon.

"And you might even pick up the greyhound vote."

They covered four streets during the next three hours, and Simon put blue lines only through those names he was certain would support him on election day.

"Why do you have to be so sure?" asked Elizabeth.

"Because when we phone them to vote on Election Day we don't want to remind the Opposition, let alone arrange a ride for someone who then takes pleasure in voting Labour."

Elizabeth laughed. "Politics is so dishonest."

"Be happy you're not going out with an American Senator," said Simon, putting another blue line through the last name in the street. "At least we don't have to be millionaires to run."

"Perhaps I'd like to marry a millionaire," Elizabeth said, grinning.

"On a parliamentary salary it will take me about two hundred and forty-two years to achieve."

"I'm not sure I can wait that long."

Four days before the election Simon and Elizabeth stood in the wings behind the stage of Coventry Town Hall with Alf Abbott, Nigel Bainbridge and their wives for a public debate. The three couples made stilted conversation. The political correspondent of the *Coventry Evening Telegraph* acted as chairman, introducing each of the protagonists as they walked onto the stage, to applause from different sections of the hall. Simon spoke first, holding the attention of the large audience for over twenty minutes. Those who tried to heckle him ended up regretting having brought attention to themselves. Without once referring to his notes, he quoted figures and clauses from Government bills with an ease that impressed Elizabeth. During the questions that followed, Simon once again proved to be far better informed than Abbott or Bainbridge, but he was aware that the packed hall held only seven hundred that cold March evening, while elsewhere in Coventry were fifty thousand more voters, most of them glued to their television watching "Ironside."

Although the local press proclaimed Simon the victor of a

one-sided debate, he remained downcast by the national papers, which were now predicting a landslide for Labour.

On election morning Simon picked up Elizabeth at six so he could be among the first to cast his vote at the local primary school. They spent the rest of the day traveling from polling hall to Party headquarters, trying to keep up the morale of his supporters. Everywhere they went, the committed believed in his victory but Simon knew it would be close. A senior Conservative backbencher had once told him that an outstanding member could be worth a thousand personal votes, and a weak opponent might sacrifice another thousand. Even an extra two thousand wasn't going to be enough.

As the Coventry City Hall clock struck nine, Simon and Elizabeth sat down on the steps of the last polling hall. He knew there was nothing he could do now—the last vote had been cast. Just then, a jolly lady, accompanied by a sour-faced man, was coming out of the hall. She had a smile of satisfaction on her face.

"Hello, Mrs. Irvine," said Simon. "How are you?"

"I'm fine, Simon." She smiled.

"Looks like she fixed the greyhound vote," Elizabeth whispered in Simon's ear.

"Now don't fret yourself, lad," Mrs. Irvine continued. "I never failed to vote for the winner in fifty-two years, and that's longer than you've lived." She winked and led the sour-faced man away.

A small band of supporters accompanied Simon and Elizabeth to the City Hall to witness the count. As Simon entered the hall, the first person he saw was Alf Abbott, who had a big grin on his face. Simon was not discouraged by the smile as he watched the little slips of paper pour out of the boxes. Abbott should have remembered that the first boxes to be counted were always from the city wards, where most of the committed Labourites lived.

As both men walked around the tables, the little piles of ballots began to be checked——first in tens, then hundreds, until they were finally placed in thousands and handed over to the town clerk. As the night drew on, Abbott's grin turned to a smile, from a smile to a poker face, and finally to a look of anxiety as the piles grew closer and closer in size.

For over three hours the process of emptying the boxes continued and the scrutineers checked each little white slip before handing in their own records. At one in the morning the Coventry town clerk added up the list of numbers in front of him and asked the three candidates to join him.

He told them the results.

Alf Abbott smiled. Simon showed no emotion, but called for a recount.

For over an hour, he paced nervously around the room as the scrutineers checked and double-checked each pile: a change here, a mistake there, a lost vote discovered, and, on one occasion, the name on the top of the pile of one hundred votes was not the same as the ninety-nine beneath it. At last the scrutineers handed back their figures. Once again the town clerk added up the columns of numbers before asking the candidates to join him.

This time Simon smiled, while Abbott looked surprised and demanded a further recount. The town clerk acquiesced, but said it had to be the last time. Both candidates agreed in the absence of their Liberal rival, who was sleeping soundly in the corner, secure in the knowledge that no amount of recounting would alter his position in the contest.

Once again the piles were checked and double-checked and five mistakes were discovered in the 42,588 votes cast. At 3:30 A.M. with counters and checkers falling asleep at their tables, the town clerk once more asked the candidates to join him. They were both stunned when they heard the result, and the town clerk informed them that there would be yet a further recount in the morning when his staff had managed to get some sleep.

All the ballots were then replaced carefully in the black boxes, locked and left in the safekeeping of the local constabulary, while the candidates crept away to their beds. Simon and Elizabeth booked into separate rooms at the Leofric Hotel.

Simon slept in fits and starts through the remainder of the night. Elizabeth brought a cup of tea to his room at eight the same morning to find him still in bed.

"Simon," she said, "you look like one of my patients just before an operation."

"I think I'll skip this operation," he said, turning over.

"Don't be such a wimp, Simon," she said rather snappily. "You're still the member, and you owe it to your supporters to remain as confident as they feel."

Simon sat up in bed and stared at Elizabeth. "Quite right," he said, stretching for his tea, unable to hide the pleasure he felt in discovering how much she had picked up of the political game in such a short time.

Simon had a long bath, shaved slowly, and they were back at the Town Hall a few minutes before the count was due to recommence. As Simon walked up the steps he was greeted by a battery of television cameras and journalists who had heard rumors as to why the count had been held up overnight and knew they couldn't afford to be absent as the final drama unfolded.

The counters looked eager and ready when the town clerk checked his watch and nodded. The boxes were unlocked and placed in front of the staff for the fourth time. Once again the little piles of ballots grew from tens into hundreds and then into thousands. Simon paced around the tables, more to burn up his nervous energy than out of a desire to keep checking. He had thirty witnesses registered as his counting agents to make sure he didn't lose by sleight of hand or genuine mistake.

Once the counters and scrutineers had finished, they sat in front of their piles and waited for the slips to be collected for the town clerk. When the town clerk had added up his little columns of figures for the final time he found that four votes had changed hands.

He explained to Simon and Alf Abbott the procedure he intended to adopt in view of the outcome. He told both candidates that he had spoken to Lord Elwyn Jones at nine that morning and the Lord Chancellor had read out the relevant statute in election law that was to be followed in such an extraordinary circumstance.

The town clerk walked up on to the stage with Simon Kerslake and Alf Abbott in his wake, both looking anxious.

Everyone in the room stood to be sure of a better view of the proceedings. When the pushing back of chairs, the coughing and the nervous chattering had stopped, the town clerk began. First he tapped the microphone that stood in front of him to be sure it was working. The metallic scratch was audible throughout the silent room. Satisfied, he began to speak.

"I, the returning officer for the district of Coventry Central, hereby declare the total number of votes cast for each candidate to be as follows:

ALF ABBOTT, (LABOUR)	18,437
NIGEL BAINBRIDGE, (LIBERAL)	5,714
SIMON KERSLAKE, (CONSERVATIVE)	18,437

The supporters of both the leading candidates erupted into a noisy frenzy. It was several minutes before the town clerk's voice could be heard above the babble of Midland accents.

"In accordance with Section Sixteen of the Representation of the People Act of 1949 and Rule Fifty of the Parliamentary Election Rules in the second schedule to that Act, I am obliged to decide between tied candidates by lot," he announced. "I have spoken with the Lord Chancellor and he has confirmed that the drawing of straws or the toss of a coin may constitute decision by lot for this purpose. Both candidates have agreed to the latter course of action."

Pandemonium broke out again as Simon and Abbott stood motionless on each side of the town clerk waiting for their fate to be determined.

"Last night I borrowed from Barclay's Bank," continued the town clerk, aware that ten million people were watching him on television for the first and probably the last time in his life, "a golden sovereign. On one side is the head of King George the Third, on the other Britannia. I shall invite the sitting member, Mr. Kerslake, to call his preference." Abbott curtly nodded his agreement. Both men inspected the coin.

The town clerk rested the golden sovereign on his thumb, Simon and Abbott still standing on either side of him. He turned to Simon and said, "You will call, Mr. Kerslake, while the coin is in the air."

The silence was such that they might have been the only three people in the room. Simon could feel his heart thumping in his chest as the town clerk spun the coin high above him.

"Tails," he said clearly as the coin was at its zenith. The sovereign hit the floor and bounced, turning over several times before settling at the feet of the town clerk.

Simon stared down at the coin and sighed audibly. The town clerk cleared his throat before declaring, "Following the decision by lot, I declare the aforementioned Mr. Simon Kerslake to be the duly elected Member of Parliament for Coventry Central."

Simon's supporters charged forward and on to the stage and carried him on their shoulders out of the City Hall and through the streets of Coventry. Simon's eyes searched for Elizabeth but she was lost in the crush.

Barclay's Bank presented the golden sovereign to the member the next day, and the editor of the *Coventry Evening Telegraph* rang to ask if there had been any particular reason why he had selected tails.

"Yes," Simon replied. "George the Third lost America for us. I wasn't going to let him lose Coventry for me."

Raymond Gould increased his majority to 12,413 in line with Labour's massive nationwide victory, and Joyce was ready for a week's rest.

Charles Hampton could never recall accurately the size of his own majority because, as Fiona explained to the old earl the following morning, "They don't count the Conservative vote in Sussex Downs, darling, they weigh it."

Simon spent the day after the election traveling around the constituency hoarsely thanking his supporters for the hard work they had put in. For his most loyal supporter, he could manage only four more words: "Will you marry me?"

6

IN MOST DEMOCRATIC COUNTRIES a newly elected leader enjoys a transitional period during which he is able to announce the policies he intends to pursue and whom he has selected to implement them. But in Britain, MPs sit by their phones and wait for forty-eight hours immediately after the election results have been declared. If a call comes in the first twelve hours, they will be asked to join the Cabinet of twenty, during the second twelve given a position as one of the thirty Ministers of State, and the third twelve, made one of the forty Under Secretaries of State, and during the final twelve, a parliamentary private secretary to a Cabinet Minister. If the phone hasn't rung by then, they remain on the back benches.

Raymond returned from Leeds the moment the count was over, leaving Joyce to carry out the traditional "thank you" drive across the constituency.

When he wasn't sitting by the phone the following day he was walking around it, nervously pushing his glasses back up on his nose. The first call came from his mother, who had rung to congratulate him.

"On what?" he asked. "Have you heard something?"

"No, love," she said, "I just rang to say how pleased I was about your increased majority."

"Oh."

"And to add how sorry we were not to see you before you left the constituency, especially as you had to pass the shop on the way to the highway."

Raymond remained silent. Not again, Mother, he wanted to say.

The second call was from a colleague inquiring if Raymond had been offered a job.

"Not so far," he said before learning of his contemporary's promotion.

The third call was from one of Joyce's friends.

"When will she be back?" another Yorkshire accent inquired.

"I've no idea," said Raymond, desperate to get the caller off the line.

"I'll call again this afternoon, then."

"Fine," said Raymond putting the phone down quickly.

He disappeared into the kitchen to make himself a cheese sandwich, but there wasn't any cheese, so he ate stale bread smeared with three-week-old butter. He was halfway through a second slice when the phone rang.

"Raymond?"

He held his breath.

"Noel Brewster."

He exhaled in exasperation as he recognized the vicar's voice.

"Can you read the second lesson when you're next up in Leeds? We had rather hoped you would read it this morning— your dear wife . . ."

"Yes," he promised. "The first weekend I am back in Leeds." The phone rang again as soon as he placed it back on the receiver.

"Raymond Gould?" said an anonymous voice.

"Speaking," he said.

"The Prime Minister will be with you in one moment."

Raymond waited. The front door opened and another voice shouted, "It's only me. I don't suppose you found anything

69

to eat. Poor love." Joyce joined Raymond in the drawing room.

Without looking at his wife, he waved his hand at her to keep quiet.

"Raymond," said a voice on the other end of the line.

"Good afternoon, Prime Minister," he replied, rather formally, in response to Harold Wilson's more pronounced Yorkshire accent.

"I was hoping you would feel able to join the new team as Under Secretary for Employment?"

Raymond breathed a sigh of relief. It was exactly what he'd hoped for. "I'd be delighted, sir," replied the new Minister.

"Good, that will give the trade union leaders something to think about." The phone went dead.

Raymond Gould, Under Secretary of State for Employment, sat motionless on the next rung of the ladder.

As Raymond left the house the next morning, he was greeted by a driver standing next to a gleaming black Austin Westminster. Unlike his own secondhand Volkswagen, it glowed in the morning light. The rear door was opened and Raymond climbed in to be driven off to the department. By his side on the back seat was a red leather box the size of a very thick briefcase with gold lettering running along the edge. "Under Secretary of State for Employment." Raymond turned the small key, knowing what Alice must have felt like on her way down the rabbit hole.

When Charles Hampton returned to the Commons on Tuesday there was a note from the Whip's office waiting for him on the members' letter board. One of the Environment team had lost his seat in the General Election and Charles had been promoted to number two on the Opposition bench in that department, to shadow the Government Minister of State. "No more preservation of trees. You'll be on to higher things now," chuckled the Chief Whip. "Pollution, water shortage, exhaust fumes . . ."

70

Charles smiled with pleasure as he walked through the Commons, acknowledging old colleagues and noticing a considerable number of new faces. He didn't stop to talk to any of the newcomers as he could not be certain if they were Labour or Conservative, and, given the election results, most of them had to be the former. As for his older colleagues, many wore forlorn looks on their faces. For some it would be a considerable time before they were offered the chance of office again, while others knew they had served as Ministers for the last time. In politics, he'd quickly learned, the luck of age and timing could play a vital part in any man's career, however able he might be. But at thirty-five, Charles could easily dismiss such thoughts.

Charles proceeded to his office to check over the constituency mail. Fiona had reminded him of the eight hundred letters of thanks to the party workers that had to be sent out. He groaned at the mere thought of it.

"Mrs. Blenkinsop, the chairman of the Sussex Ladies' Luncheon Club, wants you to be their guest speaker for their annual lunch," his secretary told him once he had settled.

"Reply yes—what's the date?" asked Charles, reaching for his diary.

"June sixteenth."

"Stupid women, that's Ladies Day at Ascot. Tell her that I'm delivering a speech at an environmental conference, but I'll be certain to make myself free for the function next year."

The secretary looked up anxiously.

"Don't worry," said Charles. "She'll never find out." The secretary moved on to the next letter.

Simon had placed the little sapphire ring surrounded by diamonds on the third finger of her left hand. Three months later a wide gold band joined the engagement ring.

After Mr. and Dr. Kerslake had returned home from their honeymoon in Italy they both settled happily into Beaufort Street. Elizabeth found it quite easy to fit all her possessions

71

into the little Chelsea house, and Simon knew after only a few weeks that he had married a quite exceptional woman.

In the beginning the two of them had found it difficult to mesh their demanding careers, but they soon worked out a comfortable routine. Simon wondered if this could continue as smoothly if they decided to start a family or he was made a Minister. But the latter could be years away; the Tories would not change their Leader until Heath had been given a second chance at the polls.

Simon began writing articles for the *Spectator* and for the *Sunday Express* center pages in the hope of building a reputation outside the House while at the same time supplementing his parliamentary salary of three thousand four hundred pounds. Even with Elizabeth's income as a doctor, he was finding it difficult to make ends meet, and yet he didn't want to worry his wife. He envied the Charles Hamptons of this world who did not seem to give a second thought about expenditure. Simon wondered if the damn man had any problems at all. He ran a finger down his own bank account: as usual there was a figure around five hundred pounds in the right-hand margin, and as usual it was in red.

He pressed on with demanding questions to the Prime Minister each Tuesday and Thursday. Even after this became routine, he prepared himself with his usual thoroughness, and on one occasion he even elicited praise from his normally taciturn Leader. But he found as the weeks passed that his thoughts continually returned to finance—or his lack of it.

That was before he met Ronnie Nethercote.

Raymond's reputation was growing. He showed no signs of being overcome by his major role in a department as massive as Employment. Most civil servants who came in contact with Raymond thought of him as brilliant, demanding, hardworking and, not that it was ever reported to him, arrogant. His ability to cut a junior civil servant off in mid-sentence or to correct his principal private secretary on matters of detail did not endear him even to his closest staff members, who always want to be loyal to their Minister.

Raymond's work load was prodigious, and even the Permanent Secretary experienced Gould's unrelenting "Don't make excuses" when he tried to trim one of Raymond's private schemes. Soon senior civil servants were talking of when, not whether, he would be promoted. His Secretary of State, like all men who were expected to be in six places at once, often asked Raymond to stand in for him, but even Raymond was surprised when he was invited to represent the Department as guest of honor at the annual Confederation of British Industries dinner.

Joyce checked to see that her husband's dinner jacket was well brushed, his shirt spotless and his shoes shining like a guard officer's. His carefully worded speech—a combination of civil-servant draftsmanship and a few more forceful phrases of his own to prove to the assembled capitalists that not every member of the Labour Party was a "raving commie"—was safely lodged in his inside pocket. His driver ferried him from his Lansdowne Road home toward the West End.

Raymond enjoyed the occasion, and, although he was nervous when he rose to represent the Government in reply to the toast of the guests, by the time he had resumed his seat he felt it had been one of his better efforts. The ovation that followed was certainly more than polite, coming from what had to be classified as a naturally hostile audience.

"That speech was dryer than the Chablis," one guest whispered in the chairman's ear, but he had to agree that with men like Gould in high office, it was going to be a lot easier to live with a Labour Government.

The man on Simon Kerslake's left was far more blunt in voicing his opinion of Raymond Gould. "Bloody man thinks like a Tory, talks like a Tory, so why isn't he a Tory?" he demanded.

Simon grinned at the prematurely balding man who had

been expressing his equally vivid views throughout dinner. At over two hundred pounds, Ronnie Nethercote looked as if he was trying to escape from every part of his bulging dinner jacket.

"I expect," said Simon in reply, "that Gould, born in the thirties and living in Leeds, would have found it hard to join the Young Conservatives."

"Balls," said Ronnie. "I managed it and I was born in the East End of London without any of his advantages. Now tell me, Mr. Kerslake, what do you do when you're not wasting your time in the House of Commons?"

Raymond stayed on after dinner and talked for some time to the captains of industry. A little after eleven he left to return to Lansdowne Road.

As his chauffeur drove slowly away from Grosvenor House down Park Lane, the Under Secretary waved expansively back to his host. Someone else waved in reply. At first Raymond only glanced out the window, assuming it was another dinner guest, until he saw her legs. Standing on the corner outside the gas station on Park Lane stood a young girl smiling at him invitingly, her white leather miniskirt so short it might have been better described as a handkerchief. Her long legs reminded him of Joyce's ten years before. Her finely curled hair and the set of her hips remained firmly implanted in Raymond's mind all the way home.

When they reached Lansdowne Road, Raymond climbed out of the official car and said goodnight to his driver before walking slowly toward his front door, but he did not take out his latchkey. He waited until he was sure the driver had turned the corner before looking up and checking the bedroom window. All the lights were out. Joyce must be asleep.

He crept down the path and back on to the pavement, then looked up and down the road, finally spotting the space in which Joyce had parked the Volkswagen. He checked the spare key on his key ring and fumbled about, feeling like a car thief. It took three attempts before the motor spluttered to life, and Raymond wondered if he would wake up the whole neighborhood as he moved off and headed back to Park Lane, not certain what to expect. When he reached Marble Arch, he traveled slowly down in the center stream of traffic. A few dinner guests in evening dress were still spilling out of Grosvenor House. He passed the gas station: she hadn't moved. She smiled again and he accelerated, nearly bumping into the car in front of him. Raymond traveled back up to Marble Arch, but instead of turning toward home, he drove down Park Lane again, this time not so quickly and on the inside lane. He took his foot off the accelerator as he approached the gas station and she waved again. He returned to Marble Arch before repeating his detour down Park Lane, this time even more slowly. As he passed Grosvenor House for a third time, he checked to be sure that there were no stragglers still chatting on the pavement. It was clear. He touched the brakes and his car came to a stop just beyond the gas station. He waited.

The girl looked up and down the street before strolling over to the car, opening the passenger door and taking a seat next to the Under Secretary of State for Employment.

"Looking for business?"

"What do you mean?" asked Raymond hoarsely.

"Come on, darling. You can't imagine I was standing out there at this time of night hoping to get a suntan."

Raymond turned to look at the girl more carefully and wanted to touch her despite the aura of cheap perfume. Her black blouse had three buttons undone; a fourth would have left nothing to the imagination.

"It's ten pounds at my place."

"Where's your place?" he heard himself say.

"I use a hotel in Paddington."

"How do we get there?" he asked, putting his hand nervously through his red hair.

"Just head up to Marble Arch and I'll direct you."

Raymond pulled out and went off toward Hyde Park Corner and drove around before traveling on toward Marble Arch once again.

"I'm Mandy," she said. "What's your name?"

Raymond hesitated. "Malcolm."

"And what do you do, Malcolm, in these hard times?"

"I . . . I sell secondhand cars."

"Haven't picked out a very good one for yourself, have you?" She laughed.

Raymond made no comment. It didn't stop Mandy.

"What's a secondhand-car salesman doing dressed up like a toff, then?"

Raymond had quite forgotten he was still in black tie.

"I've . . . just been to a convention . . . at the . . . Hilton Hotel."

"Lucky for some," she said, and lit a cigarette. "I've been standing outside Grosvenor House all night in the hope of getting some rich feller from that posh party." Raymond's cheeks nearly turned the color of his hair. "Slow down and take the second on the left."

He followed her instructions until they pulled up outside a small dingy hotel. "I'll get out first, then you," she said. "Just walk straight through reception and follow me up the stairs." As she got out of the car he nearly drove off and might have done so if his eye hadn't caught the sway of her hips as she walked back toward the hotel.

He obeyed her instructions and climbed several flights of narrow stairs until he reached the top floor. As he approached the landing, a large bosomy blonde passed him on the way down.

"Hi, Mandy," she shouted back at her friend.

"Hi, Sylv. Is the room free?"

"Just," said the blonde sourly.

Mandy pushed open the door and Raymond followed her in.

The room was small and narrow. In one corner stood a tiny bed and a threadbare carpet. The faded yellow wallpaper was peeling in several places. There was a washbasin attached to the wall; a dripping tap had left a brown stain on the enamel.

Mandy put her hand out and waited.

"Ah, yes, of course," said Raymond, taking out his wallet to find he only had nine pounds on him.

She scowled. "Not going to get overtime tonight, am I, darling?" she said, tucking the money carefully away in the corner of her bag before matter-of-factly taking off all her clothes.

Although the act of undressing had been totally sexless, he was still amazed by the beauty of her body. Raymond felt somehow detached from the real world. He watched her, eager to feel the texture of her skin, but made no move. She lay down on the bed.

"Let's get on with it, darling. I've got a living to earn."

Raymond undressed quickly, keeping his back to the bed. He folded his clothes in a neat pile on the floor as there was no chair. Then he lay down on top of her. It was all over in a few minutes.

"Come quickly, don't you, darling?" said Mandy, grinning.

Raymond turned away from her and started washing himself as best he could in the little basin. He dressed hurriedly realizing he must get out of the place as rapidly as possible.

"Can you drop me back at the gas station?" Mandy asked.

"It's exactly the opposite direction for me," he said, trying not to sound anxious as he made a bolt for the door. He passed Sylv on the stairs accompanied by a man. She stared at him more closely the second time. The Minister was back in his car a few moments later. He drove home quickly, but not before opening the windows in an attempt to get rid of the smell of stale tobacco and cheap perfume.

Back in Lansdowne Road, he had a long shower before creeping into bed next to Joyce; she stirred only slightly.

Charles drove his wife down to Ascot early to be sure to avoid the bumper-to-bumper traffic that always developed later in the day. With his height and bearing, Charles Hampton was made for tails and a topper, and Fiona wore a hat which on anyone less self-assured would have looked ridiculous. They had been invited to join the Macalpines for the afternoon, and when they arrived they found Sir Robert awaiting them in his private box.

"You must have left home early," said Charles, knowing the Macalpines lived in central London.

"About thirty minutes ago," he said, laughing. Fiona looked politely incredulous.

"I always come here by helicopter," he explained.

They lunched on lobster and strawberries accompanied by a fine vintage champagne, which the waiter kept pouring and pouring. Charles might not have drunk quite so much had he not picked the winning horses in the first three races. He spent the fifth race slumped in a chair in the corner of the box, and only the noise of the crowd kept him from nodding off.

If they hadn't waited for a farewell drink after the last race, Charles might have got away with it. He had forgotten that his host was returning by helicopter.

The long tail of cars across Windsor Great Park all the way back to the highway made Charles very short-tempered. When he eventually reached the main road he put his Daimler into fourth gear. He didn't notice the police car until the siren sounded and he was directed to pull over.

"Do be careful, Charles," whispered Fiona.

"Don't worry, old girl, I know exactly how to deal with the law," he said, and wound down his window to address the policeman who stood by the car. "Do you realize who I am, officer?"

"No, sir, but I would like you to accompany me—"

"Certainly not, officer, I am a member of . . ."

"Do be quiet," said Fiona, "and stop making such a fool of yourself."

"Parliament and I will not be treated . . ."

"Have you any idea how pompous you sound, Charles?"

"Perhaps you will be kind enough to accompany me to the station, sir?"

"I want to speak to my lawyer."

"Of course, sir. As soon as we reach the station."

When Charles arrived at the constabulary he proved quite incapable of walking a straight line and refused to provide a blood sample.

"I am the Conservative MP for Sussex Downs."

Which will not help you, Fiona thought, but he was past listening and only demanded that she phone the family solicitor at Speechly, Bircham and Soames.

After Ian Kimmins had spoken, first gently, then firmly, to Charles, his client eventually cooperated with the police.

Once Charles had completed his written statement, Fiona drove him home, praying that his stupidity would pass unnoticed by the press.

7

"YOU DON'T LIKE HIM because he comes from the East End," said Simon, after she had read the letter.

"That's not true," replied Elizabeth. "I don't like him because I don't trust him."

"But you've only met him twice."

"Once would have been quite enough."

"Well, I can tell you I'm impressed by the not inconsiderable empire he's built up over the last ten years, and frankly it's an offer I can't refuse," said Simon, pocketing the letter.

"But surely not at any cost?" said Elizabeth.

"I won't be offered many chances like this," continued Simon. "And we could use the money. The belief people have that every Tory MP has some lucrative sinecure and two or three directorships is plain daft, and you know it. Not one other serious proposition has been put to me since I've been in the House, and another two thousand pounds a year for a monthly board meeting would come in very handy."

"And what else?"

"What do you mean, what else?"

"What else does Mr. Nethercote expect for his two thousand pounds? Don't be naive, Simon, he's not offering you that kind of money on a plate unless he's hoping to receive some scraps back."

"Well, maybe I have a few contacts and a little influence with one or two people. . . ."

"I'll bet."

"You're just prejudiced, Elizabeth."

"I'm against anything that might in the long run harm your career, Simon. Struggle on, but never sacrifice your integrity, as you're so fond of reminding the people of Coventry."

When Charles Hampton's drunk-driving charge came up in front of the Reading Bench he listed himself as C. G. Hampton—no mention of MP. Under profession he entered "Banker."

He came sixth in the list that morning, and on behalf of his absent client Ian Kimmins apologized to the Reading magistrates and assured them it would not happen again. Charles received a fifty-pound fine and was banned from driving for six months. The whole case was over in four minutes.

When Charles was told the news by telephone later that day, he was appreciative of Kimmins's sensible advice and felt he had escaped lightly in the circumstances. He couldn't help remembering how many column inches George Brown, the Labour Foreign Secretary, had endured after a similar incident outside the Hilton Hotel.

Fiona kept her own counsel.

At the time, Fleet Street was in the middle of the "silly season," that period in the summer when the press is desperate for news. There had only been one cub reporter in the court when Charles's case came up, and even he was surprised by the interest the nationals took in his little scoop. The pictures of Charles taken so discreetly outside the Hamptons' country home were glaringly large the following morning. Headlines ranged from "Six Months' Ban for Drunk Driving—Son of Earl" to "MP's Ascot Binge Ends in Heavy Fine." Even the *Times* mentioned the case on its home news page.

By lunchtime the same day every Fleet Street newspaper had

tried to contact Charles—and so had the Chief Whip. When he did track Charles down his advice was short and to the point. A junior Shadow Minister can survive that sort of publicity once—not twice.

"Whatever you do, don't drive a car during the next six months, and don't ever drink and drive again."

Charles concurred, and after a quiet weekend hoped he had heard the last of the case. Then he caught the headline on the front page of the *Sussex Gazette:* "Member Faces No-Confidence Motion." Mrs. Blenkinsop, the chairman of the Ladies' Luncheon Club, was proposing the motion, not for the drunken driving, but for deliberately misleading her about why he had been unable to fulfill a speaking engagement at their annual luncheon.

Raymond had become so used to receiving files marked "Strictly Private," "Top Secret," or even "For Your Eyes Only" in his position as a Government under secretary that he didn't give a second thought to a letter marked "Confidential and Personal" even though it was written in a scrawled hand. He opened it while Joyce was boiling his eggs.

"Four minutes and forty-five seconds, just the way you like them," she said as she returned from the kitchen and placed two eggs in front of him. "Are you all right, dear? You're white as a sheet."

Raymond recovered quickly, sticking the letter into a pocket, before checking his watch. "Haven't time for the other egg," he said. "I'm already late for Cabinet committee, I must dash."

Strange, thought Joyce, as her husband hurried to the door. Cabinet committees didn't usually meet until ten, and he hadn't even cracked open his first egg. She sat down and slowly ate her husband's breakfast, wondering why he had left all his mail behind.

Once he was in the back of his official car Raymond read the letter again. It didn't take long.

DEAR "MALCOLM,"
"I enjoid our little get together the other evening and five
hundrud pounds would help me to forget it once and for
all.

Love, MANDY

P.S. I'll be in touch again soon.

He read the letter once more and tried to compose his thoughts. There was no address on the top of the notebook paper. The envelope gave no clue as to where it had been posted.

When his car arrived outside the Department of Employment Raymond remained in the back seat for several moments.

"Are you feeling all right, sir?" his driver asked.

"Fine, thank you," he replied, and jumped out of the car and ran all the way up to his office. As he passed his secretary's desk he barked at her, "No interruptions."

"You won't forget Cabinet committee at ten o'clock, will you, Minister?"

"No," replied Raymond sharply and slammed his office door. Once at his desk he tried to calm himself and to recall what he would have done had he been approached by a client as a barrister at the bar: First instruct a good solicitor. Raymond considered the two most capable lawyers in England to be Arnold Goodman and Sir Roger Pelham. Goodman was getting too high a profile for Raymond's liking whereas Pelham was just as sound but virtually unknown to the general public. He called Pelham's office and made an appointment to see him that afternoon.

Raymond hardly spoke in Cabinet committee, but as most of his colleagues wanted to express their own views, nobody noticed. As soon as the meeting was over, Raymond hurried out and took a taxi to High Holborn.

Sir Roger Pelham rose from behind his large Victorian desk to greet the junior Minister.

"I know you're a busy man, Gould," Pelham said as he fell back into his black leather chair, "so I shan't waste your time. Tell me what I can do for you."

"It was kind of you to see me at such short notice," Raymond began, and without further word handed the letter over.

"Thank you," the solicitor said courteously, and, pushing his half-moon spectacles higher up his nose, he read the note three times before he made any comment.

"Blackmail is something we all detest," he began, "but it will be necessary for you to tell me the whole truth, and don't leave out any details. Please remember I am on your side. You'll re-call only too well from your days at the bar what a disadvantage one labors under when one is in possession of only half the facts."

The tips of Pelham's fingers touched, forming a small roof in front of his nose as he listened intently to Raymond's account of what had happened that night.

"Could anyone else have seen you?" was Pelham's first question.

Raymond thought back and then nodded. "Yes," he said. "Yes, I'm afraid there was another girl who passed me on the stairs."

Pelham read the letter once more.

"My immediate advice," he said, looking Raymond in the eye and speaking slowly and deliberately, "and you won't like it, is to do nothing."

"But what do I say if she contacts the press?"

"She will probably get in touch with someone from Fleet Street anyway, even if you pay the five hundred pounds or how-ever many other five hundred pounds you can afford. Don't imagine you're the first Minister to be blackmailed, Mr. Gould. Every homosexual in the House lives in daily fear of it. It's a game of hide and seek. Very few people other than saints have nothing to *hide,* and the problem with public life is that a lot of busybodies want to *seek.*" Raymond remained silent, his anxiety showing. "Phone me on my private line immediately the next letter arrives," said Pelham, scribbling a number on a piece of paper.

"Thank you," said Raymond, relieved that his secret was at least shared with someone else. Pelham rose from behind his desk and accompanied Raymond to the door.

Raymond left the lawyer's office feeling better, but he found it hard to concentrate on his work the rest of that day and slept only in fits and starts during the night. When he read the morning papers, he was horrified to see how much space was being given to Charles Hampton's peccadillo. What a field day they would be able to have with him. When the mail came, he searched anxiously for the scrawled handwriting. It was hidden under an American Express circular. He tore it open. The same hand was this time demanding that the five hundred pounds should be deposited at a post office in Pimlico. Sir Roger Pelham saw the Minister one hour later.

Despite the renewed demand, the solicitor's advice remained the same.

"Think about it, Simon," said Ronnie as they reached the boardroom door. "Two thousand pounds a year may be helpful, but if you take shares in my real estate company it would give you a chance to make some capital."

"What did you have in mind?" asked Simon, buttoning up his stylish blazer, trying not to sound too excited.

"Well, you've proved damned useful to me. Some of those people you bring to lunch wouldn't have allowed me past their front doors. I'd let you buy in cheap . . . you could buy fifty thousand shares at one pound. When we go public in a couple of years' time you'd make a killing."

"Raising fifty thousand pounds won't be easy, Ronnie."

"When your bank manager has checked over my books he'll be only too happy to lend you the money."

After the Midland Bank had studied the authorized accounts

of Nethercote and Company and the manager had interviewed Simon, they agreed to his request, on the condition that Simon deposited the shares with the bank.

How wrong Elizabeth was proving to be, Simon thought; and when Nethercote and Company performed record profits for the quarter he brought home a copy of the annual report for his wife to study.

"Looks good," she had to admit. "But I still don't have to trust Ronnie Nethercote."

When the annual meeting of the Sussex Downs Conservative Association came around in October Charles was pleased to learn that Mrs. Blenkinsop's "no confidence" motion had been withdrawn. The local press tried to build up the story, but the nationals were full of the Abervan coal mine disaster, in which one hundred and sixteen schoolchildren had lost their lives. No editor could find space for Sussex Downs.

Charles delivered a thoughtful speech to his association, which was well received. During Question Time, he was relieved to find no embarrassing questions directed at him.

When the Hamptons finally said goodnight, Charles took the chairman aside and inquired, "How did you manage it?"

"I explained to Mrs. Blenkinsop," replied the chairman, "that if her motion of no confidence was discussed at the annual meeting, it would be awfully hard for the member to back my recommendation that she should receive an Order of the British Empire in the New Year's Honors for service to the party. That shouldn't be too hard for you to pull off, should it, Charles?"

Every time the phone rang, Raymond assumed it would be the press asking him if he knew someone called Mandy. Often it was a journalist, but all that was needed was a quotable remark on the latest unemployment figures, or a statement of where the Minister stood on devaluation of the pound.

It was Mike Molloy, a reporter from the *Daily Mirror,* who was the first to ask Raymond what he had to say about a statement phoned in to his office by a girl called Mandy Page.

"I have nothing to say on the subject. Please speak to Sir Roger Pelham, my solicitor," was the Under Secretary's succinct reply. The moment he put the phone down he felt queasy.

A few minutes later the phone rang again. Raymond still hadn't moved. He picked up the receiver, his hand still shaking. Pelham confirmed that Molloy had been in touch with him.

"I presume you made no comment," said Raymond.

"On the contrary," replied Pelham. "I told him the truth."

"What?" exploded Raymond.

"Be thankful she picked a fair journalist, because I expect he'll let this one go. Fleet Street is not quite the bunch of shits everyone imagines them to be," Pelham said uncharacteristically, and added, "They also detest two things—crooked policemen and blackmailers. I don't think you'll see anything in the press tomorrow."

Sir Roger was wrong.

Raymond was standing outside his local newsstand the next morning when it opened at five-thirty, and he surprised the proprietor by asking for a copy of the *Daily Mirror.* Raymond Gould was plastered all over page five saying, "Devaluation is not a course I can support while the unemployment figure remains so high." The photograph by the side of the article was unusually flattering.

Simon Kerslake read a more detailed account of what the Minister had said on devaluation in the London *Times* and admired Raymond Gould's firm stand against what was beginning to look like inevitable Government policy. Simon glanced up from his paper and started to consider a ploy that might trap Gould. If he could make the Minister commit himself again and again on devaluation in front of the whole House, he knew that when the inevitable happened, Gould would be left with no choice but to resign. Simon began to pencil a question on the top of his paper before continuing to read the front page, but he couldn't concentrate, as his mind kept returning to the news Elizabeth had given him before she went to work.

Once again he looked up from the article, and this time a wide grin spread across his face. It was not the thought of embarrassing Raymond Gould that caused him to smile. A male chauvinist thought had crossed his normally liberal mind. "I hope it's a boy," he said out loud.

Charles Hampton was glad to be behind the wheel again, and he had the grace to smile when Fiona showed him the photograph of the happy Mrs. Blenkinsop displaying her OBE outside Buckingham Palace to a reporter from the *East Sussex News.*

It was six months to the day of his first meeting with Sir Roger Pelham that Raymond Gould received an account from the solicitor for services rendered—five hunded pounds.

8

SIMON LEFT THE HOUSE and drove himself to Whitechapel Road to attend a board meeting of Nethercote and Company. He arrived a few minutes after the four o'clock meeting had begun, quietly took his seat and listened to Ronnie Nethercote describing another coup.

Ronnie had signed a contract that morning to take over four major city blocks at a cost of 26 million pounds with a guaranteed rental income of 3.2 million per annum for the first seven years of a twenty-one-year lease.

Simon formally congratulated him and asked if this made any difference in the company's timing for going public. He had advised Ronnie not to allow his company shares to be traded on the Stock Exchange until the Tories returned to power. "It may mean waiting a couple of years," he had told Ronnie, "but few people now doubt that the Tories will win the next election. Just look at the polls."

"We're still planning to wait," Ronnie now assured him. "Although the injection of cash that the shares would bring in would be useful. But my instinct is to follow your advice and wait to see if the Conservatives win the next election."

"I am sure that's sound," said Simon, looking around at the other board members.

"If they don't win, I can't wait that much longer."

"I wouldn't disagree with that decision either, Mr. Chairman," said Simon.

When the meeting was over he joined Nethercote in his office for a drink.

"I want to thank you," Ronnie said, "for that introduction to Harold Samuel and Hugh Ainesworth. It made the deal go through much more smoothly."

"Does that mean you'll allow me to purchase some more shares?"

Ronnie hesitated. "Why not? You've earned them. But only another ten thousand. Don't get ahead of yourself, Simon, or the other directors may become jealous."

In the car on the way to pick up Elizabeth, Simon decided to take a second mortgage out on the house in Beaufort Street to raise the extra cash needed for the new shares. Elizabeth still made little secret of her feelings about Ronnie, and now that she was pregnant, Simon decided not to worry her with the details.

"If the Government did a turnabout and devalued the pound, would the Under Secretary find it possible to remain in office?"

Raymond Gould, the Under Secretary for Employment, stiffened when he heard Simon Kerslake's question.

Raymond's grasp of the law and his background knowledge of the subject made all except the extremely articulate or highly experienced wary of taking him on. Nevertheless, he had one Achilles heel arising from his firmly stated views in *Full Employment at Any Cost?*: any suggestion that the Government would devalue the pound. Time and again eager backbenchers would seek to tackle him on the subject. But once more it was Simon Kerslake who embarrassed his opponent.

As always, Raymond gave the standard reply: "The policy of Her Majesty's Government is one hundred percent against devaluation, and therefore the question does not arise."

"Wait and see," shouted Kerslake.

"Order," said the Speaker, rising from his seat and turning toward Simon as Raymond sat down. "The Honorable Member knows all too well he must not address the House from a sedentary position. The Under Secretary of State."

Raymond rose again. "This Government believes in a strong pound, which still remains our best hope for keeping unemployment figures down."

"But what would you do if Cabinet does go ahead and devalue?" Joyce asked him when she read her husband's reply to Kerslake's question reported in the London *Times* the next morning.

Raymond was already facing the fact that devaluation looked more likely every day. A strong dollar, causing imports to be at a record level, coupled with a run of strikes during the summer of '67, was causing foreign bankers to ask "When," not "If."

"I'd have to resign," he said in reply to Joyce's question.

"Why? No other Minister will."

"I'm afraid Kerslake is right. I'm on the record and he's made sure everybody knows it. Don't worry, Harold will never devalue. He's assured me of that many times."

"He only has to change his mind once."

The great orator Iain Macleod once remarked that it was the first two minutes of a speech that decided one's fate. One either grasps the House and commands it, or dithers and loses it, and once the House is lost it can rarely be brought to heel.

When Charles Hampton was invited to present the winding-up speech for the Opposition during the debate on the Environment, he felt he had prepared himself well. Although he knew he could not expect to convert Government backbenchers to his cause, he hoped the press would acknowledge that he had won the argument and embarrassed the Government. The Administration was already rocking over daily rumors of devaluation and economic trouble, and Charles was confident that this was a chance to make his name.

91

When full debates take place on the floor of the House, the Opposition spokesman is called upon to make his final comments at nine o'clock from the dispatch box—an oblong wooden box edged in brass—resting on the table in between the two front benches. At nine-thirty a Government Minister winds up.

When Charles rose and put his notes on the dispatch box he intended to press home the Tory Party case on the Government's economic record, the fatal consequences of devaluation, the record inflation, coupled with record borrowing and a lack of confidence in Britain unknown in any member's lifetime.

He stood his full height and stared down belligerently at the Government benches.

"Mr. Speaker," he began, "I can't think . . ."

"Then don't bother to speak," someone shouted from the Labour benches. Laughter broke out as Charles tried to compose himself, cursing his initial overconfidence. He began again.

"I can't imagine . . ."

"No imagination either," came another voice. "Typical Tory."

". . . why this subject was ever put before the House."

"Certainly not for you to give us a lesson in public speaking."

"Order," growled the Speaker, but it was too late.

The House was lost, and Charles stumbled through thirty minutes of embarrassment until no one but the Speaker was listening to a word he said. Several front-bench Ministers had their feet up on the table and their eyes closed. Backbenchers sat chattering among themselves waiting for the ten o'clock vote: the ultimate humiliation the House affords to its worst debaters. The Speaker had to call for order several times during Charles's speech, once rising to rebuke noisy members, "The House does its reputation no service by behaving in this way." But his plea fell on deaf ears as the conversations continued. At nine-thirty Charles sat down in a cold sweat. A few of his own backbenchers managed to raise an unconvincing, "Hear, hear."

When a Government spokesman opened his speech by describing Charles's offering as among the most pathetic he had heard in a long political career, he may well have been exaggerating, but from the expressions on the Tory front benches not many Opposition members were going to disagree with him.

Elizabeth looked up and smiled as her husband came into the room. "I've delivered over a thousand children in the past five years, but none have given me the thrill this one did. I thought you'd like to know mother and child are doing well."

Simon took Elizabeth in his arms. "How long do I have to wait to learn the truth?"

"It's a boy," she said.

"Congratulations, darling," said Simon. "I'm so proud of you." He pushed her hair back tenderly. "So it's to be Peter, not Lucy."

"Certainly hope so, that is if you don't want the poor little blighter teased all his life."

A nurse joined them holding a small child almost swamped in a little sheet and blanket. Simon took his son in his arms and stared into the large blue eyes.

"He looks like a future Prime Minister to me."

"Good heavens, no," said Elizabeth. "He looks far too intelligent to consider anything as silly as that." She put her arms out at full stretch and Simon reluctantly released his son into the care of his mother.

Simon sat on the end of the bed admiring his wife and first-born, as Elizabeth prepared to feed him.

"Perhaps it will be possible for you to take a break for a while. You deserve a holiday."

"Not a chance," said Elizabeth, as she watched her son close his eyes. "I'm back on duty roster next week. Don't forget we still need my income while they pay members of Parliament such a pittance."

93

Simon didn't reply. He realized that if he was ever going to convince his wife to slow down, he would have to take a more gentle approach.

"Peter and I think you're wonderful," said Simon.

Elizabeth looked down at her child. "I don't think Peter's sure yet, but at least he's sleeping on it."

The decision was finally made by the inner Cabinet of twelve on Thursday, November 16, 1967. By Friday every bank clerk in Tokyo was privy to the inner Cabinet's closest secret, and by the time the Prime Minister made the announcement official on Saturday afternoon, the Bank of England had lost 600 million dollars of reserves on the foreign-exchange market.

At the time of the Prime Minister's statement, Raymond was in Leeds conducting his twice-monthly constituency office hours. He was in the process of explaining the new housing bill to a young married couple when Fred Padgett, his campaign manager, burst into the room.

"Raymond, sorry to interrupt you, but I thought you'd want to know immediately. Number Ten has just announced that the pound has been devalued from $2.80 to $2.40." The sitting member was momentarily stunned, the local housing problem driven from his mind. He stared blankly across the table at the two constituents who had come to seek his advice.

"Will you please excuse me for a moment, Mr. Higginbottom?" Raymond asked courteously. "I must make a phone call." The moment turned out to be fifteen minutes, in which time Raymond had made contact with a senior civil servant from the Treasury and had all the details confirmed. He called Joyce and told her not to answer the phone until he arrived back home. It was several minutes until he was composed enough to open his office door.

"How many people are still waiting to see me, Fred?" he asked.

"After the Higginbottoms there's only the mad major, still

convinced that Martians are about to land on the roof of Leeds Town Hall."

"Why would they want to come to Leeds first?" asked Raymond, trying to hide his growing anxiety with false humor.

"Once they've captured Yorkshire, the rest would be easy."

"Hard to find fault with that argument. Nevertheless, tell the major I'm deeply concerned but I need to study his claim in more detail and to seek further advice from the Ministry of Defense. Make an appointment for him to see me during my next office hours, and by then I should have a strategic plan ready."

Fred Padgett grinned. "That will give him something to tell his friends about for at least two weeks."

Raymond returned to Mr. and Mrs. Higginbottom and assured them he would have their housing problem sorted out within a few days. He made a note on his file to ring the Leeds borough housing officer.

"What an afternoon," exclaimed Raymond after the door had closed behind them. "One wife-beating, one electricity turned off by the Electricity Board with four children under ten in the house, one pollution of the Aire River, one appalling housing problem, never forgetting the mad major and his imminent Martians. And now the devaluation news."

"How can you remain so calm under the circumstances?" Fred Padgett asked.

"Because I can't afford to let anyone know how I really feel."

After his office hours Raymond would normally have gone around to the local pub for a pint and an obligatory chat with the locals, which would give him a chance to catch up on what had been happening in Leeds during the past few weeks. But on this occasion he bypassed the pub and returned quickly to his parents' home.

Joyce told him the phone had rung so often that she had finally taken it off the hook without letting his mother know the real reason.

"Very sensible," said Raymond.

"What are you going to do?" she asked.

"I shall resign, of course."

"Why do that, Raymond? It will only harm your career."

"You may turn out to be right, but that won't stop me."

"But you're only just beginning to get on top of your work."

"Joyce, without trying to sound pompous, I know I have many failings, but I'm not a coward, and I'm certainly not so self-seeking as totally to desert any principles I might have."

"You know, you just sounded like a man who believes he's destined to become Prime Minister."

"A moment ago you said it would harm my chances. Make up your mind."

"I have," she said.

Raymond smiled wanly before retreating to his study to compose a short handwritten letter.

Saturday, November 18, 1967

> *Dear Prime Minister,*
> *After your announcement this afternoon on devaluation and the stand I have continually taken on the issue I am left with no choice but to resign my position as Under Secretary of State for Employment.*
> *I would like to thank you for having given me the opportunity to serve in your administration. Be assured that I shall continue to support the Government on all other issues from the backbenches.*
> *Yours,*
> *RAYMOND GOULD*

When the red box arrived at the house that Saturday night, Raymond instructed the messenger to deliver the letter to Number 10 immediately. As he opened the box for the last time he reflected that his department was answering questions on employment in the House that Monday. He wondered who would be chosen to take his place.

Because of the red tape surrounding devaluation, the Prime Minister did not get around to reading Raymond's letter until late Sunday morning. The Goulds' phone was still off the hook when an anxious Fred Padgett was heard knocking on the front door later that day.

"Don't answer it," said Raymond. "It's bound to be another journalist."

"No, it's not, it's only Fred," said Joyce, peeping through an opening in the curtain.

She opened the door. "Where the hell's Raymond?" were Fred's first words.

"Right here," said Raymond, appearing from the kitchen holding the Sunday newspapers.

"The Prime Minister has been trying to contact you all morning."

Raymond turned around and replaced the phone on the hook, picked it up a few seconds later and checked the tone before dialing London WHI 4433. The Prime Minister was on the line in moments. He sounded calm enough, thought Raymond.

"Have you issued any statement to the press, Raymond?"

"No, I wanted to be sure you had received my letter first."

"Good. Please don't mention your resignation to anyone until we've met. Could you be at Downing Street by eight o'clock?"

"Yes, Prime Minister."

"Remember, not a word to the press."

Raymond heard the phone click.

Within the hour he was on his way to London, and he arrived at his house in Lansdowne Road a little after seven. The phone was ringing again. He wanted to ignore the insistent *burr-burr* but thought it might be Downing Street.

He picked the phone up. "Hello."

"Is that Raymond Gould?" said a voice.

"Who's speaking?" asked Raymond.

"Walter Terry, *Daily Mail.*"

"I am not going to say anything," said Raymond.

"Do you feel the Prime Minister was right to devalue?"

"I said nothing, Walter."

"Does that mean you are going to resign?"

"Walter, nothing."

"Is it true you have already handed in your resignation?"

Raymond hesitated.

"I thought so," said Terry.

"I said nothing," spluttered Raymond and slammed down the phone—before lifting it back off the hook.

He quickly washed and changed his shirt before leaving the house. He nearly missed the note that was lying on the doormat, and he wouldn't have stopped to open it had the envelope not been embossed with large black letters across the left hand corner—"Prime Minister." Raymond ripped it open. The handwritten note from a secretary asked him on his arrival to enter by the rear entrance of Downing Street, not by the front door. A small map was enclosed. Raymond was becoming weary of the whole exercise.

Two more journalists were waiting by the gate. They followed him to his car.

"Have you resigned, Minister?" asked the first.

"No comment."

"Are you on your way to see the Prime Minister?"

Raymond did not reply and leaped into his car. He drove off so quickly that the pursuing journalists were left with no chance of catching him.

Twelve minutes later, at five to eight, he was seated in the anteroom of Number 10 Downing Street. As eight struck he was taken through to Harold Wilson's study. He was surprised to find the senior minister in his own Department, the Secretary of State for Employment, seated in a corner of the room.

"Ray," said the Prime Minister. "How are you?"

"I'm well, thank you, Prime Minister."

"I was sorry to receive your letter and thoroughly understand the position you are in, but I hope perhaps we can work something out."

"Work something out?" Raymond repeated, puzzled.

"Well, we all realize devaluation is a problem for you after *Full Employment at Any Cost?* but I felt perhaps a move to the Foreign Office as Minister of State might be a palatable way out of the dilemma. It's a promotion you've well earned."

Raymond hesitated. The Prime Minister continued, "It may interest you to know that the Chancellor of the Exchequer has also resigned, but will be moving to the Home Office."

"I am surprised," said Raymond. "But in my case, I do not consider it would be the honorable thing to—"

The Prime Minister waved his hand. "What with the problems we are about to tackle in Rhodesia and Europe, your legal skills would come in very useful."

For the first time in his life Raymond detested politics.

Mondays usually get off to a quiet start in the Commons. The Whips never plan for any contentious business to be debated, remembering that members are still arriving back from their constituencies all over the country. The House is seldom full before the early evening. But the knowledge that the Chancellor of the Exchequer would be making a statement on devaluation at three-thirty insured that the Commons would be packed long before that hour.

The Commons filled up quickly, and by two forty-five there was not a seat to be found. The green benches accommodating just four hundred and twenty-seven members had deliberately been restored as they were before the Germans had bombed the Palace of Westminster on May 10, 1941. The intimate theatrical atmosphere of the House had remained intact. Sir Giles Gilbert Scott could not resist highlighting some of the Gothic decor of Barry, but he concurred with Churchill's view that to enlarge the chamber would only destroy the packed atmosphere of great occasions.

99

Some members huddled were even up on the steps by the Speaker's canopied chair and around the legs of the chairs of the clerks at the table. One or two perched like unfed sparrows on the empty petition bay behind the Speaker's chair.

Raymond Gould rose to answer Question Number 7 on the agenda, an innocent enough inquiry concerning unemployment benefits for women. As soon as he reached the dispatch box, the first cries of "Resign" came from the Tory benches. Raymond couldn't hide his embarrassment. Even those on the back benches could see he'd gone scarlet. It didn't help that he hadn't slept the previous night following the agreement he had come to with the Prime Minister. He answered the question, but the calls for his resignation did not subside. The Opposition fell silent as he sat down, only waiting for him to rise for a further question. The next question on the agenda for Raymond to answer was from Simon Kerslake; it came a few minutes after three. "What analysis has been made by your department of the special factors contributing to increasing unemployment in the Midlands?"

Raymond checked his brief before replying. "The closure of two large factories in the area, one in the Honorable Member's constituency, has exacerbated local unemployment. Both of these factories specialized in car components, which have suffered from the Leyland strike."

Simon Kerslake rose slowly from his place to ask his supplementary question. The Opposition benches waited in eager anticipation. "But surely the Minister remembers informing the House, in reply to my adjournment debate last April, that devaluation would drastically increase unemployment in the Midlands, indeed in the whole country. If the honorable gentleman's words are to carry any conviction, why hasn't he resigned?" Simon sat down as the Tory benches demanded, "Why, why, why?"

"My speech to the House on that occasion is being quoted out of context, and the circumstances have since changed."

"They certainly have," shouted a number of Conservatives,

and the benches opposite Raymond exploded with demands that he give up his office.

"Order, order," shouted the Speaker into the tide of noise.

Simon rose again, while everyone on the Conservative benches remained seated to insure that no one else was called. They were now hunting as a pack.

Everyone's eyes switched back and forth between the two men, watching the dark, assured figure of Kerslake once again jabbing his forefinger at the bowed head of Raymond Gould, who was now only praying for the clock to reach 3:30.

"Mr. Speaker, during that debate, which he now seems happy to orphan, the Honorable Gentleman was only echoing the views he so lucidly expressed in his book *Full Employment at Any Cost?* Can those views have altered so radically in three years, or is his desire to remain in office so great that he now realizes his employment can be achieved at any cost?"

The Opposition benches chanted, "Resign, resign."

"This question has nothing to do with what I said to the House on that occasion," retorted Raymond angrily.

Simon was up in a flash and the Speaker called him for a third time.

"Is the Honorable Gentleman telling the House that he has one set of moral standards when he speaks, and yet another when he writes?"

The House was now in total uproar and few members heard Raymond say, "No, sir, I try to be consistent."

The Speaker rose and the noise subsided slightly. He looked about him with an aggrieved frown. "I realize the House feels strongly on these matters, but I must ask the Honorable Member for Coventry Central to withdraw his remark suggesting that the Minister has behaved dishonorably."

Simon rose and retracted his statement at once, but the damage had been done. Nor did it stop members from calling "Resign" until Raymond left the chamber a few minutes later.

101

Simon sat back smugly as Gould left the chamber. Conservative members turned to nod their acknowledgment of his complete annihilation of the Government's Under Secretary of State. The Chancellor of the Exchequer rose to deliver his prepared statement on devaluation. Simon listened with horror to the Chancellor's opening words:

"The Honorable Member for Leeds North handed in his resignation to the Prime Minister on Saturday evening but graciously agreed not to make this public until I had had an opportunity to address the House."

The Chancellor went on to praise Raymond for his work in the Department of Employment and to wish him well on the back benches.

Jamie Sinclair visited Raymond in his room immediately after the Chancellor had finished answering questions. He found him slumped at his desk, a vacant look on his face. Sinclair had come to express his admiration for the way Raymond had conducted himself.

"It's kind of you," said Raymond, who was still shaking from the experience.

"I wouldn't like to be in Kerslake's shoes at this moment," said Jamie. "Simon must feel the biggest shit in town."

"There's no way he could have known," said Raymond. "He'd certainly done his homework and the questions were right on target. I suspect we would have approached the situation in the same way given the circumstances."

Several other members dropped in to commiserate with Raymond, after which he stopped by his old department to say farewell to his team before he went home to spend a quiet evening with Joyce.

There was a long silence before the Permanent Secretary ventured an opinion: "I hope, sir, it will not be long before you return to Government. You have certainly made our lives hard, but for those you ultimately serve you have undoubtedly made life easier." The sincerity of the statement touched Raymond, especially as the civil servant was already serving a new master.

As the days passed, it felt strange to be able to sit down and watch television, read a book, even go for a walk and not be perpetually surrounded by red boxes and ringing phones.

He was to receive over a hundred letters from colleagues in the House but he kept only one:

Monday, November 20, 1967

Dear Gould,

I owe you a profound apology. We all in our political life make monumental mistakes about people and I certainly made one today.

I believe that most members of the House have a genuine desire to serve the country, and there can be no more honorable way of proving it than by resigning when one feels one's party has taken a wrong course.

I envy the respect in which the whole House now holds you.

Yours sincerely,
SIMON KERSLAKE.

When Raymond returned to the Commons that afternoon, he was cheered by the members of both sides from the moment he entered the chamber. The minister who had been addressing the House at the time had no choice but to wait until Raymond had taken a seat on the back benches.

9

SIMON HAD ALREADY LEFT when Edward Heath called his home. It was another hour before Elizabeth was able to pass on the message that the Party Leader wanted to see him at two-thirty.

Charles was at the bank when the Chief Whip called, asking if they could meet at two-thirty that afternoon before Commons business began.

Charles felt like a schoolboy who had been told the head-master expected him to be in his study after lunch. The last time the Chief Whip had phoned was to ask him to make his unfor-tunate winding-up speech, and they had hardly spoken since. Charles was apprehensive; he always preferred to be told what a problem was immediately. He decided to leave the bank early and catch lunch at the House to be sure he was not late for his afternoon appointment.

Charles joined some of his colleagues at the large table in the center of the members' dining room and took the only seat available, next to Simon Kerslake. The two men had not really been on good terms since the Heath-Maudling Leadership con-test.

Charles did not care much for Kerslake. He had once told Fiona that he was one of the new breed of Tories who tried a little too hard, and he had not been displeased to see him embarrassed over the Gould resignation. Not that he expressed his true feelings to anyone other than Fiona.

Simon watched Charles sit down and wondered how much longer the Party could go on electing Etonian guardsmen who spent more time making money in the city and then spending it at Ascot than they did working in the House—not that it was an opinion he would have voiced to anyone but his closest confidants.

The discussion over the lunch table centered on the remarkable run of by-election results the Tories had had with three key marginal seats. It was obvious that most of those around the table were eager for a General Election, although the Prime Minister did not have to call one for at least another three years.

Neither Charles nor Simon ordered coffee.

At two twenty-five Charles watched the Chief Whip leave his private table in the corner of the room and turn to walk toward his office. Charles checked his watch and waited a moment before leaving as his colleagues began a heated discussion about entry into the Common Market.

He strolled past the smoking room before turning left at the entrance to the library. Then he continued down the old Ways and Means corridor until he passed the Opposition Whip's office on his left. Once through the swinging doors he entered the members' lobby, which he crossed to reach the Government Whip's office. He strode into the secretary's door. Miss Norse, the Chief's invaluable secretary, stopped typing.

"I have an appointment with the Chief Whip," said Charles.

"Yes, Mr. Hampton, he is expecting you. Please go through." The typing recommenced immediately.

Charles walked on down the corridor and found the Chief Whip blocking his own doorway.

"Come on in, Charles. Can I offer you a drink?"

"No, thank you," replied Charles, not wanting to delay the news any longer.

The Chief Whip poured himself a gin and tonic before sitting down.

"I hope what I'm about to tell you will be looked upon as good news." The Chief Whip paused and took a gulp of his drink. "The Leader thinks you might benefit from a spell in the Whip's office, and I must say I would be delighted if you felt able to join us. . . ."

Charles wanted to protest but checked himself. "And give up my Environment post?"

"Oh, yes, and more, of course, because Mr. Heath expects all whips to forgo any outside employment as well. Working in this office is not a part-time occupation."

Charles needed a moment to compose his thoughts. "And if I turn it down, will I retain my post at Environment?"

"That's not for me to decide," said the Chief Whip. "But it is no secret that Ted Heath is planning several changes in the period before the next election."

"How long do I have to consider the offer?"

"Perhaps you could let me know your decision by Question Time tomorrow."

"Yes, of course. Thank you," said Charles. He left the Chief Whip's office and drove to Eaton Square.

Simon also arrived at two twenty-five, five minutes before his meeting with the Party Leader. He had tried not to speculate as to why Heath wanted to see him, in case the meeting only resulted in disappointment. Douglas Hurd, the head of the private office, ushered him straight through to the Conservative Leader.

"Simon, how would you like to join the Environment team?" It was typical of Heath not to waste any time on small talk, and the suddenness of the offer took Simon by surprise. He recovered quickly.

"Thank you very much," he said. "I mean, er . . . yes . . . thank you."

"Good, let's see you put your back into it, and be sure the re-sults at the dispatch box are as effective as they have been from the back benches."

The door was opened once again by the private secretary; the interview was clearly over. Simon found himself back in the corridor at two thirty-three. It was several moments before the offer sank in. Then, elated, he made a dash for the nearest phone. He dialed the St. Mary's switchboard and asked if he could be put through to Doctor Kerslake. As he spoke, his voice was almost drowned by the sound of the division bells, signal-ing the start of the day's business at two thirty-five, following prayers. A woman's voice came on the line.

"Is that you, darling?" asked Simon above the din.

"No, sir. It's the switchboard operator. Doctor Kerslake's in the operating room."

"Is there any hope of getting her out?"

"Not unless you're in labor, sir."

"What brings you home so early?" asked Fiona as Charles came charging through the front door.

"I need to talk to someone." Fiona could never be sure if she ought to be flattered, but she didn't express any opinion. It was all too rare these days to have his company, and she was de-lighted.

Charles repeated to his wife as nearly verbatim as possible his conversation with the Chief Whip. Fiona remained silent when Charles had come to the end of his monologue. "Well, what's your opinion?" he asked anxiously.

"All because of one bad speech from the dispatch box," Fiona commented wryly.

"I agree," said Charles, "but nothing can be gained by tramping over that ground again. And if I turn it down, and we win the next election . . . ?"

"You'll be left out in the cold."

"More to the point, stranded on the back benches."

107

"Charles, politics has always been your first love," said Fiona, touching him gently on the cheek. "So I don't see that you have a choice, and if that means some sacrifices, you'll never hear me complain."

Charles rose from his chair saying, "Thank you, my dear. I'd better go and see Derek Spencer immediately."

As Charles turned to leave, Fiona added, "And don't forget, Ted Heath became Leader of the party via the Whip's office."

Charles smiled for the first time that day.

"A quiet dinner at home tonight?" suggested Fiona.

"Can't tonight," said Charles. "I've got a late vote."

Fiona sat alone wondering if she would spend the rest of her life waiting up for a man who didn't appear to need her affection.

At last they put him through.

"Let's have a celebration dinner tonight."

"Why?" asked Elizabeth.

"Because I've been invited to join the front-bench team to cover the Environment."

"Congratulations, darling, but what does 'Environment' consist of?"

"Housing, urban land, transport, devolution, water, historic buildings, Stansted or Maplin airport, the Channel tunnel, royal parks . . ."

"Have they left anything for anyone else to do?"

"That's only half of it—if it's out-of-doors, it's mine. I'll tell you the rest over dinner."

"Oh, hell, I don't think I can get away until eight tonight and we'd have to get a baby-sitter. Does that come under Environment, Simon?"

"Sure does," he said, laughing. "I'll fix it and book a table at the Grange for eight-thirty."

"Have you got a ten o'clock vote?"

"Afraid so."

"I see, coffee with the baby-sitter again," she said. She paused. "Simon."

"Yes, darling."

"I'm very proud of you."

Derek Spencer sat behind his massive partner's desk in Threadneedle Street and listened intently to what Charles had to say.

"You will be a great loss to the bank," were the chairman's first words. "But no one here would want to hold up your political career, least of all me."

Charles noticed that Spencer could not look him in the eye as he spoke.

"Can I assume that I would be invited back on the board if for any reason my situation changed at the Commons?"

"Of course," said Spencer. "There was no need for you to ask such a question."

"That's kind of you," said Charles, genuinely relieved. He stood up, leaned forward and shook hands rather stiffly.

"Good luck, Charles," were Spencer's parting words.

"Does that mean you can no longer stay on the board?" asked Ronnie Nethercote when he heard Simon's news.

"No, not while I'm in Opposition and only a Shadow spokesman. But if we win the next election and I'm offered a job in Government, I would have to resign immediately."

"So I've got your services for another three years?"

"Unless the Prime Minister picks an earlier date to run, or we lose the next election."

"No fear of the latter," said Ronnie, "I knew I'd picked a winner the day I met you, and I don't think you'll ever regret joining my board."

Over the months that followed, Charles was surprised to find how much he enjoyed working in the Whip's office, although he had been unable to hide from Fiona his anger when he discovered it was Kerslake who had captured his old job at Environment. The order, discipline and camaraderie of the job brought back memories of his military days in the Grenadier Guards. Charles's duties were manifold, ranging from checking that members were all present in their committees to sitting on the front bench in the Commons and picking out the salient points members made in their speeches to the House. He also had to keep an eye out for any signs of dissension or rebellion on his own benches while remaining abreast of what was happening on the other side of the House. In addition he had fifty of his own members from the Midlands area to shepherd, and had to be certain that they never missed a vote. Each Thursday he passed out a sheet of paper showing what votes would be coming up the following week. The main debates were underlined with three lines. Less important debates, those with two lines under them, made it possible for a member not to be present for a vote if paired with a member from the opposite party, as long as the Whip's office had been informed. The few that had only one line underneath were not mandatory.

Charles already knew that there were no circumstances under which a member was allowed to miss a "three-line whip," unless he had died and even then, the Chief Whip told him, the Whip's office required a death certificate.

"See that none of your members ever misses one," the Chief Whip warned him, "or they'll wish they did have a death certificate."

As whips are never called on to make speeches in the House at any time, Charles seemed to have discovered the role for which he was best cut out. Fiona reminded him once again that Ted Heath had jumped from the Whip's office to Shadow Chancellor. She was delighted to see how involved her husband had become with Commons life, but she hated going to bed each night and regularly falling asleep before he arrived home.

Simon also enjoyed his new appointment from the first moment. As the junior member of the Environment team he was given transport as his special subject. During the first year he read books, studied pamphlets, held meetings with national transport chairmen from air, sea and rail, and worked long into the night trying to master his new brief. Simon was one of those rare members who, after only a few weeks, looked as if he had always been on the front bench.

Peter was one of those noisy babies who after only a few weeks sounded as if he was already on the front bench.

"Perhaps he's going to be a politician after all," concluded Elizabeth, staring down at her son.

"What has changed your mind?" asked Simon.

"He never stops shouting at everyone, he's totally preoccupied with himself, and he falls asleep as soon as anyone else offers an opinion."

"They're being rude about my firstborn," said Simon, picking up his son and immediately regretting the move as soon as he felt Peter's bottom.

Elizabeth had been surprised to find how much time Simon had put aside for his son, and she even admitted, when interviewed by the *Littlehampton News,* that the member could change a diaper as deftly as any midwife.

By the time Peter could crawl he was into everything, including Simon's private briefcase, where he deposited sticky chocolates, rubber bands, string and even his favorite toy.

Simon once opened the briefcase in full view of a meeting of the Shadow Environment team to discover Teddy Heath, Peter's much battered bear, lying on the top of his papers. He removed the stuffed animal to reveal his "plans for a future Tory government."

"A security risk?" suggested the Opposition Leader with a grin.

"My son, or the bear?" inquired Simon.

By their second years, as Peter was feeling confident enough to walk, Simon was beginning to have his own views on the issues facing the Party. As each month passed, they both grew in confidence, and all Simon now wanted was for Harold Wilson to call a General Election.

All Peter wanted was a soccer ball.

Talk of a General Election was suddenly in the air. Just as it looked as though the Conservatives were gaining in the opinion polls, the Labour Party had a string of by-election victories in early 1970.

When May's opinion polls confirmed the trend to Labour, Harold Wilson visited the Queen at Buckingham Palace and asked her to dissolve Parliament. The date of the General Election was set for June 18, 1970.

The press was convinced that Wilson had got it right again, and would lead his party to victory for the third time in a row, a feat no man in political history had managed. Every Conservative knew that would spell the end of Edward Heath's leadership of his party.

Three weeks later political history was not made, for the Conservatives captured Parliament with an overall majority of thirty seats. Her Majesty the Queen invited Edward Heath to attend her at the Palace and asked him to form a government. He kissed the hands of his sovereign and accepted her commission.

Simon Kerslake managed a four-figure majority for the first time when he won Coventry Central by 2,118.

When Fiona was asked by the old earl how many votes Charles had won by on this occasion, she said she couldn't be certain, but she did recall Charles's telling a journalist it was more than the other candidates put together.

Raymond Gould suffered an adverse swing of only 2 percent and was returned with a 10,416 majority. The people of Leeds admire independence in a member, especially when it comes to a matter of principle.

10

WHEN SIMON AWOKE on the Friday morning after the election he felt both exhausted and exhilarated. He lay in bed trying to imagine how those Labour Ministers, who only the previous day had assumed they would be returning to their departments, must be feeling now.

Elizabeth stirred, let out a small sleep-filled sigh and turned over. Simon stared down at his wife. In the four years of their marriage she had lost none of her attraction for him, and he still took pleasure in just looking at her sleeping form. Her long fair hair rested on her shoulders and her slim, firm figure curved gently beneath the silk nightgown. He started stroking her back and watched her slowly come out of sleep. When she finally awoke she turned over and he took her in his arms.

"I admire your energy," she said. "If you're still fit after three weeks on the trail I can hardly claim to have a headache."

He kissed her gently, delighted to catch a moment of privacy between the lunacy of election and the anticipation of office. No voter was going to interrupt this rare moment of pleasure.

"Daddy," said a voice, and Simon quickly turned over to see Peter standing at the door.

"I'm hungry."

On the way back to London in the car Elizabeth asked, "What do you think he'll offer you?"

113

"Daren't anticipate anything," said Simon. "But I would hope—Under Secretary of State for the Environment."

"But you're still not certain to be offered a post?"

"Not at all. One can never know what permutations and pressures a new Prime Minister has to consider."

"Like what?" asked Elizabeth.

"Left and right wings of the Party, north and south of the country—countless debts to be cleared with those people who can claim they played a role in getting him into Number Ten."

"Are you saying he could leave you out?"

"Oh, yes. But I'll be damn livid if he does."

"And what could you do about it?"

"Nothing. There is absolutely nothing one can do, and every backbencher knows it. The Prime Minister's power of patronage is absolute."

"It won't matter that much, darling, if you continue driving in the wrong lane."

Raymond was astonished. He couldn't believe that the opinion polls had been so wrong. He didn't confide in Joyce that he had hoped a Labour victory would bring him back onto the front bench, having languished on the back benches for what seemed an interminable time.

"There's nothing to it," he told her, "but to rebuild a career at the bar. We may be out of office for a very long time."

"But surely that won't be enough to keep you fully occupied?"

"I have to be realistic about the future," he said slowly.

"Perhaps they will ask you to shadow someone?"

"No, there are always far fewer jobs available in Opposition, and in any case they always give the orators like Jamie Sinclair the lead. All I can do is sit and wait for another election."

Raymond wondered how he would broach what was really on his mind and tried to sound casual when he said, "Perhaps it's time we considered having our own home in the constituency."

"Why?" said Joyce, surprised. "That seems an unnecessary expense, and there's nothing wrong with your parents' house. And, in any case, wouldn't they be offended?"

"The first interest should be to my constituents and this would be a chance to prove a long-term commitment. Naturally, my parents would understand."

"But the cost of two houses!"

"It will be a lot easier to contemplate than when I was in Government, and it's you who have always wanted to live in Leeds. This will give you the chance to stop commuting from London every week. After I've done the rounds why don't you stay in Leeds, contact a few local real estate agents and see what's on the market?"

"All right, if that's what you really want," said Joyce. "I'll start next week." Raymond was pleased to see Joyce was beginning to warm to the idea.

Charles and Fiona spent a quiet weekend at their cottage in Sussex. Charles tried to do some gardening while he kept one ear open for the telephone. Fiona began to realize how anxious he was when she looked through the French window and saw her finest delphinium being taken for a weed.

Charles finally gave the weeds a reprieve and came in and turned on the television to catch Maudling, Macleod, Thatcher and Carrington entering Number 10 Downing Street, all looking pensive, only to leave all smiles. The senior appointments had been made. The Cabinet was taking shape. The new Conservative Prime Minister came out and waved to the crowds before being whisked away in his official car.

Would Heath remember who had organized the young vote for him before he was even the Party Leader?

"When do you want to go back to Eaton Square?" Fiona inquired from the kitchen.

"Depends," said Charles.

"On what?"

"On whether the phone rings."

115

Simon replaced the phone and sat staring at the television. All those hours of work on Environment, and the PM had offered the portfolio to someone else. He had left the television set on all day but didn't learn who it was, only that the rest of the Environment team had remained intact.

"Why do I bother?" he said out loud. "The whole thing's a farce."

"What were you saying, darling?" asked Elizabeth as she came into the room.

The phone rang again. It was the newly appointed Home Secretary, Reginald Maudling.

"Simon?"

"Reggie, many congratulations on your appointment—not that it came as a great surprise."

"That's what I'm calling about, Simon. Would you like to join me at the Home Office as Under Secretary?"

"Like to—I would be delighted to join you at the Home Office."

"Thank heavens for that," said Maudling. "It took me a dickens of a time to convince Ted Heath that you should be released from the Environment team."

Simon turned to his wife to let her know his news. "I don't think there is anything that could have pleased me more."

"Want to bet?"

Simon looked toward Elizabeth, his face showing complete puzzlement.

"Oh, poor thing, you're so slow," Elizabeth said. She patted her stomach. "We're going to have a second child."

When Raymond arrived back at his London law chambers, he let his clerk know that he wanted to be flooded with work. Over lunch with the head of the partnership, Sir Nigel Hartwell, he explained that he thought it unlikely that the Labour Party would be in government again for some considerable time.

"You've only had five years in the House, Raymond, and at

thirty-six, you must stop looking upon yourself as a veteran."

"I wonder," said Raymond, sounding uncharacteristically pessimistic.

"Well, you needn't worry about briefs. Law firms have been calling constantly since it was known you were back on a more permanent basis."

Raymond began to relax.

Joyce phoned him after lunch with the news that she hadn't yet found anything suitable, but the real estate agent had assured her that things would open up in the fall.

"Well, keep looking," said Raymond.

"Don't worry, I will," said Joyce, sounding as if she were enjoying the whole exercise.

"If we find something, perhaps we can think of starting a family," she added tentatively.

"Perhaps," said Raymond brusquely.

Charles eventually received a call on Monday night, not from Number 10 Downing Street but from Number 12, the office of the Chief Whip.

The Chief Whip was calling to say that he hoped that Charles would be willing to soldier on as a junior whip. When he heard the disappointment in Charles's voice he added, "For the time being."

"For the time being," repeated Charles and put the phone down.

"At least you're a member of the Government. You haven't been left out in the cold. People will come and go during the next five years, and you certainly have time on your side," said Fiona gamely. Charles had to agree with his wife, but it didn't lessen his disappointment.

However, returning to the Commons as a member of the Government turned out to be far more rewarding than he expected. This time his party was making the decisions, and the priorities were laid out when the Queen delivered her speech from the throne in the House of Lords at the opening of the new Parliament.

Queen Elizabeth traveled early that November morning to the House of Lords in the Irish state coach. An escort of the household cavalry accompanied her, preceded by a procession of lesser state carriages in which the King Edward crown and other royal trappings were transported. Charles could remember watching the ceremony from the streets when he was a boy. Now he was taking part in it. When she arrived at the House of Lords she was accompanied by the Lord Chancellor through the sovereign's entrance to the robing room, where her ladies-in-waiting began to prepare her for the ceremony.

At the appointed hour, Mr. Speaker, in his full court dress, a gold-embroidered gown of black satin damask, stepped down from his chair. He led the traditional procession out of the Commons and into the House of Lords. Followed by the Clerk of the House and the sergeant-at-arms bearing the ceremonial mace, then the Prime Minister, accompanied by the Leader of the Opposition, next, both front benches with their opposite numbers, and finally, as many backbenchers as could squeeze into the rear of the Lords' Chamber.

The Lords themselves waited in the Upper House, dressed in red capes with ermine collars, looking somewhat like benevolent Draculas, accompanied by peeresses glittering in diamond tiaras and wearing long formal dresses. The Queen was seated on the throne, in her full imperial robes, the King Edward III crown now on her head. She waited until the procession had filled the chamber and all was still.

The Lord Chancellor shuffled forward and, bending down on one knee, presented to the Queen a printed document. It was the speech written by the Government of the day, and although Her Majesty had read over the script the previous evening, she had made no personal contribution to its contents, as her role was only ceremonial on this occasion. She looked up at her subjects and began to read.

Charles Hampton stood at the back of the cramped gathering, but with his height he had no trouble in following the entire proceedings.

He could spot his elderly father, the Earl of Bridgewater, nodding off during the Queen's speech, which offered no more or less than had been promised by the Tories during the election campaign. Charles, along with everyone else from the Commons, was counting the likely number of bills that would be presented during the coming months and soon worked out that the Whip's office was going to be in for a busy session.

As the Queen finished her speech, Charles took one more look at his father, now sound asleep. How Charles dreaded the moment when he would be standing there watching his brother Rupert in ermine. The only compensation would be if he could produce a son who would one day inherit the title, as it was now obvious Rupert would never marry. It was not as if he and Fiona had not tried. He was beginning to wonder if the time had come to suggest that she visit a specialist. He dreaded finding out that she was unable to bear a child.

Even producing an heir would not be enough if all *he* had achieved was to be a junior whip. It made him more determined than ever to prove he was worthy of promotion.

The speech delivered, the sovereign left the Upper House followed by Prince Philip, Prince Charles and a fanfare of trumpets.

From the first day of his appointment in June, Simon enjoyed every aspect of his work at the Home Office. By the time the Queen's speech had been delivered in November, he was ready to represent his department in the Commons, although Jamie Sinclair's appointment to shadow him would insure that he could never relax completely.

As the new Tory administration took shape, the two quickly locked horns over several issues and were soon known as "the mongoose and the rattlesnake." However, in informal con-

119

ference behind the Speaker's chair, Simon and Jamie Sinclair would good-humoredly discuss the issues on which they were crossing swords. The opportunity to be out of sight of the press gallery above them was often taken by the opposing members, but once they had both returned to the dispatch box they would tear into each other, each looking for any weakness in the other's argument. When either of the names Kerslake or Sinclair was cranked up on the old-fashioned wall machines indicating that one of them had risen to start a speech, members came flooding back into the chamber.

On one subject they found themselves in total accord. Ever since August 1969, when troops had first been sent into Northern Ireland, Parliament had been having another of its periodic bouts of trouble with the Irish question. In February of '71 the House devoted a full day's business to listen to members' opinions in the never-ending effort to find a solution to the growing clash between Protestant extremists and the IRA. The motion before the House was to allow emergency powers to be renewed in the province.

Simon rose from his seat on the front bench to deliver the opening speech for the Government, and having completed his contribution, surprised members by leaving the chamber.

It is considered tactful for front-bench spokesmen on both sides of the House to remain in their places when backbenchers make their contribution to a debate. Several members began to comment when Simon hadn't returned an hour later. When he eventually came back, he only remained in his place for twenty minutes before slipping out again. He even failed to be present for the beginning of Jamie Sinclair's windup speech, to which he was expected to make a rebuttal.

When Simon eventually returned to the chamber and took his place on the front bench, an elderly Labourite rose from his seat.

"On a point of order, Mr. Speaker."

Jamie sat down immediately and turned his head to listen to the point his colleague wanted to make.

120

"Is it not a tradition of this house, sir," began the elder states-man rather ponderously, "for a Minister of the Crown to have the courtesy to remain in his seat during the debate in order that he may ascertain views other than his own?"

"That is not strictly a point of order," replied the Speaker above the cries of "Hear, hear" from the Labour benches. Simon scribbled a quick note and hurriedly passed it over the opposite bench to Jamie. On it was written a single sentence.

"I accept the point my Right Honorable friend makes," Sin-clair began, "and would have complained myself had I not known that the Honorable Gentleman, the member for Co-ventry Central, has spent most of the afternoon in the hospi-tal"—Sinclair paused to let the effect set in—"where his wife was in labor. I am rarely overwhelmed by the argument of someone who hasn't even heard my speech. But today may be the only time this child is in labor"—the House began to laugh—"as I suspect the Honorable Gentleman spent most of his afternoon converting his innocent infant to the Conservative cause." Sinclair waited for the laughter to subside. "For those members of the House who thrive on statistics and data, it's a girl, and she weighs seven pounds three ounces."

Simon returned to press his nose against the glass and to stare at his daughter once again.

He waved at her but she took no notice. On each side of her crib were howling boys. Simon smiled at the effect young Lucy was already having on the opposite sex.

11

THE CHIEF WHIP LOOKED AROUND at his colleagues, wondering which of them would volunteer for such a thankless task.

A hand went up, and he was pleasantly surprised.

"Thank you, Charles."

Charles had already warned Fiona that he was going to volunteer to be the whip responsible for the issue that had most dominated the last election—Britain's entry into the Common Market. Everyone in the Chief Whip's office realized that it would be the most demanding marathon of the entire Parliament, and there was an audible sigh of relief when Charles volunteered.

"Not a job for anyone with a rocky marriage," he heard one whip whisper. At least that's something I don't have to worry about, thought Charles, but he made a note to take home some flowers that night.

"Why is it the bill everyone wanted to avoid?" asked Fiona as she arranged the daffodils.

"Because many of our side don't necessarily back Edward Heath in his lifelong ambition to take Britain into the Common Market," said Charles, accepting a large brandy.

"Added to that we have the problem of presenting a bill to curb the trade unions at the same time, which may well prevent those in the Labour Party who support us from voting with us on Europe. Because of this, the Prime Minister requires a regular 'state of play' assessment on Europe even though legislation may not be presented on the floor of the Commons for at least another year. He'll want to know periodically how many of our side are still against entry, and how many from the Opposition we can rely on to break ranks when the crucial vote is taken."

"Perhaps I should become a member of Parliament, and then at least I could spend a little more time with you."

"Especially if on the Common Market issue you were a 'don't know.'"

Although the "Great Debate" was discussed by the media to the point of boredom, members were nevertheless conscious that they were playing a part in history. And, because of the unusual spectacle of the Whips' not being in absolute control of the voting procedure, the Commons sprang to life, an excitement building up over the weeks and months of debate.

Charles retained his usual task of watching over fifty members on all normal Government bills, but because of the priority given to the issue of entry into Europe he had been released from all other duties. He knew that this was his chance to atone for his disastrous winding-up speech on the economy, which he sensed his colleagues had still not completely forgotten.

Not that it was without risk. "I'm gambling everything on this one," he told Fiona. "If we lose the final vote I will be sentenced to the back benches for life."

"And if we win?"

"It will be impossible to keep me off the front bench," replied Charles.

"At last—I think I've found it."

After Raymond heard the news, he took the train up to Leeds the following Friday. Joyce had selected four houses for him to consider, but he had to agree with her that the one in the Chapel Allerton area was exactly what they were looking for. It was also by far the most expensive.

"Can we afford it?" asked Joyce anxiously.

"Probably not."

123

"I could go on looking."

"No, you've found the right house; now I'll have to work out how we can pay for it, and I think I may have come up with an idea."

Joyce said nothing, waiting for him to continue.

"We could sell our place in Lansdowne Road."

"But where would we live when you're in London?"

"I could rent a small flat somewhere between the law courts and the Commons while you set up our real home in Leeds."

"But won't you get lonely?"

"Of course I will," said Raymond, trying to sound convincing. "But almost every member north of Birmingham is parted from his wife during the week. In any case, you've always wanted to settle in Yorkshire, and this might be our best chance. If my practice continues to grow, we can buy a second house in London at a later date."

Joyce looked apprehensive.

"One added bonus," said Raymond. "Your being here in Leeds will insure that I never lose the seat."

Joyce smiled. She always felt reassured whenever Raymond showed the slightest need of her.

On Monday morning Raymond put in a bid for the house in Chapel Allerton before returning to London. After a little bargaining over the phone during the week, he and the owner settled on a price. By Thursday Raymond had put his Lansdowne Road house on the market and was surprised by the amount the real estate agent thought it would fetch.

All Raymond had to do now was find himself a flat.

Simon sent a note to Ronnie expressing his thanks for keeping him so well informed about what was happening at Nethercote and Company. It had been eight months since he had resigned from the board because of his appointment as a Minister, but Ronnie still saw that the minutes of each meeting were mailed to him to study in his free time. "Free time." Simon had to laugh at the thought.

His overdraft at the bank now stood at a little over seventy-two thousand pounds, but as Ronnie intended the shares should be offered at five pounds each when they went public, Simon felt there was still a fair leeway, as his personal holding should realize some three hundred thousand pounds. Elizabeth warned him not to spend a penny of the profits until the money was safely in the bank. He was thankful that she didn't know the full extent of his borrowing.

Over one of their occasional lunches at the Ritz, Ronnie spelled out to Simon his plans for the future of the company.

"Even though the Tories are in, I think I'll postpone going public for at least eighteen months. This year's profits are up again and next year's look even more promising. Nineteen seventy-three looks perfect."

Simon looked apprehensive and Ronnie responded quickly.

"If you have any problems, Simon, I'll be happy to take the shares off your hands at market value. At least that way you would show a small profit."

"No, no," said Simon. "I'll hang in there now that I've waited this long."

"Suit yourself," said Ronnie. "Now, tell me, how are you enjoying the Home Office?"

Simon put down his knife and fork. "It's the ministry most involved with people, so there's a new challenge at a personal level every day, although it can be depressing too. Locking people up in prisons, banning immigrants and deporting harmless aliens isn't my idea of fun. Still, it is a privilege to work in one of the three great offices of state."

"I bet you do Foreign Affairs and Exchequer before you're through," said Ronnie. "And what about Ireland?"

"What about Ireland?" said Simon, shrugging his shoulders.

"I would give the North back to Eire," said Ronnie, "or let them go independent and give them a large cash incentive to do so. At the moment the whole exercise is money down the drain."

"We're discussing people," said Simon, "not money."

"Ninety percent of the voters would back me," said Ronnie, lighting a cigar.

"Everyone imagines ninety percent of the people support their views, until they stand for election. The issue of Ireland is far too important to be glib about," said Simon. "As I said, we're discussing people, eight million people, all of whom have the same right to justice as you and I. And as long as I work in the Home Office, I intend to see that they get it."

Ronnie remained silent.

"I'm sorry, Ronnie," continued Simon. "Too many people have an easy solution to Ireland. If there *was* an easy solution, the problem wouldn't have lasted two hundred years."

"Don't be sorry," said Ronnie. "I'm so stupid, I've only just realized for the first time why you're in public office."

"You're a typical self-made fascist," said Simon, teasing his companion once again.

"Well, one thing's for sure. You won't change my views on hanging. Your lot should bring back the rope; the streets aren't safe any longer."

"For property developers like you, hoping for a quick killing?"

"How do you feel about rape?" asked Raymond.

"I can't see that it's relevant," Stephanie Arnold replied.

"I think they'll go for me on it," said Raymond.

"But why?"

"They'll be able to pin me in a corner, damage my character."

"But where does it get them? They can't prove lack of consent."

"Maybe, but they'll use it as background to prove the rest of the case."

"Because a person raped someone doesn't prove he murdered her."

Raymond and Stephanie Arnold, who was new to chambers,

continued discussing their first case together on the way to the Old Bailey, and she left Raymond in no doubt that she was delighted to be led by him. They were to appear together to defend a laborer accused of the rape and murder of his stepdaughter.

"Open-and-shut case, unfortunately," said Raymond, "but we're going to make the Crown prove their argument beyond anyone's doubt."

When the case stretched into a second week Raymond began to believe that the jury was so gullible that he and Stephanie might even get their client off. Stephanie was sure they would.

The day before the judge's instructions to the jury, Raymond invited Stephanie to dinner at the House of Commons. That will make them turn their heads, he thought to himself. They won't have seen anything in a white shirt and black stockings that looks like Stephanie for some time.

Stephanie seemed flattered by the invitation, and Raymond noted that she was obviously impressed when throughout the stodgy meal served in the strangers' dining room, former Cabinet Ministers came by to acknowledge him.

"How's the new flat?" she asked.

"Worked out well," replied Raymond. "I find the Barbican is convenient both for Parliament and the law courts."

"Does your wife like it?" she asked, lighting a cigarette but not looking at him directly.

"She's not in town that much nowadays. She spends most of her time in Leeds—doesn't care much for London."

The awkward pause that followed was interrupted by the sudden loud clanging of bells.

"Are we on fire?" said Stephanie, quickly stubbing out her cigarette.

"No," said Raymond laughing, "just the ten o'clock division. I have to leave you and vote. I'll be back in about fifteen minutes."

"Shall I order coffee?"

127

"No, don't bother," said Raymond. "Perhaps ... perhaps you'd like to come back to the Barbican? Then you can give me a verdict on my flat."

"Maybe it's an open-and-shut case," she smiled.

Raymond returned the smile before joining his colleagues as they flooded out of the dining room down the corridor towards the Commons chamber. He didn't have time to explain to Stephanie that he only had six minutes to get himself into either the "Ayes" or "Nos" division lobby.

When he returned to the strangers' dining room after the vote he found Stephanie checking her face in a compact mirror—a small round face with green eyes, framed by dark hair. She was replacing the trace of lipstick. He suddenly felt conscious of being a little overweight for a man not yet forty. He was totally oblivious to the fact that women were beginning to find him attractive. A little extra weight and a few gray hairs had given him an air of authority.

Once they had reached the flat, Raymond put on an Ella Fitzgerald record and retired to the small kitchen to prepare coffee.

"Well, it sure looks like a bachelor flat," Stephanie remarked as she took in the one comfortable leather chair, the pipe stand and the political cartoons that lined the dark walls.

"I suppose that's because that's what it is," he mused, setting down a tray laden with a coffee urn, coffee cups and two brandy balloons generously filled with cognac.

"Don't you get lonely?" she said.

"From time to time," he said as he poured the coffee.

"And between times?"

"Black?" he asked, not looking at her.

"Black," she said.

"Sugar?"

"For a man who has served as a Minister of the Crown and who, it's rumored, is about to become the youngest Queen's Counsel in the country, you're still very unsure of yourself with women."

Raymond blushed, but raised his eyes and stared directly into hers.

In the silence he caught the words "Your fabulous face. . . ."

"Would my Honorable friend care for a dance?" she said quietly.

Raymond could still remember the last time he had danced. This time he was determined it would be different. He held Stephanie so that their bodies touched, and they swayed rather than danced to the music of Cole Porter. She didn't notice Raymond taking off his glasses and slipping them into his jacket pocket. When he bent over and kissed her neck, she gave a long sigh.

Lucy sat on the floor and started to cry. She sat because she couldn't yet walk. Once again Peter dragged her to her feet and commanded her to walk, sounding convinced that his words alone would be enough to elicit a response. Once again Lucy collapsed in a heap. Simon put down his knife and fork as he realized the time had come to rescue his nine-month-old daughter.

"Daddy, leave her alone," demanded Peter.

"Why," asked Simon, "are you so keen that she should walk?"

"Because I need someone to play football with when you're away at work."

"What about Mum?"

"She's feeble, she can't even tackle," said Peter.

This time Simon did laugh as he picked Lucy up and put her in the high chair ready for breakfast. Elizabeth came into the room with a bowl of porridge just in time to see Peter burst into tears.

"What's the problem?" she asked, staring at her distraught son.

"Daddy won't let me teach Lucy how to walk," said Peter, as he ran out of the room.

129

"He means kill Lucy," said Simon. "I think he has plans to use her as a soccer ball."

Charles studied his chart of 330 Conservatives. He felt confident of 217, not sure about 54 and had almost given up on 59. On the Labour side, the best information he could glean was that 50 members were expected to defy the Whip and join the Government's ranks when the great vote took place.

"The main fly in the ointment," Charles reported to the Chief Whip, "is still the bill curbing the power of trade unions. The left is trying to convince those Labourites who still support the Common Market that there is no cause so important that they should enter the same lobby as those 'Tory trade-union bashers.' " He went on to explain his fear that unless the Government was willing to modify the Trade Union Bill, they might lose Europe on the back of it. "And Alec Pimkin doesn't help matters by trying to gather the waverers in our party around him."

"There's no chance of the Prime Minister modifying one sentence of the Trade Union Bill," said the Chief Whip, draining his gin and tonic. "He promised it in his campaign speech, and he intends to deliver by the time he goes to Blackpool at the end of this year. I can also tell you he isn't going to like your conclusions on Pimkin, Charles." Charles was about to protest. "I'm not complaining, you've done damn well so far. Just keep working on the undecided fifty. Try anything—threaten, cajole, bully, bribe—but get them in the right lobby. Pimkin included."

"How about sex?" asked Charles.

"You've been seeing too many American films," said the Chief Whip, laughing. "In any case I don't think we've got anyone other than Miss Norse to offer them."

Charles returned to his office and went over the list once again. His forefinger stopped at the letter P. Charles strolled out into the corridor, and looked around; his quarry wasn't there. He checked the chamber—no sign of him. He passed the library. "No need to look in there," he thought, and moved on to the smoking room where he found his man, about to order another gin.

"Alec," said Charles expansively.

The rotund figure of Pimkin turned around.

May as well try bribery first, thought Charles. "Let me get you a drink."

"That's good of you, old fellow," said Pimkin, nervously fingering his bow tie.

"Now, Alec, what's this about your voting against the European bill?"

Simon was horrified when he read the initial document. Its implications were all too evident.

The report of the new Boundary Commission had been left in the red box for him to study over the weekend. He had agreed at a meeting of Home Office officials that he would steer it through the House expeditiously so that it would make the basis for the seats to be contested at the next election. As the Secretary of State reminded him, there must be no holdups.

Simon had read the document twice. In essence the changes made sense, and, because of the movement of families from urban to rural areas, it would undoubtedly create more winnable seats for the Conservatives overall. No wonder the Party wanted no holdups. But what could he do about the decision the commission had come to on his own constituency, Coventry Central? His hands were tied. If he suggested any change from the Boundary Commission's recommendations, he would rightly be accused of rigging matters in his own favor.

Because of the city's dwindling population, the Commission had recommended that the four constituencies of Coventry become three. Coventry Central was to be the one to disappear, its voters distributed among Coventry West, Coventry East and Coventry North. Simon realized this would leave one safe seat for his sitting colleague and two safe Labour seats. It had never been far from his mind how marginal a seat he held. Now he was on the verge of being without one at all. He would have to traipse around the country all over again looking for a new seat to fight for at the next election, while at the same time taking care of his constituency in the moribund one; and at the stroke of a pen—*his* pen—they would pass on their loyalties to someone else. If only he had remained in Environment he could have put up a case for keeping all four seats.

Elizabeth was sympathetic when he explained the problem but told him not to concern himself too much until he'd spoken to the vice-chairman of the Party.

"It may even work out to your advantage," she comforted. "You might find something even better."

"What do you mean?" said Simon.

"You may end up with a safer seat nearer London."

"I don't mind where I go as long as I don't have to spend the rest of my life tossing coins."

Elizabeth prepared his favorite meal and spent the evening trying to keep up his spirits. After three portions of shepherd's pie, Simon fell asleep almost as soon as he put his head on the pillow. But she stayed awake long into the night.

The casual conversation with the head of gynecology at St. Mary's kept running through her mind. Although she hadn't confided in Simon, she could recall the doctor's every word.

I notice from the roster that you've had far more days off than you are entitled to, Dr. Kerslake. You must make up your mind if you want to be a doctor or the wife of an MP.

Elizabeth stirred restlessly as she considered the problem, but came to no conclusion except not to bother Simon while he had so much on his mind.

At exactly the time Raymond was ready to stop the affair Stephanie began leaving a set of court clothes in the flat.

Although the two of them had gone their separate ways at the conclusion of the case, they continued to see one another a couple of evenings a week. Raymond had had a spare key made so that Stephanie didn't have to spend her life checking when he had a three-line whip.

At first he began simply to avoid her, but she would then seek him out. When he did manage to give her the slip he would often find her back in his flat when he returned from the Commons. When he suggested they should be a little more discreet, she began to make threats, subtle to begin with, but after a time more direct.

During the period of his affair with Stephanie, Raymond conducted three major cases for the Crown, all of which had successful conclusions and which added to his reputation. On each occasion his clerk made certain Stephanie Arnold was not assigned to be with him. Now that his residence problem was solved, Raymond's only worry was how to end the affair.

He was discovering that getting rid of her would prove more difficult than picking her up had been.

Simon was on time for his appointment at Central Office. He explained his dilemma in detail to Sir Edward Mountjoy, vice-chairman of the Party, who was responsible for candidates.

"What bloody bad luck," said Sir Edward. "But perhaps I may be able to help," he added, opening the green folder on the desk in front of him. Simon could see that he was studying a list of names. It made him feel once again like the ambitious Oxford applicant who needed someone to die.

"There seem to be about a dozen safe seats that will fall vacant at the next election, caused either by retirement or redistribution."

"Anywhere in particular you could recommend?"

"I fancy Littlehampton."

"Where's that?" said Simon.

"It will be a new seat, safe as houses. It's in Hampshire on the borders of Sussex." He studied an attached map. "Runs proud to Charles Hampton's constituency, which remains unchanged.

133

Can't think you would have many rivals there," said Sir Edward. "But why don't you have a word with Charles? He's bound to know everyone involved in making the decision."

"Anything else that looks promising?" asked Simon, only too aware that Hampton might not be so willing to help his cause.

"Let me see. Can't afford to put all your eggs in one basket, can we? Ah, yes—Redcorn, in Northumberland." Again the vice-chairman studied the map. "Three hundred and twenty miles from London and no airport within eighty miles, and their nearest main line station is forty miles. I think that one's worth trying for only if you get desperate. My advice would still be to speak to Charles Hampton about Littlehampton. He always puts the Party ahead of personal feelings when it comes to these matters."

"I'm sure you're right, Sir Edward," he said.

"Selection committees are being formed already," said Sir Edward, "so you shouldn't have long to wait."

"I appreciate your help," said Simon. "Perhaps you could let me know if anything else comes up in the meantime."

"Of course, delighted. The problem is that if one of our side were to die during the session, you couldn't desert your present seat because that would cause two by-elections. We don't want a by-election in Coventry Central with you being accused of being a carpetbagger somewhere else."

"Don't remind me," said Simon.

"I still think your best bet is to have a word with Charles Hampton. He must know the lay of the land in that neck of the woods."

Two clichés in one sentence, thought Simon. Thank heavens Mountjoy would never have to make a speech from the dispatch box. He thanked Sir Edward again and left Conservative Party headquarters.

Charles had whittled down the fifty-nine anti–Common Market members to fifty-one, but he was now dealing with the hard kernel who seemed quite immune to cajolery or bullying. When he made his next report to the Chief Whip, Charles assured him that the number of Conservatives who would vote against entry into Europe was outnumbered by the Labourites who had declared they would support the Government. The Chief seemed pleased, but asked if Charles had made any progress with Pimkin's disciples.

"Those twelve mad right-wingers," said Charles sharply. "They seem to be willing to follow Pimkin even into the valley of death. I've tried everything, but they're still determined to vote against Europe whatever the cost."

"The maddening thing is that that bloody nuisance Pimkin has nothing to lose," said the Chief Whip. "His seat disappears at the end of this Parliament in the redistribution. I can't imagine anyone with his extreme views would find a constituency to select him, but by then he'll have done the damage." The Chief Whip paused. "If his twelve would even abstain, I would feel confident of advising the PM of victory."

"The problem is to find a way of turning Pimkin into Judas and then urge him to lead the chosen twelve into our camp," said Charles.

"You achieve that, Charles, and we'd certainly win."

Charles returned to the Whip's office to find Simon Kerslake waiting by his desk.

"I dropped by on the off chance, hoping you might be able to spare me a few moments," said Simon.

"Of course," said Charles, trying to sound welcoming. "Take a seat."

Simon sat down opposite him. "You may have heard that I lose my constituency as a result of the Boundary Commission report, and Edward Mountjoy suggested I have a word with you about Littlehampton, the new seat that borders your constituency."

"It does indeed," said Charles masking his surprise. He had not considered the problem, as his own constituency was not

135

affected by the Boundary Commission's report. He recovered quickly. "I'll do everything I can to help. And how wise of Edward to send you to me."

"Littlehampton would be ideal," said Simon. "Especially while my wife is still working here in London."

Charles raised his eyebrows.

"I don't think you've met Elizabeth. She's a doctor at St. Mary's," Simon explained.

"Yes, I see your problem. Why don't I start by having a word with Alexander Dalglish, the constituency chairman, and see what I can come up with?"

"That would be extremely helpful."

"Not at all. I'll call him at home this evening and find out what stage they've reached over selection, and then I'll put you in the picture."

"I'd appreciate that."

"While I've got you, let me give you 'The Whip' for next week," said Charles, passing over a sheet of paper. Simon folded it up and put it in his pocket. "I'll call you the moment I have some news."

Simon left feeling happier and a little guilty about his past prejudice concerning Charles, whom he watched disappear into the chamber to carry out his bench duty.

In the chamber, the European issue had been given six days for debate by backbenchers, the longest period of time allocated to one motion in living memory.

Charles strolled down the aisle leading to the front bench and took a seat on the end to check on another set of speeches. Tom Carson, the Labour member from Liverpool Dockside, was launching into a tirade of abuse against the Government. Charles rarely listened to Carson's left-wing rantings—and the under-the-breath remarks and coughing that continued during his speech proved Charles was not alone in his opinion. By the time Carson concluded, Charles had worked out a plan.

He left the chamber, but instead of returning to the

Whip's office, which afforded no privacy, he disappeared into one of the telephone booths near the cloisters above the members' cloakroom. He checked the number in his book and dialed.

"Alexander, it's Charles. Charles Hampton."

"Good to hear from you, Charles, it's been a long time. How are you?"

"Well. And you?"

"Can't complain. What can I do for a busy man like you?"

"Wanted to chew over the new Sussex constituency with you—Littlehampton. How's your selection of a candidate going?"

"They've left me to draw up a short list of six for final selection by the full committee in about ten days' time."

"Have you thought of running yourself, Alexander?"

"Many times," was the reply that came back. "But the missus wouldn't allow it; neither would the bank balance. Do you have any ideas?"

"Might be able to help. Why don't you come and have a quiet dinner at my place early next week?"

"That's kind of you, Charles."

"Not at all, it will be good to see you again. It's been far too long. Next Monday suit you?"

"Absolutely."

"Good, let's say eight o'clock, Twenty-seven Eaton Square."

Charles put the phone down and returned to the Whip's office to make a note in his diary.

Raymond had just finished making his contribution to the European debate when Charles returned to the House. Raymond had made a coherent economic case for remaining free of the other six European countries and for building stronger links with the Commonwealth and America. He had doubted that Britain could take the financial burden of entering a club that had been in existence for so long. If the country had joined at its inception, it might have been different, he argued, but he would have to vote against this risky unproven venture that he suspected could only lead to higher unemployment. Before he finished his speech, Charles put a cross by the name Gould.

A note was being passed along the row to Raymond from one of the House messengers dressed in white tie and black tails. It read "Please ring Sir Nigel Hartwell as soon as convenient."

Raymond left the floor of the House and went to the nearest telephone in the corner of the members' lobby. He called his law offices and was immediately put through to Sir Nigel.

"You wanted me to phone?"

"Yes," said Sir Nigel. "Are you free at the moment?"

"I am," said Raymond. "Why? Is it anything urgent?"

"I'd rather not talk about it over the phone," said Sir Nigel ominously.

Raymond took a subway from Westminster to Temple and was in the law chambers fifteen minutes later. He went straight to Sir Nigel's office, sat down in a comfortable chair in the spacious clublike room, crossed his legs and watched Sir Nigel pace about in front of him. He was clearly determined to get something off his chest.

"Raymond, I have been asked by those in authority about you becoming a Queen's Counsel. I've said I think you'd make a damn good QC." A smile came over Raymond's face, but it was soon wiped off. "But if you're going to take silk I need an undertaking from you."

"An undertaking?"

"Yes," said Sir Nigel. "You must stop having this damn silly, er . . . relationship with another member of our chambers." He rounded on Raymond and faced him.

Raymond turned scarlet, but before he could speak, the head of chambers continued.

"Now I want your word on it," said Sir Nigel, "that it will end, and end immediately."

"You have my word," said Raymond quietly.

"I'm not a prig," said Sir Nigel, pulling down on his waistcoat, "but if you are going to have an affair, for God's sake make it as far away from the office as possible, and, if I may advise you, that should include the House of Commons and Leeds. There's still a lot of the world left over, and it's full of women."

Raymond nodded his agreement; he could not fault the head of chambers's logic.

Sir Nigel continued, obviously embarrassed. "There's a nasty fraud case starting in Manchester next Monday. Our client has been accused of setting up a series of companies that specialize in life insurance but avoid paying out on the claims. I expect you remember all the publicity. Miss Arnold has been put on the case as a reserve junior. They tell me it could last several weeks."

"She'll try and get out of it," said Raymond glumly.

"She has already, but I made it quite clear that if she felt unable to take the case on, she would have to find other chambers."

Raymond breathed a sigh of relief. "Thank you," he said.

"Sorry about this. I know you've earned your silk, old boy, but I can't have members of our chambers going around with egg on their faces. Thank you for your cooperation. I can't pretend I enjoyed that."

"Got time for a quiet word?" asked Charles.

"You're wasting your time, dear thing, if you imagine the disciples will change their minds at this late stage," said Alec Pimkin. "All twelve of them will vote against the Government on Europe. That's final."

"I don't want to discuss Europe this time, Alec; it's far more serious, and on a personal level. Let's go and have a drink on the terrace."

Charles ordered the drinks, and the two men strolled out onto the quiet end of the terrace toward the Speaker's house. Charles stopped when he was certain there was no longer anyone within earshot.

"If it's not Europe, what is it?" said Pimkin, staring out at the Thames as he nervously fingered the rose in his lapel.

"What's this I hear about you losing your seat?"

Pimkin turned pale and touched his spotted bow tie nervously. "It's this bloody boundary business. My constituency is swallowed up, and no one seems willing to interview me for a new one."

"What's it worth if I secure you a safe seat for the rest of your life?"

Pimkin looked suspiciously up at Charles. "Anything up to a pound of flesh, dear boy," he added a false laugh.

"No, I won't need to cut that deep."

The color returned to Pimkin's fleshy cheeks. "Whatever it is, you can rely on me, old fellow."

"Can you deliver the disciples?" said Charles.

Pimkin turned pale again.

"Not on the small votes in committee," said Charles, before Pimkin could reply. "Not on the clauses even—just on the second reading, the principle itself. Standing by the Party in their hour of need, no desire to cause an unnecessary general election, all that stuff—you fill in the details for the disciples. I know you can convince them, Alec."

Pimkin still didn't speak.

"I deliver a copper-bottomed seat, you deliver twelve votes. I think we can call that a fair exchange."

"What if I get them to abstain?" said Pimkin.

Charles waited, as if giving the idea considerable thought. "It's a deal," he said, never having hoped for anything more.

Alexander Dalglish arrived at Eaton Square a little after eight. Fiona met the tall, elegant man at the door and explained that Charles had not yet returned from the Commons.

"But I expect him any moment," she added. "May I offer you a sherry?" she asked. Another thirty minutes had passed before Charles hurried in.

"Sorry I'm late, Alexander," he said, shaking hands with his guest. "Hoped I might make it just before you." He kissed his wife on the forehead.

"Not at all, dear boy," said Alexander, raising his sherry. "I couldn't have asked for more pleasant company."

"What will you have, darling?" asked Fiona.

"A strong whiskey, please. Now, let's go straight into dinner. I've got to be back at the talkshop by ten."

Charles guided his guest toward the dining room and seated him at the end of the table before taking his place below the Holbein portrait of the first Earl of Bridgewater, an heirloom his grandfather had left him. Fiona took a seat opposite her husband. During the meal of beef Wellington, Charles spent a great deal of time catching up on what Alexander had been doing since they had last met. He made no mention of the real purpose behind the meeting until Fiona provided the opportunity when she served coffee.

"I know you two have a lot to talk about, so I'll leave you to get on with it."

"Thank you," said Alexander. He looked up at Fiona and smiled. "For a lovely dinner."

She returned his smile and left them alone.

"Now, Charles," said Alexander, picking up the file he had left on the floor by his side, "I need to pick your brains."

"Go ahead, old fellow," said Charles. "Only too delighted to be of assistance."

"Sir Edward Mountjoy has sent me a pretty long list for us to consider, among them a Home Office Minister and one or two other members of Parliament who'll be losing their present seats. What do you think of . . . ?"

Dalglish opened the file in front of him as Charles poured him a generous glass of port and offered him a cigar from a gold case that he picked up from the sideboard.

"What a magnificent object," said Alexander, staring in awe at the crested box and the engraved C.G.H. along its top.

"A family heirloom," said Charles. "Should have been left to

141

my brother Rupert, but I was lucky enough to have the same initials as my grandfather."

Alexander handed it back to his host before returning to his notes.

"Here's the man who impresses me," he said at last. "Kerslake, Simon Kerslake."

Charles remained silent.

"You don't have an opinion, Charles?"

"Yes."

"So what do you think of Kerslake?"

"Strictly off the record?"

Dalglish nodded but said nothing.

Charles sipped his port. "Very good," he said.

"Kerslake?"

"No, the port. Taylor's Thirty-five. I'm afraid Kerslake is not the same vintage. Need I say more?"

"No. What a pity. He looks good on paper."

"On paper is one thing," said Charles, "but having him as your member for twenty years is quite another. And his wife . . . Never seen in the constituency, you know." He frowned. "I'm afraid I've gone too far."

"No, no," said Alexander. "I've got the picture. Next one is Norman Lamont."

"First-class, but he's already been selected for Kingston, I'm afraid," said Charles.

Dalglish looked down at his file once again. "Well, what about Pimkin?"

"We were at Eton together. His looks are against him, as my grandmother used to say, but he's a sound man, and very good in the constituency, so they tell me."

"You would recommend him then?"

"I should snap him up before one of the other safe seats gets him."

"That popular, is he?" said Alexander. "Thanks for the tip. Pity about Kerslake."

142

"That was strictly off the record," said Charles.

"Of course. Not a word. You can rely on me."

"Port to your liking?"

"Excellent," said Alexander. "But your judgment has always been so good. You only have to look at Fiona to realize that."

Charles smiled.

Most of the other names Dalglish produced were either unknown, unsuitable or easy to dismiss. As Alexander left shortly before ten, Fiona asked him if the chat had been worthwhile.

"Yes, I think we've found the right man."

Raymond had the locks on his flat changed that afternoon. It turned out to be more expensive than he had bargained for, and the locksmith had insisted on cash in advance.

The locksmith grinned as he pocketed the money. "I make a fortune doing this job, guv'nor, I can tell you. At least one gentleman a day, always cash, no receipt. Means the wife and I can spend a month in Ibiza every year, tax free."

Raymond smiled at the thought. He checked his watch, he could just catch the Thursday 7:10 from King's Cross and be in Leeds by ten o'clock for a long weekend.

Alexander Dalglish phoned Charles a week later to tell him Pimkin had made the first cut, and that they hadn't considered Kerslake.

"Pimkin didn't go over very well with the committee at the first interview."

"No, he wouldn't," said Charles. "I warned you his looks were against him and he may come across a bit too right wing at times, but he's as sound as a bell and will never let you down, take my word."

"I'll have to, Charles. Because by getting rid of Kerslake, we've removed Pimkin's only real challenger."

Charles put the phone down and dialed the Home Office. "Simon Kerslake, please."

"Who's calling?"

"Hampton, Whip's office." He was put straight through.

"Simon, it's Charles. I thought I ought to give you an update on Littlehampton."

"That's thoughtful of you," said Simon.

"Not good news, I'm afraid. It turns out the chairman wants the seat for himself. He's making sure the committee only interviews idiots."

"How can you be so certain?"

"I've seen the short list and Pimkin's the only sitting member they're considering."

"I can't believe it."

"No, I was pretty shocked myself. I pressed the case for you, but it fell on deaf ears. Didn't care for your views on hanging or some such words. Still, I can't believe you'll find it hard to pick up a seat."

"I hope you're right, Charles, but in any case thanks for trying."

"Any time. Let me know of any other seats you put your name in for. I have a lot of friends up and down the country."

Two days later, Alec Pimkin was invited by the Littlehampton Conservatives to attend a short-list interview for the selection of a Tory candidate for the new constituency.

"How do I begin to thank you?" he asked Charles when they met up in the bar.

"Keep your word—and I want it in writing," replied Charles.

"What do you mean?"

"A letter to the Chief Whip saying you've changed your mind on the main European vote, and you and the disciples will be abstaining on Thursday."

Pimkin looked cocky. "And if I don't play ball, dear thing?"

"You haven't got the seat yet, Alec, and I might find it necessary to phone Alexander Dalglish and tell him about that awfully nice little boy you made such a fool of yourself over when you were up at Oxford."

When the Chief Whip received the letter from Pimkin three days later, he immediately summoned Charles.

"*Well done,* Charles. How did you manage to succeed where we've all failed—and the disciples as well?"

"Matter of loyalty," said Charles. "Pimkin saw that in the end."

On the final day of the Great Debate on "the principle of entry" into Europe, Prime Minister Heath delivered the winding-up speech. He rose at nine-thirty to cheers from both sides. At ten o'clock the House divided and voted in favor of "the principle" by a majority of one hundred and twelve, far more than Charles could have ever hoped for. Sixty-nine Labour MPs had helped to swell the Government's majority.

Raymond Gould voted against the motion in accordance with his long-held beliefs. Simon Kerslake and Charles Hampton stood in the "Ayes" lobby. Alec Pimkin and the twelve disciples remained in their places on the Commons benches while the vote took place.

When Charles heard the Speaker read out the final result, he felt a moment of triumph. Although he realized that he still had the committee stage to go through—hundreds of clauses, any of which could go wrong—nevertheless, the first round belonged to him.

Ten days later, Alec Pimkin defeated a keen young Conservative just down from Cambridge and a local woman councillor to be selected as prospective candidate for Littlehampton.

12

RAYMOND STUDIED THE CASE once again and decided to make his own inquiries. Too many constituents had in the past demonstrated that they were willing to lie to him in office hours as happily as they would in the witness box to any judge.

He dialed the public prosecutor's office. Here was one man who could cut his work in half with a sentence.

"Good morning, Mr. Gould. What can I do for you?"

Raymond had to smile. Angus Fraser was a contemporary of his since Raymond had come to the bar, but once he was in his office he treated everyone as a stranger, making no discrimination.

"He even calls his wife 'Mrs. Fraser' when she rings the office," Sir Nigel had once told him. Raymond was willing to join in the game.

"Good morning, Mr. Fraser. I need your advice in your official capacity."

"I am always happy to be of service, sir."

This was carrying formality too far.

"I want to talk to you off the record about the Paddy O'Halloran case. Do you remember it?"

"Of course, everyone in this office remembers that case."

"Good," said Raymond. "Then you'll know what a help you can be to me in cutting through the thicket. A group of my constituents, whom I wouldn't trust further than I could throw a boulder, claim O'Halloran was framed for the Princes Street bank robbery last year. They don't deny he has criminal tendencies—" Raymond would have chuckled if he hadn't been speaking to Angus Fraser— "but they say he never left a pub called the Sir Walter Scott the entire time the robbery was taking place. All you have to tell me, Mr. Fraser, is that you are sure O'Halloran is guilty, and I'll drop my inquiries. If you say nothing, I shall dig deeper."

Raymond waited, but he received no reply.

"Thank you, Mr. Fraser. I'll see you at the soccer match on Saturday." The silence continued.

"Goodbye, Mr. Fraser."

"Good day, Mr. Gould."

Raymond settled back. It was going to be a lengthy exercise, but at least this was an opportunity to use his legal skills on behalf of a constituent, and perhaps it would even add to his reputation in the House. He started by checking with all the people who had confirmed O'Halloran's alibi that night, but after interviewing the first eight he came to the reluctant conclusion that none of them could be trusted as a witness. Whenever he came across another of O'Halloran's friends, the expression "Do anything for a pint" kept crossing his mind. The time had come to talk with the proprietor.

"I couldn't be sure, Mr. Gould, but I think he was here that evening. Trouble is, O'Halloran came almost every night. It's hard to recall."

"Do you know anyone who might remember? Someone you could trust with your cash register?"

"That'd be pushing your luck in this pub, Mr. Gould." The proprietor thought for a moment. "However, there's old Mrs. Bloxham," he said, slapping the dish towel over his shoulder. "She sits in that corner every night." He pointed to a small round table that would have been crowded had it seated more than two people. "If she says he was here, he was."

147

Raymond asked the proprietor where Mrs. Bloxham lived and then walked around the corner to 43 Mafeking Road in the hope of finding her in. He made his way through a group of young children playing football in the middle of the road.

"Is it another General Election already, Mr. Gould?" asked a disbelieving old lady as she peered through the letter slot.

"No, it's nothing to do with politics, Mrs. Bloxham," said Raymond, bending down. "I came around to seek your advice on a personal matter."

"Come on in out of the cold then," she said, opening the door to him. "There's a terrible draft rushes through this corridor."

Raymond followed the old lady as she shuffled down the dingy corridor in her carpet slippers to a room that he would have said was colder than it had been outside on the street. There were no ornaments in the room save a crucifix that stood on a narrow mantelpiece below a pastel print of the Virgin Mary. Mrs. Bloxham beckoned Raymond to a wooden seat by a table yet unlaid. She eased her plump frame into a stuffed horsehair chair. It groaned under her weight and a strand of horsehair fell to the floor. Raymond averted his glance from the old woman once he had taken in the black shawl and the dress she must have worn a thousand times.

Once settled in her chair, she kicked off her slippers. "Feet still giving me trouble," she explained.

Raymond tried not to show his distaste.

"Doctor doesn't seem to be able to explain the swellings," she continued, without bitterness.

Raymond leaned on the table and noticed what a fine piece of furniture it was and how incongruous it looked in those surroundings. He was struck by the craftsmanship of the carved Georgian legs. She noticed he was admiring it. "My great-grandfather gave that to my great-grandmother the day they got married, Mr. Gould."

"It's magnificent," said Raymond.

But she didn't seem to hear, because all she said was, "What can I do for you, sir?"

Raymond went over the O'Halloran story again. Mrs. Bloxham listened intently, leaning forward slightly and cupping her hand around her ear to be sure she could hear every word.

"That O'Halloran's an evil one," she said. "Not to be trusted. Our Blessed Lady will have to be very forgiving to allow the likes of him to enter the kingdom of Heaven." Raymond had to smile. "Not that I'm expecting to meet all that many politicians when I get there either," she added, giving Raymond a toothless grin.

"Could O'Halloran possibly have been there that Friday night as all his friends claim?" Raymond asked.

"He was there all right," said Mrs. Bloxham. "No doubt about that—saw him with my own eyes."

"How can you be so sure?"

"Spilled his beer over my best dress, and I knew something would happen on the thirteenth, especially with it being a Friday. I won't forgive him for that. I still haven't been able to get the stain out despite what those washing-powder ads tell you on the telly."

"Why didn't you tell the police immediately?"

"Didn't ask," she said simply. "They've been after him for a long time for a lot of things they couldn't pin on him, but for once he was in the clear."

Raymond finished writing his notes and then rose to leave. Mrs. Bloxham heaved herself out of the chair, dispensing yet more horsehair onto the floor. They walked to the door together. "I'm sorry I couldn't offer you a cup of tea but I'm right out at the moment," she said. "If you had come tomorrow it would have been all right."

Raymond paused on the doorstep.

"I get the pension tomorrow, you see," she replied to his unasked question.

Elizabeth took a day off to travel to Redcorn with Simon for the interview. Once again the children had to be left with the babysitter. The local and national press had made him the hot favorite for the new seat. Elizabeth put on what she called her best Conservative outfit, a pale-blue suit with a dark-blue collar that hid everything, Simon noted, and reached well below her knees.

"Well, I wouldn't have recognized you, Doctor," said Simon grinning.

"Understandably," she replied. "I've disguised myself as a politician's wife."

The journey from King's Cross to Newcastle took three hours and twenty minutes, on what was described in the timetable as "the express." At least Simon was able to catch up with a great deal of the paperwork that had been stuffed into his red box. He reflected that the civil servants who worked full-time in the bureaucracy rarely allowed politicians time to involve themselves in politics. They wouldn't have been pleased to learn that he had spent an hour of the journey reading the last four weekly copies of the *Redcorn News*.

At Newcastle they were met by the wife of the Association treasurer, who had volunteered to escort the Minister and his wife to the constituency to be sure they were in time for the interview. "That's very thoughtful of you," said Elizabeth, as she stared at the mode of transport that had been chosen to take them the next forty miles.

The ancient Austin Mini took a further hour and a half through the winding roads before they reached their destination, and the treasurer's wife never drew breath once throughout the entire journey. When Simon and Elizabeth piled out of the car at the market town of Redcorn, they were physically and mentally exhausted.

The treasurer's wife took them through to the constituency headquarters and introduced them both to the campaign manager.

"Good of you to come," he said. "Hell of a journey, isn't it?"

Elizabeth felt unable to disagree with his judgment. But on this occasion she made no comment, because if this was to be

Simon's best chance of returning to Parliament, she had already decided to give him every support possible. Nevertheless, she dreaded the thought of her husband's making the journey to Redcorn twice a month, as she feared they would see even less of each other than they did at present, let alone the children.

"Now the form is," began the campaign manager, "that we are interviewing six potential candidates, and they'll be seeing you last." The campaign manager winked knowingly.

Simon and Elizabeth smiled uncertainly.

"I'm afraid they won't be ready for you for at least another hour, so you have time for a stroll around the town."

Simon was glad of the chance to stretch his long legs and take a closer look at Redcorn. He and Elizabeth walked slowly around the pretty market town, admiring the Elizabethan architecture that had somehow survived irresponsible or greedy town planners. They even climbed the hill to take a look inside the magnificent perpendicular church that dominated the surrounding area.

As he walked back past the shops in the High Street, Simon nodded to those locals who appeared to recognize him.

"A lot of people seem to know who you are," said Elizabeth, and then they saw the display outside the local newsstand. They sat on the bench in the market square and read the lead story under a large picture of Simon.

"Redcorn's Next MP?" ran the headline.

The story volunteered the fact that although Simon Kerslake had to be considered the favorite, Bill Travers, a local farmer who had been chairman of the county council the previous year, was still thought to have an outside chance.

Simon began to feel a little sick in the stomach. It reminded him of the day he had been interviewed at Coventry Central nearly eight years before. Now that he was a Minister of the Crown, he wasn't any less nervous.

When he and Elizabeth returned to constituency headquarters they were informed that only two more candidates had

151

been seen and the third was still being interviewed. They walked around the town once again, even more slowly this time, watching shopkeepers put up their colored shutters and turn "Open" signs to "Closed."

"What a pleasant market town," said Simon.

"And the people seem so polite after London," she said.

He smiled as they headed back to party headquarters. On their way, they passed townspeople who bid them "Good evening," courteous people whom Simon felt he would have been proud to represent. Although they walked slowly, Elizabeth and he could not make their journey last more than thirty minutes.

When they returned a third time to constituency headquarters, the fourth candidate was leaving the interview room. She looked very despondent. "It shouldn't be long now," said the campaign manager, but it was another forty minutes before they heard a ripple of applause, and a man in a Harris tweed jacket and brown trousers left the room. He didn't seem happy either.

Simon and Elizabeth were ushered through, and as they entered everyone in the room stood. Ministers of the Crown did not visit Redcorn often.

Simon waited for Elizabeth to be seated before he took the chair in the center of the room facing the committee. He estimated that there were about fifty people present, and they were all staring at him, showing no aggression, merely curiosity. He looked at the weather-beaten faces. Most of the people, male and female, were dressed in tweeds. In his dark striped London suit Simon felt out of place.

"And now," said the chairman, "we welcome the Right Honorable Simon Kerslake, MP."

Simon had to smile at the mistake so many people made in thinking that Ministers were automatically members of the Privy Council and therefore entitled to the prefix "Right Honorable," instead of the plain "Honorable" accorded all MPs.

"Mr. Kerslake will address us for twenty minutes, and he has

152

kindly agreed to answer questions after that," added the chairman.

Simon felt sure he spoke well, but even his few carefully chosen quips received no more than a smile, and his more important comments elicited little response. This was not a group of people given to showing their emotions. When he had finished, he sat down to respectful clapping and murmurs.

"Now the Minister will answer questions," said the chairman.

"Where do you stand on hanging?" said a scowling middle-aged woman in a gray tweed suit seated in the front row.

Simon explained his reasons for being a convinced abolitionist. The scowl did not move from the questioner's face and Simon thought to himself how much happier she would have been with Ronnie Nethercote as her member.

A man in a brogue suit asked him how he felt about this year's farm subsidy.

"Good on eggs, tough on beef, and disastrous for pig farmers. Or at least that's what I read on the front page of *Farmer's Weekly* yesterday." Some of them laughed for the first time. "It hasn't proved necessary for me to have a great knowledge of farming in Coventry Central, but if I am lucky enough to be selected for Redcorn I shall try to learn quickly, and with your help I shall hope to master the farmers' problems." Several heads nodded their approval.

"May I be permitted to ask Mrs. Kerslake a question?" said a tall, thin spinsterish woman who had stood up to catch the chairman's eye. "Miss Tweedsmuir, chairman of the Ladies' Advisory," she announced in a shrill voice. "If your husband were offered this seat, would you be willing to come and live in Northumberland?"

Elizabeth had dreaded the question because she knew that if Simon were offered the constituency she would be expected to give up her job at the hospital. Simon turned and looked toward his wife.

"No," she replied directly. "I am a doctor at St. Mary's

153

Hospital, where I practice obstetrics and gynecology. I support my husband in his career, but, like Margaret Thatcher, I believe a woman has the right to a good education and then the chance to use her qualifications to the best advantage."

A ripple of applause went around the room and Simon smiled at his wife.

The next question was on the Common Market, and Simon gave an unequivocal statement as to his reasons for backing the Prime Minister in his desire to see Britain as part of the European community.

Simon continued to answer questions on subjects ranging from trade-union reform to violence on television before the chairman asked, "Are there any more questions?"

There was a long silence and just as he was about to thank Simon, the scowling lady in the front row, without being recognized by the chair, asked what Mr. Kerslake's views were on abortion.

"Morally, I'm against it," said Simon. "At the time of the Abortion Act many of us believed it would stem the tide of divorce. We have been proved wrong. The rate of divorce has quadrupled. Nevertheless, in the cases of rape or fear of physical or mental injury arising from birth, I would have to support the medical advice given at the time. Elizabeth and I have two children and my wife's job is to see that babies are safely delivered," he added.

The lips moved from a scowl to a straight line.

"Thank you," said the chairman. "It was good of you to give us so much of your time. Perhaps you and Mrs. Kerslake would be kind enough to wait outside."

Simon and Elizabeth joined the other hopeful candidates, their wives and the campaign manager in a small dingy room at the back of the building. When they saw the half-empty trestle table in front of them they both remembered they hadn't had any lunch, and they devoured what was left of the curling cucumber sandwiches and the cold sausage rolls.

"What happens next?" Simon asked the campaign manager between mouthfuls.

"Nothing out of the ordinary. They'll have a discussion, allowing everyone to express their views, and then they'll vote. It should be all over in twenty minutes."

Elizabeth checked her watch: it was seven o'clock and the last train was at nine-fifteen.

An hour later, when no one had emerged from the room, the campaign manager suggested to all the candidates who had a long journey ahead of them that they might like to check into the Bell Inn just over the road.

When Simon looked around the room it was clear that everyone else had done so in advance.

"You had better stay put in case you're called again," Elizabeth said. "I'll go off and book a room and at the same time call and see how the children are getting on. Probably eaten the poor baby-sitter by now."

Simon opened his red box and tried to do some work while Elizabeth disappeared in the direction of the Bell Inn.

The man who looked like a farmer came over and introduced himself.

"I'm Bill Travers, the chairman of the new constituency," he began. "I only wanted to say that you'll have my full support as chairman if the committee selects you."

"Thank you," said Simon.

"I had hoped to represent this area, as my grandfather did. But I shall understand if Redcorn prefers to choose a man destined for the Cabinet rather than someone who would be happy to spend his life on the back benches."

Simon was impressed with the directness and dignity of his opponent's statement and would have liked to respond in kind, but Travers quickly added, "Forgive me, I'll not waste any more of your time. I can see—" he looked down at the red box—"that you have a lot of work to catch up on."

Simon felt guilty as he watched the man walk away. A few

155

minutes later Elizabeth returned and tried to smile. "The only room left is smaller than Peter's and it faces the main road, so it's just about as noisy."

"At least no children to say 'I'm hungry,' " he said, touching her hand.

It was a little after nine when a weary chairman came out and asked all the candidates if he could have their attention. Husbands and wives all faced him. "My committee wants to thank you for going through this grim procedure. It has been hard for us to decide something that we hope not to have to discuss again for twenty years." He paused. "The committee is going to invite Mr. Bill Travers to fight the Redcorn seat at the next election."

In a sentence it was all over. Simon's throat went dry.

He and Elizabeth didn't get much sleep in their tiny room at the Bell Inn, and it hadn't helped that the agent told them the final vote had been 25–23.

"I don't think Miss Tweedsmuir liked me," said Elizabeth, feeling guilty. "If I had told her that I would have been willing to live in the constituency I think you'd have been offered the seat."

"I doubt it," said Simon. "In any case it's no use agreeing to their terms at the interview and then imposing your own when you have been offered the constituency. My guess is you'll find Redcorn has chosen the right man."

Elizabeth smiled at her husband, grateful for his support.

"There will be other seats," said Simon, only too aware that time was now running out. "You'll see."

Elizabeth prayed that he would prove right, and that next time the choice of constituency would not make her have to face the dilemma she had so far managed to avoid.

Joyce made one of her periodic trips to London when Raymond took silk and became a Queen's Counsel. The occasion, she decided, warranted another visit to Marks and Spencer. She recalled her first trip to the store so many years before when she had accompanied her husband to meet the Prime Minister. Raymond had come so far since then, although their relationship seemed to have progressed so little. She couldn't help thinking how much better-looking Raymond had become in middle age, and feared the same could not be said of her.

She enjoyed watching the legal ceremony as her husband was presented in court before the judges, Latin words spoken but not understood. Suddenly her husband was Raymond Gould, QC, MP.

She and Raymond arrived late in chambers for the celebration party. Everyone seemed to have turned out in her husband's honor. Raymond felt full of bonhomie when Sir Nigel handed him a glass of champagne. Then he saw a familiar figure by the mantelpiece and remembered that the trial in Manchester was over. He managed to circle the room, speaking to everyone but Stephanie Arnold. To his horror, he turned to see her introducing herself to his wife. Every time he glanced towards them, they seemed deeper in conversation.

"Ladies and gentlemen," said Sir Nigel, banging a table. He waited for silence. "We are always proud in chambers when one of our members takes silk. It is a comment not only on the man, but also on his chambers. And when it is the youngest silk—still under forty—it adds to that pride. All of you of course know that Raymond also serves in another place in which we expect him to rise to even greater glory. May I add, finally, how pleasant it is to have his wife, Joyce, among us tonight. Ladies and gentlemen," he continued. "The toast is: Raymond Gould, QC."

The applause was sustained and genuine. As colleagues came up to congratulate him, he couldn't help noticing that Stephanie and Joyce had resumed their conversation.

Raymond was handed another glass of champagne just as an earnest young pupil named Patrick Montague, who had recently joined them from chambers in Bristol, engaged him in conversation. Although Montague had been with them for some weeks, Raymond had never spoken to him at length before. He seemed to have very clear views on criminal law and the changes that were necessary. For the first time in his life Raymond felt he was no longer a young man.

Suddenly both women were at his side.

"Hello, Raymond."

"Hello, Stephanie," he said awkwardly. He looked anxiously toward his wife. "Do you know Patrick Montague?" he asked absentmindedly.

The three of them burst out laughing.

"What's so funny?" asked Raymond.

"You do embarrass me sometimes, Raymond," said Joyce. "Surely you realize Stephanie and Patrick are engaged?"

13

"CAN YOU EXPLAIN why Simon Kerslake missed the vote yesterday?"

Charles looked across the table at the Chief Whip. "No, I can't," he said. "I've been distributing the weekly 'Whip' to him the same as every member of my group."

"What's the meaning of it then?"

"I think the poor man has been spending a lot of his time traipsing around the country looking for a seat to fight at the next election."

"That's no excuse," said the Chief Whip. "Duties in the House must come first, every member knows that. The vote missed was on a vital clause, and everyone else in your group has proved reliable. Perhaps I should have a word with him?"

"No, no, I'd rather you didn't," said Charles, fearing he sounded a little too insistent. "I consider it my responsibility. I'll speak to him and see that it doesn't happen again."

"All right, Charles, if that's the way you want to play it. Thank God it can't last much longer and the damn thing will soon be law, but we must remain vigilant over every clause. The Labour Party knows only too well that if they defeat us on certain key clauses they can still sink the whole bill, and if I lost one of those by a single vote I would cut Kerslake's throat. Or anyone else who was responsible."

159

"I'll make sure he gets the message," said Charles.

"How's Fiona reacting to all these late nights?" the Chief Whip asked, finally relaxing.

"Very well, considering. In fact, now that you mention it, I have never seen her looking better."

"Can't say my wife is enjoying the 'prep school antics,' as she describes our continual late-night sessions. I've had to promise to take her to the West Indies this winter to make up for it. Well, I'll leave you to deal with Kerslake. Be firm, Charles."

"Norman Edwards?" repeated Raymond in disbelief. "The general secretary of the Lorry Union?"

"Yes," said Fred Padgett, getting up from behind his desk.

"But he burned *Full Employment at Any Cost?* on a public bonfire with every journalist he could lay his hands on to witness the conflagration."

"I know," said Fred, returning a letter to the filing cabinet. "I'm only your campaign manager. I'm not here to explain the mysteries of the universe."

"When does he want to see me?" asked Raymond.

"As soon as possible."

"Better ask him if he can come for a drink at the house at six o'clock."

Raymond had had heavy Saturday morning office hours and had only found time to grab a sandwich at the pub before going off to watch Leeds play Liverpool. Although he had never cared for soccer, now he regularly sat in the directors' box every other week in full view of his constituents while he supported his local soccer team, killing thirty thousand birds with one stone. He was careful to adopt his old Yorkshire accent when talking to the lads in the dressing room after the match, not the one he used to address a high court judge during the week.

Leeds won 3–2, and after the match Raymond joined the directors for a drink in the boardroom and nearly forgot about his meeting with Norman Edwards.

Joyce was in the garden showing the union leader her early snowdrops when Raymond returned.

"Sorry I'm late," he shouted, as he hung up his yellow-and-black scarf. "I've been to the local match."

"Who won?" asked Edwards.

"Leeds, of course, three to two. Come on in and have a beer," said Raymond.

"I'd prefer a vodka."

The two men went into the house while Joyce continued with her gardening.

"Well," said Raymond, pouring his guest a Smirnoff. "What brings you all the way from Liverpool if it wasn't to watch soccer? Perhaps you want a signed copy of my book for your next union bonfire?"

"Don't give me any trouble, Ray. I came all this way because I need your help, simple as that."

"I'm all ears," said Raymond, not commenting on the shortening of his name.

"We had a full meeting of the General Purposes Committee yesterday, and one of the brothers had spotted a clause in the Common Market Bill that could put us all out of work. The clause concerning shipment to the Channel coast."

Norman passed a copy of the bill to Raymond with the relevant clause marked in red. "If that gets through the House my boys are in deep trouble."

"Yes," said Raymond. "I can see that. Actually, I'm surprised it's been allowed to get this far."

Raymond studied the wording in detail while Edwards poured himself another vodka.

"And how much do you think this will add to the costs?" asked Raymond.

"I'll tell you, enough to make us uncompetitive, that's how much," replied the union leader.

"Point taken," said Raymond. "So what's wrong with enlisting your own member? Why come to me?"

161

"I don't trust him. He's pro-European at any cost."

"Then what about your sponsored trade-union representative in the House?"

"Tom Carson? You must be joking. He's so far to the left that even his own side is suspicious when he supports a cause." Raymond laughed. Edwards continued, "Now, what my committee wants to know is whether you would be willing to fight this clause in the House for us? Especially as we have little to offer you in return."

"I'm sure you will be able to repay me in kind sometime in the future," said Raymond.

"Got the picture," said Edwards, touching the side of his nose with a forefinger. "What do I do next?"

"You go back to Liverpool and hope that I'm as good as you think I am."

Norman Edwards put on an old raincoat and started to button it up. He smiled at Raymond. "I may have been appalled by your book, Ray. But it doesn't mean I didn't admire it."

"The damn man missed another three-line whip, Charles. It must be the last time you protect him."

"It won't happen again," promised Charles convincingly. "I would like to give him one more chance. Allow him that."

"You're very loyal to him," said the Chief Whip. "But next time I'm going to see Kerslake myself and get to the bottom of it."

"It won't happen again," repeated Charles.

"Hmm," said the Chief Whip. "Next problem is, are there any clauses on the Common Market Bill that we should be worried about next week?"

"Yes," replied Charles. "This lorry clause that Raymond Gould is fighting. He made a brilliant case on the floor of the House, and got all his own side and half of ours backing him."

"He's not the sponsored MP for the Lorry Union," said the Chief Whip, surprised.

"No, the unions obviously felt Tom Carson wouldn't help the

cause, and he's hopping mad at the slight."

"Clever of them to pick Gould. Improves as a speaker every time I hear him. And no one can fault him on points of law."

"So we had better face the fact that we are going to lose the clause?" said Charles despondently.

"Never. We'll redraft the damn thing so that it's acceptable and *seen* to be compassionate. It's not a bad time to be the defender of the union interests. That way we'll keep Gould from getting all the credit. I'll speak to the PM tonight—and don't forget what I said about Kerslake."

Charles returned to his office reflecting that in the future he would have to be more careful to tell Simon Kerslake when clauses on the Common Market Bill would be voted upon. He suspected he had carried this ploy as far as he could for the time being.

"With or without civil servants?" asked Simon as Raymond entered his office.

"Without, please."

"Fine," said Simon and pressed a switch on the intercom by his desk, "I don't want to be disturbed while I'm with Mr. Gould," he said and then ushered his colleague toward a comfortable seat. Ever since Gould had requested a meeting, Simon had been more than curious to discover what he wanted. In the years since they had locked horns over devaluation, they had had little direct contact.

"My wife was asking this morning how your search for a seat is going," said Raymond.

"Your wife is better informed than most of my colleagues. But I'm afraid the truth is, not too well. The last three constituencies to come up haven't even asked to see me. I can't put a finger on why, except that they all seem to have selected local men."

"It's still a long time to the next election," said Raymond. "You're sure to find a seat before then."

"It might not be so long if the Prime Minister decides to call a

General Election and test his strength against the unions."

"That would be foolish. He might defeat us but he won't defeat the unions," said Raymond, as a young secretary came into the office with two cups of coffee and put them on the low table.

Only when she had left the office did Raymond reveal his purpose. "Have you had time to look at the file?" he asked, sounding rather formal.

"Yes, I went over it last night between checking over my son's homework and helping my daughter to build a model boat."

"And how do you feel?" Raymond asked.

"Not very good. I can't get to grips with this new math they're now teaching, and my mast was the only one that fell off when Lucy launched the boat in the bath."

Raymond laughed.

"I think you've got a case," said Simon, sounding serious again. "Now what are you hoping to get out of me?"

"Justice," said Raymond. "That's the reason I wanted to see you privately. I feel there are no party political points to be made out of this case for either of us. I have no plans to try to embarrass the Home Office, and I consider it in the best interest of my constituent to cooperate as closely as I can with you."

"Thank you," said Simon. "So where do you want to go from here?"

"I'd like to table a planted question for your department in the hope that you would consider opening an inquiry. If the inquiry comes to the same conclusion as I have, I would expect you to order a retrial."

Simon hesitated. "And if the inquiry goes against you, would you agree to no reprisals for the Home Office?"

"You have my word."

"And if there is one thing I have learned, to my cost, about you," said Simon, "it's that you never break your word."

Raymond smiled. "I consider that long forgotten."

The following Tuesday, the Speaker looked up toward the

Labour back benches and called on "Mr. Raymond Gould."

"Number Seventeen, sir," said Raymond. The Speaker looked down to check over the question, which asked the Home Office to consider an inquiry into the case of Mr. O'Halloran.

Simon rose to the dispatch box, opened his file and said, "Yes, sir."

"Mr. Raymond Gould," called the Speaker again.

Raymond rose from his place on the Opposition back benches to ask his supplementary question.

"May I thank the Minister for agreeing to an inquiry so quickly, and ask him, if he discovers an injustice has been done to my constituent Mr. Paddy O'Halloran, that the Home Secretary order a retrial immediately?"

Simon rose again.

"Yes, sir."

"I am grateful to the Honorable Gentleman," said Raymond, half-rising.

All over in less than a minute—but older members who listened to the brief exchange between Gould and Kerslake understood that considerable preparation had gone into that minute from both sides.

Simon had read his department's final report on the O'Halloran case while Elizabeth was trying to get to sleep. He had to go over the details only once to realize that he would have to order a retrial and institute a full investigation into the past record of the police officers who had been involved in the case.

The trial was in its third day when Mr. Justice Comyns, after listening to Mrs. Bloxham's evidence, stopped proceedings and instructed the jury to return a verdict of not guilty.

Raymond received praise from all quarters of the House, but he was quick to acknowledge the support given him by Simon Kerslake and the Home Office. The London *Times* even wrote an editorial the next day on the proper use of influence by a constituency MP.

———

The only drawback to Raymond's success was that every convict's mother was lined up to see him at his twice-monthly office hours. But during the year he took only one case seriously and once again began to check into the details.

This time, when Raymond rang Angus Fraser at the prosecutor's office, he found nothing was known of Ricky Hodge beyond the fact that Fraser was able to confirm that he had no known criminal record. Raymond felt he had stumbled on a case with international implications.

As Ricky Hodge was in a Turkish jail, any inquiries had to be made through the Foreign Office. Raymond did not have the same relationship with the Foreign Secretary as he did with Simon Kerslake, so he felt the direct approach would be best, and submitted a question to be answered in the House. He worded it carefully.

"What action does the Foreign Secretary intend to take over the confiscation of a British passport from a constituent of the Honorable Member for Leeds North, details of which have been supplied to him?"

When the question was asked in front of the House on the following Wednesday the Foreign Secretary rose to answer the question himself. He stood at the dispatch box and peered over his half-moon spectacles and said:

"Her Majesty's Government is pursuing this matter through the usual diplomatic channels."

Raymond was quickly on his feet. "Does the Right Honorable Gentleman realize that my constituent has been in a Turkish prison for six months and has still not been charged?"

"Yes, sir," replied the Foreign Secretary. "I have asked the Turkish Embassy to supply the Foreign Office with more details of the case."

Raymond leaped up again. "How long will my constituent have to be forgotten in Ankara before the Foreign Secretary does more than ask for the details of his case?"

The Foreign Secretary rose again showing no sign of annoyance. "I will report those findings to the Honorable Member as quickly as possible."

"When? Tomorrow, next week, next year?" Raymond shouted angrily.

"When?" joined in a chorus of Labour backbenchers, but the Speaker called for the next question above the uproar.

Within the hour Raymond received a handwritten note from the Foreign Office. "If Mr. Gould would be kind enough to telephone, the Foreign Secretary would be delighted to make an appointment to see him."

Raymond phoned from the Commons and was invited to join the Foreign Secretary in Whitehall immediately.

The Foreign Office, known as "the Palazzo" by its inmates, has an atmosphere of its own. Although Raymond had worked in a Government department as a Minister, he was still struck by its grandeur. He was met at the courtyard entrance and guided along yards of marble corridors before climbing a fine double staircase at the top of which he was greeted by the Foreign Secretary's principal private secretary.

"Sir Alec Home will see you immediately, Mr. Gould," he said, and led Raymond past the magnificent pictures and tapestries that lined the way. He was taken into a beautifully proportioned room. The Foreign Secretary stood in front of an Adam fireplace over which hung a portrait of Lord Palmerston.

"Gould, how kind of you to come at such short notice. I do hope it has not caused you any inconvenience." Platitudes, thought Raymond.

"I know you are a busy man. Can we get down to the point at issue, Foreign Secretary?" Raymond demanded.

"Of course," Sir Alec said drily. "Forgive me for taking so much of your time." Without a further word, he handed Raymond a file marked "Richard M. Hodge—Confidential." "Although members of Parliament are not subject to the Official Secrets Act, I know you will respect the fact that this file is classified."

167

Another bluff, thought Raymond. He flicked back the cover. It was true, exactly as he had suspected: In the six months since he had been jailed, Ricky Hodge had never been formally charged.

He turned the page. "Rome, child prostitution; Marseilles, narcotics; Paris, blackmail"—page after page, ending in Turkey, where Hodge had been found in possession of four pounds of heroin, which he had been selling in small packets on the black market. It was true that he had no criminal record in England, but at only twenty-nine, Ricky Hodge had spent eleven of the last fourteen years in foreign jails.

Raymond closed the file and could feel the sweat on his forehead. It was some moments before he spoke. "I apologize, Foreign Secretary," he said. "I have made a fool of myself."

"When I was a young man," said Sir Alec, "I made a similar mistake on behalf of a constituent. Ernie Bevin was Foreign Secretary at the time. He could have crucified me in the House with the knowledge he had. Instead he revealed everything over a drink in this room. I sometimes wish the public could see members in their quiet moments as well as in their rowdy ones."

Raymond thanked Sir Alec and walked thoughtfully back to the House.

When Raymond conducted his next office hours in Leeds North two weeks later he was surprised to see that Mrs. Bloxham had made an appointment.

When he greeted her at the door he was even more surprised, for in place of her shabby clothes and carpet slippers, she was wearing a new polished cotton dress and a shiny pair of squeaky brown leather shoes. She looked as if "Our Blessed Lady" might have to wait a few more years to receive her after all. Raymond motioned her to a seat.

"I came to thank your wife, Mr. Gould," she said, once she was settled.

"What for?" asked Raymond puzzled.

"For sending that nice young man around from Chris-tees.

They auctioned Great-Grandma's table for me. I couldn't believe my luck—it fetched fourteen hundred pounds." Raymond was speechless. "So it don't matter about the stain on the dress any more. It even made up for having to eat off the floor for three months."

During the long hot summer of 1972, clause after clause of the Common Market Bill was voted on, often through the night. On some occasions, the Government managed majorities of only five or six, but somehow the bill remained intact.

Charles would often arrive home at Eaton Square at three in the morning to find Fiona asleep, only to leave again before she had woken. Veterans of the House confirmed they had never experienced any issue so demanding since the Second World War.

Then, suddenly, the last vote was taken and the marathon was over. The Common Market Bill was passed through the Commons and on its way to the House of Lords to receive their Lordships' approval. Charles wondered what he would do with all the hours that were suddenly left him in the day.

When the bill finally received the "Royal Assent" in October, the Chief Whip held a celebration lunch at the Carlton Club in St. James's to thank all of his team. "And in particular, Charles Hampton," he said, raising his glass during an impromptu speech. When the lunch broke up, the Chief Whip offered Charles a lift back to the Commons in his official car. They traveled along Piccadilly, down Haymarket, through Trafalgar Square and into Whitehall. Just as the Commons came into sight, the black Rover turned into Downing Street, as Charles assumed, to drop the Chief Whip at Number 12. But as the car stopped, the Chief Whip said, "The Prime Minister is expecting you in five minutes."

"What? Why?" said Charles.

"Timed it rather well, didn't I?" said the Chief Whip—and headed off toward Number 12.

Charles stood alone in front of Number 10 Downing Street.

169

The door was opened by a man in a long black coat. "Good afternoon, Mr. Hampton." The Prime Minister saw Charles in his study and, as ever, wasted no time on small talk.

"Thank you for all the hard work you have put in on the Common Market Bill."

"It was a tremendous challenge," said Charles, searching for words.

"As will be your next job," said Mr. Heath. "It's time for you to test your skills in another department. I want you to take over as one of the Ministers of State at the Department of Trade and Industry."

Charles was speechless.

"With all the problems we are going to encounter with the trade unions during the next few months, that should keep you fully occupied."

"It certainly will," said Charles.

He still hadn't been asked to sit down, but as the Prime Minister was now rising from behind his desk, it was clear that the meeting was over.

"You and Fiona must come and have dinner at Number Ten as soon as you've settled into your new department," said the Prime Minister as they walked toward the door.

"Thank you," Charles said before leaving.

As he stepped back onto Downing Street a driver opened the back door of a shiny Austin Westminster. It took Charles a moment to realize the car and driver were now his.

"The Commons, sir?"

"No, I'd like to return to Eaton Square for a few minutes," said Charles, sitting back and enjoying the thought of his new job.

The car drove past the Commons, up Victoria Street and on to Eaton Square. He couldn't wait to tell Fiona that all the hard work had been rewarded. He felt guilty about how little he had seen of her lately, although he could not believe it would be much better now that he was to be involved in trade-union legislation. How much he still hoped for a son—perhaps even that would be possible now. The car came to a halt outside the Georgian house. Charles ran up the steps and into the hall. He could hear his wife's voice coming from upstairs. He took the wide staircase in bounds of two and three at a time, and threw open the bedroom door.

"I'm the new Minister of State at the Department of Trade and Industry," he announced to Fiona, who was lying in bed.

Alexander Dalglish looked up. He showed no sign of interest in Charles's promotion.

PART THREE

Ministers of State

1973-1977

14

SIMON STEERED the new Boundary Commission recommendations unspectacularly through the House as an order in Council, and suddenly he had lost his own constituency. His colleagues in Coventry were understanding, and nursed those wards that would become theirs at the next election in order that he might spend more time searching for a new seat.

Seven seats became available during the year but Simon was only interviewed for two of them. Both were almost on the Scottish border, and both put him in second place. He began to appreciate what it must feel like for an Olympic favorite to be awarded the silver medal.

Ronnie Nethercote's monthly board reports began to paint an increasingly somber picture, thus reflecting in real life what the politicians were lately decreeing in Parliament. Ronnie had once again decided to postpone going public until the climate was more advantageous. Simon couldn't disagree with the judgment, but when he checked his special overdraft facility, the interest on his loans had pushed up the figures in red to over ninety thousand pounds.

When unemployment first passed the million mark and Ted Heath ordered a pay and price freeze, strikes broke out all over the country.

The new parliamentary session in the fall of 1973 was dominated by economic issues as the situation worsened. Charles Hampton once again became overworked as he negotiated far into the night with trade-union leaders. While he didn't win every argument, he was now so well briefed on his subject that he proved to be a competent negotiator for the Government. Raymond Gould rose to the occasion, making passionate speeches on behalf of the unions, but the Conservative majority beat them again and again.

Prime Minister Heath was, however, moving inexorably towards a head-on clash with the unions and a premature General Election.

When all three annual party conferences were over, members returned to the Commons aware that it was likely to be the last session before a General Election. It was openly being said in the corridors that all the Prime Minister was waiting for was a catalyst. The miners' union provided it. In the middle of a bleak winter they called an all-out strike for more pay in defiance of the Government's new trade-union legislation. Suddenly Britain was on a three-day week.

In a television interview, the Prime Minister told the nation that with unemployment now at an unprecedented 1,600,000 and the country on a three-day week, he had to call an election to insure that the rule of law be maintained. The inner cabinet advised Heath to run on February 28, 1974.

"Who runs the country?" became the Tory theme, but this only seemed to emphasize class differences, rather than uniting the country as the Prime Minister had hoped.

Raymond Gould traveled back to Leeds, convinced that the northeast industrial area would not tolerate Heath's high-handedness.

Charles felt sure that the people would back any party that had shown the courage to stand up to the unions, although the left wing, led vociferously by Tom Carson, insisted that the Government was out to crush the Labour movement once and for all. Charles drove down to Sussex to find his supporters glad of the chance to put those "Commie union bastards" in their place.

On the night of the election Simon had a quiet supper with Elizabeth and the children. He watched in silence as others learned their election fates.

Many months had passed before Charles had found it possible even to sustain a conversation with Fiona for any length of time. Neither wanted a divorce, both citing the ailing Earl of Bridgewater as their reason, although inconvenience and loss of face were nearer the truth. In public it was hard to detect the change in their relationship, since they had never been given to overt affection.

Charles gradually became aware that it was possible for marriages to have been over for years without outsiders knowing it. Certainly the old earl never found out, because even on his deathbed he told Fiona to hurry up and produce an heir.

"Do you think you'll ever forgive me?" Fiona once asked Charles.

"Never," he replied, with a finality that encouraged no further discourse.

During the three-week election campaign in Sussex they both went about their duties with a professionalism that masked their true feelings.

"How is your husband bearing up?" someone would inquire.

"Much enjoying the campaign and looking forward to returning to Government," said Fiona's stock reply.

"And how is dear Lady Fiona?" Charles was continuously asked.

"Never better than when she's helping in the constituency," was his.

177

On Sundays, at one church after another, he read the lesson with confidence; she sang "Fight the Good Fight" in a clear contralto.

The demands of a rural constituency are considerably different from those of a city. Every village, however small, expects the member to visit them and to recall the local chairmen's names. But subtle changes were taking place; Fiona no longer whispered the names in Charles's ear. Charles no longer turned to her for advice.

During the campaign, Charles would ring the photographer on the local paper to discover which events his editor had instructed him to cover that day. With the list of places and times in his hand, Charles would arrive on each occasion a few minutes before the photographer. The Labour candidate complained officially to the local editor that Mr. Hampton's photograph was never out of the paper.

"If you were present at these functions we would be only too happy to publish your photo," said the editor.

"But they never invite me," cried the Labour candidate.

They don't invite Hampton either, the editor wanted to say, but he somehow manages to be there. It was never far from the editor's mind that his proprietor was a Tory peer, so he kept his mouth shut.

All the way up to Election Day Charles and Fiona opened bazaars, attended dinners, drew raffles and only stopped short of kissing babies.

Once, when Fiona asked him, Charles admitted that he hoped to be moved to the Foreign Office as a Minister of State.

On the last day of February they dressed in silence and went off to their local polls to vote. The photographer was there on the steps to take their picture. They stood closer together than they had for some weeks, looking like a happily married couple, he in a dark suit, she in a dark suit. Charles knew it would be the main photograph on the front page of the *Sussex Gazette* the following day as surely as he knew the Labour candidate would be relegated to a half-column mention in the back, not far from the obituaries.

Charles anticipated that by the time he arrived in the Town Hall the Conservative majority in the House would already be assured. But it was not to be, and as Friday morning dawned the result still hung in the balance.

Edward Heath did not concede when the newscasters predicted he would fail to be given the overall majority he needed. Charles spent the day striding around the Town Hall with an anxious look on his face. The little piles of votes soon became larger, and it was obvious that he would hold the seat with at least his usual 21,000—or was it 22,000?—majority. He never could remember the exact figure. But as the day progressed it became more and more difficult to assess the national verdict.

The last result came in from Northern Ireland a little after four o'clock that afternoon and a BBC commentator announced:

LABOUR	301
CONSERVATIVE	296
LIBERAL	14
ULSTER UNIONISTS	11
SCOTTISH NATIONALIST	7
WELSH NATIONALISTS	2
OTHERS	4

Ted Heath invited the Liberal Leader to join him at Downing Street for talks in the hope that they could form a coalition. The Liberals demanded a firm commitment to electoral reform to help the small parties. Heath knew he could never get his backbenchers to deliver. On Monday morning he told the Queen in her drawing room at Buckingham Palace that he was unable to form a government. She called for the Labour Leader, Harold Wilson. He accepted her commission and drove back to Downing Street to enter the front door. Heath left by the back.

By Tuesday afternoon every member, having watched the drama unfold, had returned to London. Raymond had increased his majority and now hoped that the Prime Minister had long since forgotten his resignation and would offer him a job.

Charles, still unsure of the exact majority by which he had won, drove back to London, resigned to returning to Opposition. The one compensation was that he would be reinstated on the board of Hampton's, where the knowledge he had gained in Parliament as a Minister of Trade and Industry could only be of value.

Simon left the Home Office on March 1, 1974. Ronnie Nethercote immediately invited him to return to the board of Nethercote and Company at five thousand pounds a year, which even Elizabeth acknowledged as a generous gesture.

It did little to lift Simon's spirits, for an empty red box was all he had to show for nearly ten years as a member of Parliament.

Simon had gone from office to office saying goodbye, first to the senior and then to the junior civil servants, until only the cleaners were left. They all seemed certain he would return soon.

15

"His diary looks rather full at the moment, Mr. Charles."

"Well, as soon as it's convenient," Charles replied. He held the phone as he heard the pages being turned.

"March twelfth at ten-thirty, Mr. Charles?"

"But that's nearly two weeks away," he said, irritated.

"Mr. Spencer has only just returned from the States and—"

"How about a lunch, then—at my club?" Charles interrupted.

"That couldn't be until after March twelfth—"

"Very well, then," said Charles. "March twelfth at ten-thirty."

During the fourteen-day wait Charles had ample time to become frustrated by his seemingly aimless role in Opposition. No car came to pick him up and whisk him away to an office where real work had to be done. Worse, no one sought his opinion any longer on matters that affected the nation. He was going through a sharp bout of what is known as "ex-Minister's blues."

He was relieved when the day for the appointment with Derek Spencer at last came around. But although he arrived on time he was kept waiting for ten minutes before the chairman's secretary took him in.

"Good to see you after so long," said Derek Spencer, coming around his desk to greet him. "It must be nearly six years since you've visited the bank."

"Yes, I suppose it is," said Charles. "But looking around the old place, it feels like yesterday. You've been fully occupied, no doubt?"

"Like a Cabinet Minister, but I hope with better results."

They both laughed.

"Of course I've kept in touch with what's been happening at the bank."

"Have you?" said Spencer.

"Yes, I've read all the reports you've sent out over the past years, not to mention the *Financial Times*'s coverage."

"I hope you feel we've progressed in your absence."

"Oh. Yes," said Charles, still standing. "Very impressive."

"Well, now what can I do for you?" asked the chairman, returning to his seat.

"Simple enough," said Charles, finally taking an unoffered chair. "I wish to be reinstated on the board."

There was a long silence.

"Well, it's not quite that easy, Charles. I've just recently appointed two new directors and . . ."

"Of course it's that easy," said Charles, his tone changing. "You have only to propose my name at the next meeting and it will go through, especially as you haven't a member of the family on the board at the present time."

"We have, as a matter of fact. Your brother, the Earl of Bridgewater has become a nonexecutive director."

"What?" said Charles. "Rupert never told me. Neither did you."

"True, but things have changed since . . ."

"Nothing has changed except my estimation of the value of your word," said Charles, suddenly realizing that Spencer had never intended he should return to the board. "You gave me your assurance—"

"I won't be spoken to like this in my own office."

"If you're not careful, the next place I shall do it will be in your boardroom. Now, will you honor your undertaking or not?"

"I don't have to listen to threats from you, Hampton. Get out of my office before I have you removed. I can assure you that you will never sit on the board again as long as I'm chairman."

Charles turned and marched out, slamming the door as he left. He wasn't sure with whom to discuss the problem, and returned immediately to Eaton Square to consider a plan of campaign.

"What brings you home in the middle of the afternoon?" asked Fiona.

Charles hesitated, considered the question and then joined his wife in the kitchen and told her everything that had happened at the bank. Fiona continued to grate some cheese as she listened to her husband.

"Well, one thing is certain," she said, not having spoken for several minutes, but delighted that Charles had confided in her. "After that fracas, you can't both be on the board."

"So what do you think I ought to do, old girl?"

Fiona smiled; it was the first time he had called her that for nearly two years. "Every man has his secrets," she said. "I wonder what Mr. Spencer's are?"

"He's such a dull middle-class fellow, I doubt that—"

"I've just had a letter from Hampton's Bank," interrupted Fiona.

"What about?"

"Only a shareholders' circular. It seems Margaret Trubshaw is retiring after twelve years as the board secretary. Rumor has it she wanted to do five more years, but the chairman has someone else in mind. I think I might have lunch with her."

Charles returned his wife's smile.

Ronnie Nethercote had made Simon the personnel director for a company that now had nearly two hundred employees. Simon enjoyed negotiating with the trade unions at a level he had not experienced before. Ronnie made it clear how he would have dealt with the "Commie bastards" who had caused the fall of the Tory Government given half a chance.

183

"You would have lasted about a week in the House of Commons," Simon told him.

"After a week with those windbags I would have been happy to return to the real world."

Simon smiled. Ronnie, like so many others, imagined all members of Parliament were unemployable—except the one he knew.

Raymond waited until the last Government appointment was announced before he finally gave up any hope of a job. Several leading political journalists pointed out that he had been left on the back benches while lesser men had been given Government posts, but it was scant comfort. Raymond reluctantly returned to his legal office to continue his practice at the bar.

The Prime Minister, Harold Wilson, starting his third administration, made it clear that he would govern as long as possible before calling an election. But few members believed that he could hold out for more than a matter of months.

Fiona returned home after her lunch with Miss Trubshaw with a large Cheshire cat grin on her face. It remained firmly in place during the hours she had to wait for Charles to get back from the Commons after the last division.

"You look pleased with yourself," said Charles, shaking out his umbrella before closing the front door. His wife stood in the hallway, her arms crossed.

"How has your day been?" she asked.

"So-so," said Charles, wanting to hear the news. "But what about you?"

"Oh, pleasant enough. I had coffee with your mother this morning. She seems very well. A little cold in the head, otherwise—"

"To hell with my mother. How did your lunch with Miss Trubshaw go?"

"I wondered how long it would take you to get around to that."

She continued to wait just as long as it took for them to walk into the drawing room and sit down. "After seventeen years as secretary to your father and twelve years as secretary to the board, there isn't much Miss Trubshaw doesn't know about Hampton's or its present chairman," Fiona began.

"So what did you discover?"

"Which do you want to hear about first, the name of his mistress or the number of his Swiss bank account?"

Fiona revealed everything she had learned over her two-hour lunch, explaining that Miss Trubshaw usually only drank fortified wine, but on this occasion she had downed most of a vintage bottle of Pommard. Charles's smile grew wider and wider as each fact came pouring out. To Fiona, he looked like a boy who has been given a big box of chocolates and keeps discovering another layer underneath the one he's already eaten.

"Well done, old girl," he said when she had come to the end of her tale. "But how do I get all the proof I neeed?"

"I've made a deal with our Miss Trubshaw."

"You've what?"

"A deal. With Miss Trubshaw. You get the proof if she remains as secretary to the board for five more years, with no loss of pension benefits."

"Is that all she wants?" said Charles guardedly.

"And the promise of another lunch at the Savoy Grill when you're invited back on the board."

Unlike many of his Labour colleagues, Raymond enjoyed dressing up in white tie and tails and mixing with London society. An invitation to the bankers' annual banquet at the Guildhall was no exception. The Prime Minister was the guest of honor, and Raymond wondered if he would drop a hint as to how long he expected the parliamentary session to last before he felt he had to call an election.

At the pre-dinner drinks, Raymond had a quick word with the Lord Mayor of London before becoming involved in a conversation with a circuit-court judge on the problems of the parity of sentencing.

When dinner was announced, Raymond found his seat on one of the long sides stretching away from the main table. He checked his place card. Raymond Gould QC, MP. On his right was the chairman of Chloride, Michael Edwardes, and on his left an American banker who had just started work in the City.

Raymond found Michael Edwardes' views on how the Prime Minister should tackle the nationalized industries fascinating, but he devoted far more of his attention to the financial analyst from Chase Manhattan. She must have been almost thirty, Raymond decided, if only because of her elevated position at the bank and her claim to have been an undergraduate at Wellesley at the time of Kennedy's death. He would have put Kate Garthwaite at far younger, and was not surprised to learn she played tennis in the summer and swam every day during the winter—to keep her weight down, she confided. Kate had a warm, oval face, and her dark hair was cut in what Raymond thought was a Mary Quant style. Her nose turned up slightly at the end and would have cost a lot of money for a plastic surgeon to reproduce. There was no chance of seeing her legs, as they were covered by a long dress, but what he could see left Raymond more than interested.

"I see there's an 'MP' behind your name, Mr. Gould. May I ask which party you represent?" she asked in an accent common only in Boston.

"I'm a Labourite, Mrs. Garthwaite. Where do your sympathies lie on this occasion?"

"I would have voted Labour at the last election if I had been qualified," she declared.

"Should I be surprised?" he teased.

"You certainly should. My ex-husband is a Republican Congressman."

He was about to ask his next question when the toastmaster called for silence. For the first time Raymond turned his eyes to

186

the dais and the Prime Minister. Harold Wilson's speech stuck firmly to economic problems and the role of a Labour Government in the City and gave no clue as to the timing of the next election. Nevertheless, Raymond considered it a worthwhile evening. He had made a useful contact with the chairman of a large public company. And he had acquired Kate's telephone number.

The chairman of Hampton's reluctantly agreed to see him a second time, but it was obvious from the moment Charles walked in, when no hand was proffered, that Derek Spencer intended it to be a short interview.

"I thought I ought to see you personally," said Charles as he settled back in the comfortable leather chair and slowly lit a cigarette, "rather than raise my query at the annual meeting next month."

The first sign of apprehension showed on the chairman's face, but he said nothing.

"I'm rather keen to discover why the bank should pay out a monthly check for four hundred pounds to an employee called Miss Janet Darrow, whom I have never come across, although it appears she has been on the payroll for over five years. The checks, it seems, have been going to a branch of Lloyd's in Kensington."

Derek Spencer's face became flushed.

"What I am at a loss to discover," continued Charles after he had inhaled deeply, "is what services Miss Darrow has been supplying to the bank. They must be quite impressive to have earned her twenty-five thousand pounds over the last five years. I appreciate that this is a small amount when you consider the bank's turnover of one hundred and twenty-three million last year, but my grandfather instilled in me at an early age the belief that if one took care of the pennies, the pounds would take care of themselves."

Still Derek Spencer said nothing, although beads of sweat

187

had appeared on his forehead. Suddenly Charles's tone changed. "If I find I am not a member of the board by the time of the annual general meeting, I feel it will be my duty to point out this slight discrepancy in the bank's accounts to the other shareholders present."

"You're a bastard, Hampton," the chairman said quietly.

"Now, that is not accurate. I am the second son of the former chairman of this bank and I bear a striking resemblance to my father, although everyone says I have my mother's eyes."

"What's the deal?"

"No deal. You will merely keep to your original agreement and see that I am reinstated on the board before the annual meeting. You will also cease any further payments to Miss Janet Darrow immediately."

"If I agree, will you swear never to mention this matter to anyone again?"

"I will. And unlike you, I'm in the habit of keeping my word." Charles rose from his chair, leaned over the desk and stubbed out his cigarette in the chairman's ashtray.

"They've done *what?*" said Joyce.

The campaign manager repeated, "Two Communists have put their names forward for election to the General Purposes committee."

"Over my dead body." Joyce's voice was unusually sharp.

"I thought that would be your attitude," said Fred Padgett.

Joyce searched for the pencil and paper that were normally on the table by the phone.

"When's the meeting?" she asked.

"Next Thursday."

"Have we got reliable people to run against them?"

"Of course," said Fred. "Councillor Reg Prescott and Jenny Simpkins from the League."

"They're both sensible enough, but between them they couldn't knock the skin off a rice pudding."

"Shall I phone Raymond at the House and get him to come down for the meeting?"

"No," said Joyce. "He's got enough to worry about trying to reestablish himself, now that we're back in Government. Leave it to me."

She replaced the receiver and sat down to compose her thoughts. It was ironic that he was facing a threat from the extreme left just at the time when the unions were coming to respect his worth. A few minutes later she went over to her desk and rummaged about for the full list of the G.P. committee. She checked the sixteen names carefully, realizing that if two Communists were to get themselves elected this time, within five years they could control the committee—and then even remove Raymond. She knew how these people worked. With any luck, if they got bloody noses now, they might slink off to another constituency.

She checked the sixteen names once more before putting on a pair of sensible walking shoes. During the next four days she visited several homes in the constituency. "I was just passing," she explained to nine of the wives who had husbands on the committee. The four men who never listened to a word their wives said were visited by Joyce after work. The three who had never cared for Raymond were left well alone.

By Thursday afternoon, thirteen people knew only too well what was expected of them. Joyce sat alone hoping Raymond would call that evening. She cooked herself a Lancashire hotpot but only picked at it, and then later fell asleep in front of the television while watching her favorite program. The phone woke her at five past eleven.

"Raymond?"

"Hope I didn't wake you," said Fred.

"No, no," said Joyce, now impatient to learn the outcome of the meeting. "What happened?"

"Reg and Jenny walked away with it. Those two Communist bastards only managed three votes between them."

"Well done," said Joyce.

"I did nothing," said Fred, "except count the votes. Shall I tell Raymond what's been happening?"

"No," said Joyce. "No need to let him think we've had any trouble."

Joyce fell back into the chair by the phone, kicked off her walking shoes and went back to sleep.

27 Eaton Square
London SW 1
April 23, 1974

Dear Derek,
   Thank you for your letter of April 18 and your kind invitation to rejoin the board of Hampton's. I am delighted to accept and look forward to working with you again.
                 Yours sincerely,
                 CHARLES HAMPTON.

Fiona checked the wording and nodded. Short and to the point. "Shall I post it?"

"Yes please," said Charles as the phone rang.

He picked it up. "9712. Charles Hampton speaking."

"Oh, hello, Charles. It's Simon Kerslake."

"Hello, Simon," said Charles, trying to sound pleased to hear from his former colleague. "What's it like out there in the real world?"

"Not much fun, which is exactly why I'm phoning. I've been short-listed for Pucklebridge, Sir Michael Harbour-Baker's seat. He's nearly seventy and has decided not to run again in the next election. As his constituency touches the south border of yours, I thought you might be able to put in a word for me again."

"Delighted," said Charles. "I'll speak to the chairman to-night. You can rely on me, and good luck. It would be nice to have you back in the House."

Simon gave him his home number, which Charles repeated slowly, as if he were writing it down.

"I'll be in touch," said Charles.

"I really appreciate your help."

Simon put down the phone.

Elizabeth closed her copy of her medical journal.

She was lively, fun, intelligent and well informed. It had been several days before Kate Garthwaite agreed to see Raymond again, and when she eventually joined him for dinner at the House she was not overwhelmed or flattered, and she certainly didn't hang on his every word.

They began to see each other regularly. As the months passed, Raymond found himself missing her on weekends whenever he was in Leeds with Joyce. Kate seemed to enjoy her independence and made none of the demands on him that Stephanie had, never once suggesting that he spend more time with her or that she might leave clothes behind in the flat.

Raymond sipped his coffee. "That was a memorable meal," he said, falling back onto the sofa.

"Only by the standards of the House of Commons," replied Kate.

Raymond put an arm around her shoulder before kissing her on the lips. "What? Rampant sex as well as cheap Beaujolais?" she exclaimed, stretching over and pouring herself some more coffee.

"I wish you wouldn't always make a joke of our relation-ship," said Raymond, stroking the back of her shiny hair.

"I have to," said Kate quietly.

"Why?" Raymond turned to face her.

"Because I'm frightened of what might happen if I took it seriously."

Charles sat through the annual meeting in silence. The chairman made his report for the fiscal year ending March 1974 before welcoming two new directors to the board and the return of Charles Hampton.

There were several questions from the floor, which Derek Spencer had no trouble in handling. As Charles had promised, there was not even a hint of Miss Janet Darrow. Miss Trubshaw had let Fiona know that the payments had been stopped, and also mentioned that she was still worried that her contract was coming to an end on July 1.

When the chairman brought the annual meeting to a close Charles asked courteously if he could spare him a moment.

"Of course," said Spencer, looking relieved that the meeting had gone through without a hitch. "What can I do for you?"

"I think it might be wiser to talk in the privacy of your office."

The chairman glanced at him sharply but led him back to his office.

Charles settled himself comfortably in the leather chair once more and removed some papers from his inside pocket. Peering down at them he asked, "What does BX41207122, Bank Rombert, Zurich, mean to you?"

"You said you would never mention—"

"Miss Darrow," said Charles. "And I shall keep my word. But now, as a director of the bank, I am trying to find out what BX41207122 means to you?"

"You know damn well what it means," said the chairman, banging his clenched fist on the desk.

"I know it's your *private*—" Charles emphasized the word— "account in Zurich."

"You can never prove anything," said Derek Spencer defiantly.

"I agree with you, but what I am able to prove," said Charles, shuffling through the papers that now rested on his lap, "is that you have been using Hampton's money to do private deals, leaving the profits in your Zurich account without informing the board."

"I've done nothing that would harm the bank and you know it."

"I know the money has been returned with interest, and I could never prove the bank had suffered any loss. Nevertheless, the board might take a dim view of your activities, remembering that they pay you forty thousand pounds a year to make profits for the bank, not for yourself."

"When they saw all the figures, they would at worst rap me over the knuckles."

"I doubt if the director of public securities would take the same lenient attitude if he saw these documents," said Charles, holding up the papers that had been resting on his lap.

"You'd ruin the bank's name."

"And you would probably spend the next ten years in jail. If, however, you did get away with it, you would be finished in London, and by the time your legal fees had been paid there wouldn't be much left of that nest egg in Zurich."

"So what do you want this time?" demanded Spencer, sounding exasperated.

"Your job," said Charles.

"My job?" asked Spencer in disbelief. "Do you imagine because you've been a junior Minister you're capable of running a successful merchant bank?" he added scornfully.

"I didn't say I would run it. I can buy a competent chief executive to do that."

"Then what will you be doing?"

"I shall be the chairman of Hampton's, which will convince City institutions that we wish to continue in the traditions of generations of my family."

"You're bluffing," stammered Spencer.

"If you are still in this building in twenty-four hours' time," said Charles, "I shall send these to the director of public securities."

There was a long silence.

193

"If agreed," said Spencer at last, "I would expect two years' salary as compensation."

"One year," said Charles. Spencer hesitated, then nodded slowly. Charles rose to his feet and put the papers resting on his lap back into his inside pocket.

They consisted of nothing more than the morning mail from his Sussex constituents.

Simon felt the interview had gone well, but Elizabeth was not so sure. They sat huddled in a room with five other candidates and their wives, patiently waiting.

He thought back to his answers, and to the eight men and four women on the committee.

"You must admit it's the most ideal seat I've been considered for," said Simon.

"Yes, but the chairman kept eying you suspiciously."

"But Millburn mentioned that he had been at Eton with Charles Hampton."

"That's what worries me," whispered Elizabeth.

"A fifteen thousand majority at the last election, and only forty minutes from London. We could even buy a little cottage."

"If they invite you to represent them."

"At least this time you were able to tell them you would be willing to live in the constituency."

"So would anyone in their right mind," said Elizabeth.

The chairman came out and asked if Mr. and Mrs. Kerslake would be kind enough to return once more to see the committee.

Oh, God, thought Simon, what else can they want to know?

"It's too near London to be my fault this time," chuckled Elizabeth.

The Committee sat and stared at them with long faces.

"Ladies and gentlemen," said the chairman. "After our lengthy deliberations, I formally propose that Mr. Simon Kerslake be invited to contest Pucklebridge at the next election. Those in favor . . . ?"

All twelve hands went up.

"Those against . . ."

"Carried unanimously," said the chairman. He then turned to Simon. "Do you wish to address your committee?"

The prospective Conservative Member of Parliament for Pucklebridge rose. They all waited expectantly.

"I don't know what to say, except that I'm very happy and honored and I can't wait for a General Election."

They all laughed and came forward and surrounded them. Elizabeth dried her eyes before anyone reached her.

About an hour later the chairman accompanied Simon and Elizabeth back to their car and bade them goodnight. Simon wound down his window.

"I knew you were the right man," Millburn said, "as soon as Charles Hampton phoned—" Simon smiled—"and warned me to avoid you like the plague."

"Could you tell Miss Trubshaw to come in?" Charles asked his secretary.

Margaret Trubshaw arrived a few moments later and remained standing in front of his desk. She couldn't help but notice the change of furniture in the room. The modern Conran suite had been replaced by a leather clublike sofa and chairs. Only the picture of the eleventh Earl of Bridgewater remained in place.

"Miss Trubshaw," began Charles, "since Mr. Spencer has felt it necessary to resign so suddenly, I think it important for the bank to keep some continuity now that I'm taking over as chairman."

Miss Trubshaw stood like a Greek statue, her hands hidden in the sleeves of her dress.

"With that in mind, the board has decided to extend your contract with the bank for a further five years. Naturally, there will be no loss in your pension rights."

"Thank you, Mr. Charles."

"Thank you, Miss Trubshaw."

Miss Trubshaw almost bowed as she left the room.

"And, Miss Trubshaw—"

"Yes, Mr. Charles," she said, holding onto the doorknob.

"—I believe my wife is expecting a call from you. Something about inviting you to lunch at the Savoy Grill."

16

"A BLUE SHIRT," said Raymond, looking at the Turnbull and Asser label with suspicion. "A blue shirt," he repeated.

"A fortieth birthday present," shouted Kate from the kitchen.

I shall never wear it, he thought, and smiled to himself.

"And what's more, you'll wear it," she said, her Boston accent carrying a slight edge.

"You even know what I'm thinking," he complained as she came in from the kitchen. He always thought she looked so elegant in her tailored office clothes.

"It's because you're so predictable, Red."

"Anyway, how did you know it was my birthday?"

"A massive piece of detective work," said Kate, "with the help of an outside agent and a small payment."

"An outside agent. Who?"

"The local newspaper store, my darling. In the Sunday *Times* they tell you the name of every distinguished person celebrating a birthday in the following seven days. In a week during which only the mediocre were born, you were featured."

Raymond had to laugh.

"Now listen, Red."

He pretended to hate his new nickname. "Do you have to call me by that revolting name?"

"Oh, stop making such a fuss, Red, and try on your shirt."

"Now?"

"Now."

He took off his black coat and waistcoat, removed his white shirt and eased the stud on his stiff collar, leaving a small circle above his Adam's apple. Curly red hairs sprang up all over his chest. He quickly put on the new shirt. The fabric had a pleasant soft feel about it. He started to do up the buttons, but Kate walked over and undid the top two.

"You know what? You've brought a whole new meaning to the word 'uptight.' But in the right clothes, you could even pass as good-looking."

Raymond scowled.

"Now where shall we go to celebrate your birthday?"

"The House of Commons?" suggested Raymond.

"Good God," said Kate. "I said celebrate, not hold a wake. What about Annabel's?"

"I can't afford to be seen in Annabel's."

"With me, you mean?"

"No, no, you silly woman, because I'm a Labourite."

"If members of the Labour party are not allowed to indulge in a good meal, then perhaps it's time for you to change parties. In my country one only sees the Democrats in the best restaurants."

"Oh, do be serious, Kate."

"I intend to be. Now what have you been up to in the House lately?"

"Not a lot," said Raymond sheepishly. "I've been snowed under in court and . . ."

"Precisely. It's time you did something positive before your colleagues in Parliament forget you exist."

"Have you anything particular in mind?" asked Raymond, folding his arms across his chest.

"As a matter of fact, I have," said Kate. "I read in the same Sunday paper as the one in which I discovered your best-kept secret that it is proving difficult for the Labour party to repeal the Tories' trade-union legislation. It appears there are long-term legal implications which the front bench is still trying to find a way around. Why don't you set that so-called first-class mind of yours on working out the legal niceties?"

"Not such a stupid idea." Raymond had become used to Kate's political sense. When he'd remarked on it she'd only said, "Just another bad habit I picked up from my ex-husband. Now where do we celebrate?" she asked.

"Compromise," said Raymond.

"I'm all ears."

"The Dorchester."

"If you insist," said Kate, not sounding overenthusiastic.

Raymond started to change his shirt.

"No, no, no, Red, people have been known to wear blue shirts at the Dorchester."

"But I haven't got a tie to match," said Raymond triumphantly.

Kate thrust her hand into the Turnbull and Asser bag and drew out a dark-blue silk tie.

"But it's got a pattern on it," said Raymond in disgust. "What will you expect next?"

"Contact lenses," said Kate.

Raymond stared at her and blinked.

On the way out the door, Raymond's gaze fell on the brightly wrapped package that Joyce had mailed from Leeds earlier in the week. He'd completely forgotten to open it.

"Damn," said Charles, putting down the *Times* and draining his coffee.

"What's the problem?" asked Fiona as she poured out another cup.

"Kerslake's been selected for Pucklebridge, which mean he's back in the House for life. Obviously my chat with Archie Millburn had no effect."

"Why have you got it in for Kerslake?" asked Fiona.

Charles folded the paper and considered the question. "It's quite simple really, old girl. I think he's the only one of my contemporaries who could stop me from leading the Tory Party."

"Why him in particular?"

"I first came across him when he was President of the Oxford Union. He was damn good then, and now he's better. He had rivals but he brushed them aside like flies. No, despite his background, Kerslake's the one man left who frightens me."

"It's a long race yet, my darling, and he could still stumble."

"So could I, but I'll simply have to put more hurdles out for him. Damn," said Charles again, looking at his watch, "I'm late."

He picked up his *Times,* kissed his wife on the forehead and rushed out to the waiting car.

The door closed as the phone rang. Fiona answered it. "Fiona Hampton speaking."

"It's Simon Kerslake. I wondered if Charles was there?"

"No, I'm afraid you've just missed him. May I take a message?"

"Yes. I wanted to let him know that I'd been selected for Pucklebridge, and Archie Millburn left me in no doubt how much Charles did to insure that I was offered the seat. And by the same token, do thank him for delivering my whips to me so assiduously. I understand I was the only member to receive such personal attention. Be assured if ever I can return the favors I shall not hesitate to do so."

The phone went dead.

Simon listened intently to Ronnie's report at the monthly board meeting. Two tenants had not paid their quarterly rent, and another quarter deadline was fast approaching. Ronnie's solicitors had sent firm reminders, followed a month later by legal letters, but this action had also failed to elicit any money.

"It only proves what I feared most," said Ronnie.

"What's that?" asked Simon.

"They just haven't got the cash."

"So we will have to replace them with new tenants."

"Simon, when you next travel from Beaufort Street to White-chapel, start counting the 'For Rent' signs on office blocks along the way. When you've passed a hundred you'll find you still haven't reached the outskirts of the city of London."

"So what do you think we ought to do next?"

"Try and sell one of our larger properties in order to secure cash flow. We can at least be thankful that our capital assets are still considerably more valuable than our borrowings. It's the companies which have it the other way around that have started calling in the receiver."

Simon thought about his overdraft now approaching one hundred thousand pounds and was beginning to wish he had taken up Ronnie's generous offer to buy back his shares. He knew that chance had now passed.

When the board meeting was over, Simon drove to St. Mary's to pick up Elizabeth. It was to be one of their three-times-a-week journeys to Pucklebridge as Simon tried to get around to all the villages before Wilson called an election.

Archie Millburn, who had accompanied them on nearly every trip, was turning out to be a conscientious chairman.

"He's been very kind to us," said Elizabeth, on their way down to Sussex.

"He certainly has," said Simon. "Remembering he also has to run Millburn Electronics. But, as he reminds us so often, once he's introduced us to every village chairman we'll be on our own."

"Have you ever discovered why he ignored Charles Hampton's advice?"

"No, he hasn't mentioned his name since that night. All I know for certain is that they were at school together."

"So what do you intend to do about Hampton?"

"I've already dealt with that little matter."

201

Raymond was the most talked-about backbencher in the House.

He made such a penetrating speech during the second reading of the new Trade Union Bill that the Whips put him on the standing committee—the perfect medium for him to display his skills as the committee debated each clause, point by point. He was able to show his colleagues where the legal pitfalls were and how to find a way round them, and it was not long before trade-union leaders were calling him at the Commons, and even at his flat, to learn his views on how their members should react to a host of different legal problems. Raymond showed patience with each of them and, more important, gave them excellent professional advice for the price of a phone call. He found it ironic how quickly they chose to forget that he had written *Full Employment at Any Cost?*

Snippets began to appear in the national press, ranging from laudatory comments from those involved with the bill to a pointed suggestion in the *Guardian* that, whatever had happened in the past, it would be insupportable if Raymond Gould were not made a member of the Government in the near future.

"If they were to offer you a job, would it make any difference to our relationship?" Kate asked.

"Certainly," said Raymond. "I shall have found the perfect excuse not to wear your blue shirts."

Harold Wilson held the crumbling edifice together for a further six months before finally having to call a General Election. He chose October 10, 1974.

Raymond immediately returned to his constituency to fight his fifth campaign. When he met Joyce at Leeds City station he couldn't help remembering that his dumpy wife was only four years older than Kate. He kissed her on the cheek as one might a distant relative; then she drove him back to their Chapel Allerton home.

Joyce chatted away on the journey home, and it became clear that the constituency was under control and that this time Fred Padgett was well prepared for a General Election. "He hasn't really stopped since the last one," she said. Undoubtedly, Joyce was even better organized than the campaign manager and the secretary joined together. What was more, Raymond thought, she enjoyed it.

Unlike his colleagues in rural seats, Raymond did not have to make speech after speech in little village halls. His votes were to be found in the High Street, where he addressed the midday shoppers through a megaphone and walked around supermarkets, pubs, clubs, shaking hands, and then repeated the whole process.

Joyce set her husband a schedule that allowed few people in the Leeds community to escape him. Some saw him a dozen times during the three-week campaign.

Once the game was over, Raymond was back trooping around the workingmen's clubs, drinking pint after pint of bitters. He accepted it as inevitable that he would put on five or ten pounds during any election campaign. He dreaded what Kate's comment would be when she saw him.

Somehow he always found a few minutes in each day to steal away and phone her. She seemed so busy and full of news it only made Raymond feel downcast; she couldn't possibly be missing him.

The local trade unionists backed Raymond to the hilt. They may have found him stuck-up and distant in the past, but "he knows where his heart is," they confided to anyone who would listen. They banged on doors, delivered leaflets, drove cars to the polls. They rose before he did in the morning and could still be found preaching to the converted when the pubs threw them out at night.

Raymond and Joyce cast their votes in the local secondary school on the Thursday of Election Day, looking forward to a large Labour victory.

203

The Labour Party gained a working majority in the House of forty-three over the Conservatives, but only three over all the parties combined. Nevertheless Harold Wilson looked set for another five years when the Queen invited him to form his fourth administration.

The count in Leeds that night gave Raymond his biggest majority ever: 14,207 votes. He spent the whole of Friday and Saturday thanking his constituents, then prepared to travel back to London on Sunday evening.

"He must invite you to join the Government this time," said Joyce.

"I wonder," said Raymond as he kissed his wife on the cheek. He waved at her as the train pulled out of Leeds City station. She waved back enthusiastically.

"I do like your new blue shirt, it really suits you," were the last words he heard her say.

During the election campaign, Charles had had to spend a lot of time at the bank because of a run on the pound. Fiona seemed to be everywhere in the constituency at once, assuring voters that her husband was just a few yards behind.

After the little slips were counted, the swing against Charles to the Labour candidate didn't amount to more than 1 percent in his 22,000 majority. When he heard the national result, he returned to London resigned to a long spell in Opposition. As he began to catch up with his Tory colleagues in the House, he found many of them already saying openly that Heath had to go after two election defeats in a row.

Charles knew then that he would have to make up his mind once again on where he stood over the election of a new Party Leader, and that once again he must pick the right man.

Simon had a glorious campaign. He and Elizabeth had started moving into their new cottage the day the election was announced, thankful that her salary at the hospital made it possible for them to employ a nanny for Peter and Lucy now that she had to commute. A double bed and a couple of chairs sufficed as Elizabeth cooked on an old wood stove from food still packed in tea chests. They seemed to use the same forks for everything. During the campaign Simon covered the two-hundred-square-mile constituency for a second time and assured his wife that she need only take the final week off from her duties at St. Mary's.

The voters of Pucklebridge sent Simon Kerslake back to Parliament with a majority of 18,419, the largest in the constituency history. The local people had quickly come to the conclusion that they now had a member who was destined to have a Cabinet career.

Kate kept her remarks very gentle as it became obvious by Monday night that the Prime Minister was not going to offer Raymond a job in the new administration. She cooked his favorite meal of roast beef—overdone—and Yorkshire pudding in the flat that night, but he didn't comment on it; he hardly spoke at all.

17

AFTER SIMON HAD BEEN BACK at the Commons for a week, he felt a sense of *déjà vu*. The sense was heightened by finding everything unchanged, even the policeman who greeted him at the members' entrance. When Edward Heath announced his Shadow team, Simon was not surprised that he wasn't included, as he never had been known as a supporter of the Tory Leader. He was, however, mystified but not displeased to discover that Charles Hampton was not among the names to be found in the Shadow Cabinet.

"Do you regret turning him down now the full team has been published?" asked Fiona, looking up from her copy of the *Daily Mail*.

"It wasn't an easy decision, but I think it'll prove right in the long run," replied Charles, buttering another piece of toast.

"What did he offer in the end?"

"Shadow Minister of Industry."

"That sounds rather interesting," said Fiona.

"Everything about it was interesting except the salary, which would have been nothing. Don't forget, the bank still pays me forty thousand a year while I'm chairman."

Fiona folded her paper. "Charles, what's the real reason?"

Charles accepted that he could rarely fool Fiona. "The truth is that I'm far from certain Ted will be leading the Party at the next election."

"Then who will if he doesn't?" asked Fiona.

"Whoever's got the guts to oppose him."

"I'm not sure I understand," said Fiona beginning to clear away the plates.

"Everyone accepts that he has to run again for reelection now that he's lost twice in a row."

"That's fair enough," agreed Fiona.

"But as he has appointed all possible contenders to the Cabinet or Shadow Cabinet over the last ten years, someone he has selected in the past will have to oppose him. No one of lesser stature would stand a chance."

"Is there a member of the Shadow Cabinet willing to run?" asked Fiona returning to her seat at the end of the table.

"One or two are considering it, but the problem is that if they lose it could easily end their political career," said Charles.

"But if one of them wins?"

"He will undoubtedly be the next Prime Minister."

"Interesting dilemma. And what are you going to do about it?"

"I'm not supporting anyone for the moment, but I've got my eyes wide open," said Charles, folding his napkin and rising from the table.

"Is there a front-runner?" asked Fiona, looking up at her husband.

"No, not really, although Kerslake is trying to rally support for Margaret Thatcher. But that idea is doomed from the start."

"A woman leading the Tory Party? Your lot haven't got the imagination to risk it," said Elizabeth, tasting the sauce. "The day that happens I'll eat my one and only Tory hat in full view of all the delegates at the party conference."

"Don't be so cynical, Elizabeth. She's the best bet we've got at the moment."

"But what are the chances of Ted Heath stepping aside? I always thought the Leader of the party stays on until he is hit by the mythical bus. I don't know Heath very well, but I can't ever imagine him resigning."

"I agree," said Simon. "So the 1922 Committee made up of all the backbenchers will have to change the rules."

"You mean the backbenchers will pressure him to resign?"

"No, but a lot of the Committee in their present mood would be willing to volunteer as driver for that mythical bus."

"If that's true, he must realize that his chances of holding on are slim."

"I wonder if any Leader ever knows that," said Simon.

"You ought to be in Blackpool next week," said Kate, resting her elbow on the pillow.

"Why Blackpool?" asked Raymond, staring up at the ceiling.

"Because, Red, that's where they are holding this year's Labour Party conference."

"What do you imagine I could hope to accomplish there?"

"You'd be seen to be alive. At present you're just a rumor in trade-union circles."

"That's not fair," Raymond said indignantly. "I give them more advice than I give my clients."

"All the more reason to go and spend a few days with them."

"But if you're not a Minister or a trade-union leader, all you do at a party conference is spend four days eating foul food, sleeping in seedy guest houses, and applauding other people's second rate speeches."

"I've no interest in where you put your weary head at night, but I do want you to revive your contacts with the unions during the day."

"Why?" said Raymond. "That lot can't influence my career."

"Not at the moment," said Kate. "But I predict that, like my fellow Americans at their conventions, the Labour Party will one day select its Leader at the Party conference."

"Never," said Raymond. "That is and will always remain the

prerogative of elected members of the House of Commons."

"That's the sort of crass, shortsighted, pompous statement I would expect a Republican to make," said Kate as she covered his head with a pillow. She lifted up a corner and whispered in his ear, "And have you read any of the resolutions to be debated at this year's Labour conference?"

"A few," came back Raymond's muffled reply.

"Then it might serve you well to note Mr. Anthony Wedgwood Benn's contribution," she said removing the pillow.

"What's that crazy left-winger enlightening us on this time?"

"He's calling on 'conference,' as he insists on describing your gathering of the brothers, to demand that the next Leader be chosen by a full vote of the delegates, making up an electoral college from all the constituencies, the trade-union movement and Parliament—I suspect in that order."

"Madness."

"Today's extremist is tomorrow's moderate," said Kate blithely.

"A typical American generalization."

"Benjamin Disraeli, actually."

Raymond put the pillow back over his head.

As soon as Raymond stepped off the train at Blackpool Station, he knew Kate had been right to insist he attend the conference. He shared a taxi to his hotel with two trade-union leaders who treated him as if he were the local Lord Mayor.

When he checked into the hotel, he was pleasantly surprised that Jamie Sinclair, who was now a Home Office Minister, had been booked into the next room. They agreed to have lunch together the following day. Sinclair suggested an excellent restaurant just outside of Blackpool, and it soon became clear that he regularly attended the conference.

Although they had both been in the House for ten years, it was the first time they discovered how much they had in common.

"You must have been disappointed when the PM didn't ask

you to rejoin the Government," began Sinclair.

Raymond paused, staring at the menu. "Very," he finally admitted.

"Nevertheless, you were wise to come to Blackpool, because this is where your strength lies."

"You think so?"

"Come on. Everybody knows you're the trade unions' pin-up boy, and they still have a lot of influence as to who sits in the Cabinet."

"I haven't noticed," said Raymond mournfully.

"You will when they eventually choose the Leader."

"That's funny, that's exactly what . . . Joyce said last week."

"Sensible girl, Joyce. I fear it will happen in our time as members."

A waitress appeared at their side and they both ordered.

"I doubt it," said Raymond, "and I can tell you one thing. I would oppose the idea, which wouldn't make me popular with the unions."

"Perhaps. But every party needs a man like you, and the union leaders wouldn't mind if you were a card-carrying Fascist; they'd still back you."

"I'll tell you something—I'd trade it all in for your job at the Home Office. I didn't go into politics to spend my life on the benches."

As he spoke, the chairman of the Boilermakers' Union shouted across as he passed their table, "Good to see you, Ray." He showed no recognition of Jamie. Raymond turned and smiled at the man waving as Caesar might have done to Cassius.

"Have you decided how you're going to vote in the Leadership battle?" asked Fiona over breakfast.

"Yes," replied Charles. "And at this point in my career, I can't afford to make the wrong choice."

"So who have you decided on?" asked Fiona.

"While there isn't a serious contender willing to oppose Ted Heath, it remains in my best interest to continue backing him."

"Isn't there one shadow Cabinet Minister who has the guts to run against him?"

"The rumor grows that Margaret Thatcher will act as whipping girl. If she gets close enough to force a second ballot, the serious contenders will then join in."

"What if she won the first round?"

"Don't be silly, Fiona," said Charles, taking more interest in his scrambled egg. "The Tory Party would never elect a woman to lead them. We're far too hidebound and traditional. That's the sort of immature mistake the Labour Party would make to prove how much they believed in equality."

Simon was still pushing Margaret Thatcher to throw her hat in the ring.

"She certainly has enough of them," said Elizabeth.

It amused Raymond to watch the Tory Party Leadership struggle while he got on with his job. Raymond would have dismissed Thatcher's chances if Kate hadn't reminded him that the Tories had been the first and only party to choose a Jewish leader in Benjamin Disraeli, and a bachelor in Ted Heath.

"Why shouldn't they be the first to elect a woman?" she demanded. He would have continued to argue with Kate, but the damn woman had proved to be right so often in the past.

The 1922 Committee announced that the election for Tory Leader would take place on February 4, 1975. At a press conference in early January at the House of Commons, Margaret Thatcher, still the only woman in the Shadow Cabinet, announced she would allow herself to be nominated for the Leadership. Simon immediately spent his time exhorting his colleagues to support "the lady" and joined a small committee that was formed for the purpose. Charles Hampton warned his friends that the party could never hope to win a general election with a woman Leader. As the days passed, nothing became clearer than the uncertainty of the outcome.

211

At four o'clock on a particularly wet and windy day, the chairman of the 1922 Committee announced the figures:

MARGARET THATCHER	130
EDWARD HEATH	119
HUGH FRASER	16

According to the 1922 Committee rules, the winner needed a 15 percent majority, and so a second round was necessary. "It will be held in seven days' time," the Chief Whip announced. Three former Cabinet Ministers immediately declared they were candidates. Ted Heath, having been warned that he would get even fewer votes the second time around, withdrew from the second ballot.

The next seven days were the longest in Simon's life. He did everything in his power to hold Thatcher's supporters together. Charles meanwhile decided to play the second round very low key. When the time came to vote, he put his cross on the ballot paper next to the former Secretary of State he had served under at Trade and Industry. "A man we can all trust," he told Fiona.

When the votes had been finally counted, the chairman of the 1922 Committee announced that Margaret Thatcher was the outright winner with a vote of 146 to 79 for her nearest challenger.

Simon was delighted, while Elizabeth hoped he had forgotten about her promise to eat her hat. Charles was dumbfounded. They both wrote to their new Leader immediately.

February 11, 1975

Dear Margaret,
Many congratulations on your victory as the first woman Leader of our Party. I was proud to have played a

212

small part in your triumph and will continue to work for
your success at the next election.

Yours,
SIMON

27 Eaton Square
London SW 1
February 11, 1975

Dear Margaret,
   I made no secret of backing Ted Heath in the first round
of the leadership contest, having had the privilege of serv-
ing in his administration. I was delighted to have sup-
ported you on the second ballot. It illustrates how
progressive our Party is that we have chosen a woman who
will undoubtedly be Britain's next Prime Minister.
   Be assured of my loyalty.

Yours,
CHARLES

Margaret Thatcher answered all her colleagues' letters within
the week. Simon received a handwritten letter inviting him to
join the new Shadow team as number two in the Education Department.

Charles received a typed note thanking him for his letter of
support.

18

HAMPTON'S BANK had weathered the Great War, the thirties crash, and then the Second World War. Charles had no intention of being the chairman who presided over its demise in the seventies.

Soon after taking over from Derek Spencer—at the board's unanimous insistence—Charles discovered that being chairman wasn't quite as relaxed a job as he had expected. He lacked the knowledge and expertise to run Hampton's on a day-to-day basis.

While Charles remained confident that the bank could ride the storm, he wasn't taking any risks. The business news sections of the newspapers were full of stories of the Bank of England's acting as a "lifeboat" and having to step in to assist ailing financial institutions, along with the daily reports of the collapse of yet another property company. The time when property values and rents automatically increased each year had become a thing of the past.

When he had accepted the board's offer, Charles insisted that a chief executive be appointed to carry out the professional business while he remained the man with whom other City chairmen dealt. Charles interviewed several people for the position but he did not find anyone suitable. Head-hunting seemed to be the next move, the expense of which was saved when he overheard, at a conversation at the next table at White's, that the newly appointed chief executive at the First Bank of America was sick of having to report to the board in New York every time he wanted to use a first-class stamp.

Charles immediately invited the First Bank of America's chief executive to lunch at the House of Commons. Clive Reynolds had come from a background similar to Derek Spencer's: London School of Economics, followed by the Harvard Business School, and a series of successful appointments which had culminated in his becoming chief executive of the First Bank of America. This similarity did not worry Charles, as he made it clear to Mr. Reynolds that any appointee would be the chairman's man.

When Reynolds had been offered the appointment he had driven a hard bargain, and Charles looked forward to his doing the same for Hampton's. Reynolds ended up with fifty thousand pounds a year and enough of a profit incentive to insure that he didn't deal for himself or encourage any other headhunters to invite him to join their particular jungle.

"He's not the sort of fellow we could invite to dinner," Charles told Fiona, "but his appointment will enable me to sleep at night knowing the bank is in safe hands."

Charles's choice was rubber-stamped by the board at their next meeting, and as the months passed it became obvious that the First Bank of America had lost one of its prime assets below market value.

Clive Reynolds was a conservative by nature, but when he did take what Charles described as a risk—and what Reynolds called a "hunch"—more than 50 percent of such risks paid off. While Hampton's kept its reputation for caution and good husbandry under Charles, it managed a few quite spectacular coups thanks to their new chief executive.

Reynolds had enough sense to treat his new chairman with respect without ever showing undue deference, while their relationship remained at all times strictly professional.

One of Reynolds's first innovations had been to suggest that they check on every customer account over two hundred and fifty-thousand pounds, and Charles had approved.

"When you've handled the account of a company for many years," Reynolds pointed out, "it sometimes is less obvious when one of your traditional customers is heading for trouble than it would be with a newcomer. If there are any 'lame ducks,' let's discover them before they hit the ground"—a metaphor that Charles repeated at several weekend parties.

Charles enjoyed his morning meetings with Clive Reynolds, where he picked up a great deal about a profession to which he had previously only brought gut feeling and common sense. In a short time he learned enough from his new tutor to make him sound like David Rockefeller when he rose to speak in a finance debate on the floor of the House—an unexpected bonus.

Charles knew little of Reynolds's private life except what was on file. He was forty-one, unmarried, and lived in Esher, wherever that was. All Charles cared about was that Reynolds arrived each morning at least an hour before him, and left after him every night, even when the House was in recess.

Charles had studied fourteen of the confidential reports on customers with loans over two hundred and fifty thousand pounds. Clive Reynolds had already picked out two companies with whom he felt the bank should revise its current position.

Charles still had three more reports to consider before he presented a full assessment to the board.

The quiet knock on the door, however, meant that it was ten o'clock and Reynolds had arrived to make his daily report. Rumors were circulating in London that the bank rate would go up on Thursday, so Reynolds wanted to go short on dollars and long on gold. Charles nodded. As soon as the announcement had been made about the bank rate, Reynolds continued, "It will be wiser to return to dollars, as the new round of pay negotiations with the unions is about to take place. This, in turn, will undoubtedly start a fresh run on the pound." Charles nodded again.

"I think the dollar is far too weak at two ten," Reynolds added. "With the unions settling at around twelve percent, the dollar must strengthen, say, to nearer one ninety." He added that he was not happy about the bank's large holding in Slater Walker, Inc., and wanted to liquidate half the stock over the next month. He proposed to do so in small amounts over irregular periods. "We also have three other major accounts to consider before we make known our findings to the board. I'm concerned about the spending policy of one of the companies, but the other two appear stable. I think we should go over them together when you have time to consider my reports. Perhaps tomorrow morning, if you could manage that. The companies concerned are Speyward Laboratories, Blackies Limited and Nethercote and Company. It's Speyward I'm worried about."

"I'll take the files home tonight," said Charles, "and give you an opinion in the morning."

"Thank you, Chairman."

Charles had never suggested that Reynolds call him by his first name.

Archie Millburn held a small dinner party to celebrate Simon's first anniversary as the member for Pucklebridge. Although these occasions had originally been to introduce the Party hierarchy to their new member, Simon now knew more about the constituency and its flock than Archie did, as Archie was the first to admit.

Elizabeth, Peter and Lucy had settled comfortably into their small cottage, while Simon, as a member of the Shadow Education team, had visited schools—nursery, primary, public and secondary; universities—red brick, plate glass and Oxbridge; technical colleges, art institutes and correctional centers. He had read Butler, Robbins, Plowden, and had listened to children and to professors of psychology alike. He felt that after a year he was beginning to understand the subject, and only longed for a General Election so that he could once again turn rehearsal into performance.

217

"Opposition must be frustrating," observed Archie when the ladies had retired after dinner.

"Yes, but it's an excellent way to prepare yourself for Government and do some basic thinking about the subject. I never found time for such luxury as a Minister."

"But it mut be very different from holding office?" said Archie, clipping a cigar.

"True. In Government," said Simon, "you're surrounded by civil servants who don't allow you to lift a finger or give you a moment to ponder, while in Opposition you can think policy through even if you do often end up having to type your own letters."

Archie pushed the port down to Simon's end of the table. "I'm glad the girls are out," said Archie conspiratorily, "because I wanted you to know I've decided to give up being chairman at the end of the year."

"Why?" asked Simon, taken aback.

"I've seen you elected and settled in. It's time for a younger man to have a go."

"But you're only my age."

"I can't deny that, but the truth is that I'm not giving enough time to my electronics company, and the board is continually reminding me of it. No one has to tell you that these are not easy times."

"It's sad," said Simon. "Just as you get to know someone in politics, you or they always seem to move on."

"Fear not," said Archie. "I don't intend to leave Pucklebridge, and I feel confident that you will be my member for at least another twenty years, by which time I'll be quite happy to accept an invitation to Downing Street."

"You may find that it's Charles Hampton who's living at Number Ten," said Simon, as he struck a match to light his cigar.

"Then I won't get an invitation," said Archie with a smile.

Charles couldn't sleep that night after his discovery, and his tossing and turning kept Fiona awake. He had opened the

Nethercote file when he was waiting for dinner to be served. His first act with any company was to glance down the names of the directors to see if he knew anyone on the board. He recognized no one until his eye stopped at "S. J. Kerslake, MP." The cook felt sure that Mr. Hampton had not enjoyed his dinner, because he hardly touched the main course.

On his arrival at Hampton's only moments after Clive Reynolds, he called for his chief executive. Reynolds appeared a few minutes later without his usual armful of files, surprised to see the chairman in so early. Once Reynolds was seated, Charles opened the file in front of him. "What do you know about Nethercote and Company?"

"Private company. Net assets value approaching ten million pounds, running a current overdraft of seven million, of which we service half. Efficiently managed, with a good board of directors, will ride out the current problems, in my view, and should be well oversubscribed when they eventually go public."

"How much of the company do we own?"

"Seven and a half percent. As you know, the bank never takes eight percent of any company because then we would have to declare an interest under Section Twenty-three of the Finance Act. It has always been a policy of this bank to invest in a major client without becoming too involved with the running of the company."

"Who are their principal bankers?"

"The Midland."

"What would happen if we put our seven and a half percent up for sale and did not renew the overdraft facility at the end of the quarter but called it instead?"

"They would have to seek financing elsewhere."

"And if they couldn't?"

"They would have to start selling their assets, which under that sort of forced-sale position would be very damaging for any company, if not impossible in the present climate."

"And then?"

"I would have to check my file and . . ."

Charles passed over the file and Reynolds studied it carefully, frowning. "They already have a cash flow problem because of bad debts. With a sudden increased demand, they might go under. I would strongly advise against such a move, Chairman. Nethercote has proved a reliable risk over the years, and I think we stand to make a handsome profit when they are quoted on the Stock Exchange."

"For reasons I cannot disclose to you," said Charles, looking up from his chair, "I fear that remaining involved with this company may turn out to be a financial embarrassment for Hampton's." Reynolds looked at him, puzzled. "You will inform the Midland Bank that we will not be renewing this loan at the next quarter."

"Then they would have to look for support from another bank. The Midland would never agree to shoulder the entire amount on their own."

"And try to dispose of our seven and a half percent immediately."

"But that could lead to a crisis of confidence in the company."

"So be it," said Charles, as he closed the file.

"But I do feel . . ."

"That will be all, Mr. Reynolds."

"Yes, Chairman," said the mystified chief executive, who had never thought of his boss as an irrational man. He turned to leave. Had he looked back he would have been even more mystified by the smile that was spread across Charles Hampton's face.

"They've pulled the rug out from under our feet," said Ronnie Nethercote angrily.

"Who?" said Simon, who had just come into the room.

"The Midland Bank."

"Why would they do that?"

"An outside shareholder put all his stock on the market

without warning, and the Midland was unwilling to continue such a large overdraft because it was not convinced that the company's assets still covered the value of the shares."

"Have you been to see the manager?" asked Simon, unable to disguise his anxiety.

"Yes, but he can't do anything. His hands are tied by a main board directive," said Ronnie, slumping deeper into his seat.

"How bad is it?"

"They've given me a month to find another bank. Otherwise I'll have to start selling some of our assets."

"What would be the outcome if we don't manage to come up with another bank?" asked Simon desperately.

"I could be bankrupt within a month. Do you know any banker who can smell out a good deal?"

"Only one, and I can assure you he wouldn't help."

Charles put the phone down, satisfied. He wondered if there was anything that could still be regarded as secret. It had taken him less than an hour to find out the size of Kerslake's overdraft. "Banker-to-banker confidentiality," he had assured them. He was still smiling when Reynolds knocked on the door.

"The Midland were not pleased," he told Charles.

"They'll get over it," his chairman replied. "What's the latest on Nethercote?"

"Only a rumor, but everyone now knows they're in trouble and the chairman is searching around for a new backer," said Reynolds impassively. "His biggest problem is that no one is touching property companies at the moment."

"Once they've collapsed, what's to stop us picking up the pieces and making a killing?"

"A clause that was slipped through in the finance act which your government passed three years ago. The penalties range from a heavy fine to having your banking license taken away."

"Oh, yes, I remember," said Charles. "Pity. So how long do you expect them to last?"

221

"Once the month is up," said Reynolds, stroking a clean-shaven chin, "if they fail to find a backer, the creditors will swarm in like locusts."

"Aren't the shares worth anything?" asked Charles innocently.

"Not the paper they are written on at the moment," said Reynolds, watching his chairman carefully.

This time the chief executive couldn't miss the chairman's smile as Charles thought of Simon Kerslake and his overdraft of one hundred and eight thousand pounds, now backed by worthless shares. Pucklebridge would soon be looking for a new member.

At the end of a month during which no bank came to his rescue, Ronnie Nethercote caved in and agreed to call in the receiver and file a bankruptcy notice. He still hoped that he could pay off all his creditors even if the shares he and his fellow directors held remained worthless. He felt as worried for Simon and his career as he did for himself, but he knew there was nothing the receiver would allow him to do to help one individual.

When Simon told Elizabeth that night, she didn't cry. She was a fatalist at heart, and had always feared the outcome of her husband's joining the board of Nethercote's.

"Can't Ronnie help you? After all, you've supported him enough in the past."

"No, he can't," said Simon avoiding telling her where the real responsibility for his downfall lay.

"Do bankrupts automatically have to leave Parliament?" was Elizabeth's next question.

"No, but I shall because I could never be considered for further promotion—I'd always be rightly tainted with 'lack of judgment.' "

"It seems so unfair when you weren't personally to blame."

"There are different rules for those who wish to live in the spotlight," Simon said simply.

"But in time, surely—" began Elizabeth.

"I'm not willing to remain on the back benches for another twenty years only to hear whispered in the corner of the smoking room '. . . Would have made the Cabinet if it hadn't been for . . .' "

Elizabeth's next question saddened Simon. "Does that mean we will have to give up the nanny?"

"Not necessarily, but we both may have to make sacrifices in order to keep her part time."

"But my work at the hospital . . ." began Elizabeth, not completing the sentence. "So what happens next?" she asked hurriedly.

"I'll have to tell Archie Millburn tonight. I've already written my letter of resignation to hand to him. I shall make an appointment to see the Chief Whip on Monday to explain to him why I am going to apply for the Chiltern Hundreds."

"What does that mean?"

"It's one of the few ways of leaving the House in mid-session—other than dying. Officially it's a nominal office under the Crown which debars you from membership in the House."

"It all sounds rather formal to me," said Elizabeth.

"I'm afraid it will cause an embarrassing by-election in Pucklebridge," Simon admitted.

"Can nobody help?"

"There aren't a lot of people around who have a spare hundred and eight thousand pounds for a worthless bunch of shares."

"Would you like me to come with you when you go to see Archie?" Elizabeth asked, rising from her seat.

"No, darling. It's kind of you to ask."

Elizabeth leaned over and pushed back the hair that had fallen over his forehead. She couldn't help noticing some gray strands that must have appeared in the last few weeks. At that moment she felt like strangling Ronnie Nethercote.

Simon drove slowly down to Pucklebridge to keep his impromptu appointment with the chairman. Archie Millburn, standing hands on hips in his garden, listened to the tale with a sad face. "It's been happening to a lot of good people in the city lately—but what I can't understand is, if the company owns such prime properties, why has no one made a takeover bid? Sounds as if it's a divestiture specialist's dream."

"It appears to be a matter of confidence," said Simon.

"A sacred word in the City," agreed Archie, while he continued to prune his Roosevelts and Red Mistresses.

Simon handed him the prepared letter of resignation, which Millburn read over and reluctantly accepted.

"I won't mention this to anyone until you've seen the Chief Whip on Monday. I'll call a special meeting of the full committee on Tuesday evening and inform them of your decision then."

The two men shook hands. "Your misfortune is our misfortune," said Archie. "In a very short time you've gained the respect and the affection of the local people. You'll be missed."

Simon drove back to London, and, although the car radio was on, he did not take in the news flash that they kept repeating every thirty minutes.

Raymond was among the first to hear the announcement, and was stunned by it. Harold Wilson was going to resign less than halfway through the five-year Parliament, and for no apparent reason other than that he had just passed his sixtieth birthday. He proposed to remain Prime Minister only so long as the Labour Party took to select its new Leader, who would, Raymond hoped, serve out the full term. Raymond and Kate sat glued to the television, picking up every scrap of information they could. They discussed the implications far into the night.

"Well, Red, could this mean rehabilitation for our forgotten hero?"

"Who can say?"

"Well, if you can't, who can?"

"The next Leader, perhaps," said Raymond.

224

The fight for the Leadership was a straight battle between the left and right wings of the Labour Party, James Callaghan on the right and Michael Foot on the left. It was with some relief that Raymond saw Callaghan, despite losing the first ballot, come through to be elected Leader. The Queen duly called for Callaghan and asked him to form a new Government. As tradition demands, all serving Ministers of the Government sent their resignations to Downing Street to allow the new Prime Minister to select his own team.

Raymond was in court listening to the judge's summing up when his junior passed him a note: "Please call 10 Downing Street as soon as possible." The judge took a further thirty minutes to meticulously explain to the jury the legal definition of manslaughter before Raymond could escape. He ran down the corridor and stopped at one of the clerks' private boxes to make the call. The dial rotating back into place after each number seemed to take forever.

After he eventually got through three people, a voice said, "Good afternoon, Raymond": the unmistakable gravelly tones of the new Prime Minister. "I think it's time you joined the Government—" Raymond held his breath— "as Minister of State at the Department of Trade." Minister of State: only one place off the Cabinet.

"You still there, Raymond?"

"Yes, Prime Minister, and I'd be delighted to accept."

He put the phone down, immediately picked it up again and dialed the City office of the Chase Manhattan bank. They put him through to the chief systems analyst.

"Ronnie phoned while you were in the bath."

"I'll call him as soon as I reach the House."

Neither of them spoke for several minutes. Then Elizabeth asked, "Are you dreading it?"

"Yes, I am," said Simon. "I feel like a condemned man eating his last breakfast, and the worst thing is I have to drive myself to the gallows."

"I wonder if we will ever laugh about today?"

"No doubt—when I collect my parliamentary pension."

"Can we live off that?"

"Hardly. I don't get the first payment until I'm sixty-five, so we have a long wait to find out." He got up. "Can I give you a lift to the hospital?" he asked.

"No, thanks, I intend to savor the joys of being a two-car family for at least another week."

Simon kissed his wife and left for his appointment with the Chief Whip at the House of Commons.

The policeman at the gate saluted as he drove in. "Good morning, sir," he said.

"Good morning," said Simon. When you salute next time I'll have to say goodbye, he thought morosely. He parked his car on the second level of the new underground parking lot and took the escalator up to the members' entrance. He couldn't help remembering that ten years ago he would have taken the stairs. He continued through the members' cloakroom, up the marble staircase to the members' lobby. Habit made him turn left into the little post office to check whether he had any mail.

"Mr. Kerslake," the man behind the counter called into an intercom, and a few seconds later a parcel and a packet of letters held together by a thick elastic band thudded into an office basket. Simon left the parcel marked London University and the letters on the desk in his room and checked his watch: over forty minutes before his appointment with the Chief Whip. He went to the nearest phone and dialed Nethercote and Company. Ronnie answered the phone himself.

"Sacked the telephone operator last Friday," he explained. "Only me and my secretary left."

"You called, Ronnie—" a millimeter of hope in Simon's voice.

226

"Yes, I wanted to express how I felt. I tried to write you a letter over the weekend but I'm not very good with words." He paused. "Nor, it seems, with figures. I just wanted to say how desperately sorry I am. Elizabeth told me you were going to see the Chief Whip this morning. I'll be thinking of you."

"That's kind, Ronnie, but I went into it with my eyes wide open. As an advocate of free enterprise, I can hardly complain when I turn out to be one of its victims."

"A very philosophical attitude for this time of the morning."

"How are things at your end?"

"The receiver's checking the books. I still believe we can get out with all our creditors fully paid. At least that way I'll avoid the stigma of bankruptcy." There was a longer pause. "Oh, Christ, that was tactless."

"Don't worry about it, Ronnie. The overdraft was my decision." Simon already wished he had been as frank with his wife.

"Let's have lunch one day next week."

"It will have to be somewhere that takes food stamps," said Simon wryly.

"Good luck, mate," said Ronnie.

Simon decided to fill up the remaining thirty minutes at the House by going to the library and glancing over the rest of the morning papers. He settled himself in a corner of the library next to the fireplace over which hung a notice reminding members not to have overloud or prolonged conversations.

The story of the probable breakup of Nethercote and Company was detailed on the financial pages. It quoted approvingly Ronnie's view that all creditors ought to be paid in full. Not one of the articles mentioned Simon's name, but he could already anticipate the headlines in tomorrow's paper: "The Rise and Fall of Simon Kerslake." Over ten years' work quickly forgotten, he would be old news within a week.

The library clock inched toward the hour that he could no longer put off. Simon heaved himself out of the deep leather chair like an old man and walked slowly toward the Chief Whip's office.

Miss Norse, the Chief's ancient secretary, smiled benignly as he came in.

"Good morning, Mr. Kerslake," she said brightly. "I'm afraid the Chief is still with Mrs. Thatcher, but I did remind him of your appointment so I don't expect him to be long. Would you care to have a seat?"

"Thank you," he said.

Alec Pimkin always claimed that Miss Norse had a set patter for every occasion. His imitation of her saying "I hope I find you in rude health, Mr. Pimkin" had brought chuckles to the members' dining room on many occasions. He must have exaggerated, thought Simon.

"I hope I find you in rude health, Mr. Kerslake," said Miss Norse, not looking up from her typing. Simon choked back a laugh.

"Very rude, thank you," he said, wondering how many tragic stories or tales of lost opportunities Miss Norse had had to listen to over the years. She stopped suddenly and looked at her notepad.

"I should have mentioned it to you before, Mr. Kerslake—a Mr. Nethercote rang."

"Thank you, I've spoken to him already."

Simon was leafing through an out-of-date copy of *Punch* when the Chief Whip strode in.

"I can spare you one minute, Simon, one and a half if you are going to resign," he said, laughing, and marched off toward his office. As Simon followed him down the corridor, the phone by Miss Norse's side rang. "It's for you, Mr. Kerslake," she shouted to their retreating backs.

Simon turned and said, "Can you take the number?"

"He says it's urgent."

Simon stopped, hesitating. "With you in a moment," he said to the Chief Whip, who disappeared into his office. Simon walked back and took the phone from Miss Norse's outstretched hand.

"Simon Kerslake here. Who is it?"

228

"It's Ronnie."

"Ronnie," said Simon flatly.

"I've just had a call from Morgan Grenfell. One of their clients has made an offer of one pound twenty-five a share for the company and they're willing to take over the current liabilities."

Simon was trying to do the sums in his head.

"Don't bother working it out," Ronnie said. "At one twenty-five, your shares would be worth seventy-five thousand pounds."

"It won't be enough," said Simon, as he recalled his overdraft of 108,712 pounds, a figure etched in his memory.

"Don't panic. I've told them I won't settle for anything less than one pound fifty a share, and it has to be within seven days, which will give them ample time to check the books. That would bring you in ninety thousand, but you would still be eighteen thousand down the Swanee, which you'll have to learn to live with. If you sell the wife as well as the second car, you should just about survive."

Simon could tell by the way his friend was speaking that Ronnie already had a cigar between his lips.

"You're a genius."

"Not me—Morgan Grenfell. And I bet they'll make a handsome profit in the long run for their unnamed client, who seemed to have all the inside information. If you're still on for lunch next Tuesday, don't bring your food stamps. It's on me."

Simon put the phone down and kissed Miss Norse on the forehead. She was completely taken aback by a situation for which she had no set reply. She remained silent as the Chief Whip peeked his head out of his office. "An orgy in the Chief Whip's office?" he said. "You'll be on page three of the *Sun* next, Miss Norse." Simon laughed. "I've got a crisis on over tonight's vote," the Chief Whip continued. "The Government is reneging on our agreement for pairing, and I have to get a delegation back from Brussels in time for the ten o'clock division. Whatever it is, can it wait, Simon?"

"Yes, of course."

"Can you come to my office, Miss Norse—if I can drag you away from James Double-O-Seven Kerslake?"

Simon left and almost bounced to the nearest phone. He called both Elizabeth and Archie Millburn to let them know the news. Elizabeth was ecstatic, while Archie didn't sound all that surprised.

"Don't you think it might be wise for us to stop seeing each other?"

"Why?" said Raymond. "Palmerston had a mistress when he was seventy, and he still beat your precious Disraeli, came the election."

"Yes, but that was before the days of a dozen national newspapers *and* investigative journalism. Frankly, it wouldn't take a Woodward and Bernstein more than a few hours to discover our little secret."

"We'll be all right. I've destroyed all the tapes."

"Do be serious."

"You're always telling me I'm far too serious."

"Well, I want you to be now. Very."

Raymond turned to face Kate. "I love you, Kate, and I know I always will. Why don't we stop this charade and get married?"

She sighed. "We've been over this a hundred times. I shall want to return to America eventually, and in any case I wouldn't make a very good Prime Minister's wife."

"Three American women have in the past," said Raymond sulkily.

"To hell with your historical precedents—and what's more, I hate Leeds."

"You've never been there."

"I don't need to if it's colder than London."

"Then you'll have to be satisfied with being my mistress." Raymond took Kate in his arms. "You know, I used to think being Prime Minister was worth every sacrifice, but now I'm not so sure."

"It's still worth the sacrifice," said Kate, "as you'll discover when you live at Number Ten. Come on, or my dinner will be burned to a cinder."

"You haven't noticed these," said Raymond smugly, pointing down at his feet.

Kate stared at the fashionable new loafers.

"I never thought the day would come," she said. "Pity you're starting to go bald."

When Simon returned home his first words were, "We'll survive."

"But what have you done about the resignation letter?" asked Elizabeth anxiously.

"Archie Millburn said he would return it the day I became Prime Minister."

"Well, that's a relief," Elizabeth said. "And now that the worst's behind us, I want you to promise me just one thing."

"Anything."

"You will never speak to Ronnie Nethercote again."

For a moment, Simon hesitated, before saying, "That's not completely fair, because I haven't been totally straight with you from the beginning." He then sat Elizabeth down on the sofa and told her the whole truth.

It was Elizabeth's turn to remain silent.

"Oh, hell," she said eventually, looking up at Simon. "I do hope Ronnie can forgive me."

"What are you talking about?"

"I phoned him back soon after you left for the Commons and I spent at least ten minutes telling him why he was the biggest two-faced bastard I'd ever met, and that I didn't want to hear from him again in my life."

It was Simon's turn to collapse onto the sofa. "How did he respond?" he asked anxiously.

Elizabeth faced her husband. "That's the strange thing, he didn't even protest. He just apologized."

231

Charles paced up and down the room angrily. "Give me the figures again."

"Nethercote has accepted a bid of seven million five hundred thousand, which works out at one pound fifty a share," said Clive Reynolds.

Charles stopped at his desk and scribbled the figures down on a piece of paper. Ninety thousand pounds, leaving a shortfall of only eighteen thousand pounds. It wouldn't be enough. "Damn," he said.

"I agree," said Reynolds, "I always thought we were premature to lose our position in the company in the first place."

"An opinion you will not voice outside this room," said Charles.

Clive Reynolds did not reply.

"What's happened to Nethercote himself?" asked Charles, searching for any scrap of information he could find about Simon Kerslake.

"I'm told he's starting up again in a smaller way. Morgan Grenfell was delighted by the deal and the manner in which he handled the company during the takeover. I must say we let it fall into their laps."

"Can we get any stock in the new company?" asked Charles, ignoring his comment.

"I'd doubt it. It's only capitalized at one million, although Morgan Grenfell is giving Nethercote a large overdraft facility as part of the deal."

"Then all that remains necessary is to see the matter is never referred to again."

"Dad, can I have a leather soccer ball, please?"

"What's wrong with the one you've got?"

"It's made of rubber and doesn't bounce like the proper ones they use in school matches. Besides, it's too small."

"It will have to do, I'm afraid."

"But Martin Henderson's dad has given him a full-sized leather ball to start the new season."

"I'm sorry, son, the truth is that Martin Henderson's father is far better off than I am."

"I'll tell you one thing," said Peter with feeling. "I'm sure not going to be an MP when I grow up." Simon smiled as his son kicked the ball toward him. "I'll bet you can't score against me even with a small ball."

"Don't forget, we still only have small goalposts," said Simon.

"Stop making excuses, Dad, just admit you're past your prime."

Simon burst out laughing. "We shall see," he said with more bravado than conviction. At the age of eight Peter was already able to dribble and shoot with a confidence that was beginning to look ominous. An old school friend had recently warned him that "By twelve they begin to beat you, and by fifteen they hope not to show they aren't trying their hardest any more."

Simon still needed to try his hardest before he managed to score against Peter and take his place in the goal. He then watched Peter's fiercest shots safely into his arms and was again thankful that the goal was not full size.

He kept his son's best shots out for another twenty minutes before Lucy came to join them in the garden. Simon couldn't help noticing that she was wearing a dress already too tight around the shoulders. "Supper's ready, Dad," she said, and ran back inside. He cursed again at the sacrifices his own selfish greed had brought upon the family and marveled at how little they complained.

Elizabeth looked tired as she served up hamburgers and chips for the family, and then Simon remembered she had to be back on duty at St. Mary's by eight that night. Thank God he hadn't married Lavinia Maxwell-Harrington, he thought, as he looked up at his wife. Lavinia would not have hung around for hamburgers and chips.

"How did you get on?" asked Elizabeth.

"I'll survive," said Simon, still thinking about his overdraft.

"I'll kill him next time," said Peter, "once I get a real ball."

Raymond dug deeper into the red box.

"You enjoying yourself, Red?"

"It's fascinating," said Raymond. "Do you know—?"

"No, I don't. You haven't spoken to me in the last three hours, and when you do it's to tell me how you spent the day with your new mistress."

"My new mistress?"

"The Secretary of State for Trade."

"Oh, him."

"Yes, him."

"What sort of day did you have at the bank?" asked Raymond, not looking up from his papers.

"I had a most fascinating day," replied Kate.

"Why, what happened?"

"One of our customers required a loan," said Kate.

"A loan," repeated Raymond, still concentrating on the file in front of him. "How much?"

" 'How much do you want?' I said. 'How much have you got?' they asked. 'Four hundred seventeen billion at the last count,' I told them. 'That will do fine to start with,' they said. 'Sign here,' I said. But I couldn't close the deal because the lady concerned was only in possession of a fifty pound banking card."

Raymond burst out laughing and slammed down the lid of the red box. "Do you know why I love you?"

"My taste in men's clothes?" suggested Kate.

"No, no. Just your taste in men."

"I always thought that mistresses were supposed to get fur coats, trips to the Bahamas, the odd solitaire diamond, yet all I ever get is to share you with your red box."

Raymond opened the box once more, took out a small package and handed it to Kate.

"What's this?"

"Why don't you open it and find out?"

Kate slipped off the purple Asprey paper and found inside

an exquisitely made miniature solid-gold replica of the red box on a gold chain. The neat lettering on the side of the lid read, "For Your Eyes Only."

"Although they don't announce the birthdays of Ministers' mistresses in the Sunday *Times,* I haven't forgotten the anniversary of the day we met."

19

ONCE THE CHANCELLOR had presented his budget, in November 1976, the long process of the Finance Bill, confirming all the new measures proposed, fully occupied the House. Charles, although not a member of the front-bench Finance team, regularly took the lead among backbenchers on clauses on which he had a specialist's knowledge.

He and Clive Reynolds studied the new Finance Bill meticulously and between them picked out the seven clauses that would have an adverse effect on banking.

Reynolds guided Charles through each clause, suggesting changes, rewording, and on some occasions presenting an argument for deleting whole sections of the bill. Charles learned quickly and was soon adding his own ideas; one or two made even Clive Reynolds reconsider. After Charles had put forward amendments to the House on three of the clauses, both front benches became respectfully attentive whenever he rose to present a case. One morning, after the Government's defeat on a clause relating to banking loans, he received a note of congratulation from Margaret Thatcher.

The clause Charles most wanted to see removed from the bill concerned a client's right to privacy when dealing with a merchant bank. The Shadow Chancellor was aware of Charles's specialized knowledge on this subject and invited him to speak out on Clause 110 from the front bench. Charles realized that if he could defeat the Government on this clause he might be invited to join the Shadow Finance team.

The Whips estimated that Clause 110 on banking privacy would be reached some time on Thursday afternoon. On Thursday morning Charles rehearsed his arguments thoroughly with Clive Reynolds, who had only one or two minor amendments to add before Charles set off for the House. When he arrived at the Commons there was a note on the message board asking him to phone the Shadow Chancellor immediately.

"The Government is going to accept a Liberal amendment tabled late last night," the Shadow Chancellor told him.

"Why?" said Charles.

"Minimum change is what they're really after, but it gets them off the hook and at the same time keeps the Liberal vote intact. In essence, nothing of substance has changed, but you'll need to study the wording carefully. Can I leave you to handle the problem?"

"Certainly," said Charles, pleased with the responsibility with which they were now entrusting him.

He walked down the long corridor to the vote office and picked up the sheet with Clause 110 on it and the proposed Liberal amendment. He read them both through half a dozen times before he started to make notes. Parliamentary counsel, with their usual expertise, had produced an ingenious amendment. Charles ducked into a nearby phone booth and rang Clive Reynolds at the bank. Charles dictated the amendment over the phone to him and then remained silent for a moment while Reynolds considered its implications.

"Clever bunch of sharpies. It's a cosmetic job, but it won't change the power it invests in the Government one iota. Were you thinking of returning to the bank? That would give me time to work on it."

"No," said Charles. "Are you free for lunch?"

Clive Reynolds checked his diary. A Belgian banker would

237

be lunching in the boardroom but his colleagues could handle that. "Yes, I'm free."

"Good," said Charles. "Why don't you join me at White's around one o'clock?"

"Thank you," said Reynolds. "By then I should have had enough time to come up with some credible alternatives."

Charles spent the rest of the morning rewriting his speech, which he hoped would counter the Labour argument and make them reconsider their position. If it met with Reynolds's imprimatur, the day could still be his. He read through the clause once more, convinced he had found a way through the loophole the civil servants couldn't block. He placed his speech and the amended clause in his inside pocket, went down to the members' entrance and jumped into a waiting taxi.

As the cab drove up St. James's, Charles thought he saw his wife coming down the opposite side of the road. He rolled down the window to be sure, but she had disappeared into Prunier's. He wondered with which of her girlfriends she was lunching. The cab traveled on up St. James's and came to a halt outside White's.

Charles found he was a few minutes early so he decided to walk down to Prunier's and ask Fiona if she would like to come to the House after lunch and hear him oppose the finance clause. Reaching the restaurant, he glanced through the window. Charles froze on the spot. Fiona was chatting at the bar with a man whose back was to Charles, but he thought he recognized his profile. Charles noticed that his wife was wearing a dress he had never seen before. He didn't move as he watched a waiter bow, then guide the pair toward a corner table where they were conveniently out of sight. Charles's first instinct was to march straight in and confront them, but he held himself in check.

For what seemed a long time he stood alone, uncertain what to do next. Finally he crossed back over to St. James's and stood in the doorway of the Economist Building going over several

238

plans. In the end he decided to do nothing but wait. He stood there so cold and so incensed that he totally forgot about his lunch appointment with Clive Reynolds a few hundred yards up the road.

An hour and twenty minutes later the man came out of Prunier's alone and headed up St. James's. Charles felt a sense of relief until he saw him turn into St. James's Place. A few minutes later Fiona stepped out of the restaurant and followed in the man's footsteps. Charles crossed the road, causing one cab to swerve while another motorist slammed on her brakes. He didn't notice. He shadowed his wife, careful to keep a safe distance. When she reached the far end of the street he watched Fiona enter the Stafford Hotel. Once she was through the revolving doors Fiona stepped into an empty elevator.

Charles came up to the revolving doors and stared at the little numbers above the elevator, watching them light up in succession until they stopped at four.

Charles marched through the revolving doors and up to the reception desk.

"Can I help you, sir?" the hall porter asked.

"Er—is the dining room in this hotel on the fourth floor?" asked Charles.

"No, sir," replied the hall porter, surprised. "The dining room is on the ground floor to your left." He indicated the way with a sweep of his hand. "There are only bedrooms on the fourth floor."

"Thank you," said Charles and marched back outside.

He returned slowly to the Economist Building, where he waited for nearly two hours pacing up and down St. James's Place before the man emerged from the Stafford Hotel. Alexander Dalglish hailed a taxi and disappeared in the direction of Piccadilly.

Fiona left the hotel about twenty minutes later and took the path through the park before setting off toward Eaton Square. On three occasions Charles had to fall back to be certain Fiona didn't spot him; once he was so close he thought he saw a smile of satisfaction on her face.

He had followed his wife most of the way across St. James's Park when he suddenly remembered. He checked his watch, then dashed back to the roadside, hailed a taxi and shouted, "The House of Commons, as fast as you can." The cabby took seven minutes and Charles passed him two pound notes before running up the steps into the members' lobby and through to the chamber out of breath. He stopped by the sergeant-at-arms's chair.

From the table where he sat during committee of the whole House, the chairman of Ways and Means faced a packed House. He read from the division list.

THE AYES TO THE RIGHT,   294
THE NOS TO THE LEFT,   293
THE AYES HAVE IT, THE AYES HAVE IT.

The Government benches cheered and the Conservatives looked distinctly glum. "What clause were they debating?" a still out-of-breath Charles asked the sergeant-at-arms.

"Clause One hundred and Ten, Mr. Hampton."

Simon was in Manchester as a guest of the business school when he received Elizabeth's message to call her. It was most unusual for Elizabeth to phone in the middle of the day and Simon assumed the worst. Something must have happened to the children. The principal of the business school accompanied Simon to his private office, then left him alone.

Doctor Kerslake was not at the hospital, he was told, which made him even more anxious. He dialed the Beaufort Street number.

Elizabeth picked up the receiver so quickly that she must have been sitting by the phone waiting for him to call.

"I've lost my job," she said.

"What?" said Simon, unable to comprehend.

"I've been made redundant—isn't that the modern term meant to lessen the blow? The hospital governors have been instructed by the Department of Health and Social Security to make cutbacks, and three of us in gynecology have lost our jobs. I go at the end of the month."

"Darling, I'm sorry," he said, knowing how inadequate his words must sound.

"I didn't mean to bother you, but I just wanted someone to talk to," she said. "Everyone else is allowed to complain to their MP, so I thought it was my turn."

"Normally what I do in these circumstances is to put the blame on the Labour Party." Simon was relieved to hear Elizabeth laugh.

"Thanks for ringing me back so quickly, darling. See you tomorrow," she said and put the phone down.

Simon returned to his group and explained that he had to leave for London immediately. He took a taxi to the airport and caught the next shuttle to Heathrow. He was back at Beaufort Street within three hours.

"I didn't want you to come home," Elizabeth said contritely when she saw him on the doorstep.

"I've come back to celebrate," Simon said. "Let's open the bottle of champagne that Ronnie gave us when he closed the deal with Morgan Grenfell."

"Why?"

"Because Ronnie taught me one thing. You should always celebrate disasters, not successes."

Simon hung up his coat and went off in search of the champagne. When he returned with the bottle and two glasses Elizabeth asked, "What's your overdraft looking like nowadays?"

"Down to sixteen thousand pounds, give or take a pound."

"Well, that's another problem then—I won't be giving any pounds in the future, only taking."

Simon embraced his wife. "Don't be silly. Someone will snap you up."

"It won't be quite that easy," said Elizabeth.

"Why not?" asked Simon, trying to sound cheerful.

"Because I had already been warned about whether I wanted to be a politician's wife or a doctor."

Simon was stunned. "I had no idea," he said. "I'm so sorry."

"It was my choice, darling, but I will have to make one or two decisions if I want to remain in medicine, especially if you're going to become a Minister."

"You mustn't be allowed to give up being a doctor. It's every bit as important as wanting to be a Minister. Shall I have a word with Gerry Vaughan? As Shadow Minister of Health he might—"

"Certainly not, Simon. If I am to get another job, it'll be without anyone doing you or me a favor."

Raymond's first trip to the States was at the behest of the Secretary of State for Trade. He was asked to present the country's export and import assessment to the International Monetary Fund, following up a loan granted to Britain the previous November. His civil servants went over the prepared speech with him again and again, emphasizing to their Minister the responsibility that had been placed on his shoulders.

Raymond's speech was scheduled for Wednesday morning. He flew into Washington on the Sunday before and spent Monday and Tuesday listening to the problems of other nations' trade ministers while trying to get used to the dreadful earphones and the female interpreters.

The night before he was to deliver his speech, Raymond hardly slept. He continued to rehearse each crucial phrase and repeated the salient points that needed to be emphasized until he almost knew them by heart. At three o'clock in the morning he dropped his speech on the floor beside his bed and phoned Kate to have a chat before she went to work.

"I'd enjoy hearing your speech at the conference," she told him. "Although I don't suppose it would be much different from the thirty times I've listened to it in the bedroom."

All the homework and preparation proved to be worthwhile. By the time he turned the last page Raymond couldn't be certain how convincing his case had been, but he knew it was the best speech he had ever delivered. When he looked up, the smiles all around the oval table assured him that his contribution had been a triumph. As the British ambassador pointed out to him when he rose to leave, any signs of emotion at these gatherings were almost unknown.

At the end of the afternoon sessions Raymond walked out into the clear Washington air and decided to make his way back to the Embassy on foot. He was exhilarated by the experience of dominating an international conference. He quickened his pace. Just the closing day to go, followed by the official banquet, and he would be back home by the weekend.

When he reached the Embassy the guard had to double-check: they weren't used to Ministers arriving on foot and without a bodyguard. Raymond was allowed to proceed down the tree-lined drive toward the massive Lutyens Building. He looked up to see the British flag flying at half-mast and wondered which distinguished American had died.

"Who has died?" he asked the tailcoated butler who opened the door for him.

"One of your countrymen, sir, I'm sorry to say. The Foreign Secretary."

"Anthony Crosland? But I had lunch with him only last week," said Raymond. He hurried into the Embassy to find it abuzz with telexes and messages.

Raymond sat alone in his room for several hours and later, to the horror of the security staff, slipped out for a solitary dinner at the Mayflower Hotel.

Raymond returned to the conference table at nine o'clock the next morning to hear the closing speeches. He was savoring the thought of the official banquet at the White House to be held that evening when he was tapped on the shoulder by Sir Peter Ramsbotham, who indicated they must have a word in private.

"The Prime Minister wants you to return on the mid-morning Concorde," said Sir Peter. "It leaves in an hour. On arrival in Britain you're to go straight to Downing Street."

"What's this all about?"

"I have no idea. That's the only instruction I've received from Number Ten," confided the ambassador.

Raymond returned to the conference table and made his apologies to the chairman, left the room and was driven immediately to the waiting plane. "Your bags will follow, sir," he was assured.

He was back on English soil three hours and forty-one minutes later. The purser ensured that he was the first to disembark. A car waiting by the side of the plane whisked him to Downing Street. He arrived just as the Prime Minister was going into dinner accompanied by an elderly African statesman.

"Welcome home, Ray," said the Prime Minister, leaving the African leader. "I'd ask you to join us, but as you can see I'm tied up here. Let's have a word in my study."

Once Raymond had settled into a chair opposite the Prime Minister, Mr. Callaghan wasted no time. "Because of Tony's tragic death, I have had to make a few changes which will include moving the Secretary of State for Trade. I was hoping you would be willing to take over from him."

Raymond sat up straighter. "I should be honored, Prime Minister."

"Good. You've earned the promotion, Raymond. I also hear you did us proud in America, very proud."

"Thank you."

"You'll be appointed to the Privy Council immediately and your first Cabinet meeting will be at ten o'clock tomorrow morning. Now if you'll excuse me, I must catch up with Dr. Banda."

Raymond was left standing in the hall.

He asked his driver to take him back to the flat. On the journey he reflected with satisfaction that he was the first from his intake to be made a Cabinet Minister. All he wanted to do was to tell Kate the news. When he arrived, the flat was empty; then he remembered she wasn't expecting him back until the next day. He phoned her home, but after twenty continuous rings he resigned himself to the fact that she was out.

"Damn," he said out loud and after pacing around phoned Joyce to let her know the news. Once again there was no reply.

He went into the kitchen and checked to see what was in the fridge: a piece of curled-up bacon, some half-eaten Brie and three eggs. He couldn't help thinking about the banquet he was missing at the White House.

The Right Honorable Raymond Gould, QC, MP, Her Britannic Majesty's Principal Secretary of State for Trade, sat on the kitchen stool, opened a tin of baked beans and devoured them with a fork.

PART FOUR

The Labour Cabinet

1977-1978

20

CHARLES CLOSED THE FILE. It had taken him a month to gather all the proof he needed. Albert Cruddick, the private investigator Charles had selected from the yellow pages, had been expensive but discreet. Dates, times, places were all fully chronicled. The only name was that of Alexander Dalglish, the same rendezvous, lunch at Prunier's followed by the Stafford Hotel. They hadn't stretched Mr. Cruddick's imagination, but at least the private detective had spared Charles the necessity of standing in the entrance of the Economist Building once, sometimes twice a week, for hours on end.

Somehow he had managed to get through that month without giving himself away. He had also made his own notes of the dates and times Fiona claimed she was going to be in the constituency. He had then called his campaign manager in Sussex Downs and, after veiled questioning, elicited answers that corroborated Mr. Cruddick's findings.

Charles saw as little of Fiona as possible during this time, explaining that the Finance Bill was occupying his every moment. His lie had at least a semblance of credibility for he had worked tirelessly on the remaining clauses left for debate, and by the time the watered-down bill had become law he had just about recovered from the disaster of the Government's successful retention of Clause 110.

Charles placed the file on the table by the side of his chair and waited patiently for the call. He knew exactly where she was at that moment and just the thought of it made him sick to his stomach. The phone rang.

"The subject left five minutes ago," said a voice.

"Thank you," said Charles and replaced the receiver. He knew it would take her about twenty minutes to reach home.

"Why do you think she walks home instead of taking a taxi?" he had once asked Mr. Cruddick.

"Gets rid of any smells," Mr. Cruddick had replied quite matter-of-factly.

Charles shuddered. "And what about him? What does he do?" He never could refer to him as Alexander, or even Dalglish—never as anything but "him."

"He goes to the Lansdowne Club, swims ten lengths or plays a game of squash before returning home. Swimming and squash both solve the problem," Mr. Cruddick explained cheerily.

The key turned in the lock. Charles braced himself and picked up the file. Fiona came straight into the drawing room and was visibly shaken to discover her husband sitting in an armchair with a small suitcase by his side.

She recovered quickly, walked over and kissed him on the cheek. "What brings you home so early, darling? The Labourites taken the day off?" She laughed nervously at her joke.

"This," he said, standing up and holding the file out to her.

She took off her coat and dropped it over the sofa. Then she opened the buff folder and started to read. He watched her carefully. First the color drained from her cheeks, then her legs gave way and she collapsed onto the sofa. Finally she started to sob.

"It's not true, none of it," she protested.

"You know very well that every detail is accurate."

"Charles, it's you I love, I don't care about him, you must believe that."

"You're no longer someone I could live with," said Charles.

"Live with? I've been living on my own since the day you entered Parliament."

"Perhaps I might have come home more often if you had shown some interest in starting a family."

"And do you imagine I am to blame?" she said.

Charles ignored the comment and continued. "In a few moments I am going to my club, where I shall spend the night. I expect you to be out of this house within seven days. When I return I want there to be no sign of you or any of your goods or chattels, to quote the original agreement."

"Where will I go?" she cried.

"You could try your lover first, but no doubt his wife might object. Failing that, you can camp at your father's place."

"What if I refuse to go?" said Fiona, turning to defiance.

"Then I shall throw you out, as one should a whore, and cite Alexander Dalglish in a very messy divorce case."

"Give me another chance. I'll never look at him again," begged Fiona, starting to cry once more.

"I seem to remember your telling me that once before, and indeed I did give you another chance. The results have been all too plain to see." He pointed to the file where it had fallen to the floor.

Fiona stopped weeping when she realized that Charles remained unmoved.

"I shall not see you again. We shall be separated for at least two years, when we will carry through as quiet a divorce as possible in the circumstances. If you cause me any embarrassment I shall drag you both through the mire. Believe me."

"You'll regret your decision, Charles. I promise you'll regret it."

She knew she had to plan the whole operation so that her husband would never find out. She sat alone in the house considering the several alternative ways in which she could deceive

251

him. After hours of unproductive thought the idea finally came in a flash. She went over the problems and repercussions again and again until she was convinced that nothing could go wrong. She leafed through the Yellow Pages and made an appointment for the next morning.

The saleslady helped her to try on several wigs, but only one was bearable.

"I think it makes madam look most elegant, I must say."

She knew that it didn't—it made madam look awful—but she hoped it would serve its purpose.

She then applied the eye makeup and lipstick she had acquired at Harrods, and pulled out from the back of her closet a floral print dress she had never liked. She stood in front of the mirror and checked herself. Surely one would recognize her in Sussex, and she prayed that if he found out he would be forgiving.

She left and drove slowly toward the outskirts of London. How would she explain herself if she was caught? Would he remain understanding when he discovered the truth? When she reached the constituency she parked the car in a side road and walked up and down the High Street. No one showed any sign of recognition, which gave her the confidence to go through with it. And then she saw him.

She had hoped he'd be in the city that morning. She held her breath as he walked toward her. As he passed she said, "Good morning." He turned and smiled, replying with a casual "Good morning," as he might to any constituent. Her heartbeat returned to normal and she went back to find her car.

She drove off completely reassured she could now get away with it. She went over once again what she was going to say. Then all too suddenly she had arrived. She parked the car outside the house opposite, got out and bravely walked up the path.

As Raymond stood outside the Cabinet room, several of his colleagues came over to congratulate him. At exactly ten o'clock the Prime Minister walked in, bade everyone good morning and took his place at the center of the oblong table, while the other twenty-one members of the Cabinet filed in behind him and took their seats. The Leader of the House, Michael Foot, sat on his left, while the Chancellor of the Exchequer and the Foreign Secretary were placed opposite him. Raymond was directed to a seat at the end of the table between the Secretary of State for Wales and the Minister for the Arts.

"I would like to start the meeting," said the Prime Minister, "by welcoming David Owen as Foreign Secretary and Raymond Gould as Secretary of State for Trade." The other twenty-one Cabinet members murmured "Hear, hear" in a discreetly conservative way. David Owen smiled slightly; Raymond lowered his eyes.

"Perhaps, Chancellor, you would be kind enough to start us off."

Raymond sat back and decided that today he would only listen.

When Charles returned home he knew at once Fiona had left. He felt an immediate sense of relief. After a week at his club, he was glad the charade was over, a clean, irrevocable break. He strolled into the drawing room and stopped: something was wrong. It took him a few moments before he realized what she had done.

Fiona had removed every one of the family paintings.

No Wellington above the fireplace, no Victoria behind the sofa. Where the two Turners and the Constable had hung, there were nothing more than thin dusty outlines indicating the size of each picture she had removed. He walked to the library: the Van Dyck, the Murillo and the two small Rembrandts were also missing. Charles ran down the hall. It couldn't be possible, he thought, as he threw open the dining-room door. It was. He stared at the blank wall where only the previous week the Holbein portrait of the first Earl of Bridgewater had hung.

Charles scrabbled in the back of his pocket diary for the

number and dialed it frantically. Mr. Cruddick listened to the story in silence.

"Remembering how sensitive you are about publicity, Mr. Hampton, there are two avenues of approach," he began in his normal level tone and sounding unperturbed. "You can grin and bear it, or the alternative is one I have used often in the past . . ."

Because of the demands of his new job Raymond saw less of Kate, and almost nothing of Joyce apart from his twice monthly visits to Leeds. He worked from eight in the morning until he fell asleep at night.

"And you love every minute of it," Kate reminded him whenever he complained. Raymond had also become aware of the subtle changes that had taken place in his life since he had become a member of the Cabinet—the way he was treated by other people, how quickly his slightest whim was granted, how flattery fell from almost every tongue. He began to enjoy the change in status, although Kate reminded him that only the Queen could afford to get used to it.

At the Party conference that year he was nominated for a place on the national executive board of the Labour Party. Although he failed to be elected, he managed to finish ahead of several other Cabinet Ministers and polled only a few votes less than Neil Kinnock, who was fast becoming the new darling of the unions.

Jamie Sinclair and he had what was becoming their traditional lunch together on the third day of the Party conference. Jamie told Raymond of his distress at the Party's continued drift to the left.

"If some of those resolutions on defense are passed, my life will be made impossible," he said, slicing into an end cut of roast beef.

"The hotheads always put up resolutions that are never allowed more than a token discussion."

"Token discussion be damned. Some of their mad ideas are beginning to gain credence, which, translated, could become Party policy."

"Any particular resolution worrying you?" asked Raymond.

"Yes, Tony Benn's latest proposal that members must be re-elected before every election. His idea of democracy and accountability."

"Why should you fear that?"

"If your management committee is taken over by half a dozen Reds they can reverse a decision fifty thousand voters have previously agreed on."

"You're overreacting, Jamie."

"Raymond, if we lose the next election I can see a split in the Party that will be so great we may never recover."

"They've been saying that in the Labour Party since the day it was founded."

"I hope you're right, but I fear times have changed," said Jamie. "Not so long ago it was you who envied me."

"That can change again." Raymond abandoned the beef, waved his hand and asked the waitress to bring two large brandies.

Charles picked up the phone and dialed a number he had not needed to look up. The new young Portuguese maid answered.

"Is Lady Fiona at home?"

"Lady no home, sir."

"Do you know where she is?" asked Charles, speaking slowly and clearly.

"Go down to country, expect back six o'clock. Take message please?"

"No, thank you," said Charles. "I'll call this evening." He replaced the receiver.

As always, the reliable Mr. Cruddick was proved right about Fiona's movements. Charles called him immediately. They agreed to meet as planned in twenty minutes.

He drove into the Boltons, parked on the far side of the road a few yards from his father-in-law's house and settled down to wait.

A few minutes later a large anonymous moving van came around the corner and stopped outside number 36. Mr. Cruddick jumped out from the driver's seat. He was dressed in long brown overalls and a flat cap. He was joined by a young assistant who unlocked the back of the van. Mr. Cruddick nodded to Charles before proceeding up the steps to the front door.

The Portuguese maid answered when he pressed the bell.

"We have come to collect the goods for Lady Hampton."

"No understand," said the maid.

Mr. Cruddick removed from an inside pocket a long typewritten letter on Lady Hampton's personal stationery. The Portuguese maid was unable to read the words of a letter her mistress had addressed to Hurlingham Croquet Club agreeing to be their Ladies' President, but she immediately recognized the letterhead and the signature, Fiona Hampton. She nodded and opened the door wider. All Mr. Cruddick's carefully laid plans were falling into place.

Mr. Cruddick tipped his hat, the sign for Mr. Hampton to join them. Charles got out of the car cautiously, checking both ways before he crossed the road. He felt uncomfortable in brown overalls, and he hated the cap Mr. Cruddick had supplied for him. It was a little small and Charles was acutely conscious how strange he must look, but the Portuguese maid apparently didn't notice the incongruity between his aristocratic mien and his workingman's overalls. It did not take long to discover the whereabouts of the paintings. Many were stacked up in the hall, and only one or two had already been hung.

Forty minutes later the three men had located and loaded in the van all but one of them. The Holbein portrait of the first Earl of Bridgewater was nowhere to be found.

"We ought to be on our way," suggested Mr. Cruddick a little nervously, but Charles refused to give up the search. For another thirty-five minutes Mr. Cruddick sat tapping the wheel of the van before Charles finally conceded that the painting must have been taken elsewhere. Mr. Cruddick tipped his hat to the maid while his partner locked up the back of the van.

"A valuable picture, Mr. Hampton?" he inquired.

"A family heirloom that would fetch two million at auction," said Charles matter-of-factly before returning to his car.

"Silly question, Albert Cruddick," said Mr. Cruddick to himself as he pulled out from the curb and drove toward Eaton Square. When they arrived, the locksmith had replaced all three locks on the front door and was waiting on the top step impatiently.

"Strictly cash, guv'nor. No receipt. Makes it possible for the missus and me to go to Ibiza each year, tax free."

By the time Fiona had returned to the Boltons from her trip to Sussex, every picture was back in its place at Eaton Square with the exception of Holbein's first Earl of Bridgewater. Mr. Cruddick had left clutching a large check and uttering the mollifying view that Mr. Hampton would probably have to grin and bear it.

"I'm delighted," said Simon, when he heard the news. "And at Pucklebridge General Hospital?"

"Yes, I answered an advertisement in the medical journal for the post of general consultant in the maternity section."

"Our name must have helped there."

"Certainly not," said Elizabeth vehemently.

"How come?"

"I didn't apply as Dr. Kerslake. I filled out the application form in my maiden name of Drummond."

Simon was momentarily silenced. "But they would have recognized you," he protested.

"I had the full frontal treatment from Estée Lauder to insure they didn't. The final effect fooled even you."

"Don't exaggerate," said Simon.

"I walked straight past you in Pucklebridge High Street, and said 'Good morning,' and you returned the greeting."

Simon stared at her in disbelief. "But what will happen when they find out?"

"They already have," replied Elizabeth sheepishly. "As soon as they offered me the post I went down to see the senior consultant and told him the truth. He hasn't stopped telling everyone since."

"He wasn't cross?"

"Far from it. In fact, he said I nearly failed to be offered the post because he felt I wouldn't be safe let loose on the unmarried doctors."

"What about this married politician?"

21

WHEN QUEEN ELIZABETH II opened the new underground extension to Heathrow Airport on December 16, 1977, Raymond was the Minister commanded to be present. Joyce made one of her rare trips down to London, as they were invited to join the Queen for lunch after the ceremony.

When Joyce selected her new dress from Marks and Spencer, she stood in the little cubicle behind a drawn curtain to make sure it was possible for her to curtsey properly. "Good morning, Your Majesty," she practiced with a slight wobble, to the bemusement of the shop assistant waiting patiently outside.

By the time she had returned to the flat, Joyce was confident that she could carry out her part in the proceedings as well as any courtier. As she prepared for Raymond's return from the morning Cabinet meeting, she hoped he would be pleased with her efforts. She had given up any hope of being a mother, but she still wanted him to believe she was a good wife.

Raymond had forewarned her that he would have to change as soon as he arrived at the flat to be sure of being at Green Park before the Queen arrived. After they had accompanied an entourage to Heathrow on the new extension, a journey that would take thirty minutes, they were to return to Buckingham Palace for lunch. Raymond had already come in contact with his monarch on several occasions in his official capacity as a

Cabinet Minister, but for Joyce it was to be the first time she had been presented.

Once she had had her bath and dressed—she knew Raymond would never forgive her if she made him late—she began to lay out his clothes. Tailcoat, gray pinstriped trousers, white shirt, stiff collar and a silver-gray tie, all hired that morning from Moss Brothers. All that he still needed was a clean white handkerchief for his top pocket, just showing in a straight line, like the Duke of Edinburgh always wore his.

Joyce rummaged around in Raymond's chest of drawers, admiring his new shirts as she searched for a handkerchief. When she first saw the scribbled note peeking out of the breast pocket of a pink shirt lying near the bottom of the pile, she assumed it must be an old cleaning bill. Then she spotted the word "Darling." She felt suddenly sick as she looked more closely.

> *Darling Red,*
> *If you ever wear this one I might even agree to marry you.*
>
> *KATE*

Joyce sank on the end of the bed as the tears trickled down her face. Her perfect day was shattered. She knew at once what course of action she must take. She replaced the shirt and closed the drawer, after first removing the note, and then sat alone in the drawing room waiting for Raymond to return.

He arrived back at the flat with only a few minutes to spare and was delighted to find his wife changed and ready.

"I'm running it a bit close," he said, going straight into the bedroom.

Joyce followed and watched him don his morning-dress suit. When he had straightened his tie in the mirror, she faced him.

"What do you think?" he asked, not noticing the slight paleness in her cheeks.

She hesitated. "You look fantastic, Raymond. Now come along or we'll be late, and that would never do."

In 1978, the House passed a resolution allowing the proceedings in the Commons to be broadcast on the radio.

Simon had supported the motion on broadcasting, putting forward the argument that radio was a further extension of democracy, as it showed the House at work and allowed the voters to know exactly what their elected representatives were up to. Simon listened carefully to a number of his supplementary questions and realized for the first time that he had spoke a little too quickly when he had a Minister on the run.

Raymond, on the other hand, did not support the motion, as he suspected that the cries of "Hear, hear," and the heckling of the Prime Minister would sound to listeners like schoolchildren in a playground squabble. Overhearing the words with only one's imagination to set the scene would, he believed, create a false impression about the many aspects of a member's daily duties. When one evening Raymond heard a parliamentary debate in which he had taken part, he was delighted to discover that the force of his arguments carried so much conviction.

Charles found the morning program an excellent way of catching up with any proceedings he missed the previous day. As he now woke each morning alone, "Yesterday in Parliament" became his constant companion. He hadn't been aware how upper class he sounded until the time he followed Tom Carson. He had no intention of changing for the radio.

When Ronnie Nethercote invited him to lunch at the Ritz, Simon knew things must be looking up again. After a drink in the lounge, they were ushered to a corner table overlooking the park in the most palatial dining room in London. Scattered around the other tables were men who were household names in Ronnie's world as well as in Simon's.

When the head waiter offered them menus Ronnie waved his hand and said, "Order the country vegetable soup, followed by beef off the trolley, take my word for it."

"Sounds like a safe bet," said Simon.

261

"Unlike our last little venture." Ronnie grunted. "How much are you still in hock because of the collapse of Nethercote and Company?"

"Fourteen thousand three hundred pounds when I last looked, but I'm making inroads slowly. It's paying the interest before you can cut down on the capital that really hurts."

"How do you imagine I felt when we were overdrawn seven mill, and then the bank decided to pull the rug from under my feet without any warning?"

"As two of the buttons on your waistcoat can no longer reach the holes they were originally tailored for, Ronnie, I must assume those problems are now a thing of the past."

"You're right." He laughed. "Which is why I invited you to lunch. The only person who ended up losing money on that deal was you. If you'd stayed on as the other directors did, with your whack of five grand a year the company would still owe you eleven thousand pounds of earned income."

Simon groaned.

The carver wheeled the trolley of beef up to their table.

"Wait a moment, my boy, I haven't even begun. Morgan Grenfell wants me to change the structure of the new company and will be injecting a large amount of cash. At the moment Whitechapel Properties—I hope you approve of the name—is still a one-hundred-pound off-the-shelf company. I own sixty percent and the bank's got forty. Now before the new agreement is signed, I'm going to offer you—"

"Would you like it well done, as usual, Mr. Nethercote?"

"Yes, Sam," said Ronnie, slipping the carver a pound note.

"I am going to offer you—"

"And your guest, sir?" the carver said, glancing at Simon.

"Medium, please."

"Yes, sir."

"I am going to offer you one percent of the new company, in other words one share."

Simon didn't comment, feeling confident Ronnie still hadn't finished.

262

"Aren't you going to ask?" said Ronnie.

"Ask what?" said Simon.

"You politicians get dumber by the minute. If I am going to offer you a share, how much do you think I am going to demand in return?"

"Well, I can't believe it's going to be one pound," said Simon grinning.

"Wrong," said Ronnie. "One percent of the company is yours for one pound."

"Will that be sufficient, sir?" said the carver, putting a plate of beef in front of Simon.

"Hold it, Sam," said Ronnie before Simon could reply. "I repeat I'm offering you one percent of the company for one pound; now ask your question again, Sam."

"Will that be sufficient, sir?" repeated the carver.

"It's most generous," said Simon.

"Did you hear that, Sam?"

"I certainly did, sir."

"Right, Simon, you owe me a pound."

Simon laughed, removed his wallet from his inside pocket, took out a pound note and handed it over.

"Now the purpose of that little exercise," said Ronnie, turning back to the carver and pocketing the note, "was to prove that Sam here isn't the only person who could make a quid for himself this afternoon." Sam smiled, having no idea what Mr. Nethercote was talking about, and placed a large plate of well-done beef in front of him.

Ronnie took out an envelope from his inside pocket and passed it to Simon.

"Do I open it now?" asked Simon.

"Yes—I want to see your reaction."

Simon opened the envelope and studied its contents: a certificate for one share in the new company with a true value of over ten thousand pounds.

"Well, well, what do you say?" asked Ronnie.

"I'm speechless," said Simon.

"First politician I've known who's ever suffered from that problem."

Simon laughed. "Thank you, Ronnie. It's an incredibly generous gesture."

"No it's not. You were loyal to the old company—so why shouldn't you prosper with the new one?"

"That reminds me, does the name Archie Millburn mean anything to you?" Simon asked suddenly.

Ronnie hesitated. "No, no, should it?"

"Only that I thought he might be the man who convinced Morgan Grenfell that you were worth bailing out."

"No, that name doesn't ring any bells with me. Mind you, Morgan Grenfell has never admitted where they obtained their information from, but they knew every last detail about the old company. But if I come across the name Millburn I'll let you know. Enough of business. Fill me in on what's happening in your world. How's your lady wife?"

"Deceiving me."

"Deceiving you?"

"Yes, she's been putting on wigs and dressing up in strange clothes."

Finally, Charles knew he had to discuss with his lawyer, Sir David Napley, what could be done about the stolen Holbein. Six weeks and eight hundred pounds later, he was told that if he sued, the Holbein might eventually be returned, but not before the episode had been on the front page of every newspaper. Charles had Albert Cruddick's opinion confirmed: "Grin and bear it."

Fiona had been out of touch for well over a year when the letter came. Charles immediately recognized her hand and ripped open the envelope. Only one glance at her handwriting was enough to make him tear up the missive and deposit the little pieces in the wastepaper basket by his desk. He left for the Commons in a rage.

All through the day he thought of the one word he had taken in from the scrawled words: Holbein. When Charles returned from the Commons after the ten o'clock division, he searched for the remains of the letter, which the cleaning woman had conscientiously deposited in the dustbin. After rummaging among potato peelings, eggshells, and empty cans Charles spent over an hour taping the little pieces of paper together. Then he read the letter carefully.

> *36 The Boltons*
> *London SW10*
> *October 11, 1978*

> *Dear Charles,*
> *Enough time has now passed for us to try and treat each other in a civilized way. Alexander and I wish to marry and Veronica Dalglish has agreed to an immediate divorce and has not insisted we wait two years to establish legal separation.*

"You'll have to wait every day of statutory two years, you bitch," he said out loud. Then he came to the one sentence for which he was searching.

> *I realize this might not immediately appeal to you, but if you feel able to fall in with our plans I would be happy to return the Holbein immediately.*
> *Yours ever,*
> *FIONA.*

He crumpled up the paper in the ball of his hand before dropping it on the fire.

Charles remained awake into the early hours considering his reply.

The Labour Government struggled on toward the Christmas of 1978 through a session dubbed by the press as "The Winter of

Discontent." Trying to get bills through the House, losing a clause here and a clause there, it was only too delighted to reach the recess in one piece.

Raymond spent a cold Christmas in Leeds with Joyce. He returned to London early in the new year sadly aware it could not be long before the Conservatives felt assured enough to call for a vote of no confidence in the Labour Government.

The debate, when it came, caused a day of intense excitement, not least because a strike had caused the Commons bars to run dry, and thirsty members were huddled together in the lobbies, the tearoom, the smoking room and the dining rooms. Harassed whips rushed hither and thither checking lists, ringing up hospitals, boardrooms and even great-aunts in their efforts to track down the last few elusive members.

When Mrs. Thatcher rose on April seventh to address a packed House the tension was so electric that the Speaker had considerable difficulty keeping control. She addressed the House in firm, strident tones which brought her own side to their feet when she resumed her place. The atmosphere was no different when it was the turn of the Prime Minister to reply. Both Leaders made a gallant effort to rise above the petulance of their adversaries but it was the Speaker who had the last word:

THE AYES TO THE RIGHT 311
THE NOS TO THE LEFT 310
THE AYES HAVE IT, THE AYES HAVE IT.

Pandemonium broke out. Opposition members waved their agenda papers in triumph, knowing that James Callaghan would now have to call a General Election. He immediately announced the dissolution of Parliament, and after an audience with the Queen, Election Day was set for May 3, 1979.

At the end of that momentous week, those few members left at Westminster were stunned by an explosion in the members' parking lot. Airey Neave, the Shadow spokesman on Northern

Ireland, had been blown up by Irish terrorists as he was driving up the exit ramp to leave the Commons. He died on the way to the hospital.

Members hurried back to their constituencies. Raymond found it hard to escape from his department at such short notice, but Charles and Simon were out in their respective High Streets shaking hands with the voters by the morning following the Queen's proclamation.

For three weeks the arguments about who was competent to govern went back and forth, but on May 3 the British people elected their first woman Prime Minister and gave her party a comfortable majority of forty-three in the Commons.

Raymond's vote in Leeds was slightly reduced, while Joyce won the office pool for predicting most accurately what her husband's majority would be. He was beginning to realize that she knew more about the constituency than he ever would.

A few days later, when Raymond returned to London, Kate had never seen him so depressed, and decided to hold off telling him her own news once he said, "God knows how many years it will be before I can be of some use again."

"You can spend your time in Opposition making sure the Government doesn't dismantle all your achievements."

"With a majority of forty-three they could dismantle me if they wanted to," he told her. He placed the red leather box marked "Secretary of State for Trade" in the corner, next to the ones marked "Minister of State at the Department of Trade" and "Parliamentary Under Secretary at the Department of Employment."

"They're only your first three," Kate tried to reassure him.

Simon increased his majority at Pucklebridge to 19,461, notching up another record, after which he and Elizabeth spent the weekend in their cottage with the children, waiting for Mrs. Thatcher to select her team.

Simon was surprised when the Prime Minister phoned personally and asked if he could come up to see her in Downing Street: that was an honor usually afforded only to Cabinet Ministers. He tried not to anticipate what she might have in mind.

He duly traveled up from the country and spent thirty minutes alone with the new Prime Minister. When he heard what Mrs. Thatcher wanted him to do, he was impressed that she had taken the trouble to see him in person. She knew that no member ever found it easy to accede to such a request but Simon accepted without hesitation. Mrs. Thatcher added that no announcement would be made until he had had time to talk his decision over with Elizabeth. Simon was touched by her personal consideration.

Simon thanked her and traveled back to his cottage in Pucklebridge. Elizabeth sat in silence as she listened to Simon's account of his conversation with the Prime Minister.

"Oh, my God," she said, when he had finished. "She offered you the chance to be Minister of State, but in return we'll have no certainty of peace for the rest of our lives."

"I can still say no," Simon assured her.

"That would be the act of a coward," said Elizabeth, "and you've never been that."

"Then I'll phone the Prime Minister and tell her I accept."

"I ought to congratulate you," she said. "But it never crossed my mind for one moment. . . ."

Charles's was one of the few Tory seats in which the majority went down. A missing wife is hard to explain, especially when it is common knowledge that she is living with the former chairman of the adjoining constituency.

Charles had faced a certain degree of embarrassment with his local committee and he made sure that the one woman who couldn't keep her mouth shut was told his version of the story "in strictest confidence." Any talk of removing him had died when it was rumored that Charles would stand as an independent candidate if replaced.

When the vote was counted, Sussex Downs still returned Charles to Westminster with a majority of 20,176. He sat alone in Eaton Square over the weekend, but no one contacted him. He read in the Monday *Telegraph* the full composition of the new Tory team.

The only surprise was Simon Kerslake's appointment as Minister of State for Northern Ireland.

22

"WELL, SAY SOMETHING."

"Very flattering, Kate. What reason did you give for turning the offer down?" asked Raymond, who had been surprised to find her waiting for him at the flat.

"I didn't need a reason."

"How did they feel about that?"

"You don't seem to understand. I accepted their offer."

Raymond removed his glasses and tried to take in what Kate was saying. He steadied himself by holding on to the mantelpiece.

Kate continued. "I had to, darling."

"Because the offer was too tempting?"

"No, you silly man. It had nothing to do with the offer as such, but it gives me the chance to stop letting my life drift. Can't you see it was *because* of you?"

"Because of me you're going to leave London and go back to New York?"

"To work in New York and start getting my life in perspective. Raymond, don't you realize it's been five years?"

"I know how long it is and how many times I've asked you to marry me."

"We both know that isn't the answer; Joyce can't be brushed aside that easily. And it might even end up being the single reason you fail in your career."

"Given time, we can overcome that problem," Raymond reasoned.

"That sounds fine now, until the Party wins the next election and lesser men than you are offered the chance to shape future policy."

"Can't I do anything to make you change your mind?"

"Nothing, my darling. I've handed Chase my resignation and begin my new job with Chemical Bank in a month."

"Only four weeks," said Raymond.

"Yes, four weeks. I had to hold off telling you until I had severed all the bonds, had resigned and could be sure of not letting you talk me out of it."

"Do you know how much I love you?"

"I hope enough to let me go before it's too late."

Charles would not normally have accepted the invitation. Lately he had found cocktail parties to consist of nothing but silly little bits of food, never being able to get the right drink and rarely enjoying the trivial conversation. But when he glanced on his mantelpiece and saw an invitation from Lord Carrington, the Foreign Secretary, he felt it might be an amusing break from the routine he had fallen into since Fiona had left. He was also keen to discover more about the rumored squabbles in the Cabinet over expenditure cuts. Charles checked his tie in the mirror, removed an umbrella from the hat stand and left Eaton Square for Ovington Square.

He and Fiona had been apart for nearly two years. Charles had heard from several sources that his wife had now moved in with Dalglish on a permanent basis despite his unwillingness to co-operate in a divorce. He had remained discreetly silent on his wife's new life except for one or two tidbits he dropped selectively in the ears of well-chosen gossips. That way he had elicited for himself sympathy from every quarter while remaining the magnanimous loyal husband.

Charles had spent almost all of his spare time in the Commons, and his most recent budget speech had been well received by both the House and the national press. During the committee stage of the Finance Bill he had allowed himself to be burdened with a lot of the donkey work. Clive Reynolds had been able to point out discrepancies in some clauses of the bill, which Charles passed on to a grateful Chancellor. Then Charles received praise for saving the Government from any unnecessary embarrassment. At the same time, he disassociated himself from the "wets" as the Prime Minister referred to those of her colleagues who did not unreservedly support her monetarist policies. If he could keep up his work output, he was confident he would be preferred in the first reshuffle.

By spending his mornings at the bank and his afternoons and evenings in the Commons, Charles managed to combine both worlds with minimum interruption from his almost nonexistent private life.

He arrived at Lord Carrington's front door a little after six forty-five. A maid answered his knock, and he walked straight through to a drawing room that could have held fifty guests and very nearly did.

He even managed to be served with the right blend of whiskey before joining his colleagues from both the Upper and Lower Houses. He saw her first over the top of Alec Pimkin's balding head.

"Who is she?" asked Charles, not expecting Pimkin to know.

"Amanda Wallace," said Pimkin, glancing over his shoulder. "I could tell you a thing or two . . ." But Charles had already left his colleague in mid-sentence. The sexuality of the woman was attested to by the fact that she spent the entire evening surrounded by attentive men like moths around a candle. If Charles had not been one of the tallest men in the room he might never have seen the flame.

It took him another ten minutes to reach her side of the room, where Julian Ridsdale, a colleague of Charles's in the Commons, introduced them, only to be dragged away moments later by his wife.

Charles was left staring at a woman who would have looked

272

beautiful in anything from a ballgown to a towel. Her slim body was encased in a white silk dress, and her fair hair touched her bare shoulders. It had been years since he had found it so hard to make conversation.

"I expect you already have a dinner engagement?" Charles asked her in the brief interval before the vultures closed in again.

"No," she replied and smiled encouragingly. She agreed to meet him at Walton's in an hour's time. Charles dutifully began to circulate around the room, but it was not long before he found his eyes drawn back to her. Every time she smiled, he found himself responding, but Amanda didn't notice because she was always being flattered by someone else. When he left, an hour later, he smiled directly at her, and this time he did win a knowing grin.

Charles sat alone at a corner table in Walton's for another hour. He was just about to admit defeat and return home when she was ushered to the table. The anger that had developed from being kept waiting was forgotten the moment she smiled and said, "Hello, Charlie."

He was not surprised to learn that his tall, elegant companion earned her living as a model. As far as Charles could see, she could have modeled anything from toothpaste to stockings. So enchanting were her fair curls and large blue eyes that he hardly noticed that her conversation rarely strayed beyond the world's gossip columns.

"Shall we have coffee at my place?" Charles asked after an unhurried dinner. She nodded her assent and he called for the bill, not checking the addition as he normally did.

He was delighted, if somewhat surprised, when she rested her head on his shoulder in the cab on the way back to Eaton Square. By the time they had been dropped off at Eaton Square, most of Amanda's lipstick had been removed. The cabbie thanked Charles for his excessive tip and couldn't resist adding, "Good luck, sir."

Charles never did get around to making the coffee.

When he woke in the morning, to his surprise he found her even more captivating, and for the first time in weeks he quite forgot to turn on "Yesterday in Parliament."

Elizabeth listened carefully as the man from Special Branch explained how the safety devices worked. She tried to make Peter and Lucy concentrate on not pressing the red buttons that were in every room and would bring the police at a moment's notice. The electrician had already wired every room in Beaufort Street and now he had nearly finished at the cottage.

At Beaufort Street a uniformed policeman stood watch by the front door night and day. In Pucklebridge, because the cottage was so isolated, they had to be surrounded by arc lamps that could be switched on at a moment's notice.

"It must be damned inconvenient," suggested Archie Millburn during dinner. Upon his arrival at the cottage he had been checked by security patrols with dogs before he was able to shake hands with his host.

"Inconvenient is putting it mildly," said Elizabeth. "Last week Peter broke a window with a cricket ball and we were immediately lit up like a Christmas tree."

"Do you get any privacy?" asked Archie.

"Only when we're in bed. Even then you can wake up to find you're being licked; you sigh and it turns out to be an Alsatian."

Archie laughed. "Lucky Alsatian."

Each morning when Simon was driven to work, he was accompanied by two detectives, a car in front and another to the rear. He had always thought there were only two ways from Beaufort Street to Westminster. For the first twenty-one days as Minister, he never traveled the same route twice.

Whenever he was due to fly to Belfast, he was not informed of either his departure time or from which airport he would be leaving. While the inconvenience drove Elizabeth mad, the tension had the opposite effect on Simon. Despite everything, it was the first time in his life he didn't feel it was necessary to explain why he'd chosen to be a politician to anyone but Lucy.

"Why can't the North and South be friends?" she had asked her father.

"Because," replied Simon, "most of the people in the South are Catholics, while in the North they are nearly all Protestants."

"And that stops them from liking each other?" said Lucy in disbelief.

"Yes, because the Protestants in the North fear that if they separated from Britain, as the Catholics are demanding, and became part of a United Ireland, they would lose all their rights. And then the Catholics would be in control."

"I thought you told me that Christians believed all men were equal in the eyes of God."

Simon had no reply.

Inch by inch he worked to try to bring the Catholics and Protestants together. Often after a month of inches he would lose a yard in one day, but he never displayed any anger or prejudice except perhaps, as he told Elizabeth, "a prejudice for common sense." Given time, Simon believed, a breakthrough would be possible—if only he could find on both sides a handful of men of good will.

During the all-party meetings in Northern Ireland, both factions began to treat him with respect and—privately—with affection. Even the Opposition spokesman at Westminster openly acknowledged that Simon Kerslake was turning out to be an excellent choice for the "dangerous and thankless Ministry."

"This is the third time in five years," said the doctor, trying not to sound disapproving.

"I may as well book into the same clinic as before," said Amanda matter-of-factly.

"Yes, I suppose so," said the doctor. "Is there any chance the father would want you to have this child?"

"I can't be certain who the father is," said Amanda, looking shamefaced for the first time.

The doctor made no comment other than to say, "I estimate

275

that you are at least six weeks pregnant, but it could be as much as ten.

"The end of one affair and the beginning of another," said Amanda under her breath.

The doctor looked down at the confidential file. "Have you considered giving birth to the child and then bringing it up yourself?"

"Good heavens, no," said Amanda. "I make my living as a model, not as a mother."

"So be it," sighed the doctor, closing the file. "I'll make all the—" she avoided saying "usual"—"necessary arrangements. Perhaps you could give me a call in about a week rather than make the trip down again."

Amanda nodded and said, "Could you let me know what the clinic is going to charge this time? I'm sure it's suffering from inflation like the rest of us."

Somehow the doctor managed to check her temper as she showed Amanda to the door. Once Amanda had left, the doctor picked up the confidential file from her desk, walked over to the cabinet and flicked through S, T, U, until she found the right slot for Wallace. She paused and wondered if having the child might change the patient's whole cavalier attitude to life.

Peter and Lucy had certainly changed her whole life far more than she had ever anticipated.

Raymond drove Kate to Heathrow. He was wearing the pink shirt she had chosen for him; she was wearing the little red box. He had so much to tell her on the way to the airport that he hardly spoke at all. The last four weeks had gone by in a flash. It was the first time he had been grateful for being in Opposition.

"It's all right, Red. Don't fuss. We'll see each other whenever you come to New York."

"I've only been to America once in my life," he said. She tried to smile.

Once she had checked her eleven bags in at the counter, a process that seemed to take forever, she was allocated a seat.

"Flight BA one hundred seven, Gate fourteen, boarding in ten minutes," she was informed.

"Thank you," she said and rejoined Raymond, who was sitting on the end of an already crowded tubular settee. He had bought two cups of coffee while Kate had been checking in. They were both already cold. They sat and held hands like children who had met on a summer holiday and now had to return to separate schools.

"Promise me you won't start wearing contact lenses the moment I've gone."

"Yes, I can promise you that," said Raymond, touching the bridge of his glasses.

"I've so much I still want to tell you," she said.

He turned toward her. "Vice-presidents of banks shouldn't cry," he said, brushing a tear from her cheek. "The customers will realize you're a soft touch."

"Neither should future Prime Ministers," she replied. "All I wanted to say is that if you really feel . . ." she began.

"Hello, Mr. Gould."

They both looked up to see a broad smile spread across the face of someone whose tan proved that he had just arrived from a sunnier climate.

"I'm Bert Cox," he said, thrusting out his hand, "I don't suppose you remember me." Raymond let go of Kate's hand and shook Mr. Cox's.

"We were at the same primary school in Leeds, Ray. Mind you, that was a million light years ago. You've come a long way since then."

How can I get rid of him? wondered Raymond desperately.

"This is the missus," Bert Cox continued obliviously, gesturing at the silent woman in a flowery dress by his side. She smiled but didn't speak. "She sits on some committee with Joyce, don't you, love?" he said, not waiting for her reply.

277

"This is the final call for Flight BA one hundred seven, now boarding at Gate fourteen."

"We always vote for you, of course," continued Bert Cox. "The missus—" he pointed to the lady in the flowered dress again—"thinks you'll be Prime Minister. I always say—"

"I must go, Mr. Gould," said Kate, "or I'll miss my flight."

"Can you excuse me for a moment, Mr. Cox?" said Raymond.

"Delighted. I'll wait, I don't often get a chance to have a word with my MP."

Raymond walked with Kate toward the gate. "I am sorry about this, I'm afraid they're all like that in Leeds—hearts of gold, but never stop talking. What were you going to say?"

"Only that I would have been happy to live in Leeds, however cold it is. I never envied anyone in my life, but I do envy Joyce." She kissed him gently on the cheek and walked toward the security barrier before he could reply. She didn't look back.

"Are you feeling all right, madam?" asked an airport official as she went through the gate.

"I'm fine," said Kate, brushing aside her tears. She walked slowly toward Gate 14, happy that he had worn the pink shirt for the first time. She wondered if he had found the note she had left in the breast pocket. If he had asked her just one more time . . .

Raymond stood alone and then turned to walk aimlessly toward the exit.

"An American lady, I would have guessed," said Mr. Cox rejoining him. "I'm good on accents."

"Yes," said Raymond, still alone.

"A friend of yours?" he asked.

"My best friend," said Raymond.

Charles returned home after the debate feeling pleased with himself. He had received praise for his latest speech from every wing of the party, and the Chief Whip had made it quite clear that Charles's efforts on the Finance Bill had not gone un-noticed.

As he drove back to Eaton Square he wound down the car window and let the fresh air rush in and the cigarette smoke out. His smile widened at the thought of Amanda sitting at home waiting for him. It had been a glorious couple of months. At forty-eight, he was experiencing realities he had never dreamed of in fantasy. As each day passed, he expected the infatuation to wear off, but instead it only grew more intense. Even the memory the day after was better than anything he had experienced in the past.

Once the Holbein had been restored to his dining room wall, he would be willing to grant Fiona her divorce. Charles then planned to talk to Amanda about their future. He parked the car and took out his latchkey, but she was already there opening the front door to throw her arms around him.

"Let's go straight to bed," she said. "I feel in the mood."

Charles would have been shocked had Fiona uttered such feelings even once in all their years of married life, but Amanda made it appear quite natural. She was already lying naked on the bed before Charles could get his vest off. After they had made love and she was settled in his arms, Amanda told him she would have to go away for a few days.

"Why?" said Charles, puzzled.

"I'm pregnant," she said matter-of-factly. "I can always go to a clinic. Don't worry, I'll be as right as rain in no time."

"But why don't we have the baby?" said a delighted Charles, looking down into her blue eyes. "I've always wanted a son."

"Don't be silly, Charlie. There's years ahead of me for that."

"But if we were married?"

"You're already married. Besides, I'm only twenty-six."

"I can get a divorce in a moment and life wouldn't be so bad with me, would it?"

"Of course not, Charlie. You're the first man I've ever really cared for."

279

Charles smiled hopefully. "So you'll think about the idea?"

Amanda looked into Charlie's eyes anxiously. "If I had a child I would hope he had blue eyes like yours."

"Will you marry me?" he asked.

"I'll think about it. In any case, you may have changed your mind by morning."

When ten days had passed and Elizabeth had not yet heard from Miss Wallace, she decided the time had come to phone her. Elizabeth flicked through her patients file and noted the latest number Amanda Wallace had given.

Elizabeth dialed the number. It was some time before it was answered.

"9712. Charles Hampton speaking." There was a long silence. "Is anyone there?"

Elizabeth couldn't reply. She replaced the phone and felt her whole body come out in a cold sweat. She closed Amanda Wallace's file, and returned it to the cabinet.

23

Simon had spent nearly a year preparing a White Paper entitled "A Genuine Partnership for Ireland," for consideration by the House. The Government's aim was to bring North and South together for a period of ten years, at the end of which a more permanent arrangement could be considered. During the ten years both sides would remain under the direct rule of Westminster and Dublin. Both Protestants and Catholics had contributed to "the Charter," as the press had dubbed the complex agreement. With considerable skill and patience Simon had convinced the political leaders of Northern Ireland to append their names to the final draft when and if it was approved by the House.

He admitted to Elizabeth that the agreement was only a piece of paper, but he felt it was a foundation stone on which the House could base an eventual settlement. On both sides of the Irish sea, politicians and journalists alike were describing the Charter as a genuine breakthrough.

The Secretary of State for Northern Ireland was to present the White Paper to the Commons when Irish business was next scheduled on the parliamentary calendar. Simon, as the architect of the Charter, had been asked to deliver the final speech on behalf of the Government. He knew that if the House backed the concept of the document he might then be allowed to prepare a parliamentary bill and thus overcome a problem so many other politicians had failed to solve before him. If he succeeded, Simon felt that all his efforts would prove worthwhile.

When Elizabeth sat down to read through the final draft in Simon's study, even she admitted for the first time that she was pleased that he had accepted the Irish appointment.

Peter rushed in the front door covered with mud. "We won four to three. When's dinner? I'm starving."

Both Simon and Elizabeth laughed.

"As soon as you've had a bath," she said to her retreating son. "Now, embryonic statesman," Elizabeth continued, turning back to Simon, "are you also ready for your dinner like every normal human being at this time in the evening?"

"I certainly am, and I haven't won four to three yet." Simon moved his copy of the one hundred and twenty-nine page Charter onto his desk, planning to go over it again once he had finished dinner.

Peter came bounding down the stairs a few minutes later. "I scored the winning goal, Dad."

"During the half-time interval, no doubt?"

"Very funny, Dad. No, I was on the right wing when I . . ."

"Damn," they both heard Elizabeth say from the kitchen.

"What is it?" asked Simon.

"I'm out of milk."

"I'll go and buy some," Simon volunteered.

"Can I come with you?" said Peter. "Then I can tell you about my goal."

"Of course you can, son."

The two policemen on the door were chatting when Simon and Peter came out.

"Come on, one of you, my wife needs a carton of milk, so affairs of state must be held up for the time being."

"I'm sorry, Minister," said the sergeant. "When I was told you would be in for the rest of the evening I allowed the official car to go off duty. But Constable Barker can accompany you."

"That's no problem," said Simon. "We can take my wife's

car. Peter, run back and pick up Mum's car keys, and while you're at it, find out where she's parked the damned thing."

Peter disappeared back inside.

"Been in the force long?" Simon asked Constable Barker as they waited on the doorstep for Peter to return.

"Not that long, sir. Started on the beat just over a year ago."

"Are you married, Constable?"

"Fine chance on my salary, sir."

"Then you won't have encountered the problem of being milkless."

"I don't think they've ever heard of milk in the police canteen, sir."

"You should try the House of Commons sometime," said Simon. "I don't imagine you'd find it any better—the food, that is, not to mention the salary."

The constable laughed as Peter returned, jangling the car keys.

"Off we go, Constable, but I warn you, you'll have to suffer a running commentary on my son's school football match. He scored the winning goal," said Simon, winking at the policeman.

"I was going down the right wing," said Peter, oblivious to his father's sarcasm, "and first I dodged past my opposite number, then I flicked the ball to my captain before running flat out back into the center." Peter paused to make sure both men were following the details with rapt attention. Satisfied, he continued. "The captain passed the ball back to me and I took it on the full toss with my left leg, blocked it, controlled it and then shot at the far corner of the goal mouth." Peter paused again.

"Don't keep us in suspense," said Simon as they reached the car.

"The goalie dived full length, his finger touching the ball," said Peter as Simon opened the car door, "But it was too late. I . . ."

Like everyone else in Beaufort Street, Elizabeth heard the explosion, but she was the first to realize what it must be. She ran out of the front door in search of the duty policeman. She saw him running down the road and quickly followed.

The little red car was scattered all over the side street, the glass from its windows making the pavement look as though there had been a sudden hailstorm.

When the sergeant saw the severed head, he pulled Elizabeth back. Two other forms lay motionless in the road.

Within minutes, six police cars and an ambulance had arrived and Special Branch officers had cordoned off the area with white ribbon. The job of picking up the remains of the police constable needed a very resolute man.

Elizabeth was taken to Westminster Hospital in a police car, where she learned that both her husband and son were in critical condition. When she told the surgeon in charge that she was a doctor, he was more forthcoming and answered her questions candidly. Simon was suffering from multiple fractures and lacerations, a dislocated hip, and a severe loss of blood. The doctors were attempting to remove a piece of glass lodged only inches from Peter's heart.

She sat alone outside the operating room waiting for any scrap of news. Hour after hour went by, and Elizabeth kept recalling Simon's words: "Be tolerant. Always remember there are still men of good will in Northern Ireland." She found it almost impossible not to scream, to think of the whole lot of them as murderers. Her husband had worked tirelessly on their behalf. He wasn't working as a Catholic or a Protestant, just as a man trying to do an impossible task. Her son only wanted to get back home and tell her about his goal. And in the back of her mind was the knowledge that she had been the intended target.

Another hour passed. She watched a policeman steer reporters—who were arriving by the minute—into an anteroom off the main entrance. Finally a tired, gray-faced man came out into the corridor through the flapping rubber doors. "Your husband's still hanging on, Dr. Kerslake. He has the constitution of an ox; most people would have let go by now. We'll know more about your son's condition as soon as the operation is over. All I know is, they have managed to remove the piece of glass." He smiled. "Can I find you a room so that you can get some sleep?"

"No, thank you," Elizabeth replied. "I'd prefer to be near them." She added in a distracted way, "I want to hear about the winning goal."

She did not notice the doctor's puzzled look.

Elizabeth phoned home to check how Lucy was coping. Elizabeth's mother answered the phone. She had rushed over the moment she had heard and was keeping Lucy away from the radio and the television. "How are they?" she asked.

Elizabeth told her mother all she knew and then spoke to Lucy.

"I'm taking care of Grandmother," Lucy promised her.

Elizabeth couldn't hold back the tears. "Thank you, darling," she said and quickly replaced the receiver. She returned to the bench outside the operating room, kicked off her shoes, curled her legs under her body and tried to snatch some sleep.

She woke with a start in the early morning. Her back hurt and her neck was stiff. She walked slowly up and down the corridor in her bare feet stretching her aching limbs, searching for anyone who could tell her some news. Finally a nurse who brought her a cup of tea assured her that her husband and son were both still alive. What did "still alive" mean?

She stood and watched the grim faces coming out of the two operating rooms and tried not to recognize the telltale signs of despair. The surgeon told her she ought to go home and rest. They could tell her nothing definite for at least twenty-four hours.

Elizabeth didn't move from the corridor for another day and another night, and she didn't return home until the surgeon told her the news.

When she heard she fell on her knees and wept.

Simon would live; they had saved her husband's life. She continued to weep. Her son Peter had died a few minutes before. They had tried everything.

24

"GOT TIME FOR A QUICK ONE?" asked Alexander Dalglish.

"If you press me," said Pimkin.

"Fiona," shouted Alexander. "It's Alec Pimkin; he's dropped in for a drink."

Fiona came in to join them. She was dressed in a bright yellow frock and had allowed her hair to grow down to her shoulders.

"It suits you," said Pimkin, tapping his bald head.

"Thank you," said Fiona. "Why don't we all go through to the drawing room?"

Pimkin happily obeyed and had soon settled himself into Alexander's favorite chair.

"What will you have?" asked Fiona, as she stood by the bar cabinet.

"A large gin with just a rumor of tonic."

"Well, how's the constituency faring since my resignation?" asked Alexander.

"It ticks along, trying hard to survive the biggest sex scandal since Profumo," chuckled Alec.

"I only hope it hasn't harmed you politically," said Alexander.

"Not a bit of it, old fellow," said Pimkin, accepting the large Beefeater-and-tonic Fiona handed him. "On the contrary, it's taken their minds off me for a change."

Alexander laughed.

"In fact," continued Pimkin, "interest in the date of your wedding has been eclipsed only by that of Charles and Lady Di. Gossips tell me," he continued, clearly enjoying himself, "that my Honorable friend, the Member for Sussex Downs, made you wait the full two years before you could place an announcement in *The Times.*"

"Yes that's true," said Fiona. "Charles didn't even answer my letters during that period, but lately, when any problem's arisen, he's been almost friendly."

"Could that be because he also wants to place an announcement in *The Times?*" said Pimkin, downing his gin quickly in the hope of being offered a second.

"What do you mean?"

"The fact that he has lost his heart to Amanda Wallace."

"Amanda?" said Fiona in disbelief. "Surely, he's got more sense than that."

"I don't think it has much to do with sense," said Pimkin, holding out his glass. "More to do with sexual attraction."

"But he's old enough to be her father. Besides, Amanda is hardly his type."

"That may well be the case, but I am informed by a reliable source that marriage is being proposed."

"You can't be serious," said Fiona flatly.

"The subject has most certainly been broached, for she is undoubtedly pregnant and Charles is hoping for a son," said Pimkin in triumph as he accepted his second double gin.

"That's not possible," said Fiona. "I can assure you—" She caught herself and stopped.

"And I can assure you that some of the more ungenerous of our brethren are already suggesting the names of several candidates for the role of father."

"Alec, you're incorrigible."

"My dear, it is common knowledge that Amanda has slept with half the Cabinet and a considerable cross section of backbenchers."

287

"Stop exaggerating," said Fiona.

"And what's more," continued Pimkin as if he hadn't heard her, "she has only stopped short of the Labour front bench because her mother told her they were common and she might catch something from them."

Alexander laughed. "But surely Charles hasn't fallen for the pregnancy trick?"

"Hook, line and sinker. He's like an Irishman who's been locked into a Guinness brewery over a weekend. Dear Amanda has my Honorable friend uncorking her at every opportunity."

"But she's just plain stupid," said Alexander. "The only time I met her she assured me that David Frost was turning out to be an excellent chairman of the Conservative Party."

"Stupid she may be, but plain she is not. I'm told they are updating the Kama Sutra together."

"Enough, Alec, enough," said Fiona, laughing.

"You're right," said Pimkin, aware that his glass was nearly empty once again. "A man of my impeccable reputation cannot afford to be seen associating with people living in sin. I must leave immediately, darlings," he said, rising to his feet. Pimkin put his glass down and Alexander accompanied him to the front door.

As it closed, Alexander turned to Fiona. "Never short of useful information, our member," he said.

"I agree," said Fiona. "So much gleaned for such a small investment in Beefeater."

As Alexander walked back into the drawing room he added, "So what have you done about the Holbein?"

"I signed the final documents this morning, after we both agreed that at last Charles had come to his senses. He even wanted to rush the proceedings through."

"And now we know why," said Alexander. "So I see no reason why we should fall in so conveniently with his little plan."

"What do you have in mind?" asked Fiona.

"Have you seen this?" he asked, passing her a copy of Sotheby's latest catalogue of Old Master paintings.

Three weeks after the bombing, Simon left the Westminster Hospital on crutches, Elizabeth by his side. His right leg had been so shattered that he had been told he would never walk properly again. As he stepped out onto Horseferry Road, a hundred cameras flashed to meet editors' demands to capture the tragic hero. None of the photographers asked Simon and Elizabeth to smile. Normally cynical journalists were moved by the simple dignity with which both the Minister and his wife conducted themselves. The pictures the press carried the next day showed clearly they had lost their only son.

After a month of complete rest, Simon returned to his Irish Charter against doctor's orders, knowing the document was still due to be debated in the House in only two weeks' time.

The Secretary of State and the Under Secretary for Northern Ireland visited Simon at home on several occasions, and it was agreed that the Under Secretary would take over Simon's responsibilities temporarily and deliver the winding-up speech. During his absence the whole Northern Ireland office came to realize just how much work Simon had put into the Charter, and no one was complacent about taking his place.

The attempt on Simon's life and the death of his son had turned the special debate on the Charter into a national media event, the BBC scheduling a broadcast of the entire proceedings on Radio Four from three-thirty to the vote at ten o'clock.

On the afternoon of the debate, Simon sat up in bed, listening to every word on the radio as if it were the final episode in a dramatic serial, desperate to learn the outcome. The speeches opened with a clear and concise presentation of the Charter by the Secretary of State for Northern Ireland, which left Simon feeling confident that the whole House would support his plan. The Opposition spokesman followed with a fair-minded speech, raising one or two queries about the controversial Patriots' Clause with its special rights for Protestants in the South and Catholics in the North, and about how it would affect the Catholics unwilling to register in Northern Ireland. Otherwise, he reassured the House that the Opposition supported the Charter and would not call for a division vote.

Simon began to relax for the first time as the debate continued, but his mood changed as some back-bench members started to express more and more anxiety over the Patriots' Provision. One or two of them were even insisting that the Charter should not be sanctioned by the House until the need for the Patriots' Provision was fully explained by the Government. Simon realized that a few narrow-minded men were simply playing for time in the hope the Charter would be held up and in later months forgotten. For generations such men had succeeded in stifling the hopes and aspirations of the Irish people while they allowed bigotry to undermine any real progress toward peace. Elizabeth came in and sat on the end of the bed.

"How's it going?" she asked.

"Not well," said Simon. "It will now all depend on the Opposition spokesman." They both listened intently.

No sooner had the Opposition spokesman risen than Simon realized that this man had misunderstood the real purpose of the Patriots' Provision and that what Simon had agreed to with both sides in Dublin and Belfast was not being accurately explained to the House. There was no malice in the speech. The man was clearly following what had been agreed to through the usual channels, but Simon could sense that his lack of conviction was sowing doubts in the minds of members. A division vote might be called after all.

After one or two members raised further questions about the Patriots' Clause, the Shadow Minister finally suggested, "Perhaps we should wait until the Minister of State is fully recovered and able to report to the House himself."

Simon felt sick. He was going to lose the Charter if it didn't get through the House tonight. All the hard work and good will would count for nothing. His son's death would count for nothing. Simon made a decision. "I'd love a hot cup of cocoa," he said, trying to sound casual.

"Of course, darling. I'll just go and turn the kettle on. Would you like a biscuit while I'm up?"

Simon nodded. Once the bedroom door was closed, he slipped quietly out of bed and dressed as quickly as he could. He picked up his blackthorn stick, a gift from Dr. Fitzgerald, the Irish Prime Minister, which had been among the dozens of presents sent to his home awaiting his return from the hospital. Then he hobbled silently down the stairs and across the hall, hoping Elizabeth and Lucy would not hear him. He eased the front door open. When the policeman on duty saw him, Simon put a finger to his lips and closed the door very slowly behind him. He made his way laboriously up to the police car, lurched into the back and said, "Switch on the radio, please, and drive me to the House as quickly as possible."

Simon continued to listen to the Opposition spokesman as the police car weaved in and out of the traffic on a route he hadn't traveled before. They arrived at the St. Stephen's entrance to the Commons at nine twenty-five.

Visitors stood to one side as they might for royalty. But Simon didn't notice. He hobbled on as quickly as he could through the central lobby, oblivious to the awkwardness of his gait, turning left past the policeman and on toward the entrance of the House. He prayed he would reach the chamber before the Government spokesman rose to deliver his winding-up speech. Simon passed an astonished chief doorkeeper and arrived at the bar of the House as the new digital clock showed 9:29.

The Opposition spokesman was resuming his place on the front bench to muffled cries of "Hear, hear." The Speaker rose, but before he had time to call upon the Minister of State to reply, Simon stepped slowly forward onto the green carpet of the Commons. For a moment there was a stunned silence; then the cheering began. It had reached a crescendo by the time Simon arrived at the front bench. His blackthorn stick fell to the floor as he clutched the dispatch box. The Speaker called out his name *sotto voce*.

291

Simon waited for the House to come to complete silence.

"Mr. Speaker, I must thank the House for its generous welcome. I return this evening because, having listened to every word of the debate on the radio, I feel it necessary to explain to Honorable Members what was behind my thinking on the Patriots' Provision. This was not some superficial formula for solving an intractable problem, but an act of good faith to which the representatives from all sides felt able to put their names. It may not be perfect, since words can mean different things to different people—as lawyers continually demonstrate to us."

The laughter broke the tension that had been building in the House.

"But if we allow this opportunity to pass today, it will be another victory for those who revel in the mayhem of Northern Ireland, whatever their reason, and a defeat for all men of good will."

The House was silent as Simon went on to explain in detail the theory behind the Patriots' Provision and the effect it would have on both Protestants and Catholics in North and South. He also covered the other salient clauses in the Charter, answering the points that had been raised during the debate until, in glancing up at the clock above the Speaker's chair, he realized he had less than a minute left.

"Mr. Speaker, we in this great House, who have in the past decided the fate of nations, are now given an opportunity to succeed today where our predecessors have failed. I ask you to support this Charter—not unreservedly, but to show the bombers and the murderers that here in Westminster we can cast a vote for the children of tomorrow's Ireland. Let the twenty-first century be one in which the Irish problem is only a part of history. Mr. Speaker, I seek the support of the whole House."

The motion on the Charter was agreed to without a division.

Simon immediately returned home, and on arrival silently crept upstairs. He closed the bedroom door behind him and fumbled for the switch. The light by the side of the bed went on, and Elizabeth sat up.

"Your cocoa's gone cold and I've eaten all the biscuits," she said brightly, "but thank you for leaving the radio on. At least I knew where you were."

Simon started to laugh.

Elizabeth started to cry.

"What's the matter, darling?" said Simon, coming to her side.

"Peter would have been so proud of you."

25

CHARLES AND AMANDA were married at the most inconspicuous registry office in Hammersmith. They then departed for a long weekend in Paris. Charles had told his bride that he preferred not to let anyone learn of the marriage for at least another week. He didn't want Fiona to find a further excuse for not returning the Holbein. Amanda readily agreed, and then she remembered; but surely Alec Pimkin didn't count?

When they arrived on Friday night at the Plaza-Athénée, they were escorted to a suite overlooking the courtyard. Later, over dinner, Amanda astonished the waiters with her appetite as well as the cut of her dress. Paris turned out to be fun, but when Charles read in the *Herald Tribune* the next day that Mrs. Thatcher was considering a reshuffle that very weekend, he cut their honeymoon short and returned to London on Sunday, two days earlier than planned. Amanda was not overjoyed. Her husband spent Saturday evening and the whole of Sunday at Eaton Square next to a phone that never rang.

That same Sunday evening the Prime Minister called for Simon Kerslake and told him that he was to be made a Privy Councillor and would be moved from the Northern Ireland Office to the Foreign Office as Minister of State.

He had started to protest, but Mrs. Thatcher forestalled any discussion. "I don't want any more dead heroes, Simon," she said sharply. "Your family has been through enough."

Elizabeth was relieved when she heard the news—although Simon doubted if she would ever fully recover from the ordeal. Whereas his scars were visible for all to see, hers, he suspected, were deeper-grained.

Mrs. Thatcher finally called Charles Hampton on Tuesday morning while he was waiting in Eaton Square for the return of the Holbein. His lawyers had agreed with Fiona's that the first Earl of Bridgewater should be back at Charles's home by eleven that morning. Only the Queen or Mrs. Thatcher could have kept Charles from being there to receive it. The Prime Minister's call came long after he thought the reshuffle was over.

Charles took a taxi to Downing Street and was quickly ushered into the Prime Minister's study. Mrs. Thatcher began by complimenting him on the work he had carried out on successive finance bills in Opposition and in Government. She then invited him to join the front-bench team as a Minister of State at the Treasury.

Charles accepted gracefully, and after a short policy discussion with the Prime Minister drove back to Eaton Square to celebrate both his triumphs. Amanda met him at the door to tell him the Holbein had been returned. Fiona had kept her part of the bargain: the painting had been delivered at eleven o'clock sharp.

Charles strode confidently into his drawing room, delighted to find the bulky package awaiting him. He was by no means so pleased to be followed by Amanda, a cigarette in one hand and a glass of gin in the other; but this was not a day for quarrels, he decided. He told her of his appointment, but she didn't seem to take in its significance until her husband opened a bottle of champagne.

Charles poured out two glasses and handed one to his bride.

"A double celebration. What fun," she said, first finishing her gin.

Charles took a quick sip of the champagne before he began to untie the knots and tear away the smart red wrapping paper

295

that covered his masterpiece. Once the paper had been removed
he pulled back the final cardboard covers. Charles stared with
delight at the portrait.

The first Earl of Bridgewater was back home. Charles picked up
the gold frame he knew so well to return it to its place in the dining room, but he noticed that the picture had come a little loose.

"Damn," he said.

"What's the matter?" asked Amanda, still leaning against the
door.

"Nothing important, only I shall have to get the frame fixed.
I'll drop it at Oliver Swann's on the way to the bank. I've waited
nearly three years—another couple of days won't make any difference."

Now that Charles had accepted the post of Minister of State
at the Treasury he knew there was one little arrangement he
had to clear up before the appointment became public knowledge. With that in mind, he drove to the bank and summoned
Clive Reynolds to his office. It was clear from Reynolds's manner that the news of Charles's Ministerial appointment had not
yet become public.

"Clive—" Charles called him that for the first time—"I have
a proposition to put to you."

Clive Reynolds remained silent.

"The Prime Minister has offered me a post in the Government."

"Congratulations," said Reynolds, "and well deserved, if I
may say so."

"Thank you," said Charles. "Now—I'm considering offering
you the chance to stand in for me as chairman during my absence."

Clive Reynolds looked surprised.

"On the clear understanding that if the Conservatives were to
return to Opposition or I were to lose my appointment in Government, I would be reinstated as chairman immediately."

"Naturally," said Reynolds. "I should be delighted to fill the
appointment for the interim period."

"Good man," said Charles. "It can't have escaped your notice what happened to the last chairman in the same situation."

"I shall make certain that will not happen again."

"Thank you," said Charles. "I shall not forget your loyalty when I return."

"And I shall also endeavor to carry on the traditions of the bank in your absence," said Reynolds, his head slightly bowed.

"I feel sure you will," said Charles.

The board accepted the recommendation that Clive Reynolds be appointed as temporary chairman, and Charles vacated his office happily to take up his new post at the Treasury.

Charles considered it had been the most successful week of his life, and on Friday evening on the way back to Eaton Square he dropped into Oliver Swann's gallery to pick up the Holbein.

"I'm afraid the picture didn't quite fit the frame," said Mr. Swann.

"Oh, I expect it's worked loose over the years," Charles said.

"No, Mr. Hampton, this frame was put on the portrait quite recently," said Swann.

"That's not possible," said Charles. "I remember the frame as well as I remember the picture. The portrait of the first Earl of Bridgewater has been in my family for over four hundred years."

"Not this picture," said Swann.

"What do you mean?" said Charles, beginning to sound anxious.

"This picture came up for sale at Sotheby's about three weeks ago."

Charles went cold as Swann continued.

"It's the school of Holbein, of course," he said. "Probably painted by one of his pupils around the time of his death. I should think there are a dozen or so in existence."

"A dozen or so," repeated Charles, the blood quite drained from his face.

"Yes, perhaps even more. At least it's solved one mystery for me," said Swann, chuckling.

"What's that?" asked Charles, choking out the words.

"I couldn't work out why Lady Fiona was bidding for the picture, and then I remembered that your family name is Bridgewater."

"At least *this* wedding has some style," Pimkin assured Fiona between mouthfuls of sandwiches at the reception after her marriage to Alexander Dalglish. Pimkin always accepted wedding invitations as they allowed him to devour mounds of smoked-salmon sandwiches and consume unlimited quantities of champagne. "I particularly enjoyed that *short* service of blessing in the Guards' Chapel; and Claridge's can always be relied on to understand my little proclivities." He peered around the vast room and only stopped to stare at his reflection in a chandelier.

Fiona laughed. "Did you go to Charles's wedding?"

"My darling, I'm told that only Amanda was invited, and even she nearly found she had another engagement. With her doctor, I believe."

"And he certainly can't afford another divorce?"

"No, not in Charles's present position as Her Majesty's Minister of State. One divorce might go unnoticed but two would be considered habit-forming, and all diligent readers of the gossip columns have been able to observe that consummation has taken place."

"But how long will Charles be able to tolerate her behavior?"

"As long as he still believes she has given him a son who will inherit the family title. Not that a marriage ceremony will prove legitimacy," added Pimkin.

"Perhaps Amanda won't produce a son?"

"Perhaps whatever she produces will be obviously not Charles's offspring," said Pimkin, falling into a chair that had been momentarily vacated by a large buxom lady.

"Even if it was, I can't see Amanda as a housewife."

"No, but it suits Amanda's current circumstances to be thought of as the loving spouse."

"Time may change that too," said Fiona.

"I doubt it," said Pimkin. "Amanda is stupid; that has been proven beyond reasonable doubt—but she has a survival instinct second only to a mongoose's. So while Charles is spending all the hours of the day advancing his glittering career, she would be foolish to search publicly for greener pastures. Especially when she can always lie in them privately."

"You're a wicked old gossip," said Fiona.

"I cannot deny it," said Pimkin.

"Thank you for such a sensible wedding present," said Alexander, joining his wife of two hours. "You selected my favorite claret."

"Giving a dozen bottles of the finest claret serves two purposes," said Pimkin, his hands resting lightly on his stomach. "First, you can always be assured of a decent wine when you invite yourself to dine."

"And second?" asked Alexander.

"When the happy couple split up you can feel relieved that they will no longer have your present to quarrel over."

"Did you give Charles and Amanda a present?" asked Fiona.

"No," said Pimkin, deftly removing another glass of champagne from a passing waiter. "I felt your return of the bogus Earl of Bridgewater was quite enough for both of us."

"I wonder where he is now?" said Alexander.

"The Earl no longer resides in Eaton Square," said Pimkin with the air of one who has divulged a piece of information which can only guarantee further rapt attention.

"Who would want the phony Earl?"

"We are not aware of the provenance of the buyer, as he emanates from one of Her Majesty's former colonies, but the seller . . ."

"Stop teasing, Alec. Who?"

"None other than the Honorable Mrs. Amanda Hampton."

"Amanda?"

"Yes. Amanda, no less. The dear, silly creature retrieved the false Earl from the cellar, where Charles had buried him with full military honors."

"But she must have realized it was a fake?"

"My dear, Amanda wouldn't know the difference between a Holbein and Andy Warhol, but she still happily accepted ten thousand pounds for the impersonation. I am assured that the dealer who purchased this fabricated masterpiece made what I think vulgar people in the city describe as 'a quick turn.' "

"Good God," said Alexander. "I only paid eight thousand for it myself."

"Perhaps you should get Amanda to advise you on these matters in the future," said Pimkin. "In exchange for my invaluable piece of information, I'm bound to inquire if the real Earl of Bridgewater is to remain in hiding?"

"Certainly not, Alec. He is merely awaiting the right moment to make a public appearance," said Fiona, unable to hide a smile.

"And where is Amanda now?" asked Alexander, obviously wanting to change the subject.

"In Switzerland, producing a baby, which we can but hope will bear sufficient resemblance to a white Caucasian to convince one of Charles's limited imagination that he is the father."

"Where *do* you get all your information from?" asked Alexander.

Pimkin sighed dramatically. "Women have a habit of pouring their hearts out to me, Amanda included."

"Why should she do that?" asked Alexander.

"She lives safe in the knowledge that I am the one man she knows who has no interest in her body." Pimkin drew breath, but only to devour another smoked-salmon sandwich.

Charles phoned Amanda every day while she was in Geneva. She kept assuring him all was well, and that the baby was expected on time. He had considered it prudent for Amanda not to remain in England advertising her pregnancy, a less than recent occurrence to even the most casual observer. She for her part did not complain. With ten thousand pounds safely tucked away in a private Swiss account, there were few little necessities she could not have brought to her, even in Geneva.

It had taken a few weeks for Charles to become accustomed to Government after such a long break. He enjoyed the challenge of the Treasury and quickly fell in with its strange traditions. He was constantly reminded that his was the department on which the Prime Minister kept her closest eye, making the challenge even greater. The civil servants, when asked their opinion of the new Minister of State, would reply variously: able, competent, efficient, hardworking—but without any hint of affection in their voices. When someone asked Charles's driver, whose name Charles could never remember, the same question, he proffered the view, "He's the sort of Minister who never remembers your name. But I'd still put a week's wages on Mr. Hampton becoming Prime Minister."

Amanda produced her child in the middle of the ninth month. After a week of recuperation, she was allowed to return to England. She discovered that traveling with the brat was a nuisance, and by the time she arrived at Heathrow she was more than happy to turn the child over to the nanny Charles had selected.

Charles had sent a car to pick her up from the airport. He had an unavoidable conference with a delegation of Japanese businessmen, he explained, all of them busy complaining about the new Government tariffs on imports.

At the first opportunity to be rid of his Oriental guests, he bolted back to Eaton Square. Amanda was there to meet him at the door. Charles had almost forgotten how beautiful his wife was, and how long she had been away.

"Where's my child?" he asked, after he had given her a long kiss.

"In a nursery that's more expensively furnished than our bedroom," she replied a little sharply.

Charles ran up the wide staircase and along the passage. Amanda followed. He entered the nursery he had spent so much time preparing in her absence and stopped in his tracks as he stared at the future Earl of Bridgewater. The little black curls and deep brown eyes came as something of a shock.

"Good heavens," said Charles, stepping forward for a closer examination. Amanda remained by the door, her hand clutching its handle.

She had a hundred answers ready for his question.

"He's the spitting image of my great-grandfather. You skipped a couple of generations, Harry," said Charles, lifting the boy high into the air, "but there's no doubt you're a real Hampton."

Amanda sighed with inaudible relief. The hundred answers she could now keep to herself.

"It's more than a couple of generations the little bastard has skipped," said Pimkin. "It's an entire continent." He took another sip of christening champagne before continuing. "This poor creature, on the other hand," he said, staring at Fiona's firstborn, "bears a striking resemblance to Alexander. Dear little girl should have been given a kinder legacy with which to start her life."

"She's beautiful," said Fiona, picking her daughter up from the cradle to check her diaper.

"Now we know why you needed to be married so quickly," added Pimkin between gulps. "At least this child made wedlock, even if it was a close race."

Fiona continued as if she hadn't heard his remark. "Have you actually seen Charles's son?" she asked.

"I think we should refer to young Harold as Amanda's child," said Pimkin. "We don't want to be in violation of the Trade Description Act."

"Come on, Alec, have you seen Harry?" she asked, refusing to fill his empty glass.

"Yes, I have. And I am afraid he also bears too striking a resemblance to his father for it to go unnoticed in later life."

"Anyone we know?" asked Fiona, probing.

"I am not a scandalmonger," said Pimkin, removing a crumb from his waistcoat. "As you well know. But a certain Brazilian *fazendeiro* who frequents Cowdray Park and Ascot during the summer months has obviously maintained his interest in the English fillies."

Pimkin confidently held out his glass.

26

ON A SLEEPY THURSDAY in April 1982 Argentina attacked and occupied two small islands whose eighteen hundred British citizens were forced to lower the Union Jack for the first time in over a hundred years.

Mrs. Thatcher immediately dispatched a task force halfway around the globe to recapture the sovereign islands. Her fellow countrymen followed every scrap of news so intently that London theaters found themselves empty at the height of the season.

Simon felt exhilarated to be a member of the Foreign Office at such an historic moment, and Elizabeth didn't begrudge him those days when he left before she had awakened, and arrived home after she had fallen asleep. By the end of the two long months that proved necessary for the British forces to recapture the Falklands, Simon looked well placed to join the Cabinet if Mrs. Thatcher won the next election.

Under less public scrutiny but almost equal pressure, Charles beavered away at the Treasury addressing the economic problems that had previously eroded his Prime Minister's popularity. After the April budget had been presented, he spent day after day in the House helping to put the Government's case. Like Simon, he found he could only snatch moments to be at home, but unlike Elizabeth, his wife remained in bed until midday. When Charles did manage to slip away from the department, he spent all his spare time with Harry, whose progress he followed with delighted interest.

At the time when the Union Jack was raised once again in the Falklands, the budget became an act.

Charles also considered he would be a contender for a Cabinet seat if the Conservatives won a second term.

Raymond approved of Mrs. Thatcher's resolute stance on the Falklands, despite its damping effects on his own political hopes. So greatly did her personal popularity increase when the islands were reoccupied that Raymond knew there was little chance for the Labour Party to win the next General Election.

When James Callaghan had been replaced by Michael Foot as Labour Leader two years before, the Party had drifted even more to the left. Some of the more moderate members had deserted Foot to join the newly formed Social Democratic Party. Raymond himself was never tempted, as he believed Michael Foot would be quickly replaced after the next election. When Foot had invited Raymond to continue with the Shadow Trade portfolio, Raymond had accepted the assignment with as much enthusiasm as he could muster.

Raymond hated not being able to share his frustrations with Kate, as one after another of her predictions became Party policy—not least, the process of electing a Leader at the annual Party conference. In the beginning she had phoned once a week, and then it became once a month; she always sounded so happy that he refused to admit how much he missed her. Lately, he found he only contacted her on rare occasions.

A year after the recapture of the Falklands, Mrs. Thatcher found that her lead in the opinion polls remained at its all-time high. Although it was a year earlier than necessary, she called a General Election.

Once the date had been announced, Charles realized he could no longer avoid introducing Amanda to the constituency. He had explained to those who inquired that his wife had had rather a bad time of it after the birth, and had been told by her doctors not to participate in anything that might raise her blood pressure—though one or two constituents considered that the Sussex Downs Conservatives would find it hard to raise the blood pressure of a ninety-year-old with a pacemaker.

The annual garden party held in the grounds of Lord Sussex's country home seemed to Charles to be the ideal opportunity to show off Amanda, and he asked her to be certain to wear something appropriate.

He was aware that designer jeans had come into fashion, and that his clothes-conscious wife never seemed to dress in the same thing twice. He also knew that liberated women didn't wear bras. But he was nevertheless shocked when he saw Amanda in a nearly see-through blouse and jeans so tight that the outline of her underwear could be seen. Charles was genuinely horrified.

"Can't you find something a little more . . . conservative?" he suggested.

"Like the things that old frump Fiona used to wear?"

Charles couldn't think of a suitable reply. "The garden party will be frightfully dull," said Charles desperately. "Perhaps I should go on my own."

Amanda turned and looked him in the eye. "Are you ashamed of me, Charles?"

He drove his wife silently down to the constituency, and every time he glanced over at her he wanted to make an excuse to turn back. When they arrived at Lord Sussex's home, his worst fears were confirmed. Neither the men nor the women could take their eyes off Amanda as she strolled around the lawns devouring strawberries. Many of them would have used the word "hussy" if she hadn't been the member's wife.

Charles might have escaped lightly had it only been the one risqué joke Amanda told—to the Bishop's wife—or even her curt refusal to judge the baby contest or to draw the raffle; but he was not to be so lucky. The chairman of the Ladies' Advisory Committee had met her match when she was introduced to the member's wife.

"Darling," said Charles, "I don't think you've met Mrs. Blenkinsop."

"No, I haven't," said Amanda, ignoring Mrs. Blenkinsop's outstretched hand.

"Mrs. Blenkinsop," continued Charles, "was awarded the OBE for her services to the constituency."

"OBE?" Amanda asked innocently.

Mrs. Blenkinsop drew herself up to her full height. "Order of the British Empire," she said.

"I've always wondered," said Amanda, smiling. "Because my dad used to tell me it stood for 'other buggers' efforts.' "

Amanda didn't accompany her husband throughout the election campaign, but it made little difference to Charles's vast majority in Sussex Downs.

Simon was surprised by the huge 144 majority the Conservatives gained in the Commons, while Raymond resigned himself to another five years in Opposition and began to turn more of his attention to his practice at the bar and a new round of time-consuming cases. When the Attorney General offered him the chance to become a High Court judge, with a place in the House of Lords, Raymond gave the matter considerable thought before finally asking Joyce for her opinion.

"You'd be bored to tears in a week," she told him.

"No more bored than I am now."

"Your turn will come."

"Joyce, I'm nearly fifty, and all I have to show for it is the chairmanship of the Select Committee on Trade and Industry. If the Party fails to win next time, I may never hold office again. Don't forget that on the last occasion we lost this badly we were in Opposition for thirteen years."

"Once Michael Foot has been replaced, the Party will take on a new look, and I'm sure you'll be offered one of the senior Shadow jobs."

"That'll depend on who's our next Leader," said Raymond. "And I can't see a great deal of difference between Neil Kinnock, who looks unbeatable, and Michael Foot. I fear they are both too far left to win a General Election."

"Then why not run yourself?" asked Joyce.

"It's too early for me," said Raymond. "I'll be a serious candidate next time."

"Then why don't you at least wait until we know who's going to be Leader of the Party?" said Joyce. "You can become a judge anytime."

When Raymond returned to his chambers on Monday he followed Joyce's advice, let the Attorney General know that he was not interested in being a judge for the foreseeable future, and settled down to keep a watchful eye on the new Secretary of State for Trade and Industry.

Only a few days later Michael Foot announced that he would not be running again for Leader when the Party's annual conference took place. That left Neil Kinnock and Roy Hattersley the frontrunners. During the weeks leading up to the Labour Party's conference, several trade unionists and MPs approached Raymond and asked him to run but he told them all, "Next time."

As Raymond had predicted, Kinnock won handily. Hattersley was elected his deputy.

After the conference Raymond returned to Leeds for the weekend, still confident that he would be offered a major post in the Shadow Cabinet despite the fact that he hadn't supported the winner. Having completed his Leeds office hours, he hung around the house waiting for the new Leader to call him. When Neil Kinnock eventually phoned late that evening Raymond was shocked by his offer and replied without hesitation that he was not interested. It was a short conversation.

Joyce came into the drawing room as he sank back into his favorite armchair.

"Well, what did he offer you?" she asked, facing him.

"Transport. Virtually a demotion."

"What did you say?"

"I turned him down, of course."

"Who has he given the main jobs to?"

"I didn't ask, and he didn't volunteer, but I suspect we'll only have to wait for the morning papers to find out. Not that I'm that interested," he continued, staring at the floor, "as I intend to take the first place that comes free on the legal bench. I've wasted too many years already."

"So have I," said Joyce quietly.

"What do you mean?" asked Raymond, looking up at his wife for the first time since she had come into the room.

"If you're going to make a complete break, I think it's time for me to do so as well."

"I don't understand," said Raymond.

"We haven't been close for a long time, Ray," said Joyce, looking straight into her husband's eyes. "If you're thinking of giving up the constituency and spend even more time in London, I think we should part." She turned away.

"Is there someone else?" asked Raymond, his voice cracking.

"No one special."

"But someone?"

"There is a man who wants to marry me," said Joyce, "if that's what you mean. We were at school in Bradford together. He's an accountant now and has never married."

"But do you love him?"

Joyce considered the question. "No, I can't pretend I do. But we're good friends, he's very kind and understanding, and, more important, he's there."

Raymond couldn't move.

"And the break would at least give you the chance to ask Kate Garthwaite to give up her job in New York and return to London." Raymond gasped. "Think about it and let me know what you decide." She left the room quickly so that he could not see her tears.

Raymond sat alone in the room and thought back over his years with Joyce—and Kate—and knew exactly what he wanted to do, now that the whole affair was out in the open.

Harry Hampton's third birthday party was attended by all those three-year-olds in the vicinity of Eaton Square whom his nanny considered acceptable. Charles managed to escape from a departmental meeting accompanied by a large box of paint and a red tricycle. As he parked his car in Eaton Square he spotted Fiona's old Volvo driving away toward Sloane Square. He dismissed the coincidence. Harry naturally wanted to ride the tricycle around and around the dining-room table. Charles sat watching his son and couldn't help noticing that he was smaller than most of his friends. Then he remembered that Great-grandfather had only been five feet eight inches tall.

It was the moment after the candles had been blown out, and nanny had switched the light back on, that Charles was first aware that something was missing. It was like the game children play with objects on a tray: everyone shuts his eyes, nanny takes one object away and then you all have to guess which it was.

It took Charles some time to realize that the missing object was his small gold cigar box. He walked over to the sideboard and studied the empty space. He continued to stare at the spot where the small gold box left to him by his great-grandfather had been the previous night. Now all that was left in its place was the matching lighter.

He immediately asked Amanda if she knew where the heirloom was, but his wife seemed totally absorbed in lining up the children for a game of musical chairs. After checking carefully in the other rooms, Charles went into his study and phoned the Chelsea police.

An inspector from the local precinct came around immediately and took down all the details. Charles was able to supply the police officer with a photograph of the box, which carried the initials C.G.H. He stopped just short of mentioning Fiona by name.

Raymond caught the last train to London the same evening because he had to be in court to hear a verdict by ten o'clock the next morning. In the flat that night he slept intermittently as he thought about how he would spend the rest of his new life. Before he went into court the next morning he ordered a dozen red roses via Interflora. He phoned the Attorney General. If he was going to change his life, he must change it in every way.

When the verdict had been given and the judge had passed sentence, Raymond checked the plane schedules. Nowadays you could be there in such a short time. He booked his flight and took a taxi to Heathrow. He sat on the plane praying it wasn't too late and that too much time hadn't passed. The flight seemed endless, as did the taxi drive from the airport.

When he arrived at her front door she was astonished. "What are you doing here on a Monday afternoon?" she asked.

"I've come to try and win you back," said Raymond. "Christ, that sounds corny," he added.

"It's the nicest thing you've said in years," she said as he held her in his arms; over Joyce's shoulder Raymond could see the roses brightening up the drawing room.

Over a quiet dinner, Raymond told Joyce of his plans to accept the Attorney General's offer to join the Bench, but only if she would agree to live in London. They had a second bottle of champagne.

When they arrived at home a little after one, the phone was ringing. Raymond opened the door and stumbled toward it while Joyce groped for the light switch.

"Raymond, I've been trying to get you all night," a lilting Welsh voice said.

"Have you now?" Raymond said thickly, trying to keep his eyes open.

"You sound as if you've been to a good party."

"I've been celebrating with my wife."

"Celebrating? Before you've heard the news?"

311

"What news?" said Raymond, collapsing into the armchair.

"I've been juggling the new team around all day and I was hoping you would agree to join the Shadow Cabinet as . . ."

Raymond sobered up very quickly and listened carefully to Neil Kinnock. "Can you hold the line?"

"Of course," said the surprised voice at the other end.

"Joyce," said Raymond, as she came out of the kitchen clutching two mugs of very black coffee. "Would you agree to live with me in London if I don't become a judge?"

A wide smile spread over Joyce's face with the realization that he was seeking her approval. She nodded several times.

"I'd be delighted to accept," he said.

"Thank you, Raymond. Perhaps we could meet at my office in the Commons tomorrow and talk over policy in your new field."

"Yes, of course," said Raymond. "See you tomorrow." He dropped the phone on the floor and fell asleep in the chair, grinning.

Joyce replaced the phone and didn't discover until the following morning that her husband was the new Shadow Secretary of State for Defense.

Charles had heard nothing for three weeks about the missing gold box and was beginning to despair when the inspector phoned to say that the family heirloom had been found.

"Excellent news," said Charles. "Are you able to bring the box around to Eaton Square?"

"It's not quite as simple as that, sir," said the policeman.

"What do you mean?"

"I would prefer not to discuss the matter over the phone. May I come and see you, sir?"

"By all means," said Charles, slightly mystified.

He waited impatiently for the inspector to arrive, although the policeman was at the front door barely ten minutes later. His first question took Charles by surprise.

"Are we alone, sir?"

"Yes," said Charles. "My wife and son are away visiting my mother-in-law in Wales. You say you've found the gold box," he continued, impatient to hear the inspector's news.

"Yes, sir."

"Well done, Inspector. I shall speak to the commissioner personally," he added, guiding the officer toward the drawing room.

"I'm afraid there's a complication, sir."

"How can there be when you've found the box?"

"We cannot be sure there was anything illegal about its disappearance in the first place."

"What do you mean, Inspector?"

"The gold case was offered to a dealer in Grafton Street for twenty-five hundred pounds."

"And who was doing the selling?" asked Charles impatiently.

"That's the problem, sir. The check was made out to Amanda Hampton and the description fits your wife," said the Inspector. Charles was speechless. "And the dealer has a receipt to prove the transaction." The inspector passed over a copy of the receipt. Charles was unable to steady his shaking hand as he recognized Amanda's signature.

"Now, as this matter has already been referred to the Director of Public Prosecutions, I thought I ought to have a word with you in private, as I am sure you would not want us to press charges."

"Yes, no, of course, thank you for your consideration, Inspector," said Charles flatly.

"Not at all, sir. The dealer has made his position clear: he will be only too happy to return the cigar box for the exact sum he paid for it. I don't think that could be fairer."

Charles made no comment other than to thank the inspector again before showing him out.

He returned to his study, phoned Amanda at her mother's house and told her to return immediately. She started to protest, but he'd already hung up.

Charles remained at home until they all arrived back at Eaton

Square late that night. The nanny and Harry were immediately sent upstairs.

It took Charles about five minutes to discover that only a few hundred pounds of the money was left. When his wife burst into tears he struck her across the face with such force that she fell to the ground. "If anything else disappears from this house," he said, "you will go with it, and I will also make sure you spend a very long time in jail." Amanda ran out of the room sobbing uncontrollably.

The following day Charles advertised for a full-time governess. He also moved his own bedroom to the top floor so that he could be close to his son. Amanda made no protest.

Raymond gave up his flat in the Barbican, and he and Joyce moved into a small Georgian house in Cowley Street, only a few hundred yards from the House of Commons.

Raymond watched Joyce decorate his study first, then she set about the rest of the house with the energy and enthusiasm of a newlywed. Once Joyce had completed the guest bedroom, Raymond's parents came down to spend the weekend. Raymond burst out laughing when he greeted his father at the door clutching a bag marked "Gould the Family Butcher."

"They do have meat in London, you know," said Raymond.

"Not like mine, son," his father replied.

Over the finest beef dinner Raymond could remember, he watched Joyce and his mother chatting away. "Thank God I woke up in time," he said out loud.

"What did you say?" asked Joyce.

"Nothing, my dear. Nothing."

Alec Pimkin threw a party for all of his Tory colleagues who had entered the House in 1964, "To celebrate the first twenty years in the Commons," as he described the occasion in an impromptu after-dinner speech.

Over brandy and cigars the corpulent, balding figure sat back and surveyed his fellow members. Many had fallen by the way over the years, but of those that were left, he believed only two men now dominated the intake.

Pimkin's eyes first settled on his old friend Charles Hampton. Despite studying him closely, he was still unable to spot a gray hair on the Treasury Minister's head. From time to time Pimkin still saw Amanda, who had returned to being a fulltime model and was rarely to be found in England nowadays. Charles, he suspected, saw more of her on magazine covers than he ever did in his home at Eaton Square. Pimkin had been surprised by how much time Charles was willing to put aside for little Harry. Charles was the last man he would have suspected of ending up a doting father.

Certainly the coals of his ambitions had in no way dimmed, and Pimkin suspected that only one man remained a worthy rival for the Party Leadership.

Pimkin's eyes moved on to someone for whom the responsibility of high office seemed to hold no fears. Simon Kerslake was deep in animated conversation about his work on the proposed disarmament talks between Thatcher, Chernenko and Reagan. Pimkin studied the Foreign Office Minister intently. He considered that if he himself had been graced with such looks, he would not have had to fear for his dwindling majority.

Rumors of some financial crisis had long since died away, and Kerslake now seemed well set for a formidable future.

The party began to break up as one by one his contemporaries came over to thank him for such a "splendid," "memorable," "worthwhile" evening. When the last one had departed and Pimkin found himself alone, he drained the drop of brandy that remained in his balloon and stubbed out the dying cigar. He sighed as he speculated on the fact that he could now never hope to be made a Minister.

He therefore determined to become a kingmaker, for in another twenty years there would be nothing left on which to speculate.

315

Raymond celebrated his twenty years in the House by taking Joyce to the Ivy Restaurant off Berkeley Square for dinner. He admired the long burgundy dress his wife had chosen for the occasion and even noticed that once or twice women gave it more than a casual glance throughout their meal.

He too reflected on his twenty years in the Commons, and he told Joyce over a brandy that he hoped he would spend more of the next twenty years in Government. Nineteen eighty-four was not turning out to be a good year for the Conservatives, and Raymond was already forming plans to make 1985 as uncomfortable for the Government as possible.

The winter of 1985 brought further rises in unemployment and the level of inflation, which only increased the Labour Party's lead in the polls. For a short period after the Chancellor had brought in an emergency budget, Tory popularity fell to its lowest point in five years.

Mrs. Thatcher took that as a cue to introduce new blood into her Cabinet, and announced the names of those who would be formulating policy in the run-up to the next General Election. The average age of the Cabinet fell by seven years, and the press dubbed it "Mrs. Thatcher's new-lamps-for-old reshuffle."

PART FIVE

The Conservative Cabinet

1985-1988

27

RAYMOND WAS ON HIS WAY to the House of Commons when he heard the first reports on his car radio. There had been no mention of the news in the morning papers so it must have happened during the night. It began with a news flash—just the bare details. HMS *Broadsword,* a type T.K. 22 frigate, had been passing through the Gulf of Surt between Tunis and Benghazi when she was boarded by a group of mercenaries, posing as coast guard officials, who took over the ship in the name of Libya's Colonel Muammar Qaddafi. The newscaster went on to say that there would be a more detailed report in their ten o'clock bulletin.

Staying near a radio most of the morning, Raymond learned that HMS *Broadsword* was now in the hands of over a hundred guerrillas. They were demanding the freedom of all Libyan prisoners in British jails in exchange for the two hundred and seventeen-strong crew of the *Broadsword,* who were being held hostage in the engine room.

By lunch time the ticker-tape machine in the members' corridor was surrounded by members with craning necks, and the dining rooms were so full that many of them had to go without lunch.

The Palace of Westminster was already packed and buzzing with each new snippet of information. Political correspondents waited hawklike in the members' lobby seeking opinions on the crisis from any senior politicians as they passed to and from the chamber. Few were rash enough to say anything that might be reinterpreted the next day.

At three twenty-seven the Prime Minister, followed by the Foreign Secretary and the Secretary of State for Defense, filed into the House and took her place on the front bench. All three looked suitably somber.

At three-thirty the Speaker rose and called for order.

"Statements to the House," he announced in his crisp, military style. "There will be two statements on HMS *Broadsword* before the House debates Welsh affairs." The Speaker then called the Secretary of State for Defense.

Simon Kerslake rose from the front bench and placed a prepared statement on the dispatch box in front of him.

"Mr. Speaker, with your permission and that of the House, I would like to make a statement concerning Her Majesty's frigate *Broadsword*. At seven-forty GMT this morning, HMS *Broadsword* was passing through the Gulf of Surt between Tunis and Benghazi when a group of guerrillas, posing as official coast guards, boarded the ship and seized her captain, Commander Lawrence Packard, and placed the crew under arrest. The guerrillas, claiming to represent the Libyan Peoples Army, have since placed Commander Packard and the crew in the engine room of the ship. As far as it is possible to ascertain from our Embassy in Tripoli, no lives have been lost. There is no suggestion that *Broadsword* was other than going about her lawful business. This barbaric act must be looked upon as piracy under the 1958 Geneva Convention on the High Seas. The guerrillas are demanding the release of all Libyan prisoners in British prisons in exchange for the return of HMS *Broadsword* and her crew. My Right Honorable friend, the Home Secretary, informs me there are only four known Libyans in British prisons at the present time, two of whom have been sentenced to three months for persistent shoplifting, while the other two were convicted on more serious drug charges. Her Majesty's

320

Government cannot and will not interfere with the due process of law and has no intention of releasing these men."

Loud "Hear, hears" came from all sections of the House.

"My Right Honorable friend, the Foreign Secretary, has made Her Majesty's Government's position clear to the Libyan Ambassador, in particular that Her Majesty's Government cannot be expected to tolerate this sort of treatment of British subjects or of British property. We have demanded and expect immediate action from the Libyan government."

Simon sat down to loud and prolonged cheers before Raymond Gould rose from his place. The House went silent as everyone wanted to discover what the Labour Party line would be.

"Mr. Speaker," began Raymond, "we in the Labour Party also look upon this barbaric act as one of piracy on the high seas. But can I ask the Secretary for Defense if he has any plans at this early stage for the recovery of *Broadsword?*"

Simon rose again. "We are, Mr. Speaker, at present seeking a diplomatic solution, but I have already chaired a meeting of the Joint Chiefs, and I anticipate making a further statement to the House tomorrow."

Raymond rose again from his place on the front bench. "But can the Right Honorable Gentleman tell the House how long he will allow negotiations to continue when it is well known throughout the diplomatic world that Qaddafi is a master of procrastination, especially if we are to rely on the United Nations to adjudicate on this issue?" From the noise that greeted Raymond's inquiry, it seemed that his views were shared by the majority of the House.

Simon rose to answer the question. "I accept the point the Honorable Gentleman is making, but he will know, having been a Minister in the last Government himself, that I am not in a position to divulge any information which might imperil the safety of *Broadsword.*" Raymond nodded his acquiescence.

Question after question came at Simon. He handled them with such confidence that visitors in the Strangers' Gallery would have found it hard to believe that he had been invited to join the Cabinet only five weeks before.

At four-fifteen, after Simon had answered the last question the Speaker was going to allow, he sank back on the front bench to listen to the statement from the Foreign Office. The House fell silent once again as the Foreign Secretary rose from his place and checked the large double-spaced sheets in front of him. All eyes were now on the tall, elegant man who was making his first official statement since his appointment.

"Mr. Speaker, with your permission and that of the House, I too would like to make a statement concerning HMS *Broadsword*. Once news had reached the Foreign Office this morning of the plight of Her Majesty's ship *Broadsword,* my office immediately issued a strongly worded statement to the government of Libya. The Libyan ambassador has been called to the Foreign Office and I shall be seeing him again immediately after this statement and the questions arising from it have been completed."

Raymond looked up at the Strangers' Gallery from his place on the Opposition front bench. It was one of the ironies of modern diplomacy that the Libyan ambassador was in Parliament making notes while the Foreign Secretary delivered his statement. He couldn't imagine Colonel Qaddafi inviting the British ambassador to take notes while he sat in his tent addressing his followers. Raymond was pleased to see an attendant ask the ambassador to stop writing; the prohibition dated from the time when the House had jealously guarded its secrecy. Raymond's eyes dropped back to the front bench, and he continued to listen to Charles Hampton.

"Our ambassador to the United Nations has presented a resolution to be debated by the General Assembly this afternoon, asking representatives to back Britain against this flagrant violation of the 1958 Geneva Convention on the High Seas. I confidently expect the support of the free world. Her Majesty's Government will do everything in its power to insure a diplomatic solution, bearing in mind that the lives of two hundred and seventeen British servicemen are still at risk."

The Shadow Foreign Secretary rose and asked at what point the Foreign Secretary would consider once again breaking off diplomatic relations with Libya.

"I naturally hope it will not come to that, Mr. Speaker, and I expect the Libyan government to deal quickly with their own mercenaries." Charles continued to answer questions from all sections of the House but could only repeat that there was little new intelligence to offer the House at the present time.

Raymond watched his two contemporaries as they displayed over twenty years of parliamentary skill in presenting their case. He wondered if this episode would make one of them Mrs. Thatcher's obvious successor.

At four-thirty the Speaker, realizing nothing new had been said for some time, announced that he would allow one further question from each side before returning to the business of the day. He shrewdly called Alec Pimkin, who sounded to Raymond like "the very model of a modern major-general," and then Tom Carson, who suggested that Colonel Qaddafi was often misrepresented by the British press. Once Carson had sat down, the Speaker found it easy to move on to other business.

The Speaker rose again and thanked the Honorable Gentleman, the member for Leeds North, for his courtesy in informing him that he would be making an application under Standing Order Number 10 for an emergency debate. The Speaker said he had given the matter careful thought but he reminded the House that, under the terms of the Standing Order, he did not need to divulge the reasons for his decision—merely whether the matter should have precedence over the orders of the day. He ruled that the matter was not proper for discussion within the terms of Standing Order Number 10.

Raymond rose to protest, but as the Speaker remained standing, he had to resume his seat.

"This does not mean, however," continued the Speaker, "that I would not reconsider such a request at a later date."

Raymond realized that Charles Hampton and Simon Kerslake must have pleaded for more time, but he was only going to allow them twenty-four hours. The clerk-at-the-table rose and bellowed above the noise of members leaving the chamber, "Adjournment." The Speaker called the Secretary of State for Wales to move the adjournment motion on the problems facing the Welsh mining industry. The chamber emptied of all but the thirty-eight Welsh MPs who had been waiting weeks for a full debate on the principality's affairs.

Simon made his way back to the Ministry of Defense to continue discussions with the Joint Chiefs of Staff, while Charles was driven immediately to the Foreign Office.

When Charles reached his office, he was told by the Permanent Under Secretary that the Libyan ambassador awaited him.

"Does he have anything new to tell us?" asked Charles.

"Frankly, nothing."

"Send him in."

Charles stubbed out his cigarette and stood by the mantelpiece below a portrait of Palmerston. Having taken over at the Foreign Office only five weeks previously, Charles had never met the ambassador before.

Mr. Kadir, the dark-haired immaculately dressed five-foot-one ambassador for Libya entered the room.

"Foreign Secretary?" began Mr. Kadir. Charles was momentarily taken aback when he noticed the ambassador's Etonian tie. He recovered quickly.

"Her Majesty's Government wishes to make it abundantly clear to your government," began Charles, not allowing the ambassador to continue, "that we consider the act of boarding and holding Her Majesty's ship *Broadsword* against her will as one of piracy on the high seas."

"May I say—?" began Mr. Kadir again.

"No, you may not," said Charles. "And until our ship has been released, we shall do everything in our power to bring

324

pressure, both diplomatic and economic, on your government."

"But may I just say—?" Mr. Kadir tried again.

"My Prime Minister also wants you to know that she wishes to speak to your Head of State at the soonest possible opportunity, so I shall expect to hear back from you within the hour."

"Yes, Foreign Secretary, but may I—?"

"And you may further report that we will reserve our right to take any action we deem appropriate if you fail to secure the release into safe custody of HMS *Broadsword* and her crew by twelve noon tomorrow, GMT. Do I make myself clear?"

"Yes, Foreign Secretary, but I would like to ask—"

"Good day, Mr. Kadir."

After the Libyan ambassador was shown out, Charles couldn't help wondering what it was he had wanted to say.

"What do we do now?" he asked when the Permanent Under Secretary returned, having deposited Mr. Kadir in the elevator.

"We act out the oldest diplomatic game in the world."

"What do you mean?" said Charles.

"Our sit-and-wait policy. We're awfully good at it," said the Permanent Under Secretary, "but then we've been at it for nearly a thousand years."

"Well, while we sit let's at least make some phone calls. I'll start with Secretary of State Kirkpatrick in Washington and then I'd like to speak to Gromyko in Moscow."

When Simon arrived back at the Ministry of Defense from the Commons he was told that the Joint Chiefs were assembled in his office waiting for him to chair the next strategy meeting. As he entered the room to take his place at the table, the Joint Chiefs rose.

"Good afternoon, gentlemen," Simon said. "Please be seated. Can you bring me up to date on the latest situation, Sir John?"

Admiral Sir John Fieldhouse, Chief of the Defense staff, pushed up the half-moon glasses from the end of his nose and checked the notes in front of him.

"Very little has changed in the last hour, sir," he began. "The

Prime Minister's office has still had no success in contacting Colonel Qaddafi. I fear we must now treat the capture of *Broadsword* as a blatant act of terrorism, rather similar to the occupation seven years ago of the American Embassy in Iran by students who backed the late Ayatollah Khomeini. In such circumstances we can either 'jaw-jaw or war-war,' to quote Sir Winston. With that in mind, this committee will have formed a detailed plan by the early evening for the recapture of HMS *Broadsword,* as we assume the Foreign Office is better qualified to prepare for jaw-jaw." Sir John looked toward his Minister.

"Are you in a position to give me a provisional plan that I could place in front of the Cabinet for their consideration?"

"Certainly, Minister," said Sir John, pushing up his glasses again before opening a large blue file in front of him.

Simon listened intently as Sir John went over his provisional strategy. Around the table sat eight of the senior-ranking staff officers of the army, the navy and the air force, and even the first draft plan bore the stamp of their three hundred years of military experience. Simon couldn't help remembering that his call-up status was still that of a 2nd Lieutenant. For an hour he asked the Joint Chiefs questions that ranged from the elementary to those that demonstrated a clear insight into their problems. When Simon left the room to attend the Cabinet meeting at Number 10, the Joint Chiefs were already updating the plan.

Simon walked slowly across Whitehall from the Department of Defense to Downing Street, his private detective by his side. Downing Street was thronged with people curious to see the comings and goings of Ministers involved in the crisis. Simon was touched that the crowd applauded him all the way to the front door of Number 10, where the journalists and TV crews awaited each arrival. The great television arc lights were switched on as he reached the door, and a microphone was thrust in front of him, but he made no comment. Simon was surprised by how many of the normally cynical journalists called out, "Good luck," and "Bring our boys home."

The front door opened and he went straight through to the corridor outside the Cabinet room, where twenty-two of his colleagues were already waiting. A moment later, the Prime Minister walked into the Cabinet room and took her seat in the center of the table, with Charles and Simon opposite her.

Mrs. Thatcher began by telling her colleagues that she had been unable to make any contact with Colonel Qaddafi and that they must therefore decide on a course of action that did not involve his acquiescence. She invited the Foreign Secretary to brief the Cabinet first.

Charles went over the actions in which the Foreign Office was involved at the diplomatic level. He reported his meeting with Ambassador Kadir, and the resolution which had been proposed at the UN and which was already being debated at an emergency session of the General Assembly. The purpose of asking the United Nations to back Britain on Resolution 12/40, he said, was to capture the diplomatic initiative and virtually guarantee international sympathy. Charles went on to tell the Cabinet that he expected a vote to take place in the General Assembly that evening which would demonstrate overwhelming support for the United Kingdom's resolution and which would be regarded as a moral victory by the whole world. He was delighted to be able to report to the Cabinet that the foreign ministers of both the United States and Russia had agreed to back the UK in her diplomatic endeavors as long as she launched no retaliatory action. Charles ended by reminding his colleagues of the importance of treating the whole affair as an act of piracy rather than as an injury at the hands of the Libyan government itself.

A legal nicety, thought Simon as he watched the faces of his colleagues around the table. They were obviously impressed that Charles had brought the two superpowers together in support of Britain. The Prime Minister's face remained inscrutable. She called upon Simon to air his views.

He was able to report that *Broadsword* had, since the last meeting of the Cabinet, been towed into the Bay of Surt and

327

moored; there was no hope of boarding her except by sea. Commander Packard and his crew of two hundred and seventeen remained under close arrest in the engine room on the lower deck of the ship. From confirmed reports Simon had received in the last hour, it appeared that the ship's company were bound and gagged, and that the ventilation systems had been turned off. "I therefore suggest," said Simon, "that we have no choice but to mount a rescue operation in order to avoid a protracted negotiation that can only end in grave loss of morale for the entire armed forces. The longer we put off such a decision, the harder our task will become. The Joint Chiefs are putting the final touches to a plan code-named 'Shoplifter,' which they feel must be carried out in the next forty-eight hours if the men and the ship are to be saved." Simon added that he hoped diplomatic channels would be kept open while the operation was being worked out, in order that our rescue team could be assured of the greatest element of surprise.

"But what if your plan fails?" interrupted Charles. "We would risk losing not only *Broadsword* and her crew but also the good will of the free world."

"There is no serving officer in the British navy who will thank us for leaving *Broadsword* in Libyan waters while we negotiate a settlement in which, at best, our ship will be returned when it suits the guerrillas—to say nothing of the humiliation of our navy. Qaddafi can laugh at the United Nations while he has captured not only one of our most modern frigates but also the headlines of the world press. Unlike the St. James's Square siege, he has the initiative this time. These headlines can only demoralize our countrymen and invite the sort of election defeat Carter suffered at the hands of the American people after the Iranian Embassy debacle."

"We would be foolish to take such an unnecessary risk while we have world opinion on our side," protested Charles. "Let us at least wait a few more days."

"I fear that if we wait," said Simon, "the crew will be transferred from the ship to a military prison, which would only result in our having two targets to concentrate on, and then Qaddafi can sit around in the desert taking whatever amount of time suits him."

Simon and Charles weighed argument against counterargument while the Prime Minister listened, taking note of the views of her other colleagues around the table to see if she had a majority for one course or the other. Three hours later, when everyone had given his opinion, she had "14–9" written on the pad in front of her.

"I think we have exhausted the arguments, gentlemen," she said, "and having listened to the collective views around this table I feel we must on balance allow the Secretary of State for Defense to proceed with 'Operation Shoplifter.' I therefore propose that the Foreign Secretary, the Defense Secretary, the Attorney General and myself make up a subcommittee, backed up by a professional staff, to consider the Joint Chiefs' plan. The utmost secrecy will be required from us at all times, so the subject will not be raised again until the plan is ready for presentation to a full meeting of the Cabinet. Therefore, with the exception of the subcommittee, all Ministers will return to their departments and carry on with their normal duties. We must not lose sight of the fact that the country still has to be governed. Thank you, gentlemen." The Prime Minister asked Charles and Simon to join her in the study.

As soon as the door was closed she said to Charles, "Please let me know the moment you hear the results of the vote in the General Assembly. Now that the Cabinet has favored a military initiative, it is important that you are seen to be pressing for a diplomatic solution."

"Yes, Prime Minister," said Charles without emotion.

Mrs. Thatcher then turned to Simon. "When can I have a rundown on the details of the Joint Chiefs' plan?"

"We anticipate working on the strategy through the night, Prime Minister, and I should be able to make a full presentation to you by ten tomorrow."

"No later, Simon," said the Prime Minister. "Now our next

problem is tomorrow's proposed emergency debate. Raymond Gould will undoubtedly put in a second request for a full debate under Standing Order Number Ten, and the Speaker gave the House a clear hint today that he will allow it. Anyway, we can't avoid making a policy statement without an outcry from the Opposition benches—and I suspect our own—so I have decided that we will grasp the nettle and no doubt get stung."

The two men looked at each other, united for a moment in exasperation at the thought of having to waste precious hours in the Commons.

"Charles, you must be prepared to open the debate for the Government, and Simon, you will wind up. At least the debate will be on Thursday afternoon; that way some of our colleagues may have gone home for the weekend, though frankly I doubt it. But with any luck we will have secured a moral victory at the United Nations, and we can keep the Opposition minds concentrating on that. When you sum up, Simon, just answer the questions put during the debate. Do not offer any new initiative." She then added, "Report any news you hear directly to me. I shan't be sleeping tonight."

Charles walked back to the Foreign Office, thankful at least that Amanda was off somewhere in South America.

Simon returned to the Joint Chiefs to find a large map of Libyan territorial waters pinned to a blackboard. Generals, admirals and air marshals were studying the contours and ocean depths like so many children preparing for a geography test.

They all stood again when Simon entered the room. They looked at him in anticipation, men of action who were suspicious of talk. When Simon told them the Cabinet's decision was to back the Ministry of Defense, the suggestion of a smile came over the face of Sir John. "Perhaps that battle will turn out to be our hardest," he said, just loud enough for everyone to hear.

"Take me through the plan again," said Simon, ignoring Sir John's comment. "I have to present it to the Prime Minister by ten o'clock tomorrow."

Sir John placed the tip of a long wooden pointer on a model of HMS *Broadsword* in the middle of a stretch of water in a well-protected bay.

When Charles reached his office, the international telegrams and telexes of support for a diplomatic solution were piled high on his desk. The Permanent Under Secretary reported that the debate in the United Nations had been so onesided that he anticipated an overwhelming majority when they came to vote. Charles feared his hands were tied; he had to be seen to go through the motions, even by his own staff, although he had not yet given up hopes of undermining Simon's plan. He intended the whole episode to end up as a triumph for the Foreign Office and not for those warmongers at the Ministry of Defense. After consulting the Permanent Under Secretary, Charles appointed a small "Libyan task force" consisting of some older Foreign Office mandarins with experience of Qaddafi and four of the department's most promising "high fliers."

Oliver Milas, the former ambassador to Libya, had been dragged out of retirement from his comfortable Wilshire home and deposited in a tiny room in the upper reaches of the Foreign Office so that Charles could call on his knowledge of Libya at any time, day or night, throughout the crisis.

Charles asked the Permanent Under Secretary to link him up with Britain's ambassador at the United Nations.

"And keep trying to raise Qaddafi."

Simon listened to Sir John go over the latest version of Operation Shoplifter. Thirty-seven men from the crack Special Boat Service, a branch of the SAS regiment which had been involved in the St. James's Square siege in April 1984, were now in Rosyth on the Scottish coast, preparing to board HMS *Brilliant,* the sister ship to *Broadsword.*

The men were to be dropped from a submarine a mile outside Rosyth harbor and swim the last mile and a half underwater

331

until they reached the ship. They would then board *Brilliant* and expect to recapture her from a mock Libyan crew in an estimated twelve minutes. *Brilliant* would then be sailed to a distance of one nautical mile off the Scottish coast. The operation was to be completed in sixty minutes. The SBS planned to rehearse the procedure on *Brilliant* three times before first light the following morning, when they hoped to have the entire exercise down to the hour.

Simon had already confirmed the order to send two submarines from the Mediterranean full steam in the direction of the Libyan coast. The rest of the fleet was to be seen to be conspicuously going about its normal business, while the Foreign Office appeared to be searching for a diplomatic solution.

Simon's request to the Joint Chiefs came as no surprise and was granted immediately. He phoned Elizabeth to explain why he wouldn't be home that night. An hour later the Secretary of State for Defense was strapped into a helicopter and on his way to Rosyth.

Charles followed the proceedings at the United Nations live in his office. At the end of a brief debate a vote was called for. The Secretary General announced 147–3 in Great Britain's favor, with twenty-two abstentions. Charles wondered if such an overwhelming vote would be enough to get the Prime Minister to change her mind over Kerslake's plan. He checked over the voting list carefully. The Russians, along with the Warsaw Pact countries and the Americans, had kept their word and voted with the UK. Only Libya, South Yemen and Djibouti had voted against. Charles was put through to Downing Street and passed on the news. The Prime Minister, although delighted with the diplomatic triumph, refused to change course until she had heard from Qaddafi. Charles put the phone down and asked his Permanent Under Secretary to call Ambassador Kadir to the Foreign Office once more.

"But it's two o'clock in the morning, Foreign Secretary."

"I am quite aware what time it is but I can see no reason why, while we are all awake, he should be having a peaceful night's sleep."

When Mr. Kadir was shown into the Foreign Office it annoyed Charles to see the little man still looking fresh and dapper. It was obvious that he had just shaved and put on a clean shirt.

"You called for me, Foreign Secretary?" asked Mr. Kadir politely, as if he had been invited to afternoon tea.

"Yes," said Charles. "We wished to be certain that you are aware of the vote taken at the United Nations an hour ago supporting the United Kingdom's Resolution 12/40."

"Yes, Foreign Secretary."

"In which your government was condemned by the leaders of ninety percent of the people on the globe"—a fact the Permanent Under Secretary had fed to Charles a few minutes before Mr. Kadir had arrived.

"Yes, Foreign Secretary."

"My Prime Minister is still waiting to hear from your head of state."

"Yes, Foreign Secretary."

"Have you yet made contact with Colonel Qaddafi?"

"No, Foreign Secretary."

"But you have a direct telephone link to his headquarters."

"Then you will be only too aware, Foreign Secretary, that I have been unable to speak to him," said Mr. Kadir with a wry smile.

Charles saw the Permanent Under Secretary lower his eyes. "I shall speak to you on the hour every hour, Mr. Kadir, but do not press my country's hospitality too far."

"No, Foreign Secretary."

"Good night, Ambassador," said Charles.

"Good night, Foreign Secretary."

Mr. Kadir turned and left the Foreign Office to be driven back to his embassy. He cursed the Right Honorable Charles

Hampton. Didn't the man realize that he hadn't been back to Libya, except to visit his mother, since the age of four? Colonel Qaddafi was ignoring his ambassador every bit as much as he was the British Prime Minister. He checked his watch: it read 2:44.

Simon's helicopter landed in Scotland at two forty-five. He and Sir John were immediately driven to the dockside and then ferried out to HMS *Brilliant* through the misty night.

"The first Secretary of State not to be piped on board in living memory," said Sir John as Simon made his way with difficulty, his blackthorn stick tapping on the gangplank. The captain of the *Brilliant* couldn't disguise his surprise when he saw his uninvited guests, and he escorted them quickly to the bridge. Sir John whispered something in the captain's ear which Simon missed.

"When is the next raid due?" asked Simon, staring out from the bridge but unable to see more than a few yards in front of him.

"They leave the sub at three hundred hours," said the captain, "and should reach *Brilliant* at approximately three-twenty. They hope to have taken command of the ship in eleven minutes and be a mile beyond territorial waters in under the hour."

Simon checked his watch: it was five to three. He thought of the SBS preparing for their task, unaware that the Secretary of State and the Chief of the Defense Staff were on board *Brilliant* waiting for them. He pulled his coat collar up. Suddenly, he was thrown to the deck, a black and oily hand clamped over his mouth before he could protest. He felt his arms whipped up and tied behind his back as his eyes were blindfolded and he was gagged. He tried to retaliate and received a sharp elbow in the ribs. Then he was dragged down a narrow staircase and dumped on a wooden floor. He lay trussed up like a chicken for what he thought was about ten minutes before he heard the ship's engines revving up and felt the movement of the ship below him. The Secretary of State could not move for another fifteen minutes.

"Release them," Simon heard a voice say in distinctly Oxford English. The rope around his arms was untied and the blindfold and gag removed. Standing over the Secretary of State was an SBS frogman, black from head to toe, his white teeth gleaming in a wide grin. Simon was still slightly stunned as he turned to see the commander of Her Majesty's forces also being untied.

"I must apologize, Minister," said Sir John, as soon as his gag was removed, "but I told the captain not to inform the submarine commander we were on board. If I am going to risk two hundred and seventeen of my men's lives, I wanted to be sure this rabble from the SBS knew what they were up to." Simon backed away from the six foot two giant who towered over him still grinning.

"Good thing we didn't bring the Prime Minister along for the ride," said Sir John.

"I agree," said Simon, looking up at the SBS commando. "She would have broken his neck." Everyone laughed except the frogman, who pursed his lips.

"What's wrong with him?" said Simon.

"If he utters the slightest sound during these sixty minutes, he won't be selected for the final team."

"The Conservative Party could do with some back-bench members of Parliament like that," said Simon. "Especially when I have to address the House tomorrow and explain why I'm doing nothing."

By three forty-five *Brilliant* was once again beyond territorial waters.

The newspaper headlines that next morning ranged from "Diplomatic Victory" in the *Times* to "Qaddafi the Pirate" in the *Mirror*.

At a meeting of the inner Cabinet held at ten in the morning

Simon reported his first-hand experience of Operation Shoplifter to the Prime Minister.

Charles was quick to follow him. "But after the overwhelming vote in our favor at the UN, it must be sensible for us to
postpone anything that might be considered as an outright act
of aggression."

"If the SBS doesn't go tomorrow morning, we will never have
as good a chance, Prime Minister," said Simon, interrupting
him.

All eyes at the meeting of the inner Cabinet turned to Kerslake.

"Why?" asked Mrs. Thatcher.

"Because Ramadan comes to an end today, and tomorrow
the Moslems break their daylight fasts. Traditionally it's a
heavy feasting-day, which means tomorrow will be our best
chance to catch the guerrillas off guard. I have been over the
entire operation in Rosyth and by now the SBS are well on their
way to the submarines and preparing for the assault. It's all so
finely tuned, Prime Minister, that I obviously don't want to
throw away such a good opportunity."

"That's good reasoning," she concurred. "With the weekend
ahead of us we must pray that this mess will be all over by
Monday morning. Let's put on our negotiating faces for the
Commons this afternoon. I expect a very convincing performance from you, Charles."

When Raymond rose at three-thirty that Thursday afternoon to
ask a second time for an emergency debate, the Speaker granted
his request, directing that the urgency of the matter warranted
the debate to commence at seven o'clock that evening.

The chamber emptied quickly as the members scuttled off to
prepare their speeches, although they all knew that less than 2
percent of them could hope to be called. The Speaker departed
the chamber and did not return until five to seven when he took
over the chair from his deputy.

By seven o'clock, when Charles and Simon had entered the

House, all thirty-seven SBS men were aboard Her Majesty's submarine *Conqueror,* lying on the ocean bed about sixty nautical miles off the Libyan coast. A second submarine, *Courageous,* was ten miles to the rear of her. Neither had broken radio silence for the past twelve hours.

The Prime Minister had still not heard from Colonel Qaddafi and they were now only eight hours away from Operation Shoplifter. Simon looked around the House. The atmosphere resembled budget day, and an eerie silence fell as the Speaker called on Raymond Gould to address the House.

Raymond began by explaining, under Standing Order Number 10, why the matter he had raised was specific, important and needed urgent consideration. He quickly moved on to demand that the Foreign Secretary confirm that if negotiations with Qaddafi failed or dragged on, the Secretary of State for Defense would not hesitate to take the necessary action to recover HMS *Broadsword.* Simon sat on the front bench looking glum and shaking his head.

"Qaddafi's nothing more than a pirate," said Raymond. "Why talk of diplomatic solutions?"

The House cheered as each well-rehearsed phrase rolled off Raymond's tongue. Simon listened intently, privately agreeing with his sentiments and knew that, had their roles been reversed, it would have been no different.

When Raymond sat down, the cheers came from all parts of the chamber and it was several minutes before the speaker could bring the House back to order. Mr. Kadir sat in the Distinguished Strangers' Gallery staring impassively down, trying to memorize the salient points that had been made and the House's reaction to them, so that—if he were ever given the chance—he could pass them on to Colonel Qaddafi.

"The Foreign Secretary," called the Speaker, and Charles rose from his place on the Treasury bench. He placed his speech on the dispatch box in front of him and waited. Once again the House fell silent.

Charles opened his case by emphasizing the significance of

the United Nations vote as the foundation for a genuine negotiated settlement. He went on to say that his first priority was to
secure the lives of the two hundred seventeen men on board
HMS *Broadsword,* and that he intended to work tirelessly to
that end. The Secretary General was hoping to contact Qaddafi
personally and brief him on the strong feelings of his colleagues
in the General Assembly. Charles stressed that taking any other
course at the present time could only lose the support and good
will of the free world. When Charles sat down, he realized that
the rowdy House was not convinced.

The contribution from the back benches confirmed the Prime
Minister's and Simon's belief that they had gauged the feelings
of the nation correctly, but neither of them allowed the slightest
show of emotion to cross their faces and give hope to those who
were demanding military action.

By the time Simon rose to wind up for the Government at
nine-thirty that night, he had spent two and a half hours in the
chamber listening to men and women tell him to get on with
exactly what he was already doing. Blandly he backed the Foreign Secretary in his pursuit of a diplomatic solution. The
House became restive, and when the clock reached ten, Simon
sat down to cries of "Resign" from some of his own colleagues
and the more right wing of the Labour benches.

Raymond watched carefully as Kerslake and Hampton left
the chamber. He wondered what was really going on behind the
closed door of Number 10 Downing Street.

When Raymond arrived home after the debate, Joyce congratulated him on his speech and added, "But it didn't evoke
much of a response from Simon Kerslake."

"He's up to something," said Raymond. "I only wish I was
sitting in his office tonight and could find out what it is."

When Simon arrived back in his office he phoned Elizabeth
and explained that he would be spending another night at the
Ministry of Defense.

"Some women do lose their men to the strangest mistresses,"

said Elizabeth. "By the way, your daughter wants to know if you will have time to watch her play field hockey in her intramural final on Saturday."

"What's today?"

"It's still Thursday," she said, "and to think you're the one in charge of the nation's defenses."

Simon knew the rescue attempt would be all over one way or the other by lunchtime the next day. Why shouldn't he watch his daughter play in a field hockey match?

"Tell Lucy I'll be there," he said.

Although nothing could be achieved between midnight and six o'clock now that the submarines were in place, none of the Joint Chiefs left the operations room. Radio silence was not broken once through the night as Simon tried to occupy himself with the bulging red boxes containing other pressing matters which still demanded his attention. He took advantage of the presence of the Joint Chiefs and had a hundred queries answered in minutes that would normally have taken him a month.

At midnight the first editions of the morning papers were brought to him. Simon pinned up the *Telegraph*'s headline on the operations board. "Kerslake's in His Hammock Till the Great Armada Comes." The article demanded to know how the hero of Northern Ireland could be so indecisive while Britain's sailors lay bound and gagged in foreign waters, and ended with the words "Captain, art thou sleeping there below?" "Not a wink," said Simon. "Resign" was the single-word headline of the *Daily Express*. Sir John looked over the Minister's shoulder and read the opening paragraph.

"I shall never understand why anyone wants to be a politician," he said, before reporting: "We have just heard from reconnaissance in the area that both submarines *Conqueror* and *Courageous* have moved up into place."

Simon picked up the blackthorn stick from the side of his desk and left the Joint Chiefs to go over to Downing Street. He passed the morning street cleaners on their way to work before London woke up and started another day. They shouted "Morning, Simon" and "Have you got our ship back yet?"

"Ask me in three hours' time," he wanted to say but only smiled.

He found the Prime Minister sitting in the Cabinet room in her bathrobe.

"It's no use, I couldn't sleep," she said. Simon went over the final plan with her in great detail, explaining that everything was ready and would be over by the time most people were having their breakfasts.

"Let me know the moment you hear anything—however trivial," she concluded, before returning to the latest gloomy study of the economy from the Wynne Godley team, who were suggesting that the pound and the dollar would be of equal parity by 1990. "One day you may have all these problems on *your* shoulders," she said.

Simon smiled and left her to walk slowly back to his office on the other side of Whitehall. He stopped to stare at the statue of Montgomery that stood on the grass in front of the Ministry of Defense and thought how much the Field Marshal would have relished the skirmish that was about to take place. A full moon shone like an arc light above Saint Paul's Cathedral as he hurried back to his office.

At one, he joined the Joint Chiefs. None of them looked tired, although they had all shared the lonely vigil with their comrades two thousand miles away. They told stories of Suez and the Falklands and there was frequent laughter. But it was never long before their eyes returned to the clock.

As Big Ben struck one chime, Simon thought: three o'clock in Libya. He could visualize the men falling backwards over the side of the boat and deep into the water before starting the long, slow swim toward *Broadsword.*

Simon returned to his desk for what was to be the longest hour of his life.

———

When the phone rang, breaking the eerie silence like a fire alarm, Simon picked it up to hear Charles Hampton's voice.

"Simon," he began, "I've finally gotten through to Qaddafi and he wants to negotiate." Simon looked at his watch; the divers could only be a hundred yards from *Broadsword*.

"It's too late," he said. "I can't stop them now."

"Don't be such a bloody fool—order them to turn back. Don't you understand we've won a diplomatic coup?"

"Qaddafi could negotiate for months and still end up humiliating us. No, I won't turn back."

"We shall see how the Prime Minister reacts to your arrogance," said Charles and slammed down the phone.

Simon sat by the phone and waited for it to ring. He wondered if he could get away with taking the damn thing off the hook—the modern equivalent of Nelson placing the telescope to his blind eye, he considered. He needed a few minutes, only a few minutes, but the phone rang again only seconds later. He picked it up and heard her unmistakable voice.

"Can you stop them if I order you to, Simon?"

He considered lying. "Yes, Prime Minister," he said.

"But you would still like to carry it through, wouldn't you?"

"I only need a few minutes, Prime Minister."

"Do you understand the consequences if you fail, with Charles already claiming a diplomatic victory?"

"You would have my resignation within the hour."

"I suspect mine would have to go with it," said Mrs. Thatcher. "In which case Charles would undoubtedly be Prime Minister by this time tomorrow."

There was a moment's pause before she continued, "Qaddafi is on the other line, and I am going to tell him that I *am* willing to negotiate." Simon felt defeated. "Perhaps that will give you enough time, and let's hope it's Qaddafi who has to worry about resignations at breakfast."

Simon nearly cheered.

"Do you know the hardest thing I have had to do in this entire operation?"

341

"No, Prime Minister."

"When Qaddafi rang in the middle of the night, I had to pretend to be asleep so that he didn't realize I was sitting by the phone."

Simon laughed.

"Good luck, Simon, I'll phone and explain my decision to Charles."

The clock said 2:30.

On his return the admirals were variously clenching their fists, tapping the table or walking around, and Simon began to sense what the Israelis must have been feeling as they waited for news from Entebbe.

The phone rang again. He knew it couldn't be the Prime Minister this time, as she was the one woman in England who never changed her mind. It was Charles Hampton.

"I want it clearly understood, Simon, that I gave you the news concerning Qaddafi's desire to negotiate at two-twenty. That is on the record, so there will be only one Minister handing in his resignation later this morning."

"I know exactly where you stand, Charles, and I feel confident that whatever happens you'll come through your own mound of manure smelling of roses," said Simon, slamming down the phone as three o'clock struck. For no fathomable reason everyone in the room stood up, but as the minutes passed they sat back down again one by one.

At seven minutes past four radio silence was broken with the five words, "Shoplifter apprehended, repeat Shoplifter apprehended."

Simon watched the Joint Chiefs cheer like schoolchildren reacting to the winning goal at a football game. *Broadsword* was on the high seas in neutral waters. He sat down at his desk and asked to be put through to Number 10. The Prime Minister came on the line. "Shoplifter apprehended," he told her.

"Congratulations, continue as agreed," was all she said.

The next move was to be sure that all the Libyan prisoners

who had been taken aboard *Broadsword* would be discharged at Malta and sent home unharmed. Simon waited impatiently for radio silence to be broken again, as agreed, at five o'clock.

Commander Lawrence Packard came on the line as Big Ben struck five. He gave Simon a full report on the operation. One Libyan guerrilla had been killed and eleven injured. There had been no, repeat, no, British deaths and only a few minor injuries. The thirty-seven SBS men were back on board the submarines *Conqueror* and *Courageous*. HMS *Broadsword* was sailing the high seas on her way home. God Save the Queen.

Simon congratulated the commander and returned to Downing Street. As he limped up the street, journalists with no idea of the news that was about to be announced were already gathering outside Number 10. Once again Simon answered none of their shouted questions. When he was shown into the Cabinet room, he found Charles already there with the Prime Minister. He told them both the latest news. Charles's congratulations sounded insincere.

It was agreed that the Prime Minister would make a statement at seven o'clock. The draft was prepared and revised before Mrs. Thatcher stepped out onto Downing Street to give the waiting press the salient details of what had happened during the previous six hours.

Television arc lights were switched on and cameras flashed for several minutes before Mrs. Thatcher was able to speak. As she read her statement, Charles Hampton stood on her right and Simon Kerslake on her left, now the undisputed contenders as her successor.

"I must admit that my opinion of Charles Hampton has gone up," said Elizabeth in the car on the way to Lucy's field hockey match.

"What do you mean?" asked Simon.

"He's just been interviewed on television. He said he had backed your judgment all along while having to pretend to carry out pointless negotiations. He had a very good line to the effect that it was the first time in his life that he had felt honorable about lying."

Elizabeth didn't understand her husband's response. "Smelling like roses," he said sharply.

It amused Simon to watch his daughter massacred in the mud while he stood on the sidelines in the rain only hours after he had feared Qaddafi might have done the same to him. "It's a walkover," he told the headmistress when Lucy's team was down by four goals at halftime.

"Perhaps she'll be like you and surprise us all in the second half," replied the headmistress.

At eight o'clock on the following Saturday morning Simon sat in his office and heard the news that *Broadsword* had all engines on full speed and was expected to reach Portsmouth by three o'clock—exactly one week after his daughter had lost her match 0–8. They hadn't had a good second half. Simon had tried to console the downcast Lucy, and might even have succeeded if she hadn't been the goalie.

He was smiling when his secretary interrupted his thoughts to remind him that he was due at Portsmouth in an hour. As Simon reached the door, his phone rang. "Explain to whoever it is I'm already late," he said.

His secretary replied, "I don't think I can, sir."

Simon turned around, puzzled.

"Who is it?" he asked.

"Her Majesty the Queen."

Simon returned to his desk, picked up the receiver and listened to the sovereign. When she had finished Simon thanked her and said he would pass on her message to Commander Packard as soon as he reached Portsmouth. During the flight down, Simon looked out of the helicopter and watched a traffic jam that stretched from the coast to London with people who were going to welcome *Broadsword* home. The helicopter landed an hour later.

The Secretary of State for Defense stood on the pier and was able to pick out the frigate through a pair of binoculars. She was about an hour away but was already surrounded by a flotilla of small craft so that it was hard to identify her.

Sir John told him that Commander Packard had signaled to ask if the Secretary of State wished to join him on the bridge as they sailed into port. "No, thank you," said Simon. "It's his day, not mine."

"Good thing the Foreign Secretary isn't with us," said Sir John. A squad of Tornadoes flew over, drowning Simon's reply. As *Broadsword* sailed into port, the ship's company were all on deck standing to attention in full-dress uniform. The ship itself shone like a Rolls-Royce that had just come off the production line.

By the time the captain descended the gangplank a crowd of some five hundred thousand were cheering so loudly that Simon could not hear himself speak. Commander Packard saluted as the Secretary of State leaned forward and whispered the Queen's message in his ear:

"Welcome home, Rear Admiral Sir Lawrence Packard."

28

It was Joyce who left a clipping from the *Standard* for him to read when he returned from the Commons one night. She had scribbled across it: "This could end up on the front page of every national paper."

Raymond agreed with her.

Although he spent most of his time on the overall strategy for a future Labour government, like all politicians he had pet anomalies that particularly upset him. His had always been war widows' pensions, a preoccupation that dated back to his living with his grandmother in Leeds. He remembered the shock when he first realized, shortly after leaving the university, that his grandmother had eked out an existence for thirty years on a weekly widow's pension that wouldn't have covered the cost of a decent meal in a London restaurant.

From the back benches he had always pressed for the redeeming of war bonds and higher pensions for war widows. He even supported veterans' charities that worked on their behalf. His weekly mail showed unequivocally just how major a problem war widows' pensions had become. Over all his years in Parliament, he had worked doggedly to achieve ever increasing, though small, rises, but he vowed that were he ever to become Secretary of State for Defense he would enact something more radical.

With Joyce's clipping in his hand, he tried to press his view onto a reluctant Shadow Cabinet, who seemed more interested in the planned series of one-day strikes by the print unions than the case of Mrs. Dora Benson.

Raymond reread the story carefully and discovered that the case didn't differ greatly from the many others he had looked into over the years, except for the added ingredient of a Victoria Cross. By any standards, Mrs. Dora Benson highlighted Raymond's cause. She was one of the handful of surviving widows of the First World War, and her husband, Private Albert Benson, had been killed at the Somme while leading an attack on a German trench. Nine Germans had been killed before Albert Benson died, which was why he had been awarded the Victoria Cross. His widow had worked as a chambermaid in the King's Head at Barking for over fifty years. Her only possessions of any value were her war bonds; with no redemption date, they were still passing hands at only twenty-five pounds each. Mrs. Benson's case might have gone unnoticed if in desperation she had not asked Sotheby's to auction her husband's medal.

Once Raymond had armed himself with all the facts, he put down a question to the Secretary of State for Defense asking if he would at last honor the Government's long-promised pledges in such cases. A sleepy but packed House heard Simon Kerslake reply that he was giving the program his consideration and hoping to present a report on his findings to the Chancellor in the near future. Simon settled back onto the green benches, satisfied that this would pacify Gould, but Raymond's supplementary stunned him and woke up the House.

"Does the Right Honorable Gentleman realize that this eighty-three-year-old widow, whose husband was killed in action and won the Victoria Cross, has a lower income than a sixteen-year-old cadet on his first day in the armed forces?"

Simon rose once more, determined to put a stop to the issue until he had had more time to study the details of this particular case. "I was not aware of this fact, Mr. Speaker, and I can as-

347

sure the Right Honorable Gentleman that I shall take into consideration all the points he has mentioned."

Simon felt confident the Speaker would now move on to the next question. But Raymond rose again, the Opposition benches spurring him on.

"Is the Right Honorable Gentleman also aware that an admiral, on an index-linked income, can hope to end his career with a pension of over five hundred pounds a week while Mrs. Dora Benson's weekly income remains fixed at forty-seven pounds thirty-two?"

There was a gasp even from the Conservative benches as Raymond sat down.

Simon rose again, uncomfortably aware that he was unprepared for Gould's attack and must stifle it as quickly as possible. "I was not aware of that particular comparison either, but once again, I can assure the Right Honorable Gentleman I will give the case my immediate consideration."

To Simon's horror Raymond rose from the benches for yet a third time. Simon could see that Labour members were enjoying the rare spectacle of watching him up against the ropes. "Is the Right Honorable Gentleman also aware that the annuity for a Victoria Cross is one hundred pounds, with no extra pension benefits? We pay our second-string soccer players more, while keeping Mrs. Benson in the bottom league of the national income bracket."

Simon looked distinctly harassed when he in turn rose for a fourth time and made an uncharacteristic remark that he regretted the moment he said it.

"I take the Right Honorable Gentleman's point," he began, his words coming out a little too quickly. "And I am fascinated by his sudden interest in Mrs. Benson. Would it be cynical of me to suggest that it has been prompted by the wide publicity this case has enjoyed in the national press?"

Raymond made no attempt to answer him but sat motionless with his arms folded and his feet up on the table in front of him while his own backbenchers screamed their abuse at Simon.

The national papers the next day were covered with pictures of the arthritic Dora Benson with her bucket and mop alongside photos of her handsome young husband in private's uniform. Many of the papers went on to describe how Albert Benson had won his VC, and some of the tabloids used considerable license. But all of them picked up Raymond's point.

It was an enterprising and unusually thorough journalist from the *Guardian* who led her story on a different angle which the rest of the national press had to turn to in their second editions. It became known that Raymond Gould had put down forty-seven questions concerning war widows' pension rights during his time in the House and had spoken on the subject in three budgets and five social-service debates from the back benches. When the journalist revealed that Raymond gave five hundred pounds a year to the Erskine Hospital for wounded soldiers, every member knew that Simon Kerslake would have to retract his personal attack on the Shadow spokesman and make an apology to the House.

At three-thirty the Speaker rose from his chair and told a packed house that the Secretary of State for Defense wished to make a statement.

Simon Kerslake rose humbly from the front bench, and stood nervously at the dispatch box.

"Mr. Speaker," he began. "With your permission and that of the House, I would like to make a personal statement. During a question put to me yesterday I impugned the integrity of the Right Honorable Gentleman, the Member for Leeds North. It has since been brought to my attention that I did him a gross injustice and I offer the House my sincere apologies and the Right Honorable Gentleman the assurance that I will not question his integrity a *third* time."

While newer members were puzzled by the reference, Raymond understood it immediately. Aware of how rare personal statements were in anyone's parliamentary career, members looked on eagerly to see how Raymond would respond.

349

He moved slowly to the dispatch box.

"Mr. Speaker, I accept the gracious manner in which the Honorable Gentleman has apologized and hope that he will not lose sight of the greater issue, namely that of war widows' benefits, and in particular the plight of Mrs. Dora Benson."

Simon looked relieved and nodded courteously.

The following morning, the *Times* editorial declared: "In an age of militant demands from the left, Parliament and the Labour Party have found a new Clement Attlee on their front bench. Britain need have no fear for human dignity or the rights of man should Raymond Gould ever accede to the high office which that gentleman held."

Many Opposition members told Raymond he should have gone for Simon when he was down. Raymond disagreed. It was enough to know that Simon Kerslake was fallible.

The *Broadsword* factor remained in the memories of the electorate for a far shorter time than had the Falklands victory, and within six months the Conservative lead in the opinion polls had dropped to only 3 percent.

"The truth is," noted Raymond at a Shadow Cabinet meeting, "Mrs. Thatcher has had nearly eight years at Number Ten, and no Prime Minister has served two full terms in succession—let alone three—since Lord Liverpool at 1812."

Margaret Thatcher cared nothing for Lord Liverpool or historical precedent: she called an election the following June—the month that had been a winner for her in the past.

"It's time to let the nation choose who is to govern for the next five years," she declared on *Panorama*.

"Nothing to do with the fact she has regained a slight lead in the opinion polls," said Joyce tartly.

"A lead that could well disappear during the next few weeks," said Raymond.

He returned to Yorkshire for only three days of the campaign because, as one of the Party's leading spokesmen, he had to dash around the country addressing meeting after meeting in marginal seats. Many journalists went as far as to suggest that were Raymond leading the Party, they would be in a much stronger position to win the election.

Back in Leeds, however, he enjoyed his electioneering and felt completely relaxed with his constituents for the first time in his life. He also felt his age when he discovered that the new Tory candidate for Leeds North had been born in 1964, the year he had first entered Parliament. When they met, the only insult Raymond suffered at his young rival's hands was being called "sir."

"Please call me by my Christian name," said Raymond.

"Raymond—" began the young man.

"No, Ray will do just fine."

The final result of the election did not become clear until four o'clock on Friday afternoon. Only a few thousand votes determined the outcome:

CONSERVATIVES	317
LABOUR	288
LIBERAL/SDP ALLIANCE	24
IRISH	17
SPEAKER AND OTHERS	4

Although Mrs. Thatcher did not have more seats than the other parties put together, she still led the largest party in the House and remained at Number 10. She made very few changes to her front-bench team, as she clearly wished to leave an impression of unity. Charles moved to the Home Office, while Simon became Foreign Secretary. The press dubbed it "The Cosmetic Cabinet."

That post-election calm was to last a complete week before Tony Benn rolled a thundercloud across the clear blue summer sky by announcing he would contest the leadership of the Labour Party at the October conference.

Benn claimed that Kinnock's naive and gauche approach as Leader had been the single reason that the Labour Party had not been returned to power. There were many Labourites who agreed with this judgment, but they also felt they would have fared considerably worse under Benn.

What his announcement did, however, was to make respectable the claims of any other candidates who wished to run. Roy Hattersley and John Smith joined Benn and Kinnock as nominees. Many members of Parliament, trade-union leaders and constituency activists pressed Raymond to run for the Leadership. Joyce was the most vociferous of all.

"If you don't run now," she told him, "you'll have no chance in the future."

"It's the future I'm thinking about," replied Raymond.

"What do you mean?"

"I want to run for Deputy Leader. It's still the recognized number two spot, and it won't stop me from holding a key Shadow Cabinet post. And, most important, it will secure me a power base within the Party, which would give me a better chance next time."

Raymond waited another week before he launched his candidacy. At a packed Monday-morning press conference, he announced that the Lorry Union was nominating him. Norman Edwards made the motion.

With four candidates in the field for the Leadership, everyone knew that the first ballot would be inconclusive, although most prophets accepted that Benn would lead. Kinnock confided to Raymond that if he came in lower than second he would advise his supporters to vote for whichever of the other moderates looked able to beat Benn in the second ballot.

The first round went exactly as predicted, with Benn coming in first. The second ballot surprised everyone but Raymond. With Kinnock's supporters voting for Benn's closest rival, the

Party chairman was able to announce a few hours later that Tony Benn had been soundly beaten. The Labour Party had a new moderate Leader.

At eleven o'clock that same night the chairman announced that by a mere 3 percent Raymond Gould had defeated two other candidates to become the newly elected Deputy Leader of the Labour Party. The unions had agreed to allow their members to vote individually, rather than *en bloc,* but after the vote had been announced, Raymond was pleased to acknowledge a wink from Norman Edwards.

The new Leader immediately appointed Raymond Shadow Chancellor of the Exchequer. Among the many letters and telegrams Raymond received was one from Mrs. Kate Wilberhoff, which read: "Congratulations. But have you read Standing Order No. 5(4) of the Party Constitution?"

Raymond hadn't, and replied, "Hadn't. Have now. Let's hope it's an omen."

After nearly a decade of the lady from Grantham, Raymond sensed the mood was for change. In their first twelve months, the new Labour team looked fresh and innovative as Mrs. Thatcher began to look tired and out of touch.

During the long, cold winter of 1988 the Conservatives lost several votes on the floor of the House and many more upstairs in committee. The Prime Minister seemed somewhat relieved to find herself spending Christmas at Chequers.

The relief did not last long, as two elderly Conservative members died before the House convened in January. The press dubbed the Government the "lame drake" administration. Both of the pending by-elections were held in May, and the Conservatives fared far better than might have been expected in holding on to one seat and just losing the other. For a fourth time, Mrs. Thatcher plumped for a June election.

The monthly unemployment, inflation and import/export figures announced at regular intervals during their fourth cam-

353

paign all augured badly for the Conservatives. The Prime Minister's reiterated plea that a government shouldn't be judged on one month's figures began to sound unconvincing, and by the final week, the only point of contention was whether the Labour Party would end up with a large enough majority to govern.

Raymond collapsed into bed at four when the result was still unclear. He was in the middle of a dream when he was abruptly wakened by Joyce's screams from the kitchen.

"We've won. We've won."

He hadn't in his dream.

Raymond and Joyce toured the constituency that morning before joining Raymond's parents for a late lunch. When they left the little butcher shop that afternoon, awaiting Raymond on the pavement was a crowd of well-wishers who cheered him all the way to his car. Raymond and Joyce traveled down to London and were back in Cowley Street in time to watch the first Labour Prime Minister since 1979 emerge from Buckingham Palace with the television cameras following him all the way back until he took up residence at 10 Downing Street.

This time Raymond did not have long to wait for a telephone call because the first appointment the new Prime Minister confirmed was Raymond's, as his Chancellor of the Exchequer. Raymond and Joyce moved into Number 11 later that afternoon, instructing real estate agents to rent their Cowley Street house on a short-term lease. After all, the Labour Party had only won by four seats.

Leaving the Home Office came as a great blow to Charles. He informed Amanda over breakfast on the Monday after the election that he would be returning to Hampton's Bank and that his salary would be sufficient for her allowance to remain constant—as long as she behaved herself. Amanda nodded and left the breakfast table without comment, as Harry came in.

It was an important morning for Harry, as he was to be taken to his first day of school at Hill House to begin the academic course mapped out for him by his father. Though Charles tried to convince him that it would be the start of a wonderful adventure, Harry looked apprehensive. Once he had deposited a tearful eight-year-old with his first headmaster, Charles continued on to the City, cheerful at the prospect of returning to the world of banking.

When he arrived at Hampton's, he was met by Clive Reynolds's secretary, who immediately took him through to the boardroom and asked him if he would like a coffee.

"Thank you," said Charles, taking off his gloves, placing his umbrella in the stand and settling himself in the chairman's seat at the head of the table. "And would you tell Mr. Reynolds I'm in?"

"Certainly," said the secretary.

Clive Reynolds joined him a few moments later.

"Good morning, Mr. Hampton. How nice to see you again after such a long time," said Reynolds, shaking Charles by the hand.

"Good morning, Clive. It's nice to see you too. First I must congratulate you on the manner in which you have conducted the bank's affairs in my absence."

"It's kind of you to say so, Mr. Hampton."

"I was particularly impressed by the Distillers takeover; that certainly took the City by surprise."

"Yes, quite a coup, wasn't it?" said Reynolds smiling. "And there's another one in the pipeline."

"I shall look forward to hearing the details."

"Well, I'm afraid it remains confidential at the moment," said Clive, taking the seat beside him.

"Of course; but now that I have returned I had better be briefed fairly soon."

"I'm afraid shareholders cannot be briefed until we are certain the deals have been concluded. We can't afford any rumors harming our chances, can we?"

"But I'm not an ordinary shareholder," said Charles sharply. "I am returning as chairman of the bank."

"No, Mr. Hampton," said Reynolds quietly. "I am chairman of this bank."

"Do you realize whom you are addressing?" said Charles.

"Yes, I think so. A former Foreign Secretary, a former Home Secretary, a former chairman of the bank and a two percent shareholder."

"But you are fully aware that the board agreed to have me back as chairman when the Conservatives went into Opposition?" Charles reminded him.

"The composition of the board has changed considerably since those days," said Reynolds. "Perhaps you've been too busy running the rest of the world to notice minor comings and goings in Threadneedle Street."

"I shall call a board meeting."

"You don't have the authority."

"Then I shall demand an extraordinary general meeting," said Charles.

"And tell the shareholders what? That you had a standing order to return as chairman when you felt like it? That won't sound like a former Foreign Secretary."

"I'll have you out of this office in twenty-four hours," Charles continued, his voice suddenly rising.

"I don't think so, Mr. Hampton. Miss Trubshaw has completed her five years and has left us on a full pension, and it won't take you long to discover that I don't possess a Swiss bank account or have a well-compensated mistress."

Charles went red in the face. "I'll get you removed. You don't begin to understand how far my influence stretches."

"I hope I'm not removed, for your sake," said Reynolds calmly.

"Are you threatening me?"

"Certainly not, Mr. Hampton, but I would hate to have to explain how Hampton's lost over five hundred thousand pounds on the Nethercote account because of your personal whim to finish Simon Kerslake's career. It may interest you to know that the only thing the bank gained from that fiasco was good will, and we managed that because I recommended that Morgan Grenfell pick up the pieces."

"You two-timing crook. When I make that public it will finish you," said Charles triumphantly.

"Perhaps," said Reynolds calmly. "But it will also stop you from becoming Prime Minister."

Charles turned, picked up his umbrella, put on his gloves and walked away. As he reached the door, a secretary walked in holding two cups of coffee.

"I'll only be needing one, Miss Bristow," said Reynolds.

Charles passed her without a word and slammed the door.

"Don't you know any other restaurants?"

"Yes, but they don't know me," replied Ronnie Nethercote, as the two men strolled into the Ritz for the first time in a couple of years. Heads turned as people leaned forward and whispered Simon's name to their guests.

"What are you up to nowadays? I can't believe Opposition fully occupies you," Ronnie said as they took their seats.

"Not really. I might almost be described as one of the four million unemployed," replied Simon.

"That's what we're here to talk about," said Ronnie, "but first I recommend the country vegetable soup and the . . ."

"Beef off the trolley," interjected Simon.

"You remembered."

"It's the one thing you've always been right about."

Ronnie laughed more loudly than people normally did in the Ritz before saying, "Now that you no longer have the entire armed forces at your disposal or ambassadors to call you Your Eminence or however they address you now, why don't you join the board of my new company?"

"It's kind of you to ask, Ronnie, but the answer has to be no."

They broke off their conversation to give their orders.

"There's a salary of twenty-five thousand pounds a year that goes with it."

"I must admit it would help with Lucy's clothes allowance," said Simon, laughing. "Since she's been up at Oxford, Lucy seems to have been to more balls than tutorials."

"Then why not come in with us?" asked Ronnie.

"Because I'm a committed politician," said Simon, "and I no longer want to involve myself in any commercial activities."

"That might stop you from becoming Prime Minister?"

Simon hesitated at the bluntness of Ronnie's question, then said, "Frankly, yes. I've got a better-than-outside chance, and I'd be foolish to lengthen the odds by becoming involved in anything else right now."

"But everyone knows that as soon as Margaret announces she's going to pack up, you'll be the next Leader. It's as simple as that."

"No, Ronnie, it's never as simple as that."

"Then tell me, who could beat you?"

"Charles Hampton, for one."

"Hampton? He's a toffee-nosed prig," said Ronnie.

"He has a lot of friends in the Party, and his patrician background still counts for something with the Tories."

"Oh, come on," said Ronnie. "You'll kill Hampton with every elected member of the Party having a vote."

"Time will tell," said Simon. "But what have you been up to?" he asked, deliberately changing the subject.

"I've been working my backside off in preparation for the new company going public, which is why I wanted you on the board."

"You never give up."

"No, and I hope you haven't given up your one percent of the company."

"Elizabeth has it locked away somewhere."

"Then you had better find the key."

358

"Why?" asked Simon.

"Because when I put out ten million shares on the market at three quid a time, your one original share will be exchanged for one hundred thousand shares of common stock. I know you weren't ever Chancellor, but that's three hundred thousand pounds of anyone's money."

Simon was speechless.

"Well, say something," said Ronnie.

"Frankly I'd forgotten the share existed," Simon finally managed.

"Well, I think I can safely say," said Ronnie, parodying one of Mrs. Thatcher's favorite phrases, "that's not a bad investment for a pound, and one you will never regret."

As his first budget debate as Chancellor drew near, Raymond found twenty-four hours each day were not enough, even without sleep. He went over the budget changes he required with the Treasury mandarins, but it became more obvious as each week passed that he would have to make sacrifices. He was sick of being told that there would always be next year, feeling he had waited far too long already.

As the weeks passed, compromises were reached and cutbacks agreed on, but Raymond managed to cling to the changes about which he felt most passionate. The morning before the budget, the mandarins handed him his speech. It ran to one hundred and forty-three pages and they estimated it would keep him at the dispatch box for two and a half hours.

At ten past three the next day Raymond appeared on the steps of Number 11 and held the famous battered budget box, first used by Gladstone, high above his head. Dressed in a morning coat, he looked elegant and relaxed as photographers took the traditional picture before he was driven to the Commons.

By three-fifteen, the chamber had taken on the look of an opening night in the West End, for what members were about to experience was pure theater.

At three twenty-five Raymond entered the chamber to be greeted by cheers from his own side. Every place in the Commons except his had been filled. He looked up to see Joyce in the Strangers' Gallery, and smiled. At three-thirty, when the Prime Minister had finished answering questions, the Chairman of Ways and Means rose from his chair and called: "Budget statement, Mr. Chancellor of the Exchequer."

Raymond rose and placed his speech in front of him. He addressed the House for the first hour and a half without divulging any of the fiscal changes that he would be making, so abiding by the tradition that no irreversible decisions could be considered until the Stock Exchange had closed. Raymond took a sip from the glass of water by his side when he had turned page seventy-eight. He had finished with the theory and was now ready to start on the practice.

"Old-age pensions will be raised to a record level, as will allowances for single-parent families and disablement grants. War widows' pensions will go up by fifty percent and war bonds will be honored at their full face value."

Raymond paused and, taking a faded sheet from his inside pocket, read from the first speech he had ever delivered in public. "No woman whose husband has sacrificed his life for his country shall be allowed to suffer because of an ungrateful nation." The cheering after this statement lasted for some considerable time, and Raymond turned over the last page of his prize-winning essay before returning to his prepared speech.

Once the House had settled down again, he continued. "Taxes on salaries of more than thirty thousand pounds a year will be raised to eighty-five percent, and capital-gains tax to fifty percent." Several Conservatives looked glum. The Chancellor went on to announce an expansion program in the regions to stimulate employment. He detailed his plan by region, to cheers from different sections of the House.

He ended his speech by saying, "Our purpose as the first Labour Government in ten years is not to rob the rich and give to

360

the poor, but rather to make those who live in comparative ease pay taxes that will alleviate the plight of those in genuine need. Let me tell those of you who sit on the benches opposite that this is only a fifth of what we intend to achieve in the lifetime of this Parliament, and by then Britain can hope to be a more equal and just society. We intend to create a generation in which class is as outdated as debtors' prison, a generation in which talent, hard work and honesty are their own reward, a democratic society that is the envy of the East as well as the West. This budget, Mr. Speaker, is nothing more than the architect's plan for that dream. I look forward to being given enough time to build the reality."

When Raymond resumed his seat after two hours and twenty minutes—the length of time it takes to run a world-class marathon—he was greeted by cheers and the waving of agenda papers from the benches behind him.

The Leader of the Opposition was faced with the almost impossible task of an immediate response, and she couldn't hope to do more than pick up one or two weaknesses in the Chancellor's philosophy. The House did not hang on her every word.

PART SIX

Party
Leaders

1988-1990

29

MARGARET THATCHER was the first to realize changes would have to be made in the Shadow Cabinet after the success of Raymond Gould's first budget. She moved Simon to tackle Home Affairs and Charles to counter the formidable problems now raised by Raymond Gould at the Treasury.

Charles, as Shadow Chancellor, quickly gathered around him an impressive young team of economists, bankers and accountants whom he recruited mainly from the new intake on the back benches. Raymond soon discovered that his task of pushing legislation through became that much harder.

Raymond's success continued, however, even if it was at a slower pace than that for which he had hoped. Labour won the first two by-elections occasioned by member deaths. The by-election results only started a fresh round of rumors that Denis Thatcher was pressing his wife to retire.

The former Prime Minister sent a letter to the chairman of the 1922 Committee, letting him know that she would not seek reelection as Party Leader. She explained that she would be over sixty-five at the next election and had already led the party for fourteen years, the longest period for any Conservative since Churchill, and that she now felt she was ready to pass the Leadership on to new blood.

The moment everyone in the Party had said the usual phrases

about the retiring Leader being the greatest since Churchill, they proceeded to look for the new Churchill. The political journalists predicted that only two candidates had a real chance—Charles Hampton and Simon Kerslake.

Charles went about his campaign in the thorough manner in which he approached everything, appointing lieutenants to cover each intake of new members since 1964. Simon had selected Bill Travers to organize his backup team. Travers, like any farmer, rose early each morning to gather in his harvest.

Both Simon and Charles were nominated within the first twenty-four hours of the necessary seven days, and by the weekend none of the rumored third candidates had appeared in the lists, which convinced the press it would be a two-horse race.

Profiles of both men appeared in all the Sunday papers along with pictures of their wives. It was unfortunate for Charles that the only photograph the press could find of Amanda and himself together had been taken in 1981, when miniskirts were briefly the fashion, making them look even more like father and daughter.

The profiles covered Simon's rise from a middle-class Tory background to winning a marginal seat in Coventry before being offered a junior post at the Home Office. Then came his short period away from the Commons before returning to the House to hold the post of Minister of State for Northern Ireland, and subsequently Secretary of State for Defense, and finally Foreign Affairs. The high points of Simon's career that were most emphasized were the Irish Charter, which had subsequently become law, his miraculous escape and the tragedy of his son's death from an IRA bomb, and his firm stand over HMS *Broadsword*.

Charles was painted as the more traditional Tory. The younger twin of the Earl of Bridgewater, he had entered the House after Eton and Oxford and three years in the Grenadier Guards. The highlights of his career, in the press's opinion, had been his training in the Whip's office and his work as a Treasury Minister, followed by a steady traditional role at the Foreign Office, his firm stand on *Broadsword,* and now his competent, hard-working foil to Raymond Gould's budget thrusts.

The *Sunday Times* had gone one better than its rivals. Its political editor, Peter Ridell, spent the whole week trying to contact the 257 Tory members. He succeeded in reaching 228 of them and was able to report to his readers that 101 had said they would vote for Simon Kerslake, 98 for Charles Hampton, while 29 had refused to give any opinion. The article's headline read "Slight Lead for Kerslake" and went on to point out that although the two men were polite about each other in public, no one pretended that they were friends.

"King Kerslake" ran the banner headline in the Monday editions of the *Sun,* and its political editor predicted Simon would win by 130 to 127. Simon suspected that they had done little more than divide the *Sunday Times*'s "don't-knows" down the middle. With eight days to go he was being quoted at 2-1 on with Charles 11-8 against by the veteran ex-Labour MP Lord Mikardo, who had run a book on the last fourteen leadership contests irrespective of party. When Elizabeth told him the odds, Simon remained skeptical, as he knew from bitter experience that it never paid to underestimate the Right Honorable Member for Sussex Downs. Elizabeth agreed and then pointed to a small paragraph in the paper, which he had overlooked. Ronnie's new company was going public, and the shares looked certain to be well oversubscribed. "That's one prediction that's turned out to be accurate," said Simon, smiling.

With twelve hours to go to the close of nominations, a new candidate appeared in the lists, which came as a shock to everyone because until that moment the general public had been entirely unaware of Alec Pimkin. Some of his colleagues even expressed surprise that he had been able to find a proposer and a seconder. As it had been assumed that Pimkin's supporters were all men who would have backed Charles, it was considered a blow to his cause, although most political pundits doubted if Pimkin could scrape together more than seven or eight out of the two hundred and fifty-seven votes to be cast.

Charles pleaded with Pimkin to withdraw, but he stubbornly refused, admitting to Fiona that he was thoroughly enjoying his brief moment of glory. He held a press conference in the Commons, gave endless interviews to television, radio and the national press, and found he was receiving considerable political attention for the first time in his life since the Common Market debate. He even enjoyed the cartoon that appeared in the *Daily Telegraph* of the three candidates on the starting line, which had Charles portrayed as a string bean, Simon as a jumping bean, and Alec as a has-been waddling in a long way behind the other two. But Alexander Dalglish remained puzzled as to what had made Pimkin place his name in the lists in the first place.

"My majority in Littlehampton has plummeted from over twelve thousand to three thousand two hundred since I was first elected, and frankly the Social Democrats have been getting a little too close for comfort."

"But how many votes can you hope to pick up?" asked Fiona.

"Many more than those drunken scribblers realize. I have nine votes already pledged, not including my own, and I could well end up with as many as fifteen."

"Why so many?" asked Fiona, immediately realizing how tactless the question must have sounded.

"Dear, simple creature," Pimkin replied. "There are some members of our Party who do not care to be led either by a middle-class pushy minor public schoolboy or an aristocratic, arrogant snob. By voting for me they can lodge their protest very clearly."

"But isn't that irresponsible of you?" asked Fiona, annoyed by the "simple" quip.

"Irresponsible it may be, but you can't begin to imagine the invitations I have been receiving during the last few days. They should continue for at least a year after the election is over."

———

No one had thought Tom Carson would play a major role in the Leadership of the Tory Party. But when he dropped his bomb-shell, the elements of bad luck and timing came together. On the Thursday before the Leadership election the House was packed for questions to the Chancellor. Raymond and Charles were having their usual verbal battles across the dispatch box. Charles was coming out slightly on top and, as the Treasury wasn't his portfolio, all Simon could do was sit with his legs up on the table and listen while Charles scored points.

Tom Carson seemed to be extremely anxious to get in a sup-plementary on almost any financial question that was down on the order paper. Between two-thirty and five past three he had leaped up from his place no less than a dozen times. The digital clock above the Speaker's chair had reached 3:12 when, out of exasperation, the Speaker called him on a seemingly innocuous question on windfall profits.

With Prime Minister's questions just about to begin, Carson faced a packed House and a full press gallery. He paused for a moment before phrasing his question.

"What would be my Right Honorable friend's attitude to a man who invests one pound in a company and, five years later, receives a check for three hundred thousand pounds, despite not being on the board or appearing to be involved in any way with that company?"

Raymond was puzzled; he had no idea what Carson was talking about. He did not notice that Simon Kerslake had turned white.

Raymond rose to the dispatch box. "I would remind my Honorable friend that I put capital-gains tax up to fifty percent, which might dampen his ardor a little," he said. It was about the only attempt at humor Raymond had made at the dispatch box that year, which may have been the reason so few members laughed. As Carson rose a second time, Simon slipped a note across to Raymond, which he hurriedly skimmed.

"But does the Chancellor consider that such a person would be fit to be Prime Minister, or even Leader of the Opposition?"

Members started talking among themselves, trying to work out at whom the question was directed, while the Speaker stirred restlessly in his seat, anxious to bring a halt to such disorderly supplementaries. Raymond returned to the dispatch box and told Carson that the question was not worthy of an answer. There the matter might have rested, had Charles not risen to the dispatch box.

"Mr. Speaker, is the Chancellor aware that this personal attack is aimed at my Right Honorable friend, the member for Pucklebridge, and is a disgraceful slur on his character and reputation. The Honorable Member for Liverpool Dockside should withdraw his allegation immediately."

The Conservatives cheered their colleague's magnanimity, while Simon remained silent, knowing that Charles had successfully put the story on the front page of every national paper. Tom Carson, arms folded, sat back looking satisfied with himself. The Speaker quickly moved on to Prime Minister's Questions.

Charles sat back, pleased with the effect he had caused. He didn't look at Simon, who was visibly trembling.

Simon read the papers over breakfast on Friday morning. He had not overestimated the effect of Charles's bogus supplementary question. The details of his transaction with Ronnie Nethercote were chronicled in the fullest extent, and it did not read well that he had received three hundred thousand pounds from a "property speculator" for a one-pound investment. Some of the papers felt "bound to ask" what Nethercote hoped to gain out of the transaction. No one seemed to realize that Simon had been on the previous company's board for five years, had invested sixty thousand pounds of his own money in that company, and had only recently finished paying off the overdraft, ending up with a small loss.

By Sunday Simon had made a full press statement to set the record straight, and most of the papers had given him a fair hearing. However, the editor of the *Sunday Express* didn't help matters with a comment in his widely read "PM" column on the center page.

> *I would not suggest for one moment that Simon Kerslake has done anything that might be described as dishonest, but with the spotlight turned so fiercely on him, there may be some members of Parliament who feel they cannot risk going into a General Election with an accident-prone leader. Mr. Hampton, on the other hand, has made his position abundantly clear. He did not seek to return to his family bank in Opposition while he was still hoping to hold public office.*

The Monday papers were reassessing the outcome of the ballot to take place the next day and were predicting that Hampton now had the edge. Some journalists went so far as to suggest that Alec Pimkin might profit from the incident as members waited to see if there would be a second chance to give their final verdict.

Simon had received several letters of sympathy during the week, including one from Raymond Gould. Raymond assured Simon that he had not been prepared for the Carson supplementary and apologized for any embarrassment his first answer might have caused.

"It never crossed my mind that he had," said Simon, as he passed Raymond's letter over to Elizabeth.

"The *Times* was right," she said a few moments later. "He is a very fair man."

A moment later Simon passed his wife another letter.

> *15 May 1989*   *Hampton's Bank*
> *202 Cheapside*
> *London EC1*
>
> *Dear Mr. Kerslake,*
> *   I write to correct one statement to which the press has continually referred. Charles Hampton, the former chair-*

371

*man of this bank, did seek to return to Hampton's after the
Conservatives went into Opposition. He hoped to continue
as chairman on a salary of £40,000 a year.*
   The board of Hampton's did not fall in with his wishes.
                Yours sincerely,
                CLIVE REYNOLDS

"Will you use it?" asked Elizabeth, when she had finished reading the letter through.

"No. It will only draw more attention to the issue."

Elizabeth looked at her husband as he continued to read the letters and remembered the file that she still possessed on Amanda Wallace. She would never reveal its contents to Simon; but perhaps the time had come to make Charles Hampton sweat a little.

On Monday evening Simon sat on the front bench listening to the Financial Secretary moving those clauses of the short Finance Bill which were being taken in Committee on the floor of the House. Charles never let any one of Raymond Gould's team get away with a phrase, or even a comma, if he could see a weakness in his case, and the Opposition were enjoying every moment. Simon sat and watched the votes slipping away, knowing he could do nothing to stop the process.

Of the three candidates, only Pimkin slept well the night before the election.

Voting began promptly at nine o'clock the next day in the Grand Committee room of the House of Commons, the party whips acting as tellers. It became apparent that Mrs. Thatcher had decided to remain neutral, and by three-ten all but one of those entitled to vote had done so. The Chief Whip stood guard over the large black tin box until Big Ben struck four.

At four o'clock the box was removed to the Chief Whip's office, and the little slips were tipped out and checked twice in less than fifteen minutes. As the Chief Whip left his office he was followed, Pied Piperlike, by lobby correspondents hoping to learn the result, but he had no intention of divulging anything before he reached the 1922 Committee, who were keenly awaiting him.

Committee room 14 was filled to overflowing with some 250 of the 257 Conservative members of Parliament present. The chairman of the 1922 Committee rose, faced the Committee, unfolded the piece of paper the Chief Whip had handed him and pushed up his glasses. He hesitated as he took in the figures.

"The result of the ballot carried out to select the leader of the Parliamentary Party is as follows:

CHARLES HAMPTON	121
SIMON KERSLAKE	119
ALEC PIMKIN	16

There was a gasp, followed by prolonged chatter which lasted until members noticed that the chairman remained standing as he waited for some semblance of order to return among his colleagues.

"There being no outright winner," he continued, "a second ballot will take place next Tuesday without Mr. Pimkin."

The national press surrounded Pimkin as he left the Commons that afternoon, wanting to know whom he would advise his supporters to vote for in the second ballot. Pimkin, obviously relishing every moment, declared a little pompously that he intended to interview both candidates in the near future and ask them one or two apposite questions. He was at once dubbed "Kingmaker" by the press, and the phones at his home and office never stopped ringing. Whatever their private thoughts, both Simon and Charles agreed to see Pimkin before he told his supporters how he intended to cast his vote.

Elizabeth checked the faded file that she had not looked at for so many years. She sat alone at her desk willing herself to go through with it. She sipped the brandy by her side that she had removed from the medicine cabinet earlier that day. All her years of training and a total belief in the Hippocratic oath went against what she felt she must now do. While Simon slept soundly she had lain awake considering the consequences. She had made her final decision. Simon's career came first. She picked up the phone, dialed the number and waited. Elizabeth nearly replaced the phone when she heard his voice.

"9712. Charles Hampton speaking."

She felt a shudder run through her body.

"It's Elizabeth Kerslake," she said, trying to sound confident. There was a long silence in which neither of them spoke.

Once Elizabeth had taken another sip of brandy, she added, "Don't hang up, Mr. Hampton, because I feel confident you'll be interested in what I have to say."

Charles still didn't speak.

"Having watched you from a distance over the years, I am sure that your reaction to Carson's question in the Commons last week was not spontaneous."

Charles cleared his throat but still didn't speak.

"And if anything else happens this week that could cause my husband to lose the election, be assured I shall not sit by and watch."

Charles still didn't speak.

"I have in front of me a file marked Miss Amanda Wallace, and if you wish all its contents to remain confidential, I would advise you to avoid any repetition of your antics, because it's packed with names *Private Eye* would wallow in for months."

Charles still didn't speak.

Elizabeth's confidence was growing. "You needn't bother to inform me that such an action would get me struck off the medical register. That would be a small penalty for being allowed to watch you suffer the way my husband has this past week." She paused. "Good day, Mr. Hampton."

Elizabeth put the phone down and swallowed the remainder of the brandy by her side. She prayed that she had sounded convincing, because she knew she could never carry out such a threat.

Charles took Pimkin to dinner at White's—where Alec had always wanted to be a member—and was escorted to a private room on the first floor.

Charles didn't wait long to ask, "Why are you going through with this charade? Don't you realize I would have won in that first round if you hadn't stood?"

Pimkin bridled. "I haven't had so much fun in years."

"But who the hell got you your seat in the first place?"

"I well remember," said Pimkin. "And I remember the price you exacted for it. But now it's my turn to call the tune, and this time I require something quite different."

"What are you hoping for? Chancellor of the Exchequer in my first administration, no doubt?" said Charles, barely able to keep the sarcasm from his voice.

"No, no," said Pimkin, "I know my worth, for I am not a complete fool."

"So what do you want? Membership at White's? Perhaps I could fix that."

"Nothing so mundane. In return for putting you into Downing Street I expect to be translated to the House of Lords."

Charles hesitated. He could always give Pimkin his word; and who other than Pimkin would notice if he didn't carry it through?

"If you and your fifteen men vote for me next Tuesday I'll put you in the Lords," said Charles. "You have my word on it."

"Good," said Pimkin. "But one small thing, old chum," he added as he slowly folded his napkin.

"Christ—what do you want now?" asked Charles, exasperated.

"Like you, I want the agreement in writing."

Charles hesitated again, but this time he knew he was beaten. "I agree," he said.

"Good, then it's a deal," said Pimkin. Looking around for a

waiter, he added, "I rather think champagne is called for."

When Pimkin put forth the same proposition to Simon two days later, Simon Kerslake took some time before he answered. Then he said, "That's a question I would have to consider on its merits at the time, if and when I become Prime Minister."

"So bourgeois," said Pimkin as he left Simon's office. "I offer him the keys to Number Ten and he treats me like a locksmith."

Charles left the Commons that night having spent his time going around to a large cross section of his supporters, and he was reassured to discover they were standing firm. Wherever he went in the long Gothic corridors, members singly or in groups came up to pledge their support. It was true that Kerslake's windfall of three hundred thousand pounds was fast becoming yesterday's news, but Charles felt enough blood had been let from that wound to insure his final victory, even though he still cursed Pimkin for holding up the result. One anonymous note, with all the necessary details, sent to the right Labour member, had certainly proved most effective. Charles cursed again as he realized Elizabeth Kerslake had successfully stopped any further covert attacks on his rival.

When he arrived home, he was appalled to find Amanda waiting for him in the drawing room. She was the last person he was in the mood to see at the moment.

"I thought I told you to stay away until the middle of next week?"

"I changed my mind, Charlie," said Amanda.

"Why?" he asked suspiciously.

"I think I've earned a little reward for being such a good wife."

"What do you have in mind?" he asked as he stood by the mantelpiece.

"Fair exchange."

"For what?"

"For the world rights to my life story."

"Your *what?*" said Charles in disbelief. "Who is going to be the slightest bit interested in you?"

"It's not me they're interested in, Charlie, it's you. *News of the World* has offered me one hundred thousand pounds for the unexpurgated story of life with Charles Hampton." She added dramatically, "Or what it's like to live with the second son of an earl who will go to any lengths to become Prime Minister."

"You can't be serious," said Charles.

"Deadly serious. I've made quite a few notes over the years. How you got rid of Derek Spencer but failed to pull the same trick on Clive Reynolds. The extremes you went to, trying to keep Simon Kerslake out of the House. How your first wife swapped the famous Holbein picture of the first Earl of Bridgewater. But the story that will cause the most interest is the one in which the real father of young Harry Hampton is revealed, because his dad's life story was serialized in *People* a couple of years ago, and that seems to be one episode they missed out."

"You bitch, you know Harry is my son," said Charles, advancing toward her. But Amanda stood her ground.

"And perhaps I should include a chapter on how you assault your wife behind the closed doors of your peaceful Eaton Square mansion."

Charles came to a halt. "What's the deal?"

"I keep quiet for the rest of my life and you present me with fifty thousand pounds now and a further fifty thousand when you become Leader."

"You've gone mad."

"Not me, Charlie, I've always been sane. You see, I don't have a paranoia to work out on dear, harmless brother Rupert. *News of the World* will love that part, now that he's the fifteenth earl. I can just see the picture of him wearing his coronet and decked out in his ermine robes."

"They wouldn't print it."

"They would when they realize he is as queer as a three dollar note, and therefore our only son will collect the earldom when he is not entitled to it."

"No one would believe it, and by the time they print the story it will be too late to hurt me," said Charles.

"Not a bit," said Amanda. "I am assured by my agent that the true reason behind the resignation of the Leader of the Conservative Party would be an even bigger scoop than that of a one-time contestant."

Charles sank down into the nearest armchair.

"Twenty-five thousand," he said.

"Fifty," replied his wife. "It's only fair. After all, it's a double deal: no story to the press and you become Leader of the Conservative Party."

"All right," whispered Charles, rising to leave the room.

"Wait a moment, Charlie. Don't forget I've dealt with you in the past."

"What else are you hoping for?" said Charles, swinging around.

"Just the autograph of the next Tory Leader," she replied, producing a check.

"Where the hell did you get hold of that?" asked Charles, pointing to the slip of paper.

"From your checkbook," said Amanda innocently.

"Don't play games with me."

"From the top drawer of your desk."

Charles snatched it from her and nearly changed his mind. Then he thought of his brother in the House of Lords, his only son not inheriting the title, and he himself having to give up the Leadership. He took out his pen and scribbled his name on the check before leaving his wife in the drawing room holding fifty thousand pounds. She was checking the date and the signature carefully.

Simon had received a tip from a friendly journalist that Pimkin would come out in support of his old school chum. He took

Elizabeth down to the country for a quiet weekend while the photographers pitched camp in Eaton Square.

"A brilliant move," said Elizabeth over breakfast the next morning, looking at the picture on the front page of the *Observer.*

"Another photo of Hampton telling us what he will do when he's Prime Minister?" said Simon not looking up from the *Sunday Times.*

"No," said Elizabeth and passed her paper across the table. Simon stared at the Holbein portrait of the first Earl of Bridgewater under the headline: "A Gift to the Nation."

"Good God," said Simon. "Are there no depths he will sink to to win this election?"

"My dear, by any standards you have delivered the *coup de grace,*" said Pimkin to Fiona over lunch that Sunday.

"I thought you would appreciate it," said Fiona pouring him another glass of his own wine.

"I certainly did, and I particularly enjoyed the director of the National Gallery's comments—'That Charles's gesture of presenting the priceless painting to the National was the act of a selfless man.' "

"Of course—once the story had been leaked to the press, Charles was left with no choice," said Alexander Dalglish.

"I realize that," said Pimkin, leaning back, "and I would have given a dozen bottles of my finest claret to have seen Charles's face the moment he realized the first Earl of Bridgewater had escaped his clutches forever. If he had denied giving the earl to the nation, the publicity that would have followed would have certainly insured defeat in the election on Tuesday."

"Win or lose next week," said Alexander, "he daren't then suggest it was done without his approval."

"I love it, I love it," said Pimkin. "I am told that Princess Diana will be unveiling the portrait on behalf of the National at

379

the official ceremony, and rest assured I shall be there to bear witness."

"Ah, but will Charles?" asked Fiona.

On Monday morning Charles's brother phoned from Somerset to ask why he had not been consulted about donating the Holbein to the nation.

"It was my picture to dispose of as I pleased," Charles reminded him and slammed down the phone.

By nine o'clock on Tuesday morning, when the voting took place for the last time, the two contestants had spoken to nearly every member twice. Charles joined his colleagues in the members' dining room for lunch while Simon took Elizabeth to Lockets in Marsham Street. She showed him some colored brochures of a holiday on the Orient Express, which would be the most perfect way to see Venice. She hoped that they wouldn't have time to go on the trip. Simon hardly mentioned the vote that was simultaneously taking place in the Commons but it never was far from either of their minds.

The voting ended at three-fifty but once again the Chief Whip did not remove the black box until four o'clock. By four-fifteen he knew the winner but did not reveal his name until the 1922 Committee had assembled at five o'clock. He informed their chairman at one minute to five.

Once again, the chairman of the 1922 Committee stood on the small raised platform in committee room 14 to declare the result. There was no need to ask if the people at the back could hear.

"Ladies and gentlemen," he said, his words echoing around the room, "the result of the second ballot for the Leadership of the Tory Party is as follows:

CHARLES HAMPTON	119
SIMON KERSLAKE	137

Just over half the members present rose and cheered while Bill Travers ran all the way to Simon's office to be the first to report the news. When he arrived, Simon swung round and faced the open door.

"You look and sound as though you'd run a marathon."

"Like Pheidippides, I bring great news of victory."

"I hope that doesn't mean you're going to drop down dead," said Simon, grinning.

The new Leader of the Conservative Party said nothing more for a few moments. It was obvious that Pimkin had come out in favor of him. Later that night one or two other members also admitted that they had changed their minds during the second week because they hadn't liked the blatant opportunism of Charles's presenting a priceless portrait to the nation only a few days before the final vote.

The following morning Fiona phoned Pimkin to ask him why he had acted as he did. "My dear Fiona," he replied, "like Sydney Carton, I suppose I thought it would be good to go to my grave knowing I had done one honorable thing in my life."

30

It took only a week for Simon's little house on Beaufort Street to be transformed. The usually quaint and sheltered neighborhood became cluttered with ferries of cars bearing photographers, journalists and television crews. Some neighbors wondered how Elizabeth fixed such a gracious smile on her face each morning as she made her way through the hopeful interviewers who seemed permanently camped on her doorstep. Simon, they noted, handled the problem as if it had always been part of his daily routine. He had spent his first two weeks selecting the Shadow Cabinet he wanted to take into the next General Election. He was able to announce the composition of his new team to the press fourteen days after his election as Leader of the Conservative Party. He made one sentimental appointment: that of Bill Travers as Shadow Minister of Agriculture.

When asked at a press conference why his defeated rival would not be serving on the team, Simon explained that he had offered Charles Hampton the Deputy Leadership and any portfolio of his choice, but Charles had turned the offer down, saying he preferred to return to the back benches for the present.

Charles had left for Scotland the same morning for a few days' rest by the River Spey, taking his son with him. Although he spent much of their short holiday feeling depressed about the

final outcome of the Leadership struggle, Harry's original efforts at fishing helped him deaden some of the pain. Harry even
ended up with the biggest fish.

Amanda, on the other hand, realizing how slim her chances
were of catching any more fish, reopened negotiations over her
life story with *News of the World*.

When the features editor read through Amanda's notes he
decided on two things. She would require a ghostwriter, and the
paper would have to halve their original offer.

"Why?" demanded Amanda.

"Because we daren't print the better half of your story."

"Why not?"

"No one would believe it."

"But every word is true," she insisted.

"I'm not doubting the veracity of the facts," said the editor.
"Only our readers' ability to swallow them."

"They accepted that a man climbed the walls of Buckingham
Palace and found his way into the Queen's bedroom."

"Agreed," replied the editor, "but only after the Queen had
confirmed the story. I'm not so sure that Charles Hampton will
be quite as cooperative."

Amanda remained silent long enough for her agent to close
the deal.

The watered-down version of "My Life with Charles Hampton" appeared a few months later to coincide with Charles's
much-publicized divorce, but it made no more than a faint ripple in political circles. Now that Charles had no hope of leading
his party, it was very much yesterday's news.

Amanda came out of the divorce settlement with another
fifty thousand pounds but lost custody of Harry, which was all
Charles really cared about. Charles prayed that her irresponsible remarks reported in the paper concerning the boy's claim to
the title had been quickly forgotten.

Then Rupert phoned from Somerset and asked to see him
privately.

As Raymond entered his second year as Chancellor, the opinion polls showed the two main parties were once again neck and neck. A surge in Tory popularity came as no surprise after a change in Tory leadership, but Simon's first year had shown a dynamism and energy that amazed even his closest supporters. Raymond was daily made more conscious of the inroads Simon was making on the Government program. It only made him work even harder to insure that his policies became law.

No one needed to tell Simon he had a good first year as Opposition Leader. His party's percentage in the polls was now running neck and neck with the Government's.

But in the House he often found himself being frustrated. Political correspondents reported that it was the most balanced contest in years. For as long as Labour held the majority, Simon often won the argument while losing the vote.

They sat facing each other in Charles's drawing room at Eaton Square.

"I am sorry to broach such an embarrassing subject," said Rupert, "but felt it was my duty to do so."

"Duty, poppycock," said Charles, stubbing out his cigarette. "I tell you Harry is my son, and as such will inherit the title. He's the spitting image of Great-grandfather and that ought to be enough proof for anyone."

"In normal circumstances I would agree with you, but the recent publicity in *News of the World* has been brought to my notice and I feel . . ."

"That sensationalist rag," said Charles sarcastically, his voice rising. "Surely you don't take their word before mine?"

"Certainly not," said Rupert, "but if Amanda is to be believed, Harry is not your son."

"How am I meant to prove he is?" asked Charles, trying to

control his temper. "I didn't keep a diary of the dates when I slept with my wife."

"I have taken legal advice on the matter," continued Rupert, ignoring the comment, "and am informed that a blood test is all that will prove necessary to verify Harry's claim to the title. We both share a rare blood group, as did our father and grandfather, and if Harry is of that group I shall never mention the subject again. If not, then the title will eventually be inherited by our second cousin in Australia."

"And if I don't agree to put my son through this ridiculous test?"

"Then the matter must be placed in the hands of our family solicitors," said Rupert sounding unusually in control, "and they must take whatever course they consider fit."

"That must never happen," said Charles weakly.

"It will happen," said Rupert.

When the Prime Minister went into the hospital for a minor operation, the press immediately started to speculate on his resignation. Ten days later, when he walked out looking better than ever, the rumors ceased immediately. In the Prime Minister's absence, Raymond, as Deputy Leader, chaired Cabinet meetings and stood in for him during questions in the Commons. This gave the lobby correspondents a chance to proclaim, like Caesarian soothsayers plucking at entrails, that Raymond was *"primus inter pares."*

Raymond enjoyed presiding over the Cabinet and in particular the challenge of Prime Minister's Questions on Tuesdays and Thursdays.

He enjoyed the sensation of acting as Prime Minister but realized he could not afford to get used to it. Indeed, when the Prime Minister returned to Downing Street, he assured Raymond that the operation had been a success and the likelihood of any recurrence of the trouble was, in the surgeon's opinion, minimal. He admitted to Raymond that he hoped to lead the

Party to a second victory at the polls, by which time he would be within a few years of his seventieth birthday and ready to bow out quietly. He told Raymond quite bluntly that he hoped he would be his successor.

"Daddy, Daddy, open my school report."

Charles left the morning mail unopened as he hugged Harry. He knew nothing could ever part them now, but he dreaded Harry's finding out that he might not be his real father.

"Please open it," pleaded Harry, wriggling free. The school doctor had been asked to take a sample of Harry's blood along with six other boys from his year so that he would not consider the request unusual. Even the doctor hadn't been told the full significance of the action.

Harry extracted the envelope from the pile by Charles's side—the one with the school crest in the top left-hand corner—and held it out for his father to open. He looked excited and seemed hardly able to contain himself. Charles had promised he would phone his brother as soon as the result of the blood test was confirmed. He had wanted to phone the doctor a hundred times during the past week but had always stopped himself, knowing it would only add to the man's curiosity.

"Come on, Dad, read the report, and you'll see it's true."

Charles tore open the letter and removed the little book which would reveal the result of all Harry's efforts during the term. He flicked through the pages: Latin, English, History, Geography, Art, Divinity, Games, Headmaster. He read the last page, a small yellow sheet headed "Term Medical Report." It began: "Harry Hampton, Age ten, Height 4'9", weight 5 stone, 4 lbs." He glanced up at Harry who looked as if he was about to burst.

"It is true, Dad, isn't it?"

Charles read on without answering the boy's question. At the foot of the page was a typewritten note signed by the school doctor. Charles read it twice before he understood its full significance, and then a third time: "As requested, I took a sample of Harry's blood and analyzed it. The results show that Harry shares a rare blood group. . . ."

"Is it true, Dad?" asked Harry yet again.

"Yes, my son, it's true."

"I told you, Dad, I knew I'd be top in the class. That means I'll be head of the next school term. Just like you."

"Just like me," said his father as he picked up the phone by his side and began to dial his brother's home number.

31

AT THE LABOUR PARTY conference in October, Raymond delivered a keynote speech on the state of the nation's finances. He pressed the unions to continue supporting their Government by keeping the twin evils of inflation and unemployment at acceptable levels. "Let us not pass on three years of achievement to be squandered by a Conservative Government," he told the cheering delegates. "Brothers, I look forward to presenting five more Labour budgets that will make it impossible for the Tories to imagine a future victory at the polls."

Raymond received one of the rare standing ovations to be given to any Cabinet Minister at a Labour Party conference. The delegates had never doubted his ability, and over the years they had grown to respect his sincerity as well as his judgment.

Seven more days passed before Simon addressed the Tory faithful at the Conservative Party conference. By tradition, the Leader always receives a four- to six-minute standing ovation after he completes his speech on the final day. "He'd still get four minutes," said Pimkin to a colleague, "if he read them *Das Kapital*."

Simon had spent weeks preparing for the occasion since he was convinced this would be the last conference before the election. He was pleasantly surprised to find Charles Hampton

388

coming forward with new ideas on tax reform which he said he hoped might be considered for inclusion in the Leader's speech to the conference.

Charles had recently been making useful contributions in the House during finance debates, and Simon hoped that it would not be long before he would be willing to return to the front bench. Simon did not agree with most of his colleagues, who felt that his old rival had mellowed considerably during his time on the back benches. He was too wary to accept that Charles had totally lost his ambition for high office. But whatever his private misgivings, he desperately needed someone of Charles' ability to counter Raymond Gould at the Treasury. Simon included Charles's suggestions in the final draft of his speech and dropped him a handwritten note of thanks. He received no reply.

On that Friday morning in Brighton, in front of two thousand delegates, and millions more watching on television, Simon presented a complete and detailed plan of what he hoped to achieve when the Conservatives were returned to Government.

After the peroration, the delegates duly rose for a genuine six-minute ovation. When the noise had died down, Pimkin was heard to remark, "I think I made the right decision."

Sadness overcame the House in its first week back when the aging Mr. Speaker Weatherill suffered a heart attack and retired to the Lords. The Government's overall majority was only two at the time, and the Labour Party Chief Whip feared that if they supplied the new Speaker from their own ranks and the Conservatives were to retain the old Speaker's safe seat the Government majority would cease to exist. Simon reluctantly agreed that the Speaker should come from the Conservatives' own benches.

Charles Hampton asked to be granted a private interview with the Chief Whip, who agreed to see him without hesitation. Like Simon, he was hoping that Charles would now be willing to rejoin the front bench and was merely approaching him as an intermediary. Everyone in the Party was pleased that Charles had begun to regain his stature in the House since his chairmanship of Standing Committees, and he seemed more popular now than he had ever been.

Charles arrived at the Chief Whip's office the following morning and was quickly ushered through to his private room. Charles's once Odyssian locks had turned white, and the deeper lines in his face gave him a more gentle appearance. The Chief Whip couldn't help noticing that a slight stoop had replaced his ramrod bearing.

Charles's request came as a shock. The Chief Whip had gone over many reasons why Charles might want to see him, but Simon Kerslake's great rival was the last man he would have considered for this post, because it would forever deny him the chance of becoming Leader.

"But it's no secret that Simon wants you to return to the front bench and be the next Chancellor," said the Chief Whip. "You must know he would be delighted to have you back on the team."

"That's considerate of him," said Charles drily. "But I would prefer the more restful life of being an arbitrator rather than an antagonist. I fear our differences could never be fully reconciled. In any case, I've lost that desire always to be on the attack. For over twenty years Simon has had the advantage of a wife and a family to keep his feet on the ground. It's only in the last three or four that Harry has done the same for me."

The Chief Whip let out a long sigh, unable to hide his disappointment. "I will convey your request to the Party Leader," was all he said. The Chief Whip wondered if Simon would be as disappointed as he was, or if in fact he might not be relieved to see his old antagonist relegated to the sidelines.

All men are thought to have one great moment in their careers in the House, and for Alec Pimkin it was to be that day.

The election of a Speaker in the Commons is a quaint affair. By ancient tradition, no one must appear to want the honor, and it is rare for more than one person to be proposed for the post. During Henry VI's reign three Speakers were beheaded within a year, although in modern times it has been the heavy burden of duties that has often led to an early grave. This tradition of reluctance has carried on through the ages.

Alec Pimkin rose from his seat on the back benches to move "that the Right Honorable Charles Hampton does take the chair of this House as Speaker." Dressed in a dark blue suit, sporting a red carnation and his favorite pink-spotted bow tie, Alec Pimkin rose to address the House. His speech was serious yet witty, informed yet personal. Pimkin held the House in his grasp for nine minutes and never once let it go. "He's done his old friend proud," one member muttered to another across the gangway when Pimkin sat down, and indeed the look on Charles's face left no doubt that he felt the same way, whatever had taken place in the past.

After Charles had been seconded, the tradition of dragging the Speaker-elect to the chair was observed. This normally humorous affair, usually greeted with hoots of laughter and cheering, became even more of a farce at the sight of the small, portly Pimkin and his Labour seconder dragging the six-foot-four former Guards officer from the third row of the back benches all the way to the chair.

Charles began by expressing his grateful thanks for the high honor the House had bestowed on him. He then surveyed the Commons from his new vantage point. When he rose and stood his full height, every member knew they had selected the right man for the job. The sharpness of his tongue might have gone, but it had been replaced with an equally firm delivery that left none of his colleagues, however unruly, in any doubt that Mr. Speaker Hampton intended to keep "order" for many years to come.

———

Raymond was distressed when the Conservatives increased their majority in the Speaker's old seat and captured a marginal constituency on the same day. He didn't need the press to point out that were Conservatives and the Social Democratic Party to join forces, Government and Opposition would be equal in number, insuring a premature General Election. Raymond was determined that the Government hold on for at least another four weeks, so that he could deliver his third April budget and give the Party a strong platform on which to fight the election.

Simon knew that if Raymond Gould had the chance to deliver his third budget speech in April, the Labour Party might be saved at the polls. There was only one solution: to win a "no confidence" motion before the end of March. Simon picked up the phone to call the Social Democratic Party headquarters. Their Leader was all too happy to meet that afternoon.

Raymond had accepted an invitation to address a large Labour rally in Cardiff the weekend before the vote of "no confidence." He boarded the train at Paddington, settled into his compartment and began to check over his speech. As the train pulled into Swindon, a railway official stepped on board and, having discovered where the Chancellor of the Exchequer was seated, asked if he could speak to him privately for a few minutes. Raymond listened carefully to what the man had to say, replaced the speech in his briefcase, got off the train, crossed the platform and returned by the first available train to London.

On the journey back he tried to work out all the consequences of the news he had just been told.

As soon as he arrived at Paddington, he made his way through the waiting photographers and journalists, answering no questions. A car took him straight to Westminster Hospital. Raymond was shown into a private room to find the Prime Minister sitting upright in bed.

"Now don't panic," said the Prime Minister before Raymond

could speak. "I'm in fine shape considering I'm over sixty, and with all the pressure we've been under this last year."

"What's wrong with you?" asked Raymond, taking a chair next to the hospital bed.

"Recurrence of the old trouble, only this time they say it will take major surgery. I'll be out of this place in a month, six weeks at the most, and then I'll live as long as Harold Macmillan, they tell me. Now, to more important matters. As Deputy Leader of the Party, I want you to take over again, which will mean you will have to speak in my place during the 'no confidence' debate on Wednesday. If we lose the vote, I shall resign as Party Leader."

Raymond tried to protest. From the moment he had been told the Prime Minister was ill again, he had known the implications. The Prime Minister held up his hand to still Raymond's words and continued, "No party can fight an election with its Leader laid up in bed for six weeks, however well he might be when they release him. The voters have the right to know who is going to lead the Party in Parliament." As the Prime Minister spoke, Raymond remembered Kate's telegram on the day of his election as Deputy Leader. "And of course, if we are forced into an election before the Party conference in October, under Standing Order Number 5 (4), the national executive and the Shadow Cabinet would meet and automatically select you to take over as Party Leader."

Raymond raised his head. "Yes, the importance of that particular standing order had already been pointed out to me," he said without guile.

The Prime Minister smiled. "Joyce, no doubt."

"No, her name was Kate, actually."

The Prime Minister briefly looked puzzled, and then continued. "I think you must face the fact that you may well be running for Prime Minister in three weeks' time. Of course, if we win the 'no confidence' vote on Wednesday, then it's a different matter altogether, because I'll be back and guiding the ship long before the Easter recess is over. That will give us enough time to call the election after you've delivered your third budget."

"I'm unable to express how much we will miss your Leadership," said Raymond simply.

"As every member of the House will know which lobby they'll be voting in long before the debate begins, my Leadership may turn out to be less important than my single vote. Just be certain your speech is the finest you ever deliver to the House. And don't forget it will be the first occasion on which they've allowed television into the Commons, so make sure Joyce picks out one of those smart shirts you sometimes wear."

Raymond spent the final few days before the "no confidence" vote preparing his speech. He canceled all the engagements in his diary except for the Speaker's dinner to celebrate the Queen's sixty-fifth birthday, at which he would be standing in for the Prime Minister.

The Government and Opposition Whips spent Monday and Tuesday checking that every member would be present in the House by ten o'clock on Wednesday night. The political journalists pointed out that if the vote were a tie, Mr. Speaker Hampton had already made it clear that he would abide by the ancient tradition of casting his vote for the Government of the day.

The following day, members began arriving hours before the debate was due to begin. The Strangers' Gallery had been booked days in advance, with many senior ambassadors and even some privy councillors unable to be guaranteed seats. The Press Gallery was filled and editors were sitting at the feet of their political journalists' desks, while the House was taken up with lighting equipment that had been checked a dozen times that morning.

Between two-thirty and three-thirty, Mr. Speaker Hampton had been unable to stop members from chattering during questions to Mr. Meacher, Secretary of State for Education, but at three-thirty he duly shouted for order and did not have to wait long for silence before calling, "The Leader of the Opposition."

Simon rose from his place on the front bench to be greeted with cheers from his own side. He was momentarily surprised by the brightness of the arc lights, which he had been assured he would hardly notice, but soon he was into his stride. Without a note in front of him he addressed the House for fifty minutes, tearing into the Government one moment, then switching to the policies he would implement the next. He ended his peroration by describing the Labour Party as "the party of wasted opportunity," then added—jabbing his finger at Raymond—"but you will be replaced by a party of ideas and ideals."

The applause continued for some time before Charles could bring the House back to order.

When it came to Raymond's turn to wind up on behalf of the Government, members wondered how he would make himself heard above the noise that greeted him. He rose to the dispatch box and, looking grave, with head bowed, almost whispered his first few words, "Mr. Speaker, I know the whole House would wish me to open my speech by saying how sad we all are that the Prime Minister is unable to be present himself. I am sure all Honorable Members will want to join me in sending him, his wife and family our best wishes as he prepares for his operation."

Suddenly the House was silent, and, having caught its mood, Raymond raised his head and delivered for the eleventh time the speech he had prepared so assiduously. When he had seen Simon deliver his apparently impromptu speech, Raymond had torn up his notes. He spelled out the achievements of the Government during the past two and a half years and assured the House that he was only halfway through his time as Chancellor. When he reached the end of his speech, he found, like the speakers before him, that he was covered with sweat from the heat sent out by the powerful arc lights. "We, Mr. Speaker, will see the return of a Labour Government for another full Parliament." Raymond sat down as the clock reached 10:00.

The Speaker rose, and his first words were lost as he put the motion: "This House has no confidence in Her Majesty's Government.

"As many as are of that opinion say Aye; to the contrary, No. I think the Ayes have it."

"No," hollered back the voices from the Government benches.

"Clear the lobbies," called the Speaker above the cheers for Raymond Gould. Members departed to the Ayes or Nos lobbies to cast their votes. It was fourteen minutes before the tellers returned to a noisy chamber to give the result of the division to the clerk at the table, who then entered the figures on a division paper. The four tellers lined up and advanced toward the table from the bar of the House. They came to a halt and bowed. One of the Opposition whips read out: "Ayes to the right three hundred twenty-three, Nos to the left three hundred twenty-two," and passed the piece of paper to the Speaker, who tried to repeat it above the bedlam. Few members heard him say, "The Ayes have it, the Ayes have it."

Raymond sat on the front bench watching the delighted Tories, who were acting as if they had already won the election. He reflected that if the Prime Minister had been present to register his vote, the Government would have saved the day.

32

HER MAJESTY THE QUEEN visited her Prime Minister in the hospital twenty-four hours after his successful operation. He advised the monarch to dissolve Parliament in a week's time and asked that the General Election be set for May 9. He explained to the Queen that he intended to resign as Leader of his Party immediately but would remain Prime Minister until the result of the General Election was known.

When the Prime Minister thought the audience was over the Queen took him by surprise. She sought his advice on a personal matter which she realized could affect the outcome of the General Election. The Prime Minister felt that once the Labour Party had confirmed Raymond Gould as their new Leader, he should be the one to offer Her Majesty advice on such a crucial matter.

The National Executive board of the Labour Party met behind closed doors. Three hours and twenty minutes passed before the committee issued a one-line press release. "Mr. Raymond Gould has been invited to lead the Party at the forthcoming General Election."

The press was met by a unified voice once the meeting was over. As the editor of the *Sunday Express* wrote in the center page of the paper, "The Labour Party, in selecting their Leader,

397

resembled nothing less than the old-fashioned magic circle of the Tory party in their determination to prove unity." The only leak he had managed to gather from the meeting was that "Raymond Gould's acceptance speech had impressed everyone present."

But the editor went on to point out that if the Labour Party should lose the General Election, Raymond Gould could be the shortest-serving Leader in its history, as under Standing Order 5 (4) of the Constitution his appointment must be confirmed by the delegates at the next Party conference in October.

It had been two hours before Raymond was able to leave the committee room and escape the press. When he eventually got away he went straight to Westminster Hospital to visit the Prime Minister. The operation had visibly aged him. He was in good spirits, but he admitted that he was glad not to be facing a grueling election campaign. After he had congratulated Raymond on his new appointment he went on to say, "You're dining with the Queen tonight?"

"Yes, to celebrate her sixty-fifth birthday," said Raymond.

"You must be prepared for more than that," said the Prime Minister gravely, and he then revealed the private conversation that he had had with the monarch the previous day.

"And will her decision depend on the three people in that room?"

"I suspect it will."

"And where do you stand?"

"That's no longer relevant. It's more important what you consider is best for the country."

For the first time Raymond felt like the Leader of the Party.

Elizabeth straightened Simon's white tie and took a pace back to look at him.

"Well, at least you *look* like a Prime Minister," she said, smiling.

Her husband checked his watch. Still a few minutes to spare before he needed to be at the Speaker's private apartments—not that he was willing to risk being late for this particular birthday celebration. Elizabeth helped him on with his overcoat and after a search realized he had lost another pair of gloves.

"I do hope you can take care of the nation's belongings a little better than you do your own," she sighed.

"I'm sure I'll find it harder to lose a whole country," said Simon.

"Do remember that Raymond Gould will be trying to assist you," said Elizabeth.

"Yes, that's true. I only wish I was fighting the present Prime Minister."

"Why?" she said.

"Because Gould was born into the wrong party," said Simon as he kissed his wife and walked toward the front door, "and a lot of voters are coming to the same conclusion."

The policeman at the gates of New Palace Yard saluted as Simon was driven into the courtyard and dropped at the members' entrance. He glanced at his watch again as he strode through the swinging doors: ten minutes to spare. The Commons had the feel of a funeral parlor, with most of the members already back in their constituencies preparing for the General Election.

Simon peeked into the smoking room. A few members were scattered around, mainly from safe seats that they felt did not need nursing. Pimkin, surrounded by his usual cronies, hailed his Leader. His face lit up when he saw Simon formally dressed. "I say, waiter, mine's a double gin and tonic." His companions duly laughed. Simon responded by asking the barman to give Mr. Pimkin a large gin and tonic and to charge it to his account.

Simon spent a few minutes moving from group to group, chatting to members about how the election might go in their constituencies. Pimkin assured Simon that the Tories would win easily. "I wish everyone was as confident as you are," Simon told him before leaving for the Speaker's private apartments as Pimkin ordered another gin.

Simon strolled along the library corridor, lined from floor to ceiling with venerable old journals of the House, until he reached the Speaker's private rooms. When he came to the grand stairway dominated by Speaker Addington's portrait, he was met by the Speaker's train bearer clad in white tie and black tails.

"Good evening, Mr. Kerslake," he said and led Simon down the corridor into the antechamber where a relaxed Charles Hampton stood ready to receive his guests. Charles shook Simon's hand formally. Simon thought how well his colleague looked compared with the way he looked in those days following the Leadership battle. Both men were still ill at ease with each other.

"Gould did himself proud today," said Charles. Simon shifted uncomfortably from foot to foot. "Wouldn't make a bad Prime Minister," Charles added. His face was unreadable. Simon couldn't decide if the statement had been made matter-of-factly or if his old rival simply still harbored a desire to see his downfall.

He was about to test him when the train bearer announced, "The Right Honorable Raymond Gould."

Charles went over to greet his guest. "Many congratulations on your election as Leader," were his first words. "With all you've been through this week, you must be exhausted."

"Exhilarated, to be honest," replied Raymond. Raymond moved toward Simon, who, in turn, offered his congratulations. The two men shook hands, and for a moment they looked like medieval knights who had lowered their visors before the final joust. The unnatural silence that followed was broken by Charles.

"Well I hope it's going to be a good, clean fight," he said, as if he were the referee. Both men laughed.

The train bearer came to the Speaker's side to inform him

that Her Majesty had left Buckingham Palace and was expected in a few minutes. Charles excused himself, while the two Leaders continued their conversation.

"Have you been told the real reason why we are bidden this evening?" asked Raymond.

"Isn't the Queen's sixty-fifth birthday enough?" inquired Simon.

"No, that's just an excuse for us to meet without suspicion. I think it might be helpful for you to know that Her Majesty has a highly sensitive proposition to put to us both."

Simon listened as Raymond revealed the substance of his discussion with the Prime Minister.

"It was considerate of you to brief me," was all Simon said after he had taken in the effect such a decision might have on the General Election.

"I feel sure it's no more than you would have done in my position," said Raymond.

Charles waited in the entrance of the courtyard of the Speaker's house to welcome the Queen. It was only a few minutes before he spotted two motorcycle escorts entering the gates of New Palace Yard, followed by the familiar maroon Rolls-Royce which displayed no license plate. The tiny white light in the center of its roof blinked in the evening dusk. As soon as the car had come to a halt, a footman leaped down and opened the door.

The Queen stepped out, to be greeted by the commoner whom history had judged to be the monarch's man. She was dressed in a simple aqua cocktail dress. The only jewelry she wore was a string of pearls and a small diamond brooch. Charles bowed before shaking hands and taking his guest up the carpeted staircase to his private apartments. Her two Party Leaders stood waiting to greet her. She shook hands first with her new Labour Leader, the Right Honorable Raymond Gould, congratulated him on his new appointment that afternoon and inquired how the Prime Minister was faring. When she had listened intently to Raymond's reply, she shook hands with her Leader of the Opposition, the Right Honorable Simon Kerslake, and asked how his wife was coping at Pucklebridge General Hospital. Simon was always amazed by how much the Queen could recall from her past conversations, most of which never lasted for more than a few moments.

She took the gin and tonic proffered her on a silver tray and began to look around the magnificent room. "My husband and I are great admirers of the Gothic revival in architecture, though, being infrequent visitors to Westminster, alas, we are usually forced to view the better examples from inside railway stations or outside cathedrals."

The three men smiled, and after a few minutes of light conversation Charles suggested they adjourn to the state dining room, where four places were set out at a table covered with silver that glittered in the candlelight. They all waited until the Queen was seated at the head of the table.

Charles had placed Raymond on the Queen's right and Simon on her left, while he took the seat directly opposite her.

When the champagne was served, Charles and his colleagues rose and toasted the Queen's health. She reminded them that her birthday was not for another two weeks and remarked that she had twenty-four official birthday engagements during the month, which didn't include the private family celebrations. "I would happily weaken, but the Queen Mother attended more functions for her ninetieth birthday last year than I have planned for my sixty-fifth. I can't imagine where she gets the energy."

"Perhaps she would like to take my place in the election campaign," said Raymond.

"Don't suggest it," the Queen replied. "She would leap at the offer without a second thought."

The chef had prepared a simple dinner of smoked salmon followed by lamb in red wine and aspic. His only flamboyant gesture was a birthday cake in the shape of a crown resting on a portcullis of sponge. No candles were evident.

After the meal had been cleared away and the cognac served, the servants left them alone. The three men remained in a warm spirit until the Queen stopped proceedings abruptly with a question that surprised only Charles.

She waited for an answer.

No one spoke.

"Perhaps I should ask you first," said the Queen, turning to Raymond, "as you are standing in for the Prime Minister."

Raymond didn't hesitate. "I am in favor, ma'am," he said quietly, "and I have no doubt it will meet the approval of the nation."

"Thank you," said the Queen. She next turned to Simon.

"I would also support such a decision, Your Majesty," he replied. "At heart I am a traditionalist, but I confess that on this subject I would support what I think is described as the modern approach."

"Thank you," she repeated, her eyes finally resting on Charles Hampton.

"Against, ma'am," he said without hesitation, "but then I have never been a modern man."

"That is no bad thing in Mr. Speaker," she said, and paused before adding, "but as I seem to have a consensus from my Party Leaders, I intend to go through with it. Some years ago I asked a former Lord Chancellor to draw up the necessary papers. He assured me then that if none of my parliamentary Leaders was against the principle, the legislation could be carried through while Parliament was still in session."

"That is correct, ma'am," said Charles. "It would require two or three days at most if all the preparations have already been completed. It's only a matter of proclamation to both Houses of Parliament; your decision requires no vote."

"Excellent, Mr. Speaker. Then the matter is settled."

PART SEVEN

Prime Minister

1991

33

HER MAJESTY'S PROCLAMATION was passed through the Lords and the Commons. When the initial shock had been absorbed by the nation, the election campaign once again took over the front pages.

The first polls gave the Tories a two-point lead. The press attributed this to the public's relatively unfamiliarity with the new Labour Leader, but by the end of the first week the Tories had slipped a point, while the press had decided that Raymond Gould had begun his stewardship well.

"A week is a long time in politics," he quoted. "And there are still two to go."

The pundits put forward the theory that Raymond had increased his popularity during the first week because of the extra coverage he had received as the new Leader of the Labour Party. He warned the press department at Labour Party headquarters that it might well be the shortest honeymoon on record, and they certainly couldn't expect him to be treated like a bridegroom for the entire three weeks. The first signs of a broken marriage came when the Department of Employment announced that inflation had taken an upturn for the first time in nine months.

"And who has been Chancellor for the last three years?" demanded Simon in that night's speech in Manchester.

Raymond tried to dismiss the figures as a one-time monthly hiccough, but the next day Simon was insistent that there was more bad news just around the corner. When the Department of Trade announced the worst deficit in the balance of payments for fourteen months, Simon took on the mantle of a prophet and the Tories edged back into a healthy lead.

"Honeymoon, broken marriage and divorce, all in a period of fourteen days," said Raymond wryly. "What can happen in the last seven?"

"Reconciliation, perhaps?" suggested Joyce.

For some time the Social Democratic Party had considered Alec Pimkin's seat in Littlehampton vulnerable. They had selected an able young candidate who had nursed the constituency assiduously over the past three years and couldn't wait to take on Pimkin this time.

Alec Pimkin eventually made an appearance in Littlehampton—only after the local chairman had tracked him down to his London flat to say they were becoming desperate. The SDP yellow lines were almost as abundant on the canvas returns as the Conservative blue ones, he warned.

"Don't you realize that I have had grave responsibilities in the Commons?" Pimkin declared. "No one could have anticipated that members would have been called back for a special declaration."

"Everyone knows about that," said the chairman. "But the bill commanded by the Queen went through all its three readings last week without a division."

Pimkin inwardly cursed the day they had allowed television into the House. "Don't fuss," he soothed. " 'Come the hour, cometh the man,' and surely the voters will remember that I have had a long and distinguished parliamentary career. Damn it, old thing, have you forgotten that I was a candidate for the Leadership of the Tory party?"

No—and how many votes did you receive on that occasion?

the chairman wanted to say, but instead he took a deep breath and repeated his urgent request that the member visit the constituency as soon as possible.

Pimkin arrived seven days before the election and, as in past campaigns, settled himself in the private bar of the Swan Arms—the only decent pub in the town, he assured those people who took the trouble to come over and seek his opinion.

"But the SDP candidate has visited every pub in the division," wailed the chairman.

"More fool he. We can say that he's looking for any excuse for a pub crawl," said Pimkin, roaring with laughter.

Any temporary misgivings Pimkin might have had were allayed when he noted in the evening paper that the national polls showed that Labour and Conservative were neck and neck at 42 percent, while the SDP had only 12 percent.

Raymond spent the last week traveling from Liverpool to Glasgow and then back to Manchester before he returned to Leeds on the eve of the election. He was met at the station by the Mayor and driven to the Town Hall to deliver his last appeal to the electorate before an audience of two thousand.

Introducing him, the Mayor said, "Ray has come home."

The zoom lens of the TV cameras showed clearly the fatigue of a man who had only caught a few hours' sleep during the past month. But it also captured the energy and drive that had kept him going to deliver this, his final speech.

When he came to the end, he waved to his supporters who cheered themselves hoarse. Suddenly he felt his legs beginning to give way. Joyce and Fred Padgett took the exhausted candidate home. He fell asleep in the car on the way back, so the two of them helped him upstairs, undressed him and let him sleep on until six the next morning.

Simon returned to Pucklebridge on the eve of the election to deliver his final speech in the local village hall. Four hundred and eighteen voters sat inside to hear him; four thousand others stood outside in the cool night air listening to his words relayed on a loudspeaker; and fourteen million more viewed it on "News at Ten." Simon's powerful speech ended with a rallying call to the electorate: "Be sure you go to the polls tomorrow. Every vote will be vital."

He did not realize how accurate that prophecy would turn out to be.

On Election Day both Leaders were up by six. After interviews on the two breakfast television channels, both stood for the obligatory photo of the candidate arriving at a polling hall with his wife to cast his vote. Simon enjoyed being back in Pucklebridge, where for a change he had the chance to shake the hands of his own constituents. Neither Leader ever sat down that day other than in a car as they moved from place to place. At 10 P.M. when the polls closed, they collapsed, exhausted, and allowed the computers to take over.

Raymond and Joyce stayed in Leeds to follow the results on television while Simon and Elizabeth returned to London to witness the outcome at the Conservative central office.

The first result came from Guilford at eleven twenty-one, and showed a 2 percent swing to the Conservatives.

"Not enough," said Simon in the Party chairman's study at central office.

"It may not be enough," said Raymond when the next two seats delivered their verdict, and the swing switched back to Labour.

It was going to be a long night.

When the first hundred seats had been declared, the analysts were certain of only one thing: that they were uncertain of the final outcome. Opinions, experts and amateur, were still fluid at one o'clock that morning, by which time two hundred results were in, and remained so at two o'clock when over three hundred constituencies had been reported.

Raymond went to bed with a lead of 236–191 over Simon, knowing it might not be enough to offset the country shires the next day. Neither Raymond nor Simon slept. The next morning pundits were back on radio and television by six o'clock, all agreeing with the *Daily Mail*'s headline, "Stalemate." Raymond and Joyce returned to London on the early afternoon train after they learned Raymond had retained Leeds North with a record majority. Simon traveled back down to Pucklebridge where he, too, acknowledged a record majority.

By three forty-seven, when Raymond had reached Number 11 Downing Street, the Labour lead had fallen to 287–276. At four, the Social Democrats notched up a victory in Brighton East by a mere 72 votes. It was more than the loss of the seat that saddened Simon. "The House won't be quite the same without Alec Pimkin," he told Elizabeth.

At four twenty-three that Friday afternoon, both the major parties had three hundred and three seats, with only twenty seats still to be heard from. Simon won two and smiled. Raymond won the next two and stopped frowning. With six results still to come in, even the computer had stopped predicting the results.

At five the BBC's veteran commentator announced the final vote of the 1991 election:

CONSERVATIVE	313
LABOUR	313
SDP	18
IRISH	19
SPEAKER	1

He pointed out that there had never before been a tie in British political history. He went on to say, "There simply is no precedent to fall back on as we await word from Buckingham Palace."

He closed with the observation, "This only makes Her Majesty's recent decision even more fateful than we could have anticipated."

In the audience room of Buckingham Palace, the Lord Chancellor was advising the monarch on the legal position that the election results had created. He pointed out that although in the past the sovereign's ratification had merely served as a symbol to confirm the people's wishes, on this occasion the choice itself had to come direct from the palace.

There was, however, one man whose advice he suggested might prove invaluable. Whatever his past party loyalty or personal prejudices, the Speaker of the House could always be relied upon to offer an unbiased judgment as to which candidate would be most able to command the support of the House.

The monarch nodded thoughtfully and later that evening called for Charles Hampton. Mr. Speaker spent forty minutes alone with the sovereign. Just as the Lord Chancellor had predicted, Hampton gave a fair and accurate assessment of the strengths and weaknesses of the two leaders. However, Mr. Speaker left the monarch in no doubt as to which of the two men he believed would make the most able Prime Minister. He added that the man in question enjoyed his utmost personal respect.

After Charles Hampton had left, the sovereign requested that the private secretary contact both Simon Kerslake and Raymond Gould and explain that his decision would be made by the following morning.

When Raymond learned that Charles Hampton had been consulted, he couldn't help worrying that despite the Speaker's traditionally neutral role, Hampton's Tory background would cloud his final judgment.

When Simon watched Charles being driven from the Palace on "News at Ten" that night, he switched off the television and, turning to Elizabeth, said, "And I really believed that man had harmed me for the last time."

412

34

KING CHARLES III MADE the final decision. He requested his private secretary to call upon the Right Honorable Raymond Gould and invite him to attend His Majesty at the Palace.

As Big Ben struck ten o'clock on that Saturday morning, Raymond stepped out of the Labour Party headquarters on the corner of Smith Square and into the clear morning sunlight to be greeted by crowds of well-wishers, television cameras and journalists. Raymond only smiled and waved, knowing it was not yet the occasion to make a statement. He slipped quickly through the police cordon and into the back seat of the black Daimler. Motorcycle escorts guided the chauffeur-driven car through the dense crowds slowly past Conservative Party headquarters. Raymond wondered what was going through Simon Kerslake's mind at that moment.

The chauffeur drove on to Millbank past the House of Commons, round Parliament Square, and left into Birdcage Walk before reaching the Mall.

Scotland Yard had been briefed that the Labour Party Leader had been called to see King Charles, and the car never stopped once on its journey to the Palace.

The chauffeur then swung into the Mall, and Buckingham Palace loomed up in front of Raymond's eyes. At every junction a policeman held the traffic and then saluted. Suddenly it was

413

all worthwhile: Raymond went back over the years and then considered the future. His first thoughts were of Joyce, and how he wished she could be with him now. He frowned as he recalled the low points of his career. The near-disastrous brush with blackmail. His resignation and the subsequent years of political exile. He smiled as his thoughts turned to the high points: his first ministerial appointment; being invited to join the Cabinet; presenting his first budget; the political exhilaration of his climb to the Leadership of the Party. And Kate. He could anticipate the telegram she would send by the end of the day. Finally, he recalled the little room above the butcher shop, where he was first guided by his grandmother onto the path that would lead him to Number 10.

The Daimler reached the end of the Mall and circled the statue of Queen Victoria before arriving at the vast wrought-iron gates outside Buckingham Palace. A sentry in the scarlet uniform of the Grenadier Guards presented arms. The huge crowds that had been waiting around the gates from the early hours craned their necks hoping to find out who had been chosen to lead them. Raymond smiled and waved. In response some of them waved back and cheered more loudly while others looked sulky and downcast.

The Daimler continued on its way past the sentry and across the Courtyard through the archway and into the quadrangle before coming to a halt on the gravel outside a side entrance. Raymond stepped out of the car to be met by the King's private secretary. The silent equerry led Raymond up a semicircular staircase, past the Alan Ramsey portrait of George III. The equerry guided Raymond down a long corridor before entering the audience room. He left Raymond alone with his new sovereign.

Raymond could feel his pulse quicken as he took three paces forward, bowed and waited for the King to speak.

The forty-three-year-old monarch showed no sign of nervousness in carrying out his first official duty, despite its unusual delicacy.

414

"Mr. Gould," he began, "I have taken advice from many quarters, including Mr. Speaker, and having done so, I wanted to see you first.

"I thought it would be courteous to explain to you in detail why I shall be inviting Mr. Simon Kerslake to be my first Prime Minister."

ABOUT THE AUTHOR

Born in 1940 and educated at Wellington School and Brasenose College, Oxford, Jeffrey Archer became the youngest member of Britain's House of Commons in 1969. He served there through 1974, when he went on to a career as the author of such bestselling novels as *Kane and Abel* and *The Prodigal Daughter*. He is married, has two children, and lives in London and Cambridge.